LORI G. ARMSTRONG
HALLOWED GROUND

Gold Imprint
Medallion Press, Inc.
Printed in USA

Previous accolades for Lori G. Armstrong's first novel, BLOOD TIES:

2006 Private Eye Writers of America SHAMUS Award Nominee for Best First Novel!

". . . a fascinating tale of intrigue that will sweep you into a world of horror and suspense."
— *NY Times Best selling author, Clive Cussler*

"Lori G. Armstrong's BLOOD TIES is a gripping debut mystery, vividly set in The Black Hills of South Dakota."
— *Kathleen Taylor, Author of the* TORY BAUER MYSTERIES

"Hard as nails, a barroom brawler — and a chick! Lori Armstrong's creation is born of the Black Hills. Tough, sensitive and smart, Julie Collins is a welcome addition to the private eye genre. In BLOOD TIES she breaks all the rules."
— *Stephanie Kane, Author of* SEEDS OF DOUBT

"I highly, highly recommend Ms. Armstrong's debut read. She provides plenty of edge of your seat reading."
— *K. Ahlers, Independent Reviewer*

"Lori Armstrong writes a compelling story that will hold your interest from the first page. I was glued to my chair from the prologue and couldn't stop reading until I finished it. BLOOD TIES is a roller coaster ride of danger and excitement that will have your heart pumping and your emotions twisting like a wet dish rag. I loved this book, and if you like kick-butt heroines and a fast paced mystery, you will too."
— *C.Cody, www.romancejunkies.com*

"If you want to walk on the seamier side with a good murder mystery, you will enjoy BLOOD TIES."
—Romance Reviews Today

"BLOOD TIES by Lori G. Armstrong is a thrilling roller of a mystery that taunts you to try and solve the riddle. The suspense was superb, keeping you glued to the page. Your subconscious urging you to read just one more page, get one more piece of the puzzle."
—In The Library Reviews

TOP PICK! 4 1/2 stars!
"This engrossing tale of murder and deceit — with it's razor-sharp characterization and well-defined sense of place — delivers from beginning to end."
—Romantic Times BOOKclub Magazine

"BLOOD TIES will linger in my memory as a mystery, and I can only hope Ms. Armstrong will have more books published with Julie Collins as the main character. With BLOOD TIES, Medallion Press has been cemented in my mind as a quality publisher, and Ms. Armstrong as an author I'll be looking for in the future."
—The Romance Studio

"Lori Armstrong provides a fabulous mystery starring an intriguing protagonist with a climax that will stun the audience."
—Midwest Book Review

"This was an emotionally driven novel with insider views of the north prairies' culture. We rated it four hearts."
—Heartland Reviews

Published 2006 by Medallion Press, Inc.

The MEDALLION PRESS LOGO
is a registered tradmark of Medallion Press, Inc.

Printed in the United States of America

Typeset in Adobe Garamond Pro

10 9 8 7 6 5 4 3 2 1
First Edition

ACKNOWLEDGEMENTS:

Thanks to Medallion Press — Helen, Leslie and Wendy.

My gratitude to Supermom, Super Lawyer and an awesome friend, Jane Wipf Pfeifle, who eagerly tracked down answers to some strange legal questions. I want to be you when I grow up!

A shout out to the mechanics, nurses, law enforcement personnel, gunsmiths, and state agencies that shared their expertise with me. Any legal, medical, procedural, political, technological errors are strictly my own.

Thanks to my yoga teacher, K.D. for keeping me sane every day.

A huge thank you to my critique partners, Mary LaHood and Arianna Hart.

Thanks to my friends and family for the love and enthusiasm.

Praise be to my super daughters Lauren, Haley and Tessa, for believing I'm Supermom even when I'm not.

To my husband, Erin, the love of my life . . . twenty years and counting baby!

PROLOGUE

Late afternoon

ATONEMENT DAY.

Anticipation streamed down his spine in a river of sweat.

He blotted moisture from his neck with a stained bandana, cursing the heat. It was like being in a pressure cooker. His gaze darted like a spooked jackrabbit, never stopping long in one place.

Weeds sprouted inside the shack, trailed up the buckled walls and poked through the broken rafters. Shards of glass, dulled by rodent and bird droppings covered the wooden floor.

Hard to believe people ever lived in this shithole.

The door hinge screeched. Dim, watery light sliced the dimness, creating a morass of fleeting shapes and

1

shifting shadows.

Two figures were herded to the center.

"Jesus, it reeks in here. Didja hafta pick a place that smells like an outhouse?"

"You wanted remote." The man scrunched his nose, his eyes eclipsed by the fleshy folds of his face. His blood pulsed, synchronized to his footsteps as he clomped over the planked floor.

He ripped off her gag. A single beam of sunlight reflected off the metal barrel.

"Please. Don't hurt us."

Her shrill voice grated on him; a broken tree limb scraping a windowpane.

A hard knot of enmity tightened his grip on the pistol. "On your knees."

The man huddled next to her dropped to the ground like a sack of wet grain.

"Come on, I ain't got all day."

"Don't do this," she pleaded, swaying to the filth beneath her feet. "I'll tell you anything you want. Just let him go. He had nothin' to do with it."

"Shut up." He swung the long, silver barrel toward her companion. "Ain't got nothin' to say? Gonna let her beg for your worthless life?"

"My ancestors were Sioux warriors. I don't beg."

"Ooh," he taunted, "tough guy."

The other man stationed by the door laughed.

"Where were your superior warrior skills when I hogtied you, huh?"

The Lakota man stared ahead without blinking.

Furious at the haughty attitude, the man kneed the Indian in the face.

Blood spurted. The blow knocked him sideways.

Satisfaction was short-lived when he realized his captive hadn't uttered a sound.

Grabbing the braid, he yanked him vertical again. "Still feeling invincible, *Tonto?*"

"No." Blood, a brighter red than his skin poured from his misshapen mouth. "I won't lay down, waitin' for you to shoot me like some diseased dog."

"Lucky for you, the wait is over. Enjoy the happy hunting grounds."

He fired.

The first shot struck the forehead, slicing off the top of his skull, sending blood, bone, and brain matter splattering across the floor.

Across her face.

The second shot ripped through his chest. His heart exploded upon impact, darkening his skin in a grotesque tribal tattoo. The force of the blast jerked him backward, a discarded marionette.

Her shrieks cut through the deafening aftermath of gunfire.

Pungent clouds of gun smoke hung, momentarily obscuring the man's vision, but not his objective.

Dangling the big pistol by his thigh, he slanted his head to inspect his marksmanship. "Appears the brave warrior done been scalped. Ain't that right, sweetheart?"

Obscenities flew from her mouth. Snot and tears tracked the crimson spatters. Retching and weeping, she struggled to escape, slipping in the dirt and fluids coating the floor.

"Didja hafta make such a fuckin' mess? Why didn't ya use a .22?"

"Thought we were supposed to make a statement. Nothing makes a statement like a Smith and Wesson .44 mag."

He snorted. "Who the fuck you think you are, Eastwood? Come on. Grab her and let's go."

The man polished the warm muzzle against his cheek, relishing the familiar aroma of gun oil that couldn't mask the stench of dust and despair.

"What're you waitin' for? She's scared shitless. Now she'll tell us what we wanna know. Let's get outta here. This place gives me the fuckin' creeps."

The man cradling the gun casually twisted his body.

He riddled the guy with the four remaining bullets before the fool had a chance to raise his weapon.

Fitting, the man thought, as he stood over the twitching form, the Swiss cheese body now matched his face.

He reloaded the cylinder. Six more bullets.

Glass crunched as he tracked the woman cowering in the corner like a whipped pup.

Cocking the hammer, he sited her trembling lips. Her slender throat. Her breasts. The notch between her thighs, which had enthralled lesser men.

"Don't kill me."

He bent forward until her hair flowed against his cheek soft as goose down. Her fear was potent; the ultimate rush.

"Beg me," he whispered.

"Please. Let me go. No one will ever know. I won't tell nobody he did it. Ever. I swear."

"Yeah, I know you won't."

He fired. Twice.

After wiping the sticky blend of sweat, blood, and gunpowder residue from his jowls, he jammed his gun in the holster.

Slippery fingers punched in a number on his cell phone.

"It's done."

The bandana fluttered to the floor, forgotten in his haste to escape into the blistering sun.

CHAPTER 1

One week earlier . . .

THE DOG DAYS OF SUMMER DIDN'T INCITE THE EUPHOria I remembered from my youth.

No agenda except endless hours of swimming and bike riding. Running through the sprinkler. Stretching out in the freshly mown grass, watching clouds billow into mysterious shapes or form towering thunderheads. Drinking Kool-Aid. Making mud pie masterpieces and dandelion necklaces.

A wave of sleepiness washed over me. What I wouldn't give for a nap right about now. I lifted my hair, letting the gentle breeze cool my sweaty neck and soothe my over-worked adult soul.

The breeze turned gusty, shearing the documents on my desk into a mini-tornado. Pity, the paper that had landed on my cigarette didn't immediately burst into flames, like the cool burning map at the start of *Bonanza*. But, the edges did start to char quite nicely.

I grabbed the smoking paper and accidentally tipped over my Big Swig. Crap. Four hours worth of paperwork now swam in a lake of Diet Mountain Dew. Looked like the Jolly Green Giant had pissed on my desk.

"Fuck," I yelled to nobody in particular, complete with hand gestures. "Fuck, fuck, fuck!"

Two raps sounded on the open door adjoining my office to the reception area.

I glanced up.

Tony Martinez leaned against the jamb.

Hello. My heart did a slow roll then a hard thump.

He lifted a dark brow. "So, blondie, was that an invitation?"

"Not for you." I resisted the urge to smooth my hair, check my teeth for lipstick smears, pop a TicTac.

"Shame," he said, flashing perfect white teeth at me, complete with a sexy dimple deep enough to fall into. "And here I'd hoped you'd changed your mind."

I gave him a cool once-over, which he allowed.

Martinez and I had gotten tangled up in a case a few months back. I hadn't seen him since, but I remembered, and had seriously considered, his open-ended invitation to get tangled up in his sheets. His offer still held a certain appeal, which my common sense refused to acknowledge—an attitude my body tried to change.

Despite his badass biker appearance, Martinez is, for lack of a better term, a businessman. He owns two bars, Fat Bob's, a biker hangout, and Bare Assets, a strip joint. Oh, and he's the president of the Hombres, a local motorcycle "club" rumored to control nefarious commerce in our area.

I busied myself scooping up the soggy mess. "What brings you to the respectable side of town?"

"Just checking to see how the private dick business is treating you."

"Swell." The Cromwell report made a soft, wet thud as it plopped into the metal wastebasket.

"Nice office. Great artwork." His astute gaze passed over rust-colored walls, showcasing my collection of local artists and lingered on the large green and blue Sioux pottery wedding vase nestled next to the golden buffalo skin chair.

"Thanks." I'd slaved to create a warm, welcoming space, unlike the austere, utilitarian office I'd left behind three months ago.

After quitting my secretarial job at the Bear Butte County Sheriff's Department, I'd hoped the mundane part of my life had ended. Truthfully, the working hours of a PI were worlds apart from TV shows. My days were spent verifying and documenting research. Followed by piles of paperwork to fill out and file. Endless phone calls. Snooze city.

With the Internet, I had access to information from my brand-spanking new Gateway.

No wire taps, no confrontations between jilted lovers, no aha! moments. My hard-hittin'-hard-livin'-PI fantasies had been dealt a serious blow. I'd wrinkle up like Jessica Fletcher if I waited for trouble to stumble in. Few clients crossed our humble threshold, preferring to conduct business via telephone, fax, or email.

Tony Martinez was far from humble. Why he chose today to cross my threshold remained to be seen. Pathetic, that I'd gladly embrace his brand of trouble just to relieve the tedium.

"You been busy?" I asked, remembering my manners.

"Hit a slow patch this time of year." He shrugged. "It'll pick up next month."

August. Sturgis Rally. Bike week. A motorcyclist's version of heaven, my personal vision of hell. Half a million bikers descended on the sleepy South Dakota town that boasts 7,000 full-time residents. Shuddering, I made a mental note to pencil in vacation time.

Liquid oozed between my knuckles as I wadded up more squishy paper. "Why are you here?"

"I want to hire you."

I peered at him over my accidental papier-mâché' project. "What?"

"Before you say no, give me a chance to explain." He briefly disappeared, returning with a stack of cheap brown paper towels from the bathroom and helped me mop up the mess.

Okay, for the Mr. Clean impersonation I'd at least listen to his spiel.

I sat, motioning him to the chair opposite the desk. Silently praising the cellophane wrapper that had saved my smokes, I lit up and considered him through the haze.

"You want to hire me? This isn't that same bullshit

offer about me riding around on the back of your Harley, is it?" I inhaled.

"You sound disappointed."

I blew smoke in his face.

He waved a meaty hand through it. "You interested or not?"

"I'm all ears."

For a second, tough guy Martinez almost seemed . . . bewildered. My eyes locked on him, waiting for the expression to reappear. When it didn't, I wondered if I'd imagined it.

After a time, he said, "Remember Harvey?"

The man in question popped into my head. Huge, rude, and tattooed. "Kung fu man? Second in command of your clandestine operations and purveyor of all things evil?" I expelled another smoke cloud.

Brown eyes went from indulgent to cold. "I'm not kidding around."

Chastised, I said, "Sorry, habit. Go ahead."

"Why aren't you taking notes?"

I tapped my forehead, taking another long drag.

He sighed. "First off, I know you and Harvey don't see eye to eye—"

"Does Harvey know you're here?" I did not want, in any way, shape, or form, to get on Harvey's other bad side; being on one was plenty.

"This is about his sister, Rondelle. She's gotten herself into a situation that makes Harvey see red and makes him worthless to me. His reaction time is slow. I've had to call in reinforcements just to handle normal bar problems."

If Harvey, bouncer and all-around mean mother extraordinaire wasn't doing his job keeping peace in Fat Bob's, a bar even the cops avoided, Tony's tense posture was understandable.

Martinez continued, "So far, I've stopped him from heading down to the rez to handle the situation on his own. He'll break bones first, ask questions second. I don't need him in jail."

As the chief enforcer, Harvey knew the Hombres organization inside out. I doubted he'd betray Martinez, but I wouldn't want to take that chance either.

"Tell me about his sister."

"Rondelle isn't the problem. It's her daughter, Chloe. She's sort of missing."

My cigarette made it halfway to my mouth before it stopped short. Oh hell no. Not another case about a missing kid. I choked, "*Sort of* missing?"

"Before you freak, you should understand this is nothing like the Samantha Friel case."

I grudgingly unearthed a slightly damp legal pad and a feathered pen. "Let's start at the beginning with full names and a full explanation."

Martinez pulled out a photo and a crumpled piece of floral stationery from the pocket of his black leather vest. He handed them to me across my desk. "The mother's name is Rondelle Eagle Tail."

Fairly common Lakota name. I frowned. As siblings did she and Harvey share the same surname? Funny, I'd never considered that Harvey *had* a last name. I'd built him up into an entity unto himself with a singular

12

moniker, like Elvis. Or Charo. Or Hitler.

"Daughter's name is Chloe Black Dog."

"How did it happen that Chloe is 'sort of' missing?"

"Rondelle dropped off Chloe at the Smart Start program in Sturgis. When she swung by to pick Chloe up after her shift at a casino in Deadwood, the daycare worker told her that Chloe's father had already been there."

Dread settled in my stomach as I studied the moon-faced, dark-eyed girl in the picture. "Don't most daycare facilities have safeguards to prevent that situation?"

"That's the problem. Donovan had authorization to pick up his daughter, without restrictions. Rondelle didn't think anything of it until it became obvious Donovan wasn't planning on returning Chloe any time soon."

When had it become obvious to Rondelle that Chloe was missing? An hour? A day? A week? Or when the Department of Social Services credit didn't appear in her bank account?

Cynical? Yep. Welcome to my world.

"This situation stem from child support issues?"

"No. Before you ask, there's no suspected abuse on either side. For whatever reason, we're guessing he took her to Pine Ridge. He used to live there, and his family still does."

"Where does Donovan live now?"

"Doesn't matter," he said.

"Let me decide that." I drummed my pen and waited. The don't-fuck-with-me aura Martinez projected usually scared the hell out of me, but at times it pissed me off. Stoicism wasn't winning him points. He'd

13

better play nice and cough up more substantial details or I'd kick him to the curb.

His resigned gaze caught mine. "Fine. He'd been renting a trailer in Black Hawk. But we know he hasn't shown up there in the last few days."

"If you've already got someone doing surveillance on his place what do you need me for?"

A calculating smile deepened his dimple. "Blondie, I'm gonna keep that very intriguing question in a strictly professional context." He sobered quickly. "I need someone who won't spook Donovan the minute they set eyes on him. Unfortunately, Harvey doesn't fit that bill."

"I assume Donovan has a job?"

"He's foreman for Brush Creek Construction Company. Travels between the Pine Ridge, Rosebud, and White Plain reservations, overseeing projects."

"So no one has talked to him?"

He shook his head. "We've tried. Left messages with the business office, his cell phones and his pager, but he hasn't responded."

No kidding. I wouldn't respond either if I knew Harvey *and* Martinez were hot on my tail. But with that much professional responsibility, it wouldn't be easy for Donovan to vanish.

"Tell me about Donovan."

Martinez rattled off info: the vehicle Donovan drove, his general physical description, favorite hangouts, friends. Something was missing.

I ground out my smoke. "Has Rondelle contacted the authorities? Child welfare?" Why wasn't she here, hysterical, demanding the father's head on a pike?

"No. Not only is Rondelle Lakota, she's a single mother with an arrest record dating back to juvenile. The courts or the tribal police won't do a damn thing. Do you know how many kids get shuffled from foster home to foster home on the reservations?" he countered. "Or passed off from one family member to another?"

"But the FBI—"

"Don't give a damn about one five-year old Indian girl. I do. Harvey does." He paused. "And I thought you would, too."

Shit. He'd reeled me in and he knew it.

He angled forward, tattoos rippling on his forearms as he rested them on his knees, the picture of sincerity. "Go down to Pine Ridge and find her."

"And if I can't?"

"You will."

His confidence in my abilities didn't inspire the same ballsy feeling within my own skin.

I scanned the crumpled paper and the scant notes. Three names. An unclear chain of events. Phone numbers that might be disconnected. "With this little scrap of information?"

"All I could come up with. That's why I need you to use your contacts to find her."

"My contacts?" Being new to the PI biz, I hadn't cultivated many contacts, and my partner Kevin hadn't been around enough to share his. That was another no-confidence admission I kept to myself.

"Wasn't your half-brother Lakota?"

Clever, how Martinez had one-upped me on personal stats. I'd do a little digging on him to level the field. "Ben was from White Plain, not Pine Ridge."

"Doesn't matter."

Yes, it did, and Martinez damn well knew it. Individual tribes were as particular about their bloodlines and sub bands as the English were about their titles and estates.

"I'll make it worth your while," he added.

I sank back in my chair. "It's not that."

Did I admit to Martinez my wounds hadn't healed from the last time I'd (unsuccessfully) involved myself in a child's life? Or, more importantly, maybe Kevin wouldn't want me to accept this type of case?

As the senior partner, Kevin had assigned me projects, corporate stuff mostly. I never complained. Then again, I hadn't taken any initiative to bring in new clients. This case offered me a chance to get out of the office.

Would it restore my self-confidence after the way I'd handled the screwed up situation with my neighbor, Kiyah?

As I battled my ghosts, Martinez floated a personal check in front of me.

My stomach jumped at the sight of all those zeroes. "Five thousand bucks?"

"A retainer. You find her, you keep it, plus I'll pay your normal fees."

Why did it feel like a bribe? The beige check bearing his name in neat, block letters, sans address and phone number, stared back at me like a dare. I picked it up.

16

"It won't bounce, I guarantee it."

Sad to admit his wicked grin clinched the deal, sucker that I am for a handsome face. Five thousand smackers would go a long way in proving the case's worthiness to Kevin.

But I hedged. This was too . . . pat.

"What?"

"If I do find Chloe, what do I do with her?"

"Nothing. Keep track of her until Harvey and I can get to wherever you are. Then we'll return her to Rondelle."

"Sounds good in theory. In reality it's a felony called kidnapping."

Martinez reclined back in the chair. "So is Donovan keeping Chloe from her custodial parent in the first place."

He had a point.

"You in?" he asked tightly.

"Maybe. Two things." I held up my hand, halting his questions. "First, is that if I take this case, I run the investigation my way without complaint from you, or interference from Harvey. That means if I see one of your henchmen following me at any time, then the deal is off and I keep this." I fluttered the check like a yellow warning flag.

His mouth twitched. "Henchmen?"

"Bodyguards, or whatever the hell you call them."

"Deal. What's the second thing?"

All the fury, hurt, and frustration I'd felt about Samantha's murder and Kiyah's sad life darkened the sunny room like a cloud of sulfur. "If this missing child angle is

17

bogus and you're using me to do your dirty work because Donovan somehow double-crossed you and the Hombres, I will make it my mission to take you down."

Pointed silence weighted the air.

"I'd expect nothing less, blondie."

"Then I'm on it."

I whirled my chair toward my computer and opened the standard contract document file. "Hang tight for a sec while I print out the agreement."

Outside on the street below, air brakes from a tour bus *whooshed*, followed by squealing tires, angry voices, and blaring horns. The smell of diesel fuel and burnt rubber drifted in. Gotta love tourist season.

"Where's your partner?" he asked.

"In and out. Why?"

"Curious. His girlfriend still hanging on?"

My hands froze on the keyboard. How had Martinez found out Lilly lingered at death's door? Far as I knew, hoods and librarians did *not* run in the same circles. Then again, it had been awhile since I'd stepped foot in either crowd. Might be a new literacy program, "Books for Bikers" or some damn thing.

Before I could ask specifics, he said, "Jimmer told me."

Jimmer. Our mutual friend: pawnshop owner, suspected commando for hire, and other sketchy occupations I didn't waste brainpower contemplating. "You seen him lately?"

"Yeah, last week at Bare Assets."

Don't ask. I bit my tongue and wheeled around as the printer kicked out the paper.

18

I managed not to leap to the rafters when I saw Martinez lounging with one hip cocked on my desk.

"Almost done," I said brightly.

"Good." His rapt gaze roamed my face. "You cut your hair."

"Uh. Yeah." *Smooth, Julie.*

"Looks good."

"Thanks." I grabbed the contract. Handed it over along with a feather-tipped pen and watched as he scrawled his signature across the bottom.

When he finished, he lightly drew the feather down my bare arm from my shoulder to my wrist. "Seeing anyone these days?"

With Martinez as a client, I had a legitimate reason for rejecting his advances, much as it secretly pained me. There'd been a powerful one-two punch between us from the start. I pretended to be oblivious to it. He didn't.

I'd successfully avoided all memories of it until now.

"Actually, I am," I said, snatching the pen from him. "How about you?"

His low, sexy chuckle stirred a hormonal response in me, which I virtuously ignored.

"No one I wouldn't ditch in a hot minute for a shot at you."

On the outside I didn't blink. On the inside? My heart revved into high gear like a nitro drag bike at the starting line.

Luckily, Kim chose that moment to stumble into my office.

"Hey, Jules, are we—" She skidded to a halt on

magenta spike heels. Her startled gaze traveled from Martinez, to me, and then back to him.

She drank in his maze of tattoos, the thick mane of black hair, the heavy soled biker boots, the leather, the attitude, the heady tang of danger that clung to him, a scent more potent than cologne.

Her back snapped straight. She bared her teeth. I expected her to circle him, lick his neck, and call "dibs."

Glossy peach lips pouted. "Damn. I suppose he's yours, too?"

Thankfully, Martinez smiled. "Not that I haven't tried, but I can't claim Ms. Collins attentions . . ."

Yet. The unspoken word hung in the air. Part challenge, part promise.

He stretched away from the desk and offered his hand. "Tony Martinez. And you would be?"

"Very happy to meet you, sugar," she drawled, grasping his hand, wiggling closer as she teetered and lost her balance.

"This is my friend, Kim Carpenter. Kim runs Classic Cuts, downstairs," I said, amused that his palm on her breast had immediately stabilized her precarious sense of balance.

Kim used her maroon talons to fluff up her flawlessly tousled hairdo.

Glad I wasn't the only female with the impulse to primp for Martinez. Usually I drew the line at groping a hot man after the obligatory exchange of "nice-to-meet-yous."

Usually, but not always.

"Ah." He cast me an appreciative glance. "Julie's knock-out new look is your handiwork?"

Kim preened and all but buffed her knuckles above her cleavage. "Took me a month to convince her to tame that mop of hair, but Lord, she still won't let me do a blessed thing about the sorry state of her nails."

"And you won't." I shoved the receipt in a file, automatically curling my fingers into my palms. God forbid the day came that I'd even *consider* a French manicure.

"So, Mr. Martinez," Kim said, then switched the conversation to Spanish, smirking at me.

He answered in kind.

How sweet.

I tuned them out until I heard, "—you ladies into having a drink with me?"

Behind his back, I vehemently shook my head. Unfortunately, Kim's good eye was firmly anchored on Martinez, leaving the glass one staring back at me in that sightless, creepy manner I'd never get accustomed to.

"You buying, sugar?" Kim cooed.

"Absolutely."

"Sorry," I said with forced sweetness, just to compete with the gooey tone Kim had affected. "But Kim and I have plans. You know, girl stuff."

Hah. Let him think we were giving each other facials. Not his business that our night out would likely consist of slurping margaritas, cheating at pool, and trying like hell not to drink on our own dime. Face down in salt and lime *was* my ideal facial treatment.

He shrugged. "Another time then." To me he said,

"You'll be in touch?"

The reminder of my task tomorrow dimmed some of my enjoyment. "As soon as possible."

He left as swiftly as he'd arrived.

Kim sighed and sprawled into the seat he'd just vacated. "That man is proof that God exists, and She wants every woman to experience the pleasures of a virile Latin male." She squirmed. "Mmm. Mmm. Mmm. I believe I can still feel his body heat."

"Spare me your overheated imagination. Kevin said no sex in that chair, and I think that includes solo acts."

Her fake eyelashes swept up as she rolled her good eye. "Girl, one of these days you are going to share whatever little trick that makes all these hunky men kowtow to you."

Only a southern belle like Kim could get away with using the word *kowtow* in casual conversation. "What men?"

"Hmm. Let's see. Your partner, Kevin. Boy-toy, Kell. GI Joe stud Jimmer, although he scares the bejesus out of me."

"Jimmer isn't nearly as scary to me as Martinez."

"Scary how?"

"On more levels than I can explain."

"Interesting. Didn't think any man made 'Julie the Invincible' shake in her Doc Martens."

"Shut up."

"Well, anyway, you could have your own . . ." She frowned. "What's the female equivalent of a harem?"

"There isn't one. Women aren't supposed to enjoy

the carnal pleasures of the flesh with more than one man at a time, remember?"

Kim sniffed. "Stupid decree made by men, I'll bet."

"Yep. The old double standard is alive and well," I said.

"That sucks." She sailed to her feet, nimble as a cat. "What do you say we try to break that rule tonight?"

Words to live by. No wonder Kim and I had become such fast friends.

I grinned. "You're on."

CHAPTER 2

HANGOVERS WERE NEVER FUN.

The next morning, after a scalding shower, a pot of high-octane coffee, and four Excedrin, I barely felt human.

I watched as Kell slept in total oblivion to the throbbing in my head.

How he'd managed to avoid becoming a raging alcoholic after performing in bars every night was beyond me.

How I'd hooked up with him was equally baffling.

One thing for sure, Kell was mighty easy on the eyes. Long golden hair, a tight ass, a toothy grin. With a guitar slung around his neck, the man fulfilled every one of my hair band/Kip Winger fantasies from the 1980's.

Plus, he was truly a gentle soul; tolerant, non-confrontational, everything I'm not. Maybe opposites did attract, although, Kevin claimed the only reason I'd hooked up with Kell was because his spine was made of tofu.

Perched on the mattress beside him, I brushed sun-

24

streaked tangles from his cheekbone, and then nudged his ribs hard with my elbow. Sadistic? Yes. A personality defect I blamed on too many tequila shooters.

He stretched, squinting at the clock. "What time is it?"

"Nine."

He groaned.

"I wanted to say good-bye."

"Man. I am so wiped."

"You should be. It was a great set last night."

"Thanks. Glad someone thought so." His disapproving gaze skimmed my periwinkle Josephine Chaus pantsuit. "Off to work?"

"Yeah, then follow-up on a new case. You know, the usual," I lied. Nothing usual about tracking down a man who'd abducted his own kid, especially when my part in locating the missing girl fell outside normal legal channels for the first time.

Kell frowned. "I've got rehearsal this afternoon and tonight. Don't know if I'll be back today."

"Whatever," I said, which pretty much defined our relationship.

Yawning in my face, he rolled over, burrowed under the star quilt and was out like a light.

As I sped toward Rapid City, I smoked and formulated a plan for tracking down Donovan Black Dog. Just because Martinez had suggested I start my search in Pine Ridge didn't mean I would.

Yeah, yeah, Kevin had attempted to ingrain in me the "customer is always right" philosophy he followed, but I thought it a complete line of bullshit. Weren't *we* supposed to be the experts? In my book, depositing a check didn't give the client the right to call the shots. With Kevin rarely in the office, I called all the shots.

I zoomed into my designated spot in the sunny lot behind the office building. Kevin's spot remained empty.

No surprise. A pang of disappointment squeezed my throat. In the last few months he hadn't spilled his guts to me about the personal shit he was dealing with, a set of circumstances that had to be sheer hell.

Kevin had been in the trenches for most of my major life crises. Was it so wrong I wanted to return the support he'd given me? Granted, I'd never liked Lilly. Didn't mean I wanted her dead. It meant I geared my sympathy toward Kevin, not her.

My biggest fear was that Lilly's terminal cancer had nothing to do with the gulf separating Kevin from me. Had the rapid change from friends to business partners shoved that wedge between us? Or did he regret the steamy—albeit drunken—kiss we'd shared a few months back, a kiss that we'd yet to address?

If this were a typical situation with him, I'd nag, yell, whine, and bitch. Piss him off. Force a confrontation to get any kind of reaction. It appeared my *Jerry Springer* approach to therapy would have to wait another day.

Our suite of offices was dark and cool. I retrieved voice mail messages and booted up Kevin's computer. Three new file folders were stacked in the center of his desk. A day-glow blue sticky note read:

"Jules, please finish these today. I'll be in touch. K."

Hmm. Apparently Kevin *had* been in the office. When?

I checked the security log. He'd come in at midnight and clocked out at eight this morning, the time I usually rolled in.

Was he avoiding me? Or was the middle of the night the only time he could escape Lilly's clutches? Not a particularly nice thought. The truth rarely was.

My gaze swept the dim room. Not only were the couch cushions rumpled, the dove-gray fleece blanket I'd given him for his birthday dangled drunkenly between the arm and the side table. Kevin had been sleeping at the office. Why?

Curious, I examined the security log for the whole week. He'd been here for the last five nights. Again, why?

I reached for the phone, but my paranoia stopped the motion mid-air. Even if I got lucky and tracked him down, he'd hedge his reasons and avoid any explanation.

I channeled my frustration into work. Took me four hours to finish Kevin's assignment. Either he'd underestimated my PI skills, or those skills were improving.

Heels kicked off, caffeine within reach, and cigarettes at hand. Time to concentrate on finding Donovan Black Dog.

During my last disastrous relationship—with a psycho passing himself off as a carpenter—I'd learned a few things about the construction business. A hierarchy exists in blue-collar jobs. At the top is the general contractor. Since most general contractors run multiple projects, one person is designated to handle it all: The foreman.

27

A foreman is God on site. He oversees structural stages, plumbing, electrical, drywall subcontractors, roofers, bricklayers; he is the "go to" guy for everything. Hence, he could never be too far out of touch.

So how had Donovan Black Dog eluded Martinez and company?

Within minutes of tapping into the local county database listing building permits, I'd discovered a list of Brush Creek Construction's current projects, all from the comfort of my cushy office chair.

I skimmed the records. Why hadn't a shrewd man like Martinez staked out Donovan's various jobsites? The housing developments in Rosebud and Pine Ridge would've been tricky, especially if those jobs were federally funded, with stipulations about exactly who could be on site. But Brush Creek had several operations close to Rapid City.

Interesting. Brush Creek had landed the contract on the highly controversial new Indian casino under construction on the reservation land owned by the Sihasapa tribe. Land loosely linked to Bear Butte.

Only one mile from where my brother's body had been found.

Shit. I leaned back in my chair and closed my eyes. I did not want to make this another case about Ben.

In recent months, I'd made great strides in not letting Ben's murder continue to consume my life. Not a natural or easy progression. Part of me felt a traitor for not pursuing justice. Part of me needed a break from the black vortex of pain and misery that engulfs me

28

whenever I think of what I'd lost.

I rubbed grit from my eyes and refocused.

Contrary to what Martinez claimed, it isn't contacts that lead to information on a case, but a methodical strategy. Find a thread, jerk it and see how strong it is. Sometimes it unravels; sometimes it leads to a bigger knot with more dangling threads.

My list started with the basics. To erect a building a variety of materials are needed. Concrete. Steel. Lumber.

Common sense said Brush Creek would use local resources. For lumber, that meant the mill outside of Whitewood. The yellow pages for Sturgis listed two building supply companies.

Utilizing my tenth grade acting skills, I called the first store, pretending to inquire about a lost invoice for Brush Creek Construction. They had no record of a current account.

I hit pay dirt with the second call. Not only did they connect me directly to Luanne, supervisor at the contractor sales desk, but she informed me that a custom window order was waiting for a delivery confirmation time from the foreman.

Armed with that information, I phoned the main office of Brush Creek Construction.

"Hi. This is Luanne with contractor sales at Dakota Warehouse. We got in those custom windows Mr. Black Dog has been waiting for on the Bear Butte job. He wanted to know when they came in and I've tried calling him on his cell," I rattled off the number Martinez had scribbled, "and his pager, but he's not answering."

29

Talk about suspicious. The secretary immediately challenged me. "Yeah? Exactly what number *do* you have for his pager?"

I recited the second line scrawled on the paper.

"Those are the right ones," she admitted. "He hasn't been in the office for days. With the crappy cell service between Rosebud and Pine Ridge, we don't talk to him much."

"I can imagine. Look. Is he planning to check in at the Bear Butte jobsite any time soon so I can get these windows off my loading dock?" Ooh. Didn't I sound efficient?

"Hang on."

Papers rustled in the background. Deep voices murmured.

Maybe my cockiness had been premature.

She returned to the line. "He checked in an hour ago and said he'd be onsite after five today. Give me your number and I'll have him call you for a delivery time."

"That'd be great, thanks." Despite my sense of elation at the topnotch detective work, it'd almost been too easy.

The afternoon dragged. I finished the Cromwell report and tidied the offices. Called Kevin. When his voice mail kicked in, I withstood the temptation to leave yet another message.

At 4:00 I drove home, changed clothes, and switched vehicles.

Clouds of red dirt swirled behind my beat up Ford truck as I trekked down the gravel road leading to the new casino. A parking lot had mushroomed kitty-corner to where the building stood. Staggered lines of pickups, SUVs, and heavy equipment trailers provided perfect cover.

I parked diagonally to keep an eye on incoming traffic as well as the clusters of men milling around outside blowing off steam.

Equal rights and all that jazz aside, a construction site was a boys' club. Men worked hard, sweated, shouted, swore and talked dirty without worrying about offending some woman's delicate sensibilities. The few times I'd visited Ray I'd noticed women were a scarce commodity.

My presence could raise a few red flags, so I'd dressed in Wranglers, a white tank top, faded flannel shirt, tucked my hair beneath an old ball cap, and hid in the truck.

Binoculars in hand, I settled in. A grimy layer of dust coated the inside of the dashboard and stuck to the sweat dampening my face and neck. Doing a stakeout with the windows up when it's 90 degrees wasn't an option. I suffered the additional dust blowing through the open window in silence.

Workers laughed and joked, gathered stained coolers and dented lunchboxes, stowed mystery tools in scarred toolboxes. The day starts early in the summer when mornings are cool. Might seem like bankers' hours, knocking off at 5:00. But after putting in eleven or twelve hours of physical labor, these guys deserved every second of happy hour.

Once the workers scattered into the parking area, I set aside my binoculars and flipped open *Entertainment Weekly*. No one paid attention to me. I was just someone's old lady, idly passing the time until my man finished his shift.

About 5:15 a dually pickup bumped into view. I scooted down in my seat, but kept my gaze trained on the man behind the wheel of the white Dodge Ram. He drove through slowly and parked behind a dump truck, which completely obscured his vehicle from view.

Interesting.

A short, lean man, I assumed Donovan, headed straight for command central, the dilapidated 10 X 13 trailer, obviously salvaged after it'd been hit by a twister. Cap pulled down, sunglasses covered his eyes. He blended in with the rest of the workforce, except for the butt-length braid and the reddish-brown hue of his skin.

With the shades drawn inside the trailer, my binoculars were useless. I suspected my original plan of following Donovan, in hopes he'd lead me to Chloe, was overly optimistic. I'd have to make direct contact with him. An unsettling prospect, a woman, out here alone without backup. But if there were any chance Donovan would talk to me, I'd risk it.

So I waited, feeling superior that I didn't slack in my watchdog duties even to smoke one lousy cigarette.

Twenty minutes passed. My truck and one rusted-out Buick LeSabre were the only vehicles left in the lot. Eerie, how fast this place resembled a Black Hills ghost town.

It was the perfect time to make my move.

I scooted out the passenger's side and situated myself in the shade of the dump truck, smack dab in a patch of skunkweed. Gnats buzzed around my head. Dust particles tickled my nose. Metal rivets dug into my back. What's not to love about surveillance?

Donovan emerged from the trailer.

His keys jangled. He shifted his black backpack (no pansy-ass briefcases for construction guys), and his long strides ate the distance with enough speed to cause a race walker envy.

When he reached the truck I sidled from the shadows. "Donovan Black Dog?"

"Shit!" He leapt back like a startled cat. "Where did you come from? Who are you?"

Although my heart knocked in my chest, I offered a friendly smile and my hand. "I'm Julie Collins."

He ignored my hand and harrumphed, "What do you want?"

"To talk to you about Chloe."

"Not interested." He attempted to maneuver around me.

Naturally, I propped myself against the driver's side door, blocking his escape. "Too bad."

"What makes you think I'll talk to you?" A statement, not a threat.

"You know, that *is* a good question. I'll even give you two options: You can talk to me," I waggled my cell phone between us, "or you can talk to the Bear Butte County Sheriff and explain to *him* why you violated your custody agreement and snatched your daughter."

My sunglasses slid down my nose; I peered at him over the pink plastic rims. "FYI: Sheriff Richards' number is on my speed dial. It'd take him about three minutes to have a deputy here."

Donovan didn't say a word.

"What's it gonna be?"

"You work for the county?" he demanded.

I said, "Suit yourself," and pretended to dial.

He backtracked. "Okay, okay, put the phone away. I'll talk."

I clicked it shut. "Look. I'm here . . ." Much easier to offer proof. I reached into my back pocket for a business card.

"Whoa." His hands came up in surrender. Bet as a kid he killed at freeze tag, his immediate statue impression was superb. "No need to flash your piece."

He thought I was packin'? Way cool. Instead of disabusing him of that notion, I shrugged. "Fine. But I've got cuffs"—a complete lie, I'd forgotten them at home— "so don't try anything."

"Not a problem," he assured me.

"Tell me where I can find Chloe and I'll be on my way."

A thin line of sweat tracked down Donovan's temple and neck, adding to the damp stain below his yellowed T-shirt collar. A muscle jumped in his jaw. The man was as skittish as a calf at branding time. "Who sent you?"

Nervous usually meant unstable. An unarmed woman, alone in a field with a man I didn't know, great plan, Julie. I'd have to win his trust pretty damn fast. "Someone who's very concerned about Chloe's well-being."

Disparaging laughter boomed. "That narrows it down some, 'cause it sure as shit ain't Chloe's mother."

34

CHAPTER 3

"You sure about that?" With a bored sigh, I removed my sunglasses and tucked them in the pocket of my flannel shirt. "Rondelle won't file charges against you if Chloe is returned to her immediately."

Donovan studied me from behind mirrored shades, which was disconcerting as hell. I preferred fear to curiosity.

"Yeah? Maybe I oughta file charges against *her*."

Color me surprised he'd finally called my bluff. "Why? *You're* the one who snatched Chloe from her daycare in the first place."

"Who tole you that buncha horseshit?"

At my blank look—which wasn't entirely faked—he swore again.

"Let me tell you a little story 'bout how I happened to 'snatch' my daughter. More than two weeks ago, Rondelle dumped Chloe off at Smart Start, on a day Chloe wasn't supposed to be there."

Donovan paused, ripped off his sunglasses so I could see the aggravation in his eyes.

My breath stalled. I knew what he was about to say before the words huffed passed his lips.

"Rondelle never showed to pick her up. When they got a hold of me, as a *last resort*," he stressed, "I was in Pine Ridge, three hours away."

He glanced at a fluffy white cloud passing overhead, a temporary reprieve from the burning sun, but nothing shielded his heated words. "Had to talk fast to convince the supervisor, Cindy, not to call Social Services or the cops, which might've been the best choice, but at the time, I decided enough was enough."

"Couldn't you have called someone else to pick her up? Like another family member who lives close by?"

Donovan's gaze snapped back to mine. Hardened like cement.

I blinked innocently, an offhand comment, but he saw right through it.

"Rondelle didn't hire you." Donovan's impassioned denial sent his braid slithering over his shoulder like a fat, black snake. "No fuckin' way am I lettin' that psycho Harvey get his hands on my daughter, I don't care how much he's payin' you."

Clarifying who'd actually written the check wouldn't set Donovan's mind at ease.

And why in the hell did Donovan's state of mind matter to me? He'd been thrust into the villain's role in this melodrama, ripping the poor child away from her loving mother. But if what he'd told me was true, I

36

didn't blame him.

Once again I only had half the story. Hell, I didn't know who to believe, which did not bode well for client relations. Despite my conflicting feelings, I asked, "Do you have any intention of returning Chloe to Rondelle?"

Equally belligerent, he said, "Why should I tell you anything?"

I considered reaching for my nonexistent gun, just to see if he'd flinch again, but with my luck, he'd probably call me on it. Screw client confidentiality. I used the only leverage I had left.

"Because if you don't, I'll call Tony Martinez and you can explain it to him."

Stunned silence buzzed between us equal to the distant hum of traffic on I-90.

"All right," he said grudgingly. "I'll talk to you. But not here."

The empty parking lot seemed the ideal place to hash through this mess. "Why not here?"

Donovan's nervous gaze swept the area. "Might look deserted, but there's things goin' on here you don't want no part of." He pointed to Bear Butte. "There's a picnic area near the creek where the north trailhead starts. We'll have some privacy there."

My insides squeezed like an orange in a juicer.

I'd avoided Bear Butte since Ben's murder. In fact, most days I pretended Bear Butte didn't exist—quite an accomplishment since the 1000-foot volcanic rock formation cast its shadow over everything and everyone in our small county.

"Absolutely not. No fucking way."

Donovan stared at me like I'd grown hooves. "What?"

I blurted, "How about if we go to Dusty's? It's down the road. Happy hour. I'll even buy." I'd rather chance running into my former abusive boyfriend, Ray, than lounge around where my brother had been murdered and pretend I was on a fucking picnic.

He shook his head. "Sorry. I'm part of the Sacred Buffalo sobriety movement and never go anywhere alcohol is served."

I freaked.

Oh God. Was I really going to have to sit at a puke green picnic table and pretend I wasn't hearing Ben's last scream as someone slashed his throat and dumped his lifeless body into the creek?

Heat rushed to my face. I had to grit my teeth to stop from throwing up the buffalo jerky churning into stew in my stomach.

"Well?" he snapped. "Make up your mind."

Anger helped me regain my bearings, didn't necessarily have to be mine.

"Fine. I'll follow you. Don't try to skip out on me because I *will* call the sheriff."

"Yeah, I know." He unlocked his door and swung it open. Clods of mud wrapped in long strings of ditchweed plopped beneath the chrome running board. "But if I end up in jail, I guarantee Chloe'll stay gone for a long, long time."

"That a threat?"

"Nope. Jus' a fact." Donovan heaved himself into

his truck.

My mouth hung open like a broken cellar door; I literally ate his dust as he roared off.

The amount of traffic on the gravel road between the new casino and Bear Butte had quadrupled. I hadn't noticed since for the last few months I'd spent most of my time in Rapid City.

I smoked with the windows up. Orangish-red dirt enfolded me in a void making it impossible to see. I wished the dust could seep into my brain and block my thoughts as easily.

Through the pall, I spotted the turn-off and braked.

The blacktop with its crater-sized potholes was smooth in comparison to the rutted county road. I concentrated on following the hand-carved signs, purposely not gawking at the scenery. Especially not at the creek.

Sweat poured down my back, my muscles were tight, a hundred crisscrossing rubber bands stretched to the breaking point. An ominous warning droned in my head like a swarm of cicadas.

And still I drove.

Scowling at the cheerful two-story visitor center, I hung a sharp right. My gaze flicked over the squat, skeletal ceremonial sweat lodges, the fire pits ringed with chunks of vanilla-colored shale. Strips of red, yellow, black, and white fabric—symbolic of the four directions—flapped in the breeze. Bulging prayer pouches filled with tobacco weighted the branches of bearberry bushes, trees, and tangled vines.

I popped the clutch into neutral and coasted downhill, around a cluster of chokecherry and scrubby pine trees to a plateau where rolling prairie met clear blue sky as far as the eye could see.

Donovan's pickup stood out in the parking area like a white elephant.

I parked. Peeled my fingers from the death grip on the steering wheel. Took a deep breath.

My trembling hands gathered up cigarettes, lighter, two bottles of water, and my cell phone. As I exited my truck, I forced my stubborn feet to move across the chalky gray earth and silently willed myself not to wig out.

But questions bombarded me from all directions anyway. Why had my brother been here? Had he been dragged to *Mato Paha*, this Lakota holy place, for a specific reason? Would I ever find out why?

"Let me help ya," Donovan said, reaching for the water bottles and scattering my thoughts like buckshot.

"Thanks."

"You all right?" he asked.

I met his gaze. "No."

He said nothing, just waited for me to explain, which I did.

"My brother was killed up here a few years back. Not my favorite place, so I'd like to get this over with, if you don't mind."

"Shit. I'm sorry. I 'member something 'bout that. Guy from White Plain." His concern changed to doubt.

40

"He was your brother?" Assessing black eyes raked my fair skin, blond hair, blue eyes, and utter lack of Native American attributes.

"Technically, he was my half-brother. We share the same white father."

"You're not Lakota?"

"Not a bit."

"What was your brother's name?"

"Ben Standing Elk." I watched for any sign of recognition. Chances were slim they'd known each other, but hey, South Dakota *was* a small state.

Donovan whistled. "Man. Bet the Standing Elk family treated you like you'd pissed in their gene pool, eh?"

I laughed, a bit too quickly, a bit too loudly. "Got it on the first try. How'd you know?"

"*Shee*. They've got a rep for tryin' to keep their bloodline pure. That why they didn't raise a stink about him bein' killed?"

His observation floored me. I'd often wondered if one of Ben's full-blooded Lakota brothers had been murdered, if his family would've been more concerned about finding the killer.

"Beats me. I'm not exactly in their inner circle." The few times Ben had dragged me to family functions on the reservation, I'd been as welcome as General Custer.

Heat shimmered from the hot pavement as I followed him across the road. At the scarred picnic table, I claimed the side without a creekside view. The warped bench seat gouged my butt. The forlorn cry of a mourning dove gouged my soul.

41

Donovan gulped a swig of water. "So's his sister Leticia Standing Elk?"

"Yeah."

"You know her?"

"Not really." Petty to point out Leticia was also Ben's *half*-sister, so I refrained.

"Count yourself lucky. My boss has to deal with her all the time, and accordin' to him, she's a bitch on wheels."

Leticia Standing Elk worked for the South Dakota Gaming Consortium; she'd probably crossed paths with Brush Creek Construction dozens of times. Leticia and I didn't travel in the same social circle. In fact, I hadn't seen her since the day she'd slapped me after refusing to admit me to Ben's memorial service, a Lakota mourning tradition that marked a year after a person's passing.

I refocused on the task at hand but it didn't help. My grief swamped me as I watched Donovan. His mannerisms, speech patterns, and attitude reminded me so much of Ben, for a brief, crazy moment I believed I'd drifted into an alternate reality and he *was* Ben.

I dispensed a mental slap and moved on.

"Donovan. We're here to talk about Chloe."

"I know."

He didn't avoid the subject, but jumped right in.

"Here's what happened that night I supposedly 'snatched' her and she ain't been returned. Those Smart Start people kicked Chloe outta the program. Know why?"

He twisted the cap off the water bottle; his slender thumb tracked the grooves in the blue plastic lid. "Cindy showed me a copy of Chloe's records. Rondelle had been more'n four hours late pickin' Chloe up, twelve times in one month. Instead of makin' a point of bein' there, Rondelle authorized people I ain't ever heard of to have access to my daughter." His brittle tone matched the bitterness in his eyes. He reached for my cigarettes and lit up.

I followed suit. My hands shook almost as much as his did, although for different reasons.

We smoked in silence until he said, "No matter what shit she pulls, she gets to do whatever the hell she wants with Chloe. It ain't right." He tossed the half-smoked cigarette on the cement slab, grinding it beneath his steel-toed work boot.

A maroon minivan drove past and my eyes tracked it to the creek. Too late I remembered I wasn't supposed to be gawking around until the leaves rustled a whisper of warning.

Donovan swatted a big, black carpenter ant, then flicked it off the table. "So, yeah, I sent Chloe someplace safe, away from her sorry-ass excuse of a mother. If Harvey wants to come after me, let him."

"Right or wrong, Rondelle does have legal custody."

He scooted forward, startling me.

"Let me ask you this: Does Harvey know who Rondelle's workin' for up'n Deadwood?"

Where had that come from? "Some casino."

"He mention that casino is owned by the Carlucci family?"

My vacant look made him laugh.

"No, course Rondelle didn't tell him. Which means

43

Martinez don't know either, or else *you* wouldn't be here."

I bristled. "Why should I give a damn about the Carlucci family?"

He folded his arms over his chest. His feet bumped mine beneath the table. "You wouldn't, but I guarantee the Hombres care a whole bunch. Territorial pissing match going on there. Rumor has it the Carluccis are goin' after other income sources which currently belong to the Hombres."

A bad feeling emerged. Had Martinez lied to me? "The Carluccis a rival Italian bike gang or something?"

"No. Crime family from the east coast. They bought into a casino in Deadwood last year. Ain't nobody happy 'bout that."

"Crime family?" I repeated inanely. "Like in *The Sopranos*?"

"Yep."

Ping. He'd just pegged my bullshit meter. "Get real, that crap doesn't happen in South Dakota."

"Guess again. We got problems, same as big cities." Donovan puffed up a bit. "In my position I hear stuff."

"Yeah? Like what kind of stuff?"

"Building stuff mostly. Who's funding what project. Who needs money, who's got money. Where it came from. What strings are attached. Little Joe Carlucci is jus' another vulture, like that blowhard Bud Linderman who'd like to own every damn building and video gambling machine in Deadwood."

"What does that have to do—"

"Don't you get it? Ever since the White Plain Tribal

44

Council signed the compact with the governor to wedge a casino on this strip of land, they've managed to piss off jus' 'bout everyone."

That was true. The controversy over building the casino had raged for the last year. The Sihasapa tribe controlled White Plain, the smallest South Dakota reservation. They were the only South Dakota tribe without a gaming facility or gambling revenues. Crying foul, they had petitioned the governor and the chairperson of the National Native American Gaming Commission to recognize a small parcel of land that had been held in trust, specifically for their tribe, by the U.S. Government for more than a century. They had to have it designated as "Indian land" to be eligible to build a casino. The land in question just happened to be at the base of Bear Butte, a place Lakota tribes considered holy.

Ben's sister Leticia had been revered and reviled for her involvement in getting the land successfully recognized. I hadn't faulted her or the Sihasapa tribe for utilizing *their* land in a manner that benefits their people. Had I been naïve to think anyone else cared, when other, more serious Native American issues—poverty, alcoholism, violence, abuse—weren't being addressed at all?

"Who else is this pissing off?" I asked.

"Ever'one." He ticked off names on his slender fingers. "The tribal members and councils from Pine Ridge, Rosebud, and Standing Rock who don't want no more Indian gaming 'cause it takes money away from their casinos. The Medicine Wheel Holy Society who wants to keep this site and everything surroundin' it sacred

45

ground. The local ranchers and the county government officials who are now dealin' with the reservation as a sovereign nation. Even the casino owners in Deadwood. With this building right off I-90, it'll suck tourists away from Deadwood."

Donovan had built up quite a head of steam so I let him roll with it, even when questions bounced in my brain like a pinball.

"Crazy, e'en it? That's not all. Someone's been sabotagin' the construction site since the moment we broke ground. Puttin' sugar in the gas tanks of the heavy equipment. Breakin' windows. Ax gouges in the trusses, delayed deliveries, missin' deliveries. We're runnin' two months behind schedule and way over budget. No one wants the casino to open."

"You have any idea who's responsible?"

"*Shee*. Could be any of them people." He sighed. "It ain't right. We're jus' doin' our job. We took on this project cause no one else wanted it. Slim profit margin and Brush Creek can't afford round the clock security. I've had employees up'n quit a good payin' job for no good reason. Whoever is behind this has gone from vandalism to terrorism."

This was too far out to believe. I figured it was a diversion to steer me away from the real issue. "Interesting theory. But what the fuck does it have to do with Chloe?"

A look of fear crossed his face and despite the heat, I shivered. Something had spooked this man, a man I suspected wasn't easily spooked.

"Never mind. You wouldn't understand." He swung

46

his feet around as if to leave.

I placed my hand on his arm. "Then stay and talk to me. Let me help you. Help me understand."

Donovan regarded me, gauging my sincerity. "Okay. After a sobriety meeting a coupla weeks back, two men approached me. Approach ain't the right word. They beat the livin' shit out of me. Dark parkin' lot, late at night, I was alone, bleedin', my face grindin' the pavement, thought I was dead for sure."

"What did they want?"

"To warn me to keep my mouth shut 'bout what was goin' on at the construction site. They had pictures of Chloe. Close-ups. None of that long range shit."

If Donovan was lying, then he was the most accomplished liar I'd ever met. His retelling made the fine hair on the back of my neck stand up.

Anger built in him; quickly, like a summer storm. His fist beat the table until the chipped paint flaked from the force of the blows.

"They had pictures of my daughter. Asked me if I knew how easy it'd be to make her cry. To make her disappear. Then they tole me they'd be in touch. Goddamn Rondelle. Between fuckin' around with that wannabe Frankie Ducheneaux—"

"Wait a sec. Who is Frankie Ducheneaux?"

"Guy Rondelle used to date. Guy who used to be my friend."

Was this whole custody issue a ruse to mask a bout of jealousy? "How'd you know him?"

"Through the Medicine Wheel Society a few years

back."

"*You* were a member?" Why hadn't Martinez told me this?

"Yeah." He shifted, almost with embarrassment. "Got it in my head I needed to save the world after I sobered up. Joined the Society. Was great for a while, felt like I was makin' a difference. We got that shootin' range stopped, but I couldn't stand the politics. Frankie was the worst, actin' like he was 'Heap Big Chief' or something." His smile was there and gone. "Then I got the job at Brush Creek and I hadta quit."

"You helped them get the shooting range shot down, but you're helping to build a casino that the Medicine Wheel Holy Group wants even *less* than that range?"

"Yeah."

"Why?"

"Can't eat or feed your kid on your principles."

I had nothing to say to that one.

"Don't matter what I think 'cause this is all Rondelle's fault. Between workin' for a hard-ass like Bud Linderman and now the Carluccis, she's in a mess 'o trouble and it's spreadin' fast. I ain't 'bout to let Chloe get caught in the shitstorm."

God. Talk about a massive headache. Not only from the twist this case had taken, but also from the stress of pretending I was anywhere besides sitting in the shadow of Bear Butte.

A breath of sage-scented air wafted by. I inhaled but the calming properties were slow to kick in.

Donovan sighed. "Didja tell me about your brother

48

'cause I'm Lakota?"

I let his change of topic slide. "Yeah. You remind me of Ben."

He sat up taller, as if I'd given him a compliment.

"Can I ask you somethin'?"

Never an easy way to deflect that request. "Sure."

"Didja really used to work for the sheriff?"

"Yeah."

"You really carryin' a gun?"

A smile crept up. "No."

"*Shee*. The girl can bluff." He paused, mirth gone. "Can I ask you somethin' else?"

I nodded, warily.

"Could you have done anything to prevent Ben's murder?"

I'd have been less shocked if he'd have reached across the table and slapped me. "No."

"Then that's where we're different. 'Cause I *can* keep Chloe safe, and I will, no matter what it takes. You won't find her. Trust me."

He unfolded his long legs, faded denim brushing the warped pine underbelly of the picnic table. Kicking aside yucca seedpods, flat pieces of shale crunched beneath his booted feet. He wandered to the barbecue grill, his back straight as a section of rebar.

I fiddled with the plastic covering my cigarette package, processing everything. Had Donovan told me the truth? Or an elaborate lie to get back at Rondelle?

One thing was for certain, sharing this new information with Martinez wasn't going to be a picnic.

Donovan turned, his silhouette perfectly aligned with the striking backdrop of Bear Butte. He started toward me, a funny sort of smirk on his face.

A distinctive pop cut the tranquility.

Donovan's smile changed into a grimace. His body jerked once, twice, three times and he pitched backward.

Horror froze me to the spot. I might have screamed, a shriek might've actually forced itself from my shriveled lungs and out my open mouth. But all I heard was the ringing thud as his head clipped the corner of the steel barbecue grill before he crashed to the ground.

CHAPTER 4

I HIT THE DIRT.

Listened for more gunshots.

Silence mocked me.

I couldn't cower in the dirt waiting for bullets that might not come.

Donovan needed help.

On my elbows, I crawled across the uneven terrain, through pine needles, patches of dead grass and cactus until I reached Donovan.

His body was splayed like a broken mannequin.

I had the overwhelming urge to throw up at the sight of all that blood.

Think, Julie, just breathe through it. You can do this.

Gritting my teeth, I lifted myself onto my hands and knees to gauge the damage.

Without jostling Donovan from the weird position he'd landed in, I checked his vitals. The little self pep talk had kicked my emergency medical skills into gear.

Was he still breathing? Yep. Move down. My fingers pressed against the carotid artery in his neck; a thready pulse, but a pulse nonetheless. Good.

Despite my squeamishness, I examined his body, trying to figure out where the hell all the blood was coming from. I found one entrance point in his left shoulder. Another, on his left thigh. The worst injury was in the middle of his stomach. Blood darkened his T-shirt, spreading out like a dreamcatcher the size of a compact disc.

Shit. This was bad, and I couldn't even see the back of his head, where he'd nailed the barbecue grill. I assumed he'd have a bump the size of a cantaloupe, or he'd cracked his skull open.

I peered at the dirt beneath his head. No puddles of liquid oozed out. Was that worse? Could he be hemorrhaging internally?

Automatically, I patted my hip for my cell phone. My fingers connected with air. Crap. I'd left it on the picnic table.

I hadn't heard any additional shots. With my pulse booming in my ears and adrenaline crashing through my system, the damn shooter could've skipped up behind me whistling show tunes and I wouldn't have noticed.

Chills raced down my spine at the silence, like the earth was holding its breath.

After another quick glance around, I crouched and ran the twenty feet to the table. Snatching up my cell phone, I flipped it open, and hit speed dial for the sheriff's office.

belonged. Squeezed my eyes shut to stop the tears.

Goddamn it. He wasn't Ben, but Donovan wasn't going to die. Not here. Not like this. Not if I could help it.

Talk to him, a voice whispered in my head.

"Hang on," I pleaded. "You're doing fine. Just hold out a little bit longer until the cavalry arrives."

The chittery caw of a crow answered, chastising me.

A hysterical giggle escaped.

"Although, being Native American and all, you might not appreciate the term *cavalry*."

Donovan didn't laugh.

"The emergency crew in this county makes those guys on *Third Watch* and *ER* look like slackers," I added.

Off in the distance I heard the wails of sirens: ambulance, patrol car, and fire truck.

"See? I told you they'd come, o ye of little faith. They'll have you fixed up in no time." I sniffed, wiping my running nose on my bare shoulder. "But I hope you weren't fond of this T-shirt, my friend, 'cause the sucker is toast."

I knew I was babbling; yet I couldn't seem to stop.

The sirens got closer, loud enough I couldn't hear myself think. Loud enough to drown out the grateful sobs bursting from my mouth.

Gentle hands pulled me away from Donovan's body. I stumbled backward, brushing the grill. I yelped and staggered into the picnic table. Someone shoved my head between my knees before everything went black.

"Collins, wake up."

I opened my eyes to the cloudless sapphire sky spread out above me. Then Sheriff Richards' ugly face moved over mine, destroying the beautiful view.

"Hey," he said. "Lost you there for a minute. You okay?"

A sharp stick poked my back. I turned my head, got a mouthful of dust for my trouble. Great. I was lying on the dirt, among the pinecones, rocks, and weeds.

But not in a pool of my own blood.

Coughing, I sat up, accepting a paw-sized hand from the sheriff. "What happened to me?"

"Damndest thing. You stood, then toppled to the ground like a ragdoll. Afraid you'd gone into shock." When I wobbled, he firmed his grip. "Easy, girl. Come on. Sit over here."

My butt connected with the wooden bench of the picnic table hard enough my teeth clacked together.

"I'm assuming the blood on you isn't yours?"

I looked down. My jeans had dark, sticky splotches in odd places. My once-white tank top was now a mix of red splatters and smears. Blood and dirt were caked on my hands. "No. It's not mine."

"Had me worried there for a second. Thought I might have to call another ambulance." He hunkered in front of me, his single black eyebrow scrunched above his eyes in a manner I took for worry. "You sure you're okay?"

I didn't answer. Minor aches, pains, scrapes, and

bruises aside, I'd fared far better than Donovan. My gaze swept the area.

The sheriff noticed my panicked look. "I've got three guys trying to track the shooter."

Glancing over the sheriff's shoulder at the ambulance, I watched as the EMT shut the back door. He raced to the passenger's side of the cab, jumped in, and they sped off, sirens blaring.

"Donovan?" I asked.

"Alive. Just barely."

"Where they taking him?"

"Sturgis. They've already called the medivac chopper from Rapid City. It'll meet them there with a trauma unit."

At least they hadn't spent time arguing about getting him to the Indian Health Service hospital at Sioux San in Rapid City, standard operating procedure when dealing with most Native American injury situations in our county.

"Need anything? Water?"

I nodded. "And my cigarettes."

He snorted a bull-like sound of disgust, but grabbed the pack and my lighter anyway, dropping them in my lap.

Someone shouted his name and he ambled off.

I lit up. My gut pitched at the blood crusted on my palms and under my nails. Eyes closed, I inhaled and let the nicotine work its magic.

Deputy John brought me a blanket. And a cylinder of handi-wipes. After convincing him I wasn't about to go into shock, he told me to stay put and assured me

Sheriff Richards would return soon.

Right. I knew a stock response. Heck, I'd even used it. I might be here for hours.

I smoked, one right after another. My brain was determined to torture me by re-living the shooting, in super slow-mo.

Last spring, Kevin and I had been used for target practice. Fortunately for us, the man responsible had only been trying to scare us. Didn't seem to be the case this time.

More than an hour later, the sheriff plopped down beside me. The poor bench groaned. He's a big man—6'8", 300 odd pounds—who looks like an escapee from WWE "Smackdown!" His girth blocked the fading sunlight, throwing me in shadow. I shivered.

"You up to making a statement now?"

I nodded.

"You knew the victim?"

"Yes."

"How?"

"He's connected to a case I'm working on." Most people over-explained things when interviewed by law enforcement. I knew better. I smoked and waited for the inevitable question.

"How long had you been at this location before the shots were fired?"

"Thirty minutes, give or take."

"Did the victim," he flipped through his notebook, "this Donovan Black Dog, have a gun?"

"Not that I know of."

58

"You have a gun with you?"

I exhaled before I faced him. "Why? You gonna dust me for gunpowder residue? You think I shot him and then tried to save his ass in an effort to cover my own?"

"Knock off the indignant act, Collins. You know procedure. Just answer the question."

"No. My gun is at the office." I turned away, mentally kicking myself for forgetting it, or for believing I wouldn't need it, but mostly for giving into Kell's paranoia.

The reason the handgun wasn't in my possession was because Kell had asked me to leave it at the office. Said it freaked him out to have a weapon around.

Normally, I couldn't have given a shit what he wanted, but lately I'd begun to wonder if my belligerent stance was a roadblock to a decent relationship, not the quirky, charming enhancement I'd imagined.

Right now, I'd rather have the damn gun.

Sheriff Richards sighed. "I don't suppose you're gonna tell me what this case is about?"

"I can't."

"Then maybe you'll tell me what the hell you're doing up at Bear Butte, when I know you avoid this place like Sunday dinner at your father's house."

Took him longer to get to the point than I'd predicted. Damn, I'd forgotten how dead-on his instincts were. Scared me how much better he'd known me than he'd ever let on.

"Trust me, Sheriff. This place was not my first choice."

"Is this case connected to your brother's?"

I snuffed my smoke on the concrete slab. "No. Just

59

a coincidence Donovan's Native." I stared him in the eye. "Sheriff, we both know it's a pipe dream any new information will turn up on Ben's murder. Donovan was too paranoid to talk to me where he works. He suggested here, since it was close by. I stupidly agreed."

What had possessed me to say yes? Now I had another event surrounding Bear Butte to add to my nightmares.

"This wasn't a predetermined meeting place?"

I shook my head.

His eyes narrowed. "Nobody knew you two were coming here?"

"Someone might have followed us, but I wouldn't have noticed a presidential motorcade through that much dust."

"Donovan work around here then?"

He'd find out sooner or later. I'd earn cooperation points if that information came from me. "Sort of. He's the foreman for Brush Creek Construction. They're general contractors on the Bear Butte Casino." I pointed to the parking lot across the road where the white Dodge had been blocked in by emergency vehicles. My ugly-ass Ford sat alone, like it'd developed chronic wasting disease.

"Great," he muttered.

"What?"

"Don't pretend you don't remember what a pain in the ass it is to deal with the Feds."

"Why drag them into this? This section of Bear Butte isn't their jurisdiction."

His look read: Like that matters.

"Any sign of the shooter?" My abrupt topic switch didn't erase his grumpy expression.

"No comment."

Touché.

"I will say, I doubt this was a random shooting." He paused, watching my face intently to see if I'd crack.

I blinked, wide-eyed, an unfortunate bystander.

The sheriff knew me better and called me on it. "You piss off anyone lately?"

"Gee, there've been so many I lost count."

He slapped the notebook against his thigh. "Goddamn it, this is serious."

I bristled, but cut the smart comments.

"Do you think the shots could have been meant for you?"

"No." I hadn't even considered that crazy idea.

"You have any idea why someone would be shooting at *him*?"

"No."

Deputy John loped over, garnering the sheriff's attention. After a brief, intense discussion, the sheriff came back and said, "You're free to go for now. I'll be in touch."

And he was gone.

Gathering my stuff without enthusiasm, I trudged to my pickup and climbed inside. The windows stayed rolled up, not due to dust, but because a bone-chilling cold had burrowed deep inside me. An iciness that owed nothing to the air temperature outside the cab.

I peeled out of the parking lot and gunned it up the

steep incline, glaring at the scenery, the creek, the herd of grazing buffalo, all the beautiful, horrible things about this sacred place.

The sheriff's last question kept popping up like a wayward bobber: *"You have any idea why someone would be shooting at him?"*

I had a really great idea who to ask.

As the rage simmered inside me, I began to get warm.

CHAPTER 5

THE SUN HAD SET, SWIRLING ORANGE, PINK, AND PURPLE together in the sky like rainbow sherbet. It wouldn't last; once the sun dropped behind the jagged hills, daylight disappeared like someone had flipped a switch.

I turned on my headlights and pulled onto I-90 going east toward Rapid City. My truck protested when I punched the accelerator to seventy. It wasn't used to highway miles; mostly I used it to creep along Forest Service roads. Or the occasional trip up County Road 7 to the landfill where the speed limit topped out at a whopping thirty-five.

I should've stopped at home, changed cars, changed clothes, but I was so hell-bent on my mission to kick some ass it didn't occur to me to do so until I'd passed the halfway mark.

The thirty-minute drive did nothing to calm me. By the time I'd reached my destination, my rage had intensified to the point my eyeballs pulsated. God. It'd be my luck if I had an embolism after surviving an evening of gunfire.

Would Donovan survive?

My belly clenched. I had to focus on other things now.

As I watched the neon motorcycle spinning on top of Fat Bob's, I struggled with the best way to get into the club without being recognized.

Yeah, right. Being covered in blood and dirt was a surefire way to remain inconspicuous.

I rooted around under the seats until I'd unearthed an old sweatshirt. I shook it out hoping spiders or stink-bugs hadn't invaded and slipped it over my head.

Eww. The damn thing smelled like motor oil and the mustiness of decaying vegetation. Upending my purse on the seat, I found a sample bottle of Poison perfume—a joke gift from Kim—and liberally spritzed myself. Stinky stuff lived up to the name. It almost smelled worse than the "Eau de 1982 Ford."

After retrieving the black case from the glove compartment, I shoved it in my left pocket, wallet in the right. At the last minute I remembered my ball cap. I slapped it on and jumped from the truck, the theme song from *Alias* playing in my head at my brilliant impromptu disguise.

Fear and anger made an interesting hormonal cocktail in my system.

Poker face in place, I marched up to the tin-covered entryway like I had every right to be there.

Six bikers stood in line ahead of me. I peeked around one super skinny chick—undoubtedly intimately acquainted with meth—to see if I knew the bouncers. My plan would be a no-go if Roger worked the door. He'd remember me, since I'd knocked him on his ass once, which was part of the reason I'd been banned from the club.

Thankfully, both guys were new. I doubted they'd posted a big sign by the cash box with my name, picture, and transgressions. Even though the incident in question had happened months ago, I had no clue how long the ban stayed in effect. Had these guys been warned about little ol' me?

Four people. Then two. I didn't smile as I passed over my ID and five bucks.

The cute blond guy with muscles bigger than his head studied my driver's license. I could almost hear him counting backward, to verify if I was old enough to drink. Ironic, since *he* looked about the same age as my paperboy.

His baby blues met mine. "You don't look thirty-four."

"Thanks."

He smiled broadly, a dimple winked in his smooth cheek, no doubt a practiced mannerism he considered charming, and probably got him laid on a regular basis.

I had no choice but to remain unaffected.

"Any relation to Tom Collins?" he asked, elbowing the other body-builder bouncer, and they both guffawed.

"Yep." I held out my hand, reminding him to fork over my ID. "He's my first cousin."

His merriment gave way to confusion, but I'd already

sidled past him into the main part of the bar.

The place wasn't packed yet, not good for my intent to blend in. I snagged an empty glass from a deserted table, settled back against the wall by the broken pay phone. Pretended to nurse my drink as I scoped out the joint.

Fat Bob's is three separate bars lumped together in one space. The main room is made up of the usual cheap tables, chairs, and booths lining the walls. A "U" shaped counter-style bar is in the middle of the room. The back area has a dance floor, juke box (all Skynard, all the time), pool tables, and dart boards. Beyond the back room is a beer garden, or so I'd heard. The last time I'd skulked in here I hadn't had much time to learn the layout. I'd been too busy picking fights and getting tossed out on my rear.

Some things never change.

According to the Harley clock above the bar, a mere ten minutes had elapsed. I'd forgotten my cigarettes and decided to chance buying a pack from the bartender in the back room, when I saw him.

His back was to me, but I'd recognize that hair and those tattoos anywhere.

No big surprise he wasn't alone.

Despite the blood pulsing in time to "Two Steps" blaring from the speakers, I inched forward. Tricky, acting in a stealthy manner without it seeming like that was my game.

A mere twenty feet separated us. Fifteen. Ten. I switched the black case from my left pocket to my right.

66

For all intents and purposes, it looked like a cell phone.

Two rotund floozies at the table beside me brayed with drunken laughter.

He twisted slightly, gauging if the disturbance required his attention.

I latched onto the back of an empty barstool, acting part of the revelry, but kept my chin tucked to my chest so he couldn't see my face.

He twisted back around and adjusted his stance.

Perfect. I made my move.

Four steps. I tapped him on the right shoulder. Before he'd turned completely, I inhaled and sucker-punched him as hard as I could, in the jaw, just like in the movies.

Caught unaware, he staggered back. In the split second it took to regain his equilibrium, I shoved him against the wall, and jammed the stun gun underneath his chin.

"Don't fucking move a muscle, Harvey, or I swear to God I will fucking blast you."

Harvey blinked, which I assumed meant he understood.

I figured I had maybe a minute, tops, before the bouncers showed up.

He said, "Long time no see."

"Shut up." My hand ached from where I'd hit him but I pressed the stun gun deeper into his neck anyway. "I can't fucking believe you had someone follow me."

"What?"

"Don't play stupid, asshole."

"Ms. Collins. I have no earthly idea what you're talking about. Put down the stun gun and I promise we'll talk." His voice stayed calm, Zen-like.

Which just infuriated me. "Your promises aren't worth shit."

"Fine. Back away and we'll go talk to Martinez."

"His promises don't mean dick, either."

"Then at least tell me what you want?"

"I want to know why you put a hit on Donovan."

"Donovan?" he repeated.

"Yeah, Donovan." I brandished my left hand in his face like a red flag. "Want proof? See that blood? I'm covered in it. Does it make you happy? Did you get off thinking about Donovan's blood splattered all over me, you sick fucking bastard?"

"For the last time. What are you babbling about?"

I saw movement out of the corner of my eye.

"Call off your fucking lapdogs, Harvey. Anyone touches me and I'll keep blasting you with this until I can pull out my gun."

"Back off," he said to whoever was behind me. His remote gaze never left mine. "What about Donovan?"

"Want the gory details on how your hired assassin took him out?" My finger itched on the silver button. I scooted in until I smelled garlic on his breath. "First shot hit his shoulder, the second his leg. Oh, and then he fell backward and whacked his head on a steel barbecue grill.

"But the best shot was the slug he took in the gut. That one bled like crazy. You wanna hear how I managed to keep his intestines inside *with my bare hands* until the fucking ambulance arrived? Or shall we skip that part?"

His face finally showed emotion, not fear like I'd hoped, but something akin to surprise. "Contrary to what you think, I didn't have anything to do with it."

Rage erupted in me and I smashed the stun gun into his throat even harder. "You are a fucking liar."

"Julie."

Martinez's voice. I didn't dare look to see where it was coming from.

"What? I'm a little busy right now."

"Julie, back off."

"Go away, Martinez. This is between me and Harvey."

"No. Put down the stunner."

"Fuck you."

"Don't do this."

"Why not? You lied to me. You used me. I told you what would happen if you double-crossed me, Martinez."

"I know. But you're wrong."

"Know what's wrong? I'm wearing Donovan's blood, that's what's wrong, *amigo.* So now I'm calling the shots and Harvey's gonna pay."

"Listen to me. We didn't have anything to do with it."

"Why should I believe you?"

Martinez shuffled closer. I felt him. Hell, I *smelled* him.

I waited, figuring he'd pile on flattery.

He didn't disappoint me.

"Blondie, you know I'd never purposely put you in

the line of fire. Ever."

Don't fall for it.

God, I wasn't wrong. I couldn't be wrong. Someone had to take the blame for what had happened tonight. Harvey was as good a candidate as anyone.

"Think about it. If Harvey took out Donovan, how would he find Chloe?"

Just like that, Martinez knew he had me.

His voice took on a husky timbre. "Come on. Put it down."

Okay. So maybe my arm was tired. My knuckles hurt. Before I zapped Harvey just to see him flop around like a landed trout, my hand wilted.

A heartbeat later I found myself flat on my back, staring at the air above me for the second time in so many hours.

Harvey, that sneaky ninja bastard, had kicked my feet out the millisecond I'd given him the chance. An added benefit of knocking me on my ass; it'd knocked the wind out of me and rendered me unable to speak.

Soon as I caught my breath, I would zap him. I didn't give a rat's ass what Martinez thought.

Harvey leaned over me. The end of his braid brushed my nose.

I flinched.

His eyes were as dark and cold as a January night. "Don't you ever come in here and threaten me in front of a bar full of customers. Try it again, Ms. Collins, and I *will* kill you."

No beating around the bush for Harvey.

He straightened and barked orders at the bouncers. The back room emptied as people scattered past me.

At least no one stuck around to watch the tough girl struggle to her feet.

Except Martinez. And he didn't offer a hand to help me up.

I stood next to him, breathing hard, smelling bad, covered in dirt, blood, and God-knew-what sticky substance from the grungy bar floor. I just wanted to go home, end this awful day by drinking myself into oblivion.

He picked up my ball cap and tossed it on the bar. "This is your disguise?"

"It worked. I'm in here, aren't I?"

"I'd have recognized you."

I didn't have a snappy response for that.

"Come to my office. You need a drink."

My brain wasn't firing on all cylinders and a valid excuse to decline his offer eluded me.

Taking my silence as a yes, Martinez's warm, rough hand circled my wrist. He unlocked a door between the bathrooms, which opened into a large storage area with three enormous walk-in coolers.

We moved past floor-to-ceiling metal shelves filled with bar supplies, and stopped at another door—reinforced steel, marked "Private."

He ushered me inside.

The space wasn't what I'd expected. No posters of scantily clad chicks hawking beer. No neon bar signs. No big screen TV blaring ESPN. No greasy Harley parts strewn across the floor. It was nice. Neater than my house and a helluva lot cleaner than the bar.

Gray tweed sofas were arranged around a square coffee table. A big black desk took up one entire wall. A small chrome cart packed with liquor bottles was shoved in the corner. It was bizarre to think we were in the middle of a busy biker hangout.

He pointed to a wooden door off to the right. "Bathroom is through there if you wanna clean up."

"Does seeing me covered in Donovan's blood bother you, Martinez?"

"I thought it might bother you."

Just when I'd decided he was an asshole, he acted . . . well, less assholish. Without responding, I slipped down the short hallway.

Holy crap. Not only was there a full size bathroom in here, there was a bedroom right next to it. His bedroom? Did he live here?

I shut the bathroom door and paused in front of the black pedestal sink, taking a half-assed glance in the mirror.

Oh yeah. I looked like shit. Felt like it too.

I stripped off the raggedy sweatshirt. Scrubbed the blood and dirt from my hands, my arms, my face until my flesh stung. Some small cuts reopened and began to bleed. Scraped skin and a few bruises were trivial in comparison to Donovan's wounds. I watched pink soapsuds swirl down the drain until the water ran clear.

Martinez had his back to me when I returned to his office. A bottle of Don Julio sat on the coffee table. I was absurdly touched he'd remembered my drink of choice.

He turned and gave my bloodstained tank top and

jeans a once-over. "Is that all from Donovan?"

I nodded, feeling oddly exposed, which naturally I hated, so I crossed my arms over my chest and glared at him.

His gaze zoomed in on my scratched forearms. "Didn't the EMTs check you out?"

"They didn't have time."

"I do." He pointed to the loveseat. "Sit."

"Blood and dirt aside—"

"Sit your ass on that couch, Julie. Now."

Grumbling, I perched on the edge of the cushion. I wasn't giving in, I told myself. I'd just moved closer to the tequila.

Martinez left, came back with a medical kit. He crouched in front of me. "Give me your hands."

I didn't have the energy to act churlish and refuse.

He inspected my palms, my forearms from elbow to wrist. When he finished, he poured me a shot and handed it over.

I knocked it back. Before the first drop lined my stomach, I held out the glass for more.

Martinez poured another slug for me, then one for himself.

The silver liquid disappeared without the obligatory toast. After the third mouthful, I set the empty glass on the table.

"More?" he asked.

"No."

"You sure? This might sting." He ripped open an antiseptic cleansing pad.

"Shit. I hate this part."

"You'll hate it worse tomorrow if it's not taken care of tonight."

I knew he was right. But why had he designated himself my personal first aid station?

As he applied antibiotic cream to the cuts, he said, "Tell me what happened."

So I did. It distracted me from the too-tight feeling of my skin and Martinez's surprising gentleness.

When I finished, he said, "Why didn't you start in Pine Ridge, like I told you?"

"For the same reason you wouldn't have."

Those deep brown eyes hooked mine.

"Because following someone else's plan drives you bat shit. I do things my way, Martinez, you knew that when you hired me."

"If you hadn't met with Donovan—"

"He'd be dead." I signaled for more tequila. "I'm still not positive Harvey didn't set this up without your knowledge. With Donovan out of the picture, Rondelle will keep full custody of Chloe. Which, quite frankly, after talking to Donovan, I'm not sure she deserves."

"Not your decision. Your job is to find Chloe, period."

I stalled, braced myself with a shot.

"Even if Rondelle's working for the Carlucci family?"

As I expected, that got his attention.

CHAPTER 6

"Donovan was confused. Rondelle doesn't work for the Carluccis," Martinez said.

"You know for sure? You've been up there lately? Seen her in action?"

The tiniest bit of annoyance showed. "No. She's a cocktail waitress at The Golden Boot. Bud Linderman owns it."

"Who's Bud Linderman? A friend of yours?"

"Hardly. A business acquaintance."

"Or business rival?"

"No. He owns a couple of cowboy bars in Spearfish and Wyoming, but his main dealings are in real estate. Apartment complexes, retirement resorts, and nursing homes. Couple of car dealerships." His gaze cut through me. "What else?"

"According to Donovan, she hadn't told Harvey she'd switched jobs because she knew he'd have a shit fit. He said she's been working the cage at Trader Pete's

75

for a while."

He said nothing, just eased back onto his haunches, expecting an explanation.

God. I needed a cigarette. I finished telling him the little bit I'd learned.

Although his expression hadn't changed, I sensed anger. Danger. His silence frightened me more than a burst of rage.

"I'll look into it," he said, rising to his feet. "You'll be at the office tomorrow?"

I nodded.

"Good. I'll call you." He extended his hand to help me up. "You're exhausted. Go home, get some sleep."

"That's it?"

"For now." Martinez walked to the door, fiddled with the locks. "You can go out the back."

Not that I wanted to saunter through the main bar. Raggedy appearance aside, it bothered me I'd been dismissed. Okay, it really bugged me that I wouldn't get to stick around and see if Martinez ripped Harvey a new one.

I glanced up; he'd already exited the room. I followed and watched him unlock about two hundred locks on another steel door at the back of the storage area.

Once I'd stepped outside, I shivered from the chill in the night air. My tank top didn't cover much skin and I'd accidentally left my sweatshirt on the bathroom floor. I spun back toward him.

He reached out; a blunt fingertip softly tracked my profile from temple to chin.

I shivered again.

"We'll talk tomorrow, blondie."

Then he shut the door in my face.

I smoked all the way to Wendy's. No comment on my horror movie escapee appearance from the chubby girl manning the drive-thru window. When she handed over my bacon cheeseburger combo with a genuine smile, I figured her as a new hire. Nobody gets that much joy from slinging burgers.

Although, it beat the shit out of watching someone get shot.

I ate while I drove home, wishing I had three hands so I could call Kevin. The strange twist in this case left me unsettled. Antsy. I needed Kevin's opinion.

Was it really Kevin's expertise I needed? Or did I just want his attention? Either way, whatever advice he'd impart would have to wait until morning, or whenever the hell I saw him again. Depressed, I balled up the sandwich wrapper and chucked it on the floor mat.

No lights burned inside my house. Good thing Kell wasn't here. I had no desire to explain my bloody clothes or justify the brutality that creeps into my life when I least expect it.

My reluctance went beyond client confidentiality. The one time I'd brought up my brother's murder, he'd gotten a look of revulsion I'd rather forget.

Right. I had baggage. Who didn't?

Kell didn't, but he had principles in spades. Didn't

77

take any drugs, only ate organic food, and practiced random acts of kindness. In his shiny, happy bubble guns aren't allowed, violence is a dirty word, and killing a chicken is as bad as killing a human.

I'd begun to feel like a pin, waiting to pop his illusions.

So far I'd managed not to get defensive with him. The hippie-type credo he lived by was good in theory; in reality, seemed one person got stuck paying more than their fair share of the bills while the other person touted their ideology.

For now, he crashed here, more often on my couch than in my bed.

I made a beeline for the shower and let the water beat on my head until icicles practically dripped from my nose. The water only washed away the blood; it didn't go through my skull and numb my brain.

My bloody clothes on the fluffy pink bathroom rug sent my mind spinning. I needed something to help me wind down.

Jumbo bottle of Excedrin, birth control pills, and Power-Puff girl band-aids stared at me from inside the medicine cabinet. Pretty pathetic selection of pharmaceuticals. Too much trouble to dig for the cough syrup stashed under the sink by the plunger. And I'd save my cache of Tylenol with codeine for serious injuries.

I tossed my clothes in the garbage. My gaze landed on the bottle of tequila sitting on the kitchen counter. Granted, I'd had a few slugs with Martinez, but they didn't count; I'd been under duress. Plus, the calming effects hadn't lasted near long enough.

Two substantial, no frills shots later, I'd relaxed. Drowsy, I slipped between my cool sheets. I'd start keeping a bottle of tequila in the bathroom for medicinal purposes.

I woke alone when the alarm beeped at 4:30. Still sore, I stumbled out of bed. Coffee brewing, I half-dozed on the couch beneath my grandmother's wedding ring quilt for ten minutes until the aroma beckoned me. Five cups went down the hatch as I made myself presentable. By 5:30, I was in my car, Godsmack blasting the last bit of sleep from my brain.

First stop: Black Hills Bagels. Armed with two of everything—bagels, hummus, and onion flavored cream cheese—I pulled into the office parking lot.

Bingo. Kevin's car was still there.

I nearly skipped inside. Juggling keys and Styrofoam to-go boxes, I unlocked the main door and decoded the alarm.

Thoughtful, showing up early with Kevin's favorite breakfast?

Nope. Bribery, pure and simple. I'd need every advantage when I told him about Chloe and Donovan Black Dog. And Tony Martinez. And Harvey. And Rondelle. And the Carlucci angle.

Crap. Maybe I should've bought cinnamon rolls from the Colonial House too.

He'd left the door to his office cracked. No lights

shone beyond the fingers of tangerine sun creeping through the blinds.

I knocked softly. "Kevin?"

A groan, then, "Jules?"

I pushed on the door. "You decent?"

"Yeah." Fabric rustled, sofa springs creaked.

In the dim light I watched as he tried to orient himself. It was an odd sight. Kevin, Mr. Meticulous, shoeless, sockless, prone on the couch with his hair sticking up like Calvin from *Calvin and Hobbes*, and a fleece blanket ruched around his waist.

I crossed to him, perching on the middle cushion so my hip touched his. Heavy stubble covered his jaw. Instinctively, I ran my hand across his face, taming his hair. His eyes remained closed.

"Your hand is cold," he said.

"Sorry."

"Don't be." He sniffed. "And you smell good."

He hadn't flinched at my touch or pushed me away, which was a novelty of late. I kept my hand in place. "Do I usually smell bad?"

"You usually smell like cigarettes."

"Damn. I knew there was something I'd forgotten."

"You haven't even sucked down one death stick yet this morning?"

"Nope."

"You sick or something?"

"Ha ha."

"Then granola boy *is* influencing you. Maybe he'll convince you to quit smoking."

"Don't bet on it."

He opened his eyes.

God. My stomach knotted. Exhausted didn't begin to describe his change in appearance over the past month. His skin had lost the golden glow of summer, his dark hair lacked the usual sheen, his green eyes were pale, as if caring for Lilly in her last days on this earth had sucked the life and the color right out of him.

"How is Kell, by the way?" Kevin asked. "Still making bean cakes and writing angst-ridden folk tunes?"

I whapped him on the arm, which earned me a rare grin.

"I don't know. He didn't grace me with his presence after his gig last night. Besides, I'm not his keeper."

His grin faded. "Consider yourself lucky."

My hand stilled at the bitterness in his tone. I could say something flip, or I could buck up and ask the question we usually avoided. "How *is* Lilly?"

"The same." Pause. "Actually, that's not true. She gets worse every day."

"Kev, I'm so—"

"Don't say it. If another person tells me how fucking *sorry* they are, I swear to God I'll snap." He struggled to get up.

I pushed him back down. "Fine. Then I'll ask why the hell you've been sleeping in your office for the last week."

"Shit. How'd you know?"

"Wouldn't be much of an investigator if I couldn't figure that out, now would I?"

"You learned from the best."

"Damn straight."

He grabbed my hand and held my gaze for the longest time. "I've missed you."

"Yeah? Well, you know what they say. A day without Julie is like a day without—"

"Hemorrhoids," we finished together.

I smiled. Our inside jokes didn't seem forced, even when we'd had sixteen years of them. I brushed my lips across his forehead.

The moment lingered; a connection we hadn't allowed ourselves for months. Reluctantly, I sat up. "Come on. Over bagels you can tell me why you're crashing on this crappy couch. And I'll bring you up to speed on the latest case."

His eyes lit with interest. "You brought bagels? If I weren't already overpaying you, I'd give you a raise."

I stood.

Kevin deposited his feet on the floor and attempted to put himself back together, slowly, clumsily.

Weird, seeing him befuddled.

"Well, my *liege*, while you do something with your hair, I'll be in the reception area."

No smart-ass comeback. Just a muttered, "Thanks."

I set out the bagel stuff and snuck into my office for a smoke.

Ah. Nothing in the world like that first hit of nicotine. While I smoked, I opened Martinez's file. Not much in there: copy of the contract, copy of the check, and my scant notes. Didn't feel like writing down the horrific details from last night.

In the doorway separating my office from the reception area, I watched Kevin.

A chunk of bagel liberally smeared with hummus and cream cheese disappeared in his mouth, the other half was already gone. Was he starving as well as sleep deprived?

I poured myself a cup of coffee and sat across from him.

"Aren't you having one?" he asked.

I shook my head. "Too early."

He shrugged and snagged the other bagel, neatly slicing it in half. "Why *are* you here so early?"

"Because I wanted to catch you." I blew on my coffee, staring at him over the steam but he wouldn't meet my eyes. "Kev, are you avoiding me?"

He picked at the poppy and sesame seeds on the top of the bagel before he admitted, "Yeah, I'm avoiding you."

Animosity surfaced; I managed to gulp it down with a swig of coffee. I waited for an explanation, or a clarification, hell, anything, but he silently, meticulously destroyed his breakfast seed by seed.

"As your partner I deserve to know why."

More silence.

I chanced it and put my hand over his, hoping he wouldn't rebuff me. "As your best friend I demand you tell me why I've suddenly developed the plague, or else I'll kick your ass."

Kevin looked up at me, a ghost of a smile on his lips. "Try it, tough girl. I'm spoiling for a good fight." Lines around his mouth drew taut. "Truth is, I've been avoiding everyone, not just you."

"And here I thought I was special," I murmured. He pulled his hand away, pulled back into his shell. "That doesn't tell me why."

"Because I don't want to talk about it."

"It" being Lilly's cancer, her imminent death.

Death had made a habit of knocking on my door every few years just to make sure I knew nothing was sacred, no one was safe. But in my case, those losses had been instantaneous, the grief immediate. I'd never had to watch death destroy someone I loved, slowly, piece by piece. Helpless. Waiting. Wondering. Hoping either for a quick end or a miraculous recovery.

Neither was an option for Lilly.

Where was Kevin at now, three months after her terminal diagnosis? Since Lilly had opted not to repeat chemotherapy, for the first month they'd traveled: Greece, Spain, Italy. When she'd gotten too sick to continue, Kevin had brought her home.

Between Lilly's parents, her sister, the hospice workers, and Kevin, Lilly had round the clock care. He'd never given me details on what that care entailed. In hindsight, maybe I should've asked.

"See," Kevin continued, as if there hadn't been a lull in our conversation, "whenever I go somewhere and run into someone I know, they ask how Lilly is *doing*. How am I supposed to respond to that? If I said, 'Just great, she's dying but her spirits are up,' people would think I'd lost it, which, sadly, isn't too far from the truth."

He draped his forearms on his thighs and talked to the carpet. "Some asshole actually had the balls to ask how much time she's got left. Like I'd know. Like if I did I'd tell him." He dry-washed his face. "God, Jules, this is so fucked up."

Tears burned behind my lids. It was so unfair. I sucked them up because Kevin would know they weren't for Lilly, but for him, and I doubted he'd appreciate them.

"So, to answer your question, the reason I'm sleeping here is I can't stand to be in Lilly's house twenty-four hours a day. Even though I know every time I leave she might die and I won't be there for her." His feeble laugh curdled the coffee in my stomach. "That makes me the biggest bastard on the planet, doesn't it?"

"No. It makes you human."

"Her parents don't understand why I can't sit at her side, hour after hour, just holding her hand. I know they think if I loved her—"

"You do," I said, overlooking the ripping sensation in my heart. "Just not in the same way they do. They can't expect you to stop living because she's dying. The only person's expectations you have to live up to are your own."

"Easier said than done." He slapped his hands on his legs. "Enough. Let's talk about this new case."

Kevin focused his attention on me. Completely. Totally. Like a guided missile that'd found the target.

"Why the hell are we working for Tony Martinez?"

CHAPTER 7

"THE INFORMATION IS IN MY OFFICE." SO WERE MY cigarettes. Yeah, pretty pathetic I'd need a crutch to get through this conversation.

Kevin followed me and eased into the chair across the desk.

I lit up and opened the file.

"Martinez hired me to find Harvey's niece. I laid out the company rules up front and he still gave us a big retainer, so I figured what the hell?" I passed over the copy of the check. "It started out as the basic child custody situation: father snatches kid, mom wants kid back."

"Started out?" he asked, frowning at the paper in his hand.

"Things got complicated big time last night."

Kevin's gaze snapped to mine. Sharpened. "Explain complicated."

There was the Kevin I knew: shrewd, focused. Ready to chew my ass. I'd gladly welcome it if it would chase the shadows from his face.

By the time I'd finished explaining, his mouth hung open.

"For Christ's sake, Julie, someone shot at you?"

I attempted to defend myself but he beat me to the punch.

"Then you waltzed into Fat Bob's and threatened Harvey with a stun gun? What the hell were you thinking?"

"I wasn't thinking. Between Donovan getting shot and bleeding all over me, dealing with Sheriff Richards, and the fact this all went down at Bear Butte."

The "Enrich Your Word Power" calendar on the corner of my desk caught my eye. Yesterday's word, *imprudent*, seemed particularly apt for the way I'd handled things.

"The bottom line is I don't know if I'm still on the case. If Rondelle is working for the Carluccis, I doubt Martinez will help her."

"When will you know for sure?"

"He's supposed to call me today. Either way, we'll probably get to keep the retainer."

"I don't give a crap about the money."

I whipped my head around to look over my shoulder, then craned my neck to look beyond him.

"What?"

"Just wondering what the hell you did with my partner."

He scowled. "Funny."

"Not really." I snatched the paper from his hands, waving it in his face. "I know the drill. We're in the business to make money, not self-fund lost causes."

87

"Is this a lost cause?"

I gaped at him. Who was this man? Where were recriminations? The lecture on maintaining the company's reputation? I knew I'd fucked up. He knew I'd fucked up. Why didn't he point it out?

"Julie?"

"What?"

"God. Don't bite my head off."

"Why aren't you mad?" I demanded. "I thought you'd come in here and tell me to drop this case, no matter what Martinez decides."

Kevin's back conformed to the chair as he considered his response.

Finally, he said, "I left you in charge of the agency. That means you make the day-to-day decisions regarding clients, not me. I won't second-guess those decisions because strangely enough, I do trust your judgment where the business is concerned. You wouldn't have taken on this case if you didn't believe it had merit." He paused. "After what you went through last night, do you want to continue searching for Chloe Black Dog if Martinez gives you the all-clear?"

Despite my misgivings on whether that'd actually happen, I answered, "Yes."

"Then keep me posted." Kevin stood slowly; his gaze swept the room, landing anywhere but on me. "Look. I've got to go."

He waited until he'd reached the door to turn around. "Thanks. For the breakfast, for . . ." He rested his forehead against the doorframe, the picture of weariness.

"For making me feel human for a little while."

Didn't he know, didn't Lilly tell him he was the epitome of humanity every damn minute he sat by her bedside and watched her die?

"You'll keep in touch?"

"I'll try."

"Let me know if there's anything I can do."

Those green eyes focused on me with an intensity that made me squirm. "Actually, there is one thing you can do."

"What?"

"Keep Tony Martinez out of your bed. I trust you, but he's a different story."

He shut the door softly behind him.

I smoked and stared at the fake wood grain pattern for a long, long time.

Martinez called and set up a meeting. When I asked questions, he cut me off. His phone manners left something to be desired.

Hoo-ray. I'd be hanging out in Fat Bob's again. As I'd suspected, I wouldn't be allowed in the front entrance. Back door all the way for a bad girl like me.

I closed the agency and popped in to say howdy to Kim. Saturday in a beauty shop is crazy, so my suggestion we hook up later and drink ourselves into a stupor met with little more than a half-hearted grunt.

No sign of Kell at my house. He'd left a message on

my machine telling me to come to Jasper's Bar for the last set. The next message was from Sheriff Richards updating me on Donovan's condition. Critical. Not critical, but stable, just plain critical. Well, at least he was still alive.

Hearing the last call, from my father, made me wish I'd forgotten to check my messages. He and Martinez were in a dead-heat for shitty phone etiquette. In his usual terse manner, he said he'd expect me for dinner Sunday at 1:00.

Just what I didn't need on my day off. When I absolutely, positively couldn't get out of a family dinner, I dragged Kevin along. Not an option for tomorrow and I couldn't take Kell. Cattle ranchers and card carrying PETA members were not a good mix.

Recently I'd seen a bumper sticker that read:

"VEGETARIAN: LAKOTA WORD FOR BAD HUNTER."

Ben would've gotten a huge kick out of it. Kell didn't find it funny. My father has no sense of humor, either. Hey, maybe they did have something in common.

Several blissful months had elapsed since I'd been forced to pass the potatoes and the pleasantries with dad, his wife and their two kids. I had no excuse not to go. I'd worry about it tomorrow since I had plenty of other things to worry about tonight.

Sipping a Coors, I listened to Marilyn Manson's "Beautiful People" while I chose an ensemble. Hmm. Saturday night in a biker bar, what to wear? Leather? Lace? Chains? Technically, I wouldn't be *in* the bar so it really didn't matter.

I slipped on a pair of Cruel Girl black denim jeans, a black camisole under a royal blue long-sleeved silk shirt, buttoned just enough to cover my bruises and scratches. Black satin stiletto mules made the outfit professional and sexy. I was ready to rock and roll.

Watery early evening sun cut through the dirt devils when I arrived at Fat Bob's. Even though serious partiers came out after dark, I got a few catcalls as I skirted the beer garden to the steel door.

I knocked. It opened immediately.

I didn't recognize the guy who'd let me in. A swarthy, no-necked bruiser wearing an Hombres leather vest and a big pistol.

His mistrust was apparent. "You come alone?"

"Yes."

"Got any weapons?" He motioned me in, I followed.

"Just my charm."

No response. He slammed the door and locked it. "This way. Mr. Martinez is waiting."

Did I detect a note of reproach? Five minutes didn't count as late in my book. And what was up with the "Mr. Martinez" stuff? Then again, I hadn't seen Tony in action as president of the Hombres. Maybe he did have a throne and scepter.

No-neck led me to the same office suite I'd been in last night. He knocked. Locks tumbled and the door swung open.

Another goon blocked the doorway. I mean completely blocked it.

The increase in security gave me the creeps.

"That her?" goon #2 asked.

"Yep," No-neck answered.

"You check her ID?"

No-neck opened his mouth, but I'd tired of the game. "For Christsake, if I wanted Martinez dead I'd have strangled him with my pantyhose last night when we were alone."

Neither man budged.

Martinez laughed from inside the room. "It's her."

I batted my lashes at both men.

Goon #2 stepped aside. I sauntered in.

Two different guys, also sporting Hombres jackets, and mean-eyed distrust, were congregated in front of the desk, pouring over file folders. They gave me a cursory glance, then resumed shuffling papers.

Martinez's once-over wasn't as casual. "You look better than you did last night."

"Thanks."

"How do you feel?"

"Better than Donovan does, I'm sure."

"Any news on his condition?"

"No change."

"Pity. Can I get you something to drink?"

"A Coors."

"Light?"

I shuddered. "God no."

With his warm palm in the small of my back, he steered me toward the conversation area. Didn't introduce the other men. To goon #2 he said, "Have Big Mike fetch Ms. Collins a Coors." Martinez asked, "On tap?"

Not falling for that old trick. Too easy to slip something hinky in a frosty mug. "Bring me a bottle."

He grinned. "You have trust issues, blondie."

"Oh that's rich, coming from the man with a bodyguard."

"Two actually. One is on break."

Was he serious? I angled my chin toward the guys in the corner with their heads bent close. "And them?"

"They're in my marketing and distribution division."

The type of things the Hombres were purported to control in this area weren't the type of things a normal marketing executive handled or brought up at the monthly board meeting.

Don't ask, Julie, just keep your damn mouth shut for a change.

Martinez offered, "Hard for you not to comment on my business practices, isn't it?"

I gave him a gimlet stare.

"Fortunately, a standard business model works for whatever . . . ah, *merchandise* one is selling."

"Who told you that line of bullshit?"

"Economics Prof in college."

"*You* went to college?"

He nodded.

Yikes. An organized lawbreaker.

"Surprised?"

"Yeah."

"Thought you might be."

A cold six-pack appeared before I got more uncomfortable.

93

Martinez snapped his fingers. The room emptied. Neat trick. Okay, *scary* trick.

The twist-off lids hissed as he opened the beers. He handed one to me.

I fished my cigarettes from my purse and looked around for an ashtray.

"No one smokes in here," he said.

"There's a first time for everything."

He scooted forward, invading my space. "Yes, there is."

Those watchful dark brown eyes caused my heart to skip a beat or three. "What?"

"Nothing." Clinking his bottle against mine, he drained the whole thing in about four swallows. He set his empty on the table. "Now you've got an ashtray."

I was almost too paranoid to light up now. Almost. In the name of addiction I soldiered on. Two puffs, two drinks, and my tongue loosened, oh happy day.

"I get that you're a big, scary dude not to be messed with. Fat Bob's is a fortress. So why am I here?"

"Get to the point, why don't you?"

"You're not paying me to be your drinking buddy, Martinez." I paused, sipped. "I guess the question is: are you still paying me?"

"Your partner didn't advise you to drop this case, after what happened last night?"

How the hell had he known about my early morning meeting with Kevin? I shrugged, shooting for nonchalant. "Partner being the operative word. He left it up to me."

"Why wouldn't you keep the five grand and tell me to go fuck myself? I wouldn't blame you."

I waited motionless, a rabbit caught in a snare.

Martinez wasn't finished poking me with a stick to see if I was really dead or just playing dead. "I got the distinct impression you'd taken Donovan's side."

He was still in my face and I had too much pride to retreat.

"*You* hired me to find Chloe. I've got your take on the situation and Donovan's, neither of which is entirely accurate. We're still missing information. I need that information before I make a final decision. Isn't our priority to find Chloe and make sure she's safe?"

Finally, Martinez sat back, but in no way was he relaxed. He unclipped a cell phone and punched in a number. "Harvey. Bring Rondelle in."

I finished the beer to wet my suddenly dry mouth.

Irritating, the whole locking/unlocking the door process. I'd half-hoped No-neck would escort Rondelle, saving me from another confrontation with kung fu man.

No such luck.

Harvey stepped inside first, a woman, I assumed Rondelle, a beat later.

Martinez had placed a hard-backed chair inside the conversation area and he motioned for her to sit down.

She did, reluctantly, throwing petulant glares at

95

Harvey, fidgeting like a two-year old in church.

Rondelle was striking, if a bit on the thin side. Younger than I'd imagined, shorter too. Her features, from what I could see beneath the black hair obscuring her face, were more Native American princess, less Asian than Harvey's.

Wearing skimpy rumpled clothes, her waist-length hair in knots, she personified a bad-mannered teenager reluctantly dragged out of bed.

Harvey bypassed the couch and leaned against the wall behind me. I didn't like having him at my back, but complaining wouldn't be in my best interest.

Martinez remained standing. "Rondelle, this is Julie Collins."

Her head came up. She had a wide forehead and high cheekbones that tapered into a sharp chin. Bleary hazel eyes stared down a blade-thin nose. She folded her arms, took my measure. Apparently finding me lacking, she scoffed, "Who's she?"

"I hired her to find Chloe."

She harrumphed and glared at Harvey. Twitched like she had fleas.

Where to start? With empathy? Not my strong suit, but worth a try.

"Thanks for coming here. I know you've got lots of other things on your mind. Not knowing where Chloe is, and now with Donovan in the hospital—"

"What?" Her head snapped up so fast I heard her neck bones crack.

The beer in my stomach fizzed. Surely she knew

96

about Donovan. If not from the newspaper or TV, Harvey would have told her, wouldn't he?

"Donovan is in the hospital?" she repeated. "Why? Since when?"

"Someone shot him last night," I said carefully.

"No!" She sprang, knocking over the chair. Shot across the room, swinging her tiny fists at Harvey, screaming, "I told you, you bastard, I told you not to look for her!"

Stunned, I watched Rondelle punch Harvey in the head until Martinez caught her and wrenched her arms behind her back. She kicked and screamed, twisting her body, trying to get away from him and back at Harvey.

"Goddammit, Rondelle, that's enough," Tony said.

Harvey made no move to help Martinez contain Rondelle. He hadn't defended himself from Rondelle's blows, either.

"Let go of me!"

"Not until you calm down."

"Fuck you. And fuck you too, Harvey." She spit at him.

"Knock it off or I'll call Big Mike in here to deal with you," Martinez warned.

"I don't care." She lunged for Harvey again. "If they kill her it'll be your fault."

What the hell was going on? Rondelle hadn't wanted Harvey to find Chloe? Why had I been hired?

A sob broke from Rondelle's throat.

I'd had enough of them manhandling her. I said: "Let her go."

She quit struggling.

Martinez released her, and for good measure blocked her access to her brother. Strange turn of events since it was Harvey's job to protect him.

Rondelle pushed her hair out of her eyes and curled in the love seat opposite me, hugging her knees to her chest.

After a few uncomfortable seconds I prompted, "Rondelle? Are you gonna tell me what the hell is really going on here?"

"Julie—" Tony started.

"Shut up, Martinez," I said without taking my eyes off Rondelle. "I'm not talking to you."

Harvey growled at me. I doubted anyone ever spoke to El Presidente that way.

"Can I get a drink first?"

Without comment, Martinez grabbed a bottle of Stoli's, a lowball glass from the bar cart in the corner, and set it in front of Rondelle.

"Classy guy like you always has the good stuff." Her hands shook as she poured, tossed it back and repeated the process.

Harvey's revulsion with her actions pulsed through the room like a sonic wave.

By the third shot of vodka, the rigid set to her mouth relaxed and she seemed less fidgety.

Wasn't the case with me. I was starting to get pissed off. "Talk."

"Start when you changed jobs." This from Martinez.

"While back, I got sick of the Linderman's crap at The Golden Boot. I filled out an app at Trader Pete's."

She sent a semi-panicked look to Martinez. "Swear I didn't know I was workin' for the Carluccis until 'bout three weeks later.

"Robin, the head cashier, was short-handed. She asked me to work one of the private cocktail parties upstairs." She sent Harvey a crafty look. "Told me no one minded if the girls wanted to earn a little extra money by being 'friendly' with some of the Carlucci's special customers."

I'd never met a local woman who openly admitted she took money for sex. With the very public FBI bust of Pam's Purple Door in 1980, Deadwood's last working brothel, prostitution had left Deadwood. Or maybe not.

"Did you take Robin up on her offer?"

"Yes."

Harvey was shaking Rondelle like a stuffed toy before I'd realized he'd moved. "What the fuck is wrong with you? Now you're whoring yourself?"

I leapt to my feet, itching for the chance to knock Harvey on his ass, but Martinez beat me there. Wow. He was fast if he got the jump on kung fu man.

With one fist wrapped in Harvey's tank top, Martinez jerked him away.

"Back off," Harvey snarled. "She's my fucking sister."

"So what?" Rondelle snarled back. "You think it was the first time I did it for money? Or for food? Or to pay my goddamn rent? Get real."

Tony didn't say a word. Harvey's face remained stoic.

I placed myself between Rondelle and Harvey, directing my anger toward Martinez. "Get him out of here."

He shook his head. "No can do, blondie. He

deserves to know what's going on."

"Fine. But if he can't keep his stupid mouth shut, or keep his meat hooks off his sister, he goes. You hired me, he didn't. I might have to put up with your shit, but I won't put up with his."

"Understood." His eyes narrowed at something behind me.

I turned. Rondelle had poured herself another slug of vodka. Or five. With my back to her I couldn't tell how many shots she'd glugged down. This was not going well.

I sat and lit a cigarette, searching for calm.

"Okay, Rondelle, get to the point."

She traced the rim of her empty glass with a dirt-caked fingernail. "I worked two, three, of those parties. Top shelf booze, catered by some fancy chef. Slick guys in shiny suits, like you see on TV, the ones who polish their shoes with the same junk they polish their hair. Late one night, I was in the bathroom, and I heard a couple of guys talkin' in the other room." She scowled. "Them walls are as paper thin as the cheap-ass government ones on the rez."

"What were they talking about?"

"The Bear Butte Casino. See, that's why I listened. Donovan had been bitchin' 'bout the problems he'd been havin' with threats, meetin' deadlines and stuff on the jobsite so he couldn't take Chloe 'cause he was workin' so much overtime. I kept listenin' and this one guy bragged his 'inside man' would keep causin' problems with construction delays."

"Sounds like a Carlucci specialty," Harvey said.

"I didn't know that," Rondelle retorted. "Anyways, I didn't see the guys who was talkin'."

Rondelle reached for the vodka bottle and emptied every drop into her glass.

"Chloe was with Donovan that weekend. When I picked her up, I told him what I'd heard. He didn't say nothin', told me to forget about it, so I did."

"Then I got a package delivered to me by name at Trader Pete's. Inside were pictures of Chloe with some men I'd never seen before comin' out of Smart Start and a warning to keep my mouth shut about what I'd heard."

"What'd you do with the pictures?"

Her gaze flicked to the right by the floor. "Burned 'em."

Harvey muttered. Martinez murmured something back.

"Shut up." She glared at her brother. "It ain't your business. *I* told Donovan to take Chloe and hide her. Even from me. That's why I didn't want you lookin' for her."

CHAPTER 8

THAT'S HOW DONOVAN HAD KNOWN IMMEDIATELY Rondelle hadn't hired me.

Anger rose from the dark place inside me, thick, black, potent.

Why hadn't anyone listened to Rondelle? She was the child's mother. She'd made a decision, probably the right decision for the first time in her life. Harvey should've been supporting her, not circumventing her.

Rondelle bit her lip, a childish habit which drove home the point she was little more than a child herself.

My head ached. The shitty games people played never changed. To think I'd wanted something different and dangerous in my humdrum PI life. Doing background checks didn't seem like such a bad gig.

"Rondelle, do the Carluccis know Harvey is your brother?" Martinez asked.

I paused, fresh cigarette in hand. Now, there was a problem I hadn't considered. Rondelle could be in even

102

deeper trouble if what Donovan told me about the bad blood between the Hombres and the Carluccis was true.

"I don't list Harvey as a reference. Can you see it? Yeah, call my brother. He's an enforcer with the Hombres. Oh, sure, everything in his job is illegal, but he can vouch for *my* character."

"With all your whoring, boozing, and lying, you've got no right questioning my character, little sis."

"Enough," Martinez said.

I agreed. "Rondelle, do you have any idea where Donovan might have sent Chloe?"

"No."

Harvey swore.

Rondelle straightened her hunched shoulders. "Can I go now?"

Martinez nodded, escorted her to the door, handed her off to No-neck with murmured instructions. He neatly stopped Harvey in his tracks when he attempted to follow Rondelle out.

"Let her go."

For the first time I saw something on Harvey's face besides contempt: deep-seated sorrow.

Then Martinez did the strangest thing; he put his arm around Harvey's shoulder in a half-hug.

And Harvey let him.

Huh? A genuine gesture of affection from one baddie to another? This night just got weirder and weirder.

Martinez caught me staring at him after Harvey left the room. Without a word, he headed for the bar cart, poured three fingers of Bacardi Silver and downed it.

I waited. Eyed the four full bottles of warm Coors sweating on the coffee table.

"I'm sorry," Martinez said, shocking the hell out of me. He sank into the opposite corner of the couch, putting his ostrich skin cowboy boots on the table.

"You should be."

"Don't pull any punches, do you?"

"Wrong." I pointed at him with my cigarette. "I didn't get to zap Harvey last night, that was pulling a punch."

"True," he murmured.

Martinez, this close, sent my protective instincts haywire. I dropped the cigarette butt in the bottle. Swished it around as it hissed out.

"I ought to walk away from this case."

"I know."

"You didn't tell me when you hired me that Rondelle didn't know about it."

"If I told you at the time I didn't think it mattered, would you believe me?"

I shrugged.

"I thought I was doing Harvey a favor."

"Harvey has a shitty way of showing his gratitude."

He lifted his hands in resignation. "That's why I'd rather have the reputation of being a bastard. Every time I play nice guy it turns around and bites me in the ass."

Oh I didn't touch that comment. Not nearly enough space between me and his very bitable ass.

Jesus, Julie, just focus, would you?

"Harvey should've listened to Rondelle in the first

place," I said.

"Let me explain something about Harvey."

I held up a hand. "Don't." *Don't make me feel sorry for him; don't humanize him.* I needed Harvey to be the bad guy because if he wasn't, who was?

"Don't what? Tell you that his mother killed herself by driving drunk? How Rondelle survived but their sixteen-year old brother Lonnie didn't?"

"Martinez, don't do this."

His boots whumped the floor. "She was ten years old and Harvey couldn't get custody of her because he had a felony. He had to watch his only surviving family member shuffled from foster home to foster home on the reservation, and he couldn't do a damn thing about it."

I squeezed my eyes shut and was tempted to clap my hands over my ears.

He scooted closer; his melodious voice held a knife's edge. "Rondelle believed he'd abandoned her. Nothing he did for her was ever enough. She totally rejected him."

An image of my father appeared. Ben had dealt with his rejection from our father by establishing a relationship with me. Not for the first time I wondered if Ben's motives in getting to know me were fuelled by revenge on our father.

"When she got pregnant at nineteen," Martinez continued, "she had nowhere else to go—"

"So she finally came to Harvey."

"Yes."

"Where was Donovan during this time?"

"In Pine Ridge. Drunk, unemployed, unable to take

on the responsibility of a baby. Harvey mostly kept Rondelle off the booze during her pregnancy. After Chloe was born, Rondelle became the party girl again."

I opened my eyes. "How long did Harvey take care of Chloe?"

"A year. While Rondelle played at being a mother, Harvey changed diapers and made sure Chloe had food in her belly."

Don't ask, my brain warned. My mouth opened like a drawbridge anyway. "Rondelle's mother was dead. Where was her father?"

"In the state pen."

I examined the silver buckles on my shoes. "Shit."

"Considering the alternatives, it was a good thing Donovan sobered up and stepped up to his responsibilities. Still, Rondelle saw an opportunity to hurt Harvey like she believed he'd hurt her."

"Oh no."

"Oh yes," Martinez mocked. "She moved. Didn't stay in one place more than a few months. Drove Harvey nuts when he didn't know where they were."

I'd been through that when Ben disappeared. It'd driven me crazy and driven a wedge in my marriage that had splintered it completely.

"Things haven't improved. Rondelle still uses Chloe as leverage. Harvey, being Harvey, pushes the issue and ends up pushing Rondelle further away."

Silence weighed between us while I processed the information. Everyone I came in contact with had family issues. Nothing easy and simple like Mom and Dad occasionally playing favorites, but deep-rooted hatred stemming from tragedy—whether accidental or intentional.

I sighed. "This is so fucked up. Is everybody's family like this?"

"Guess we're just the unlucky ones."

"Yours too?"

"You have no idea."

I waited for him to elaborate. He didn't.

"I'll get started on this again Monday."

Martinez lifted both brows. "Not tomorrow?"

"I wish. Instead I get to suffer through a *family* thing." The clock on the far side of the room caught my attention as it clicked to 9:00. "Look. I've gotta go."

Maybe I could block this night, last night, and tomorrow from my memory banks with earsplitting music and cold beer.

He placed his palm on my knee. "Stay."

A simple request. But hanging around would be a stupid move on my part, despite my body going soft simply from the heat of his hand.

"I can't," I said with genuine regret.

His hand slid away. A heartbeat later his fingers were on my chin, turning my face toward his. "I wish you'd stop running from this."

"Why?"

"Because it's gonna catch us eventually."

I wanted to deny it. I didn't.

He smiled. "Be careful."

Unnerved by his confidence, I blurted, "Why? Think the Carluccis shot Donovan?"

All the teasing warmth bled from his eyes. "Concentrate on finding Chloe and let me worry about the Carluccis."

"They know who I am, don't they?"

"Yes."

He didn't lie, another point in his favor.

Before I asked another question I didn't want the answer to, I snapped my mouth shut, gathered my stuff and left before I did something foolish and stayed.

I'd barely made it to my car when I sensed someone behind me.

I whirled around in the darkness, automatically dropping into a fighting stance. I'd been involved in a brawl in this parking lot before. Although I'd won that particular battle, I wasn't anxious for a repeat performance, especially in heels.

Rondelle materialized, her hands held up in surrender. "Please. Don't hurt me."

"God, Rondelle. Don't sneak up on me like that."

"You sound just like Harvey," she scoffed.

Comparing me to her brother was not a wise move. "What are you doing skulking around in the parking lot?"

"Waiting to talk to you."

"About?"

She sidled closer, fingers twisted in a knot, gaze aimed at the tips of her Keds. "Chloe."

I leaned back against my car, crossing my arms over

108

my chest. Didn't care if it looked belligerent, because I was definitely feeling it. "Excuse me for acting stupid, but weren't we just talking about Chloe?"

She raised her wet eyes to mine, firmed her trembling lip. Her despair—whether real or feigned—was quite a performance. "You think I don't care about her, don't you?"

I shrugged.

"I do care." Tears trickled out; she wiped them with the heel of her hand. "It's just when you told me that Donovan had been shot . . . it shocked me and I sorta went crazy."

"Bullshit."

Her gaze flew to me. "W-w-what?"

"Don't play the 'I-was-so-upset-I-didn't-know-what-I-was-saying' card with me, Rondelle. Unlike Harvey and Martinez, I can see right through you."

The internal debate showed on her face. Continue to act like a spoiled child? Or reveal the real Rondelle? Little girl lost disappeared. "You ain't very sympathetic, are ya?"

"Nope. I'm saving my small amount of sympathy for Donovan. It'll be a miracle if he lives."

"I never meant for him to get hurt." Her sorrow actually looked real.

"A little late for that now, don't you think?"

"Yeah." Rondelle focused on the bar behind us and said thoughtfully, "Interestin' that you ain't still in there with Tony."

"Why is that interesting?"

"You're out here in under thirty minutes and you ain't wearin' that 'I-just-got-laid' smile."

"Gee, thanks," I said dryly. "How do you know we didn't just have a quickie?"

"He likes to take his time."

It was on the tip of my tongue to ask how she knew Martinez's sexual preferences, but the bottom line was I really didn't want to hear a second hand answer.

"That's why you're acting like you trust me all of a sudden? Because I'm not screwing Tony Martinez?"

"That, and because Harvey don't trust you."

So much for my ego.

"Man." She dragged her hand through her tangled hair. "I fucked up. I never shoulda let him make me do that job."

Who made her do what? Had she been forced into prostitution? "How did you . . . I mean . . . Hell, were you really taking money for sex at those parties?"

Her lips curled with contempt. "Nah. I just like fuckin' with Harvey's head. Asshole deserves it. Thinks the worst of me anyway. When I wasn't workin' the cage I really was just a cocktail waitress."

Why would she tell such a big lie?

A rusted Buick LeSabre cruised right toward us. She watched it cagily, slouching out of sight.

It braked in front of us anyway. The driver's side window rolled down. A man poked his head out.

"Rondelle. Come on. We gotta go."

He was a good-looking Native American male, about thirty, cocky, with intense eyes. On second thought, shifty eyes.

"Frankie, I told you to stay over there. No one's supposed to know I'm here."

"This is boring as shit. How much longer I gotta wait?"

"Until I'm done."

Like an angry stallion he tossed his head; a long black mane cascaded over his broad shoulder. "Who the fuck is she?"

"Who the fuck are you?" I retorted.

Frankie sneered and said something to Rondelle in Lakota. I caught *wasicu*, the derogatory name for a white person. Great.

Her abrupt response to him included hand gestures.

Lip curled, he glared at me, destroying his previous beauty. Bald tires spun gravel as he sped away.

"Frankie Ducheneaux, I presume?"

"Yeah." She watched his taillights disappear. "How'd you hear about him?"

"Donovan." I settled back against the car door. "What's the deal? You dating him?"

"I did for awhile, after we met at a meeting."

With the way Rondelle had knocked back the vodka I'd bet my last fifty bucks it wasn't a Sacred Buffalo Sobriety meeting. "A church social?" I joked.

"Sort of. Medicine Wheel Holy Society."

"The group that opposes the casino? You're a member?"

"Used to be. Frankie still is." She closed her eyes. "Lately he's worked at Trader Pete's in the restaurant."

Seemed strange Frankie wouldn't have told her who she was working for.

"Know what's pathetic? The only reason he hooked up with me was to get me to feed him information from Donovan about what was goin' on at the building site. Then he could share it with the Medicine Wheel Society and act like a big man with the leaders. When I wouldn't tell him nothin' anymore, he dumped me."

"Then why are you here with him now?"

"Not my choice. Harvey tracked him down and told him to bring me here. Frankie ain't stupid enough to tell the Hombres *no*. Jerk knew where I'd been hidin' out."

"Do you trust him?"

She laughed. "No. I ain't leavin' with him, either."

I counted to ten, patting myself on the back for my uncharacteristic patience. "You sure you should be telling me this, Rondelle?"

"No, but there's some other stuff you oughta know. It's about the Carluccis. Somethin' I didn't want them to hear."

Withholding more information? Not a smart move. "Martinez is better equipped to deal with any problems you're having with them."

"No. You'll understand because . . . "

"I'm a woman?"

"Yeah." She gnawed on her lip for a second, debating. "See, there's a reason I didn't tell them the guy's name I was with when I overheard that stuff about the sabotage. I wasn't s'posed to be in the private meeting room."

I waited; alarm bells rang in my head. "Who

brought you there?"

"Little Joe Carlucci," she said softly.

"Oh shit."

"Exactly."

"How did you get mixed up with him?"

"He started buggin' me the first week on the job. I was sorta flattered, I mean, he's a good lookin' guy, smooth, has money. And everyone called him 'Junior', not Little Joe. My boss, Robin, just told me to be nice to him."

"So, how nice *were* you?"

"Guess."

On her knees or naked on her back kind of nice.

I didn't want to ask, but I had to know what she'd been dealing with. "Straight sex?"

"Mostly."

"How long did this go on?"

"Too long. I got sick of it real fast. Didn't need his bullshit with all the other junk goin' on in my life, so I gave notice."

Rondelle didn't strike me as the type who'd give warning before she left a crappy job. "Why didn't you just quit?"

"Would've put my boss, Robin, in a bind, tryin' to fill my shifts. I trusted her to keep it quiet."

Half a dozen Harleys roared in, making conversation impossible until they parked.

Finally, she said, "'Course, someone told him."

My brows lifted.

"Not Robin. She was the only friend I had up there."

"What happened?"

"On the day before my last shift, he called me upstairs. Stupid me, I went. He must've been on something, cause he dragged me outta his office by the hair into the next room and raped me. First . . . then, the other, right after." She shuddered so hard she rocked my car. "He was in such a hurry he forgot to—"

Rondelle's eyes flicked to me, the stark fear in them made me sick.

"He forgot to what, Rondelle?"

"Never mind. He scared me. I never felt so . . ."

Dirty. Helpless. Used.

"So stupid. I shoulda known better." She cleared her throat. "Anyway, you get the picture."

A picture I didn't want.

"And so did I. I got the picture." At my baffled look she said, "You ever noticed all them cameras in casinos watching everything goin' on?"

I nodded.

"They're even upstairs. They change them disks every twenty-four hours but they gotta keep records for seven days."

My mouth dropped. "The whole thing is on disk?"

"Yep. He got so riled up he forgot 'bout the security camera." Her voice trickled to a whisper. "But I didn't forget. I'll never forget."

I forced myself to focus on the details, not the distress in her every movement. "How'd you get the disk?"

She fidgeted. "Lifted it from the security room."

"By yourself? Weren't the security guards suspicious?"

"Nah. I'd been hangin' out with them ever since I started the job. Nice guys. Lonely. Told me more than they shoulda about the security system. I knew those upstairs cameras were on a different video feed. Little Joe didn't like no one checkin' up on him so the monitors in the security room were always off.

"Plus, since I worked the cage and was around money all the time I had security clearance to be in there. They didn't have no reason not to trust me. Nobody ever goes back and checks them disks anyway. Especially the ones from upstairs."

"Where is the disk now?"

"Safe."

"Like Chloe is safe?"

Her chin drooped to her chest and I felt like a total bitch.

I softened my tone. "Rondelle, this is beyond dangerous."

"I know. That's why I wanna ask you something important."

A strange foreboding seized me: This case would change drastically in the next ten seconds.

"Stop lookin' for Chloe for a couple of days."

Wasn't expecting that.

"After, when you find her, call me and I'll disappear with her for awhile."

I thought about Donovan, fighting for his life in the hospital. How would he feel if he woke up and realized he might never see his daughter again? Wouldn't he rather have her gone, than dead? How could I possibly have a hand in making that decision?

"Can I ask you something?" she said softly.

"I guess."

"Who's the one person you'd trust with your life? Trust to do the right thing by you no matter what?"

I didn't hesitate. "Sheriff Tom Richards."

"Yeah? Why him? 'Cause he's a cop?"

"No. Because his sense of right and wrong is black and white. Mine isn't. That's why I had to stop working for him, but I'd put my life in his hands any day."

What did it say for my partnership with Kevin that his name wasn't at the top of my list?

"I only got one other person I can rely on."

The way she worded the sentence led me to believe she'd decided to put her faith in me. "Whoa, whoa, whoa. Back up. Why am I on the short list?"

Her doe-like eyes held trust I didn't want and sure as hell hadn't earned.

"Because you didn't roll over for Tony or Harvey or Donovan, or for me for that matter. But mostly because you understand what it's like."

Despite the balmy night my blood ran cold. Not rape. *It*.

Jesus. How the hell had she recognized the victim in me when I tried so damn hard to keep her hidden?

"I keep tellin' myself it ain't so bad." Sour laughter followed. "I'm sure he don't think he did nothin' wrong since I'd been with him before. But not like that. I'd never let him do that to me."

Rondelle was a lot tougher than I was, facing her

rapist after the fact.

"How do you deal with it?" Her staccato breath cut the balmy air as she toed the gravel with her girlish pink tennis shoe.

I could lie, or deny, but I heard myself saying, "The usual. I drink. Smoke. Pretend it never happened."

"What a coincidence. Me too."

The parallels between us hit me then. Left motherless. Floating through life with sporadic support. But she'd turned on her brother and I'd turned to mine.

"Rondelle—"

"Please. Don't say no. I need your help. If somethin' comes up, promise you'll call my friend, the one I trust. He's the only one who can get in touch with me."

"Why would he trust *me*?"

"He won't. Not until you give him the code word."

Rondelle had code words and escape routes set up? Crap. I felt myself sinking deeper.

If Martinez found out all the lies Rondelle told, and that I was covering for her . . . I couldn't think about that. Chloe was her kid. She did have a right to make decisions for her, more so than Harvey or Tony, no matter who was paying the bills.

That attack of conscience dealt with, I snagged a notebook and pen from inside my purse. "Write it down."

She scribbled, then held the notebook tightly to her chest. "Who's gonna see this?"

"Just me. I'll transfer the information to my computer at the office just as soon as I leave here."

"Promise?"

"I promise."

"Okay." Rondelle's chin trembled. "This is really, really important. Don't talk to no one 'bout this. If anyone calls you or contacts you and claims to be my friend, don't believe 'em. I ain't got no friends."

Sorrow punched a hole in my heart. So young to be without hope and so alone. "Have you told me everything?"

"Everything you need to know for now." She passed me the notebook. I looked at the single word she'd written: *tiblo*. Lakota for brother. Shivers raced down my spine.

What else could I say? I handed her a business card. "If you need anything, or think of anything else, call me. Day or night."

"Thanks," she whispered as she disappeared into the night like smoke, just like Harvey.

Maybe they were more alike than she cared to admit.

I stopped at the office and transferred the information Rondelle had given me into my computer. Kevin hadn't been in his office, but I suspected he would be later. I updated the case and whined about having to face my father without him.

Paperwork done, alarm reset, I headed straight to Jasper's.

Music and beer did make for interesting distractions, but I wasn't in the party mood after talking to Rondelle. I left early and went home alone.

The next morning, coffee and a shower stimulated my brain cells, but didn't exactly speed me along to start my day. I stared at myself in the bathroom mirror debating on whether I should bother with make-up. Depending on my dad's mood, he'd either tell me I looked like a whore or like my dead mother.

Around 12:30 Kell called. "I'm going hiking with T-Rex today."

Kell's friend T-Rex was a total loser. His (usually illegal) excursions into the great outdoors involved a cooler of beer, loud tunes, and minimal physical activity.

I didn't use a hiking trip as an excuse to party. It saved my sanity, spiriting me away from my mental demons.

Female laughter echoed in the receiver and Kell managed an offhand, "Maybe we can hook up later."

Maybe not. Maybe it was time to admit Kell and I were over.

I couldn't put off the trip to my dad's any longer.

The county road to the ranch ran parallel to Bear Butte. It bisected the new gravel road leading to the casino. Increased traffic also increased the amount of dust, even way out here. With my windows rolled up and the vents shut, red motes swirled inside my Sentra, making me cough and leaving a powdery residue on everything.

I held my breath until I passed the grove of dead cottonwood trees marking the turnoff to my dad's place. Good practice since I figured I'd be holding my breath a lot today.

Scrub oaks lined the rutted lane. I pulled into the yard next to the machine shed, a habit from my teen years.

After my mother's death, my dad had started over. Sold the only home I'd ever known in Rapid City and bought a ranch in Bear Butte County. I knew he'd been raised on a farm, but I hadn't had a clue he intended to return to that rural lifestyle. Not that living anywhere in South Dakota isn't a rural experience.

I didn't adjust well to life on the ranch. My father didn't care. He wouldn't let me do outside chores. Instead, I cooked, cleaned, and undertook more household responsibilities than should be expected of a grieving young girl.

After a year of hard labor, I'd decided if Dad expected me to act like an adult, then I'd take on an adult persona. I started smoking. Drinking. Lost my virginity at age sixteen in the back seat of a Pontiac Firebird to a guy twelve years older than me.

I liked the rebellious Julie.

My father hadn't.

More and more often he began to give his opinion on my new transformation with his fists. He'd been stingy with physical punishment before my mom had died, waiting until she'd left the house. Then he'd find some sign of disobedience and mete out my discipline with his belt or his hands or whatever was close by.

Clever man that he was, he'd warned me that if I cried to mommy, the next time the punishment would double in severity. I never doubted him. Out of some perverse need to protect my mother from the ugly truth about the monster she'd married, I managed to hide the bruises, and the utter shame.

The punishment was always worse after Ben had been around.

After Mom died all safety parameters vanished.

Kevin began to believe I had turned into the world's biggest klutz—until one spring night when he came out to the ranch and found me beaten, lying on the kitchen floor.

I'd convinced him not to call 911, begged him not to tell, afraid that somehow my father would destroy our friendship if anyone knew the truth about his violent streak.

Kevin had cleaned and bandaged me and let me cry. But he warned me if it happened again, he'd tell his father—a real threat since at that time Kevin's dad was a cop with the RCPD.

Of course it happened again. Kevin never knew. He also hadn't known that night he'd come to my rescue I'd fallen a little bit in love with him.

The screen door on the porch banged open, startling me from the past. I glanced out the car window and waved to Brittney, my father's ten-year old daughter. Her twelve-year old brother, DJ—short for Doug Junior, naturally—wasn't on the welcoming committee. He didn't like me any more than I liked him.

DJ was the spitting image of my father right down to the mean, cold blue stare, black hair, and temper.

Brittney favored her mother, Trish, in appearance. Frizzy copper curls, pale green eyes, her square face spotted with freckles. She seemed a nice enough girl, but I hadn't gone out of my way to befriend her, either.

I suppose that made me a hypocrite. Maybe it was resentment. I knew my father's wife would never let him treat their kids the way he'd treated me. Their lives, their perception of our father, was one I'd never share and certainly never understand.

I climbed out of the car, stopping to admire a yellow rose bush bursting with blooms. Trish had spruced up the sixty-year old farmhouse and made the ideal ranch wife. She gardened, canned, cooked, and liked being hauled out of bed at two in the morning when a blizzard threatened the livestock.

I didn't resent her. She was smart enough not to expect me to be a regular part of their family or to ask why I didn't try to mend the rift with my dad.

Brittney met me halfway. "Mom said to tell you dinner's done."

"I'm a little late."

"That's okay. Church got out late today too."

Another mark against me in my father's holier-than-thou book. I no longer attended church. The whole "spare the rod, spoil the child" philosophy didn't sit well with someone who'd met the business end of the rod on too many occasions. The best way I could honor my father was to stay the hell away from him.

Balto, the family Australian blue heeler, raced down the steps to greet me. I braced myself. He sniffed me and kept sniffing until Brittney jerked him back by his braided collar. I don't like dogs. I'm not afraid of them, just don't understand people's fascination with something that sheds, shits, and drools.

The scent of roast beef, onions, cooked carrots, and bay leaves teased me as I followed Brittney to the cheerful red and yellow kitchen.

Trish was mashing potatoes. Without looking up from the mixer, she said, "Hi, Julie. Go on in to the dining room. I'm about finished."

"Anything I can do?"

"Nope, but thanks."

I wandered into the dining room, as ill at ease as if I were in a stranger's house. Few traces remained of the years I'd lived here. Trish had decorated this house in country kitsch that fit the surroundings in a way I never had.

Heavy footsteps stopped behind me.

Every muscle in my body went on the defensive.

Taking a deep breath, I turned around and faced my father.

CHAPTER 9

"BEEN AWHILE."

No, "Nice to see you" or even a "Hello." I couldn't force a smile, but I did meet his eyes, a frosty blue identical to mine.

"Yeah, well, I've been busy."

"So I've heard."

That stopped me. Dad and I didn't have any mutual friends.

Perplexed, his gaze encompassed the room. "You come alone?"

"Yep."

"Huh. Thought you didn't go nowhere without Kevin in tow."

So this was how it was going to be, *pick pick pick*. Skipping my usual smart-ass answer, I glommed onto the ladder-back chair farthest from his and sat down at my grandmother's trestle table.

He jerked back his padded captain's throne and kept yapping.

"When you gonna quit screwin' around and get married again? It ain't right, a woman bein' a man's *partner* that ain't her husband."

With his emphasis on partner, he might as well have said *whore*.

"You know Kevin and I are just friends and business associates."

Trish breezed into the room with a platter of meat. "How is Kevin, by the way?"

Nicely deflected, Trish.

"Not so good. His girlfriend Lilly doesn't have much time left."

"That's too bad," she said. "Cancer doesn't discriminate against the young."

Dad opened his mouth but Trish shot him a look that shut it.

I wanted to pump my fist in the air and shout, "You go, girl!" but I refrained.

Brittney carried in the potatoes, DJ hot on her heels with the gravy boat and a basket of hot, homemade biscuits.

Everyone settled in. Heads bowed as Dad began the prayer. After the last "Amen" we were finally allowed to eat.

The kids chattered through the meal. I half-listened, busy as I was shoving ranch raised beef in my mouth. Trish is an excellent cook, the one thing I enjoyed in this situation. Since I'd met Kell my red meat intake dropped. I frowned. Why had I let him dictate what I ate?

Trish made dessert, too, double chocolate brownie bars with hand-churned vanilla ice cream.

I'd barely licked the spoon clean when Trish said, "You two go on outside and catch up. Too nice a day to get stuck inside."

Guess my food wouldn't digest before Dad had a chance to upset my stomach. Hell, I even offered to help Trish with the dishes, but she shooed us out.

An after dinner cigarette would've been the perfect capper to the delicious meal. Except Dad frowned on my smoking, and in his present prickly mood, if I lit up, I'd never hear the end of another one of my sins.

Restless, I stuck my hands in my pockets and wondered why I was here. How long would it take him to get to the reason for the summons?

"Let's take a walk," he said.

The afternoon was gorgeous. Temp in the high seventies, with the occasional gentle breeze heavy with the scent of sweet clover. Perfect summer days like this on the ranch made you forget about the harshness of winter, the stress of calving season, the exhaustion of planting and harvesting. I'd always appreciated the appeal of the land, the solitude, if not the work it took to maintain it.

We passed the swing set, the barn, the fragrant black chunk of earth that was Trish's vegetable garden. Silence hung, permeated by everyday outdoor ranch sounds: cattle lowing, meadowlarks chirping, mourning doves cooing, and the constant, annoying buzz of insects.

Dad stopped by the metal gate to the north pasture, placing his worn boot on the bottom rung.

I studied him as he stared across the field. He'd turn sixty-six this year. I supposed he could still be considered a handsome man. Tall, at 6'2", his build was rangy rather than muscular. Thick, dark hair showed neither signs of gray nor of thinning. Square face, aquiline nose, and a broad forehead illustrated years worth of frown lines. Weathered lines also creased the corners of his full mouth and around his eyes.

"Black Irish" was the term my mother had bandied about in those rare instances when she'd called him on his temper. Had she been making it an excuse for his behavior? Or a description of his heart? Although I'd inherited my mother's Scandinavian looks, my eyes were all his.

I tipped my head back, letting the sun warm my face. "I've forgotten how beautiful it is here."

He snorted. "You'd remember if you showed up more n' twice a year."

I could've talked back. I knew that's what he wanted. Naturally, I clamped my teeth together.

A prairie hawk swooped, catching a mouse in its talons before it soared again beating wings across the sky. I wished something, anything would come down and whisk me away.

"Ain't even been out here to shoot your bow." He shifted his weight and the metal latch on the fence rattled. "Or didja give it up?"

"No, I haven't given it up." I'd thought about it, but he wouldn't care about my conflicted feelings.

Finally, he said, "What were you doin' up at Bear

127

Butte when that Injun got shot?"

Injun. He'd used the term to rile me. Again, I ignored the taunt. "Where did you hear about it?"

"Everybody with a scanner heard it. This county ain't that big. Besides, don't get stuff like that happenin' round here very often."

During hunting season there was the occasional accidental shooting, usually some guy from out of state who paid heavily for the right to hunt, in more ways than one. We had our share of domestic calls, drunk driving arrests, vandalism, to name a few. When I worked for the sheriff's department I recorded every incident, so I knew the secrets in Bear Butte County better than most.

I also knew my dad wasn't one of those guys glued to the police scanner hoping to be the first to call his pals to pass along the latest news or misfortune. Forget the tough, loner stereotype of cowboys. Ranchers were as gossipy as churchwomen. "Who called you?"

"Maurice Ashcroft."

NRA poster child and my dad's closest buddy. Surprised me that old Maurice hadn't sped to the scene with guns blazing, dog tags from Vietnam clanking, acting as representative of the Bear Butte County militia—which as far as I knew didn't exist. Then again, the ranchers around here had enough guts and guns to make it a reality.

"'Course, he wasn't the only one. Don and Dale heard it too. Said that Injun worked over where they're buildin' that casino. How'd you know him?"

"From a case I'm working on."

"You'd better not be workin' for those savages that're

buildin' that eyesore."

And my calm facade cracked. "Or what?"

He faced me, his pupils reduced to tiny silver pin-pricks of pure meanness. "Watch your tone."

Again I said, "Or what? You gonna show me who's boss?" I knew my eyes were as cold and mean as his. I gave him a disdainful once-over before I confined my gaze to his face. "Try it, old man; I'll knock you flat on your ass."

He smiled, spitefully. "You ain't so tough, girl. But I'm glad your mother ain't around to hear your foul mouth."

"If she were around, we wouldn't be standing here, would we?" A barbed reminder he'd used the money from her life insurance policy to buy the ranch. If not for her death, he'd still be driving a cement truck.

He didn't have a response for that.

A few minutes passed, which seemed like an hour. God, I wanted a cigarette so bad my lungs were weeping.

"So, are you workin' for the White Plain tribe?" he asked, as if we hadn't just been exchanging heated words.

I could've told him my client information was confi-dential, just to see him lose what remained of his temper, but I didn't. I merely said, "No."

"Good."

"Why do you care?" Some day, I'd find the back-bone to ask him why he hated Native Americans. Because that hatred had been in place long before Ben's birth and my mother's passing.

He pointed across the field. "Take a look around. You seen what the traffic has done, you oughta see the grazing areas. We never used to have dust like that out here. Everything is covered with red dirt. For miles. Maurice had to call the vet out sixteen times in the last month. His calves are eatin' the grass and it's makin' them sick. Hell, four of 'em even died. We're all sufferin' from it."

If I mentioned western South Dakota had been in a severe drought, he'd find some way to dispute it. "The price of growth, I guess."

"Yeah, 'cept none of us asked for this type of growth. And the growth we wanted, we didn't get."

"Bring it up with your county commissioner. Red Granger, right?"

"We tried. Red said there ain't nothin' he can do since the casino is on tribal land. Sovereign nation or some such."

He used his forearm to wipe the moisture from his brow.

"Even though anybody that goes to that casino has to use County Road 9, Red says the county doesn't have the funds to put oil on the gravel, say nothin' of coverin' it with blacktop."

"Did Red talk to Sihasapa Tribal Council? See if they'd be willing to pay for part to keep the dust down?"

"They said it wasn't their problem."

"You'd think they'd want to keep the dust down as much as everybody else."

He sneered. "They can do whatever the heck they want 'cause they don't answer to nobody, least of all the people that're payin' the taxes in this county."

Big bone of contention for everyone. Any revenue from the new casino wouldn't benefit our tiny county. I knew how deep budget cuts affected law enforcement and our limited services. Truthfully, even a small amount of income would be welcome. "Won't some of the traffic spill over to the other businesses?"

"No. Not like when we had a chance to bring some real money in."

"Wal-Mart wasn't serious about building a super center out here, were they?"

"No. I'm talkin' about the outdoor shootin' range."

"Not everyone wanted that."

"Most folks did, in spite of that group takin' it to court." He snorted again. "Dumbest thing I ever heard, getting an injunction because the noise might disrupt their 'meditation.' Then the whole project fell apart when the state got spooked and pulled fundin'. The county lost out on easy money that would've benefited *everybody*, not just one group.

"Now, instead, some slick tribal members found a loophole to build that Injun casino on that land after all. Same thing all over again. The stock growers'll be the ones strugglin'. It ain't right. Something needs to be done."

"Like what?"

"Like stopping that casino from ever openin'."

I didn't like the sound of that. Doug Collins prided himself on voting (Republican) in every local, state, and national election, but he'd never been particularly political. Or much of a joiner.

"Dad, what are you up to?"

"Ain't only me. Lots of people in this area don't want that casino here, includin' other tribes." He harrumphed. "For once some of those redskins are showin' a lick of sense."

"Who else is involved in this?" I demanded.

"Like I'd tell you, *Miss Pee Eye*. I know you'd run straight to your buddy, Sheriff Richards."

It constantly puzzled me why he'd taken a dislike to my former boss. The sheriff was elected, not appointed. "Damn right I would, if I thought your plan would put innocent people in danger."

"Oh I see. It's okay if the tribe puts a hard workin' rancher's livelihood in danger. But the minute your poor, misunderstood Injuns are threatened, then you jump to their defense, don't cha? Couldn't be that *they* were the ones doin' something wrong, no sirree."

"That's not fair."

"But it's the truth." He sniffed, rubbed his nose then scratched the middle of his back like some bug had crawled inside his shirt and was biting him. "I knew better'n to try and talk to you about this."

"That's why I'm here? So you can warn me off?"

"No. I wanted to warn you not to mess in something you don't understand, something you've never cared about."

Never cared about? Just because I hadn't married a rancher and popped out a passel of kids didn't mean I didn't have roots here. My gaze traveled over the pasture. Clumps of creamy yarrow grew along the old fenceline

132

and waved in the breeze. I knew if I walked through the buffalo grass I'd find gopher holes, crusty cow pies, chunks of rock, patches of wild mint. I'd hear birds twittering, rabbits scurrying, and bees buzzing. All the sights and scents and sounds that made up everything and nothing in this chunk of earth wasn't something I'd wanted to forget. I'd always cared about the ranch, and this land, in a way he'd never understand.

Fury rose inside me. My mouth opened to unleash it when my cell phone rang.

Angry, I unclipped it from my waistband and stomped away from him, not bothering to check the caller ID. "Hello."

"I called just in time," Kim drawled. "You sound madder than a wet cat, sugar."

"Hey. What's up?" My lungs labored to control my breathing. I wouldn't give him the satisfaction of anger. I didn't have to prove the violence I hated in him always lurked below the surface in me.

"Ran into Kevin in the parking lot. Told me you probably needed rescuing from your asshole father, and since he couldn't be there with you, he asked me to give you a call and run interference."

I closed my eyes. As usual Kevin had found a way to come through when I needed it. I missed him more than was healthy.

"Julie, hon, you all right?"

"No."

"Ah, sugar, what can I do?"

I paused to clear the anger scrambling my brain. "I

133

didn't plan on going into the office today. Can't you take care of it?" I said loudly, so Dad didn't have to try so hard to eavesdrop.

Kim chuckled. "Ooh. I love this fake 'em out spy stuff. Come on over to my place. We'll eat ice cream, and cry in our satin hankies about how Daddy done us wrong."

"You had the same problem?"

"Yes." Her syrupy sweet southern voice had acquired an acidic edge. "You're not the only one with a nasty daddy, Julie. Maybe someday after I've had a martini or five I'll tell you about mine."

Hell, not another person in my life with issues. Didn't anyone have a normal family?

"Sounds like a plan. I'll be there in a little bit."

"Good. The Ben & Jerry's oughta be thawed by the time you get here. Ta."

I snapped my phone shut and turned toward him. "Look. I gotta go."

"Figured as much."

In his best sentry pose, arms crossed, feet braced apart, face stoic, he waited for me to give him a plausible excuse for why I was taking off.

I didn't.

A beat passed, and I tired of the contest of wills. "Tell Trish thanks for lunch."

"Don't think I won't know if you don't heed my advice, girly. Maybe you could do something right for the first time in your life."

I gave him my back as I walked away, when I really wanted to give him the finger.

CHAPTER 10

WITH HELP FROM KIM AND A PINT OF NEW YORK SUPER Fudge, I managed to shove aside the disturbing conversation with my father. We hunkered down in her pastel house, on her pastel couch, popped "light" popcorn and immersed ourselves in the world of *Oh Brother Where Art Thou?*

Kim understood my Clooney fixation far more than Kevin ever had.

Still, it was weird to have a girlfriend to pal around with.

My mother had died before she'd been able to school me on the subtleties of dealing with other women. Since my friends were guys, I'd acted like one; straightforward, using my competitive streak in athletic and academic situations, not as a conversational skill.

I'd soon learned that was the wrong tack. Women, for all their talk of it, do not appreciate honesty—especially from other women. It only took me the first week in high school to figure out I didn't need the constant validation from other females that most of the girls my age relied on.

Worries about bad hair days and who wore what brand name clothing paled in comparison to my worries on whether my father would use a belt or his fists on me to express his grief.

Besides, Ben, Kevin, and Jimmer had been more than enough. When I didn't have them to count on, I realized I needed, and finally wanted that female camaraderie I'd always avoided.

Luckily Kim and I had clicked right away. Although at times, I suspected the easygoing nature of our new friendship would be tested, just like every other relationship in my life. For right now, I was glad we both worked to keep it light, easy, and fun.

Later, I rolled down the windows as I bumped down the road leading home, reveling in the rare summer air that brushed across my skin like warm velvet. In my housing development few of my adult neighbors were outside on the front stoop enjoying the evening like they did on TV in big city ghettos.

Kids screamed from the playground, a couple of pre-teen boys played basketball on a cracked driveway, three girls wheeled past on their pink bicycles, baby dolls sticking out from the dirty baskets attached between the handlebars.

Most residents were blue-collar workers who'd achieved the American dream of owning a home. Too bad they thought so little of those homes that the majority had fallen into a serious state of disrepair.

My house was no castle, but at least I bothered to mow the lawn and pick up the trash that collected in the drainage ditch running parallel to my property. Rusted car parts, neglected toys, and busted lawn furniture did not decorate my yard.

I parked behind my old Ford. Unlike some of the larger homes, mine didn't have a garage. Made for a smaller house payment and property taxes, but not a fun task in the winter months to sweep off snow and scrape ice from the windshield.

Shades drawn, lights off; the house looked unoccupied. An unexpected happiness bubbled up inside me. Although I'd spent the afternoon on Kim's couch, it wasn't the same as sprawling on my own couch, blissfully eating an entire bag of Dakota Style chips and catching an episode of *The Wire*.

I practically skipped up the sidewalk. When I reached the bottom step, I froze at the sad bundle of wilted dandelions carefully tied with a scrap of yellow lace.

Kiyah.

My heart fell.

The year before I'd befriended the young girl who lived next door. She'd filled some latent mothering gene in me I usually ignored; I'd filled her belly when her mother was too drunk to care whether or not she ate.

Through a bizarre set of circumstances a few months

back, Kiyah's mother, Leanne, had filed a restraining order against me, barring me from contact with Kiyah. I'd quit my job in the sheriff's office shortly after; however, the restraining order had remained in effect.

As much as I wanted to know if Kiyah's life had improved in the months since the Department of Social Services had become involved in her case, I could do nothing. Thinking about Kiyah effectively burst my small bubble of happiness. I reached for the flowers.

"Julie?"

I jumped and the bundle slipped behind the steps where I couldn't reach it.

"Oh dear, I didn't mean to scare you."

I whirled around toward my seventy-something neighbor, Eleanor Babbitt. "You just surprised me."

Actually, it was no surprise she'd snuck up on me; the woman maintained pro status in matters of stealth. She had the snoopy manner of Mrs. Kravitz on *Bewitched* mixed with the personality of Ned Flanders from *The Simpsons*, so it was hard to be mad at her. Especially when I suspected the highlight of her day was picking up her mail.

"Did you need something?" I asked sweetly.

"Not really." Cracked skin on her fingertips looked raw and sore as she fiddled with the bullet-shaped buttons on her Oriental print housedress. "Wanted to remind you we're on the two-day water restriction schedule starting tomorrow."

Ah hah. A lie. As my next-door neighbor she knew firsthand I *never* watered the crabgrass masquerading as my lawn.

She rushed to continue, "You might want to tell that fella that's been staying here sometimes, you know, in case he isn't aware of it."

Fishing for information on Kell. Interesting. I smiled. "I'll be sure to remind him."

Before she had the chance to ask any other questions, a jacked-up black Chevy Blazer turned into my driveway. It was Kell's friend T-Rex's rig, but why wasn't bass thumping through the tinted windows?

T-Rex, an idiotic name for a grown man even if he was a fossil hunter, hopped out of the driver's side, circled around back and opened the passenger door.

First thing to emerge was a set of crutches.

"Steady," he warned as Kell slid from the cab to stand on one leg.

"Thanks," Kell said.

The next thing I noticed was the stretchy tan tape wrapped from the top of Kell's bare left foot up around his ankle. Then the bright blue sling holding his right arm.

"What the hell happened to you?"

Kell winced.

Okay. So maybe I could have been more sympathetic.

T-Rex said, "When we were hiking he tripped and twisted his ankle. Dumb schmuck broke his fall with his hand and managed to sprain his arm too."

Finally my feet moved. But even as I stood in front of him I was speechless.

"I'm all right," Kell said.

"Or he will be in a week or so."

"What?"

T-Rex shouldered Kell's backpack. "That's what the emergency room doc said. He's supposed to elevate his foot, restrict the movement of his arm, and rest for the next seven days. Looks like the band will have to find a fill-in guitar player for the time being."

Seven days? In my house? I knew if I demanded, "Why did you bring him *here*? He doesn't even live here!" I'd come off as an unfeeling bitch. Normally I couldn't give a crap what T-Rex thought of me, but Mrs. Babbitt clucked her tongue, reminding me of her presence.

"You poor thing," she soothed. "My boy Robbie had a nasty sprain once. Took him two weeks to get back on his feet."

Two weeks? Surely Kell didn't expect me to play Florence Nightingale the entire time? Had he told T-Rex I'd take care of him? Or had he just assumed I would?

She patted me on the shoulder. "Call me if you need anything."

"Come on," T-Rex said, starting for the porch, "let's get you settled in." He spun toward me in afterthought. "Any place in particular you want him?"

Motel 6 wasn't the appropriate answer so I shook my head.

Kell shuffled forward. "I'll be fine on the couch. Maybe TV will take my mind off the pain."

T-Rex snorted. "Mr. Natural here wouldn't take any pain killers. Ought to be a real treat in another few hours."

Great.

I think Kell tried not to be difficult. He might've pulled it off if he'd taken any pain medication and become co-matose. But he couldn't get comfortable, he couldn't sleep, and I was the one who suffered.

Mrs. Babbitt brought over a casserole. Thoughtful gesture, though I suspected she wanted to know whether Kell really was sleeping on the couch, and if my windows were as dirty on the inside as they were on the outside.

Of course, Kell wouldn't eat the Italian casserole she'd made because it contained meatballs.

Then I had to make him something else to eat, which he didn't eat because he was in too much pain.

Needless to say, I hopped out of bed the next morning before my alarm went off, skipped the coffee, and escaped to the office.

Grumpy without my customary morning kick start, I wasn't paying attention as I crossed the parking lot, especially after I spotted Kevin's car and hurried to catch him before he returned to his nurse duties.

Two shadows moved in front of me, then solidified.

I looked up.

The guys wore identical shiny suits and twin expressions of doom. "Ms. Collins. We'd like to have a word with you."

This wasn't a pleasant addition to my already crappy day, facing goons that were obviously muscle for somebody. Not Martinez. His bodyguards wore clothes and tattoos touting their allegiance to the Hombres.

A momentary stab of fear jabbed my empty gut. Wouldn't be in my best interest to show it.

"Sorry. I'll have to pass. I'm late." I attempted to skirt the smaller of the two goons; he stepped right into my path.

"I don't think you understand. That wasn't a suggestion."

My hand dropped to the pocket of my suit jacket. "No, I don't think you understand. I don't care who the hell you work for, or what you want, get out of my way."

He didn't budge.

I backed up.

The other goon must've seen it as a sign I'd decided to cooperate. He said, "Good choice. Our car is right over there."

"Please. Tell me you don't think I'm stupid enough to get in a car with you guys?"

"It'd be in your best interest."

"Yeah? It'd be in your best interest to walk away and leave me the fuck alone."

Without a word, big goon guy unbuttoned his suit coat, flashing the piece attached to his hip. Smaller goon guy did the same.

"Is that supposed to make me tremble with fear? How do you know I don't have a gun in my pocket?" I'd bluffed with Donovan and it'd worked then, so I figured I'd give it a shot.

They exchanged a puzzled look.

"You ain't carrying," small goon scoffed in a nasal tone, which confirmed his east coast roots.

I'd suspected, but now I knew for sure who I was dealing with: the Carlucci contingent. Fear manifests in different ways in different people at different times. Mine resembled verbal diarrhea.

"You sure? Maybe I've got a can of pepper spray. Or a stun gun. I could take one of you out before either of you took those guns out of the holster."

I wiggled the hand inside my jacket pocket, watching their beady eyes follow the movement. All I had in there was a pack of cigarettes, a lighter, and my cell phone, but hey, they didn't know that. "You want to take that chance?"

"She's bluffing," small goon said.

"Look around guys." With my left hand I pointed to the security camera hidden beneath an ivy-covered downspout on the side of the building. A fake. The building owners were too cheap to install the real thing and it fooled most people.

"If you were lucky enough to get the drop on me, after I disabled one of you, I guarantee I'd scream like a banshee. Someone would hear it. I also guarantee that unlike on the east coast, some Midwestern Samaritan would call the cops."

I paused to consider them coolly while sweat coated my back.

"I have a feeling you don't have a permit to carry concealed or a registration in your rental car, do you, boys? Do those guns even *have* serial numbers?"

Another quick exchanged glance.

"Bet the cops would love busting you guys. Oh,

143

and since you're obviously not local, I doubt you could convince them to look the other way. Especially since I would have no qualms about pressing harassment charges against your sorry asses." My voice dropped to a loud whisper. "Did I mention I had dinner with the head of the violent crimes division just last month?"

"Shut up," big goon finally said.

"Or what?"

Evidently they weren't used to women, or anyone else standing up to them. I might've cooperated at first, but dammit, I hadn't had a cup of coffee yet and I wasn't thinking too clearly.

They backed off, even when I sensed they'd rather grab me by the hair and shove me face first in the car.

"Look. We just want to talk to you."

"And now you have."

Big goon sighed. "You don't get it. If you talk to us now, my boss won't get involved. Trust me, you don't want him to take a personal interest in you."

"You tell your boss if he wants to talk to me he can make an appointment."

"You don't know who you're dealing with, you stupid bitch," small goon sneered. "Mr. C. will cut your tongue out for showing such disrespect—"

"Shut the fuck up, Tommy," big goon warned.

"I don't see why we gotta put up with her bullshit, Reggie," Tommy said. "Smack her and let Mr. C—"

I retreated toward the building. "I'm going inside now. Follow me and I'll shoot you. You tell your boss, Mr. C—I'm assuming it stands for Carlucci?—that if he tries this intimidation shit with me again, I'll track him down and shoot him. I don't give a fuck who he thinks he is."

No one said a word.

The sound of a steel door hitting a brick wall broke the standoff. But I didn't dare take my eyes off these guys to see who'd joined our little party. I noticed they didn't either.

"Hey," Kevin said, his footsteps picking up speed until he stood beside me. "What the hell is going on?"

God. I hated to lie to him, but I had no choice. I hoped he wouldn't notice the nervous sweat breaking out on my forehead. "Nothing. These guys were just leaving."

Kevin glanced over at Reggie, the big guy. "Is there a problem?"

"No problem." His smile dried up like Wonder bread the minute his gaze landed on me. "We will talk again, Ms. Collins. Count on it. In the meantime . . . " He crossed the ten feet separating us and stopped directly in front of me, his frigid, deadly eyes locked to mine. "Have a nice day. We'll be in touch. Soon."

They climbed in a black Lincoln Towncar and disappeared down the alley.

I exhaled.

"Who were those guys?" Kevin asked.

"Insurance salesmen."

"Yeah?"

"You know how pushy they get when you try to switch companies. Mention something about purchasing a 'whole life' policy and they'll follow you through the gates of hell."

"Hmm," he said, clearly not buying it.

Before he voiced the questions I saw in his eyes, I said, "I was hoping to catch you today. Where are you going?"

Kevin frowned and brushed his hand over my temple. "Babe, why are you sweating?"

He *had* noticed. "Because we're standing in the sun?"

His frown deepened. "It's not that hot out here yet."

"Sure it is," I said, pulling him into the building's shadow. "Let's go inside. Get me something cold to drink I'll perk right up."

"Sorry." Kevin leaned against the brick beside the door. Instead of his usual dapper self—suit, tie, perfectly shined shoes, he looked like a beach bum who'd been on a weeklong bender. "I'd planned on finishing up some employment checks for Greater Dakota Gaming, but, big surprise, I've been summoned."

"By Lilly?"

"No. By Violet."

My eyes widened.

"Her mother. And before you ask, no, nothing's changed with Lilly's condition."

"Then why the summons?"

"Because she can."

I kept my mouth firmly closed.

Kevin's gaze focused on the oak trees in the park beyond the two-story concrete parking ramp. "I'd hoped . . . Hell, I wanted a normal day. Paperwork, catching up on phone calls, shooting the breeze with you.

Drinking a cup of the sludge you pass off as coffee."

"But?"

"But I've got to go because Lilly needs me."

The words, *I need you too,* stuck in my throat.

I fumbled for my cigarettes.

He laughed—an abrasive bark that didn't suit him. "I sound like a whiny prick, huh?"

"Kev, you're entitled."

"It's one entitlement that sucks."

"No doubt." My gaze followed his to the bright green leaves shimmering in the sun, shifting on the morning breeze. "Want me to finish the Greater Dakota employment stuff?"

"Yeah. It's on your desk." He turned and looked at me. "I know you've got the Black Dog case, but I promised Bill in Human Resources I'd get those files to him."

"When?"

"Last Friday."

If Kevin had missed a major client deadline, he was more messed up than I'd imagined.

"How many?"

"Nine."

Figuring an hour for each check, I'd be here . . . until they were finished. Chloe's case would go on the back burner since Greater Dakota was our biggest contract.

"No problem. I'll call Bill and have their courier pick them up before 5:00."

"Thanks. You've been a great partner."

Good thing the bricks dug into my back, holding me up. Made me a little queasy to realize the business was Kevin's tether to a normal life, not me.

Kevin lightly chucked me under the chin. "I'm nominating you for 'Employee of the Month.'"

"Too late, pal. I nominated myself, voted for myself, and spent the bonus check on myself."

His cell phone rang. He checked the caller ID and swore, "Damn intrusive things. I'll check in tomorrow." As if in afterthought, he said, "Consider wearing your gun in case those 'insurance agents' come back."

I smiled. "Never been one to fall for a hard sell."

"Watch your back, tough girl, since I'm not here to watch it for you." Guilt exposed frown lines by his mouth I hadn't noticed before. "Better yet, call Jimmer."

As I watched him drive away with a hollow feeling, my cell phone rang. My home number glowed on the blue screen. Kell. Big surprise.

Damn intrusive things, indeed.

CHAPTER 11

I WORKED THROUGH LUNCH AND FINISHED THE REPORTS by 3:00, even when Kell had called and interrupted me a hundred times.

Okay, more like six times. I knew he hurt, I knew he was bored, but how was that my problem? Like I had time to go home, put on a big red nose and a squirting carnation to keep him entertained.

Things were strained between us after one day.

If I was honest with myself, the more time we spent together with our clothes on, the more I realized we had absolutely nothing in common.

I'd left the answering service on to keep distractions to a minimum. Now that I had a minute, I propped my feet on my desk and indulged in a leisurely smoke. For the first time my mind wandered to the morning's bizarre events in the parking lot.

God. Had I really been so stupid as to mouth off to mafia bodyguards? What if they were still waiting for me out there? And there were two of them and one of me. Bad odds.

I called Jimmer, the great odds equalizer.

He answered on the second ring. "Julie! Been thinking about kicking your ass. Surprised you remembered my phone number, it's been so long."

Oh, the curse of caller ID. "Well, I've been busy."

"Ain't we all. So. What's up?"

"Can't I just call up an old friend to chat?"

His snort of disbelief nearly shattered my eardrum. "Not since you've been hanging out with that musician pussy."

Jimmer didn't like Kell any more than my father would have. If I defended Kell, Jimmer would be more determined to maim him, so I changed the subject.

"Must be your lucky day. How would you like to see me in person?"

"Sure. When?"

"How about now?"

"Now? What's the rush? Did Lilly finally kick the bucket or something?"

Jimmer had less tact than I did. "Nope. Still hanging on."

"Pity."

I slurped my Diet Pepsi, and peeked out the window to the street below. No black-suited guys hovering by the lamppost. "So, you coming over to the office or what?"

He sensed something wasn't right. "What's the deal, Jules?"

"I need you to walk me to my car."

"Why? You got unpaid parking tickets and a meter maid gunning for ya?"

I held back a laugh. "No."

He paused. "Then where is your car?"

"Right below in the office parking lot."

"This some kind of dumb ass joke?"

"I wish. See, I had a little trouble this morning, and with Kevin out of commission, he suggested I call you."

"Who'd you piss off now, little missy?"

His pet name brought a quick smile. "Big Joe Carlucci's bodyguards."

The silence on the line lasted about two seconds.

"Fuck. Don't move. I'll be there in ten." He hung up.

I retrieved my gun from the filing cabinet and shoved it in my purse. Screw Kell. No matter what he claimed, words were not more effective than a Browning High Power. I locked up the office and waited in the hallway for Jimmer.

Permanent solution, hairspray, and shampoo blended with the sharp scent of Pine Sol and the smell of wet wool carpet. Our building janitor, Ricky, must've been busy last night. Though it looked like he'd skipped scrubbing the windows again.

Jimmer bounded up the stairs two at a time. Even wearing camo he didn't fade into the background. At 6'6", and all 300 odd pounds of it solid muscle, Jimmer never blended. From his buzz cut to his combat boots he embodied military.

I had my suspicions he was still involved with some "black ops" section of the government. Not only did he own a pawnshop specializing in military type weapons, he'd disappear for weeks at a time. And he'd never sent me a postcard from his travels.

It didn't surprise me he knew of the Carluccis, since he knew everyone who was anyone. Most people were afraid of him, with good reason. As he bore down on me, I was glad he was on my side.

"Hey," I said. In his shadow I felt like a munchkin from *The Wizard of Oz*.

And he wasn't even winded from running up two flights of stairs. Big hands rested on his hips. "You wanna tell me why the fuck you're messing with those Italian assholes?"

Jimmer pronounced Italian, *Eyetalian*.

"Not intentionally, believe me," I said.

He waited for me to explain, his "talk-or-I'll-rip-you-to-shreds" glare burned into me until I blurted, "Tony Martinez hired me to find Harvey's sister's kid. Only no one knew Harvey's sister, Rondelle, had been working for the Carluccis up in Deadwood. It's gotten more complicated."

"Complications Martinez didn't know about?"

"Yeah, he wasn't really happy when he found out."

"I'll bet. Christ, you really can pick 'em, can't you, little missy?"

I shrugged.

"Does Martinez know someone from the Carlucci

family paid you a visit this morning?"

"No."

"He will." His hard gaze went to my purse and he studied it like he had X-ray vision. "Your Browning in there?"

"Yep."

"Loaded?"

I nodded.

"Stun gun?"

"Ah, no."

He sighed his disappointment.

"Before you ask, couldn't fit my bow in here either."

"Smart-ass. What about your knife?"

"I don't have a knife."

His cool gray eyes met mine. One hand reached behind his back, then he handed me a knife sheathed in a camouflage nylon case. "Now you do."

Holy crap. The thing had to be at least ten inches long. And if Jimmer freely handed it over, I knew it wasn't the only blade he had.

"Thanks." I unzipped my purse and dropped it next to the gun since it wouldn't fit in my jacket pocket. "Do you really think I'll need it?"

"You always need it."

That was Jimmer; he figured everyone should be armed to the teeth at all times. It was endearing, in a psychotic kind of way.

"Ready?"

"As I'll ever be."

"Want me to hold your hand?" he asked snidely.

"No, but you could give me a piggyback ride," I retorted just as snidely.

"Don't push it." Luckily he only took the steps one at a time on the way downstairs, giving my smoker's lungs a break.

Before we opened the steel door leading to the parking lot, Jimmer stopped and said, "I made a quick sweep of the area."

"You did?"

"Course, that don't mean nothin'. They could be waiting on a side street. Or anywhere else, for that matter."

Comforting.

He tossed me a set of keys. "Just to be safe, I want you to drive this."

Be still my heart. Were these the keys to his beloved Hummer? Not a "pussified" one like GM was making, no, his was the real deal, a military issue. I wasn't entirely sure it wasn't fully armed.

"And no," he said, as if reading my mind, "you ain't getting your girlie hands on my Hummer." He pointed to a black Toyota Highlander. "That's your ride."

I couldn't complain. It was much nicer than my Sentra. Still, it wasn't Jimmer's usual style. "Where'd you get that?"

He rolled his eyes. "Didja forget I own a damn pawn shop?"

"Someone pawned their *car*?"

"Car is nothin'. Some people would sell their kid for a fix."

Not touching that one. I really didn't want to know

about any more desperate people. I had enough in my life already. "You don't mind driving my car?"

Jimmer grinned. "You got insurance, right? In case I gotta take evasive maneuvers in that rice burner?"

My gaze narrowed. I started to ask specifics on what qualified as "evasive maneuvers" but my cell phone rang.

Taking it out of my jacket pocket, I flipped it open. My home phone number lit up the screen. Kell again. Great. I debated on ignoring it.

Guilt gnawed at me and I answered cheerily, "Hey Kell, what's up? I'm just on my way home."

"Good to hear, Ms. Collins. We've been waiting for you."

Not Kell. The blood drained from my face. My vision distorted even as I established the voice; Reggie, the big Carlucci bodyguard from this morning.

His laugh left grease stains on my ear. "Surprised? I told you we'd be in touch. We've been having the most enlightening conversation with your friend. Wanna listen in?"

In the background I heard Kell whimpering, then a sharp crack of flesh hitting flesh. Followed by a scream.

The knots in my stomach untied and lashed my throat.

I curled my hand into a fist until the car keys bit into my skin. "You bastard. He has nothing to do with this. Leave him alone."

Jimmer was by my side; his big hand steadied mine after I'd bobbled the phone. He hunkered down, holding the receiver out, pressing his head to mine so he could hear every awful word.

"We just want to talk to you."

"Fine. Let him go and I'll meet you anywhere you want."

"Nope. We tried that this morning, remember? Here's the deal: Tommy won't rearrange his pretty face if you get here within the next, oh, twenty minutes. We'll talk then."

I swallowed. My voice still came out choked. "If I'm late?"

A muffled whump; another cry of pain echoed in my ear. "It'd be in your best interest to hurry."

Click.

Fury surged in me. Not only were those bastards in my house, invading my sacred space, they'd decided to take out their frustration on a man who hadn't done anything wrong except hook up with me.

I spun toward the Highlander; an enormous palm in front of my face stopped the motion.

I glared at Jimmer. "Didn't you hear them? Get out of my way. If I leave right now it'll still take me over twenty fucking minutes to get there."

"Julie, listen to me."

He didn't loosen his grip, but his voice had turned cold and precise. He snatched the keys from me and pocketed them.

"Change of plans. You drive your car. I'll follow you."

I blinked. "You're coming along?"

"Hell, yeah, like I'd leave you to deal with these assholes with one gun and one little knife."

"You don't have to get involved in this, Jimmer."

"Too late for that now." He patted his belt and removed a black box. "Besides, those fuckers need to find out we don't do things that way here."

His confidence bolstered mine. "Damn straight. I'll cut their balls off with my knife and make them wear 'em as earrings."

"That's my girl. Be your usual pissy self. Then they won't suspect you aren't alone."

I watched as he pounded a number on the tiny buttons on his cell phone. "What are you doing?"

"Calling for backup."

I didn't ask who. I just got in my car and drove.

As I sped home, I cursed. I muttered. I smoked like a prescribed burn.

If Kell came out all right, I swore I'd become attentive, helpful, sympathetic. I'd fluff his pillows, cook tofu stir-fry, watch endless hours of FUSE and listen to his dreams of grandeur about when his rock band finally scored a record deal.

Why are you trying to be who he wants you to be and not who you are?

Bad time to have an identity crisis.

I checked the digital clock as I stubbed out yet another cigarette. Five minutes.

Jimmer had called me with last minute instructions. Keep my gun tucked in the small of my back, keep them talking and keep my head down. Like I couldn't have figured out the last one on my own.

What I couldn't figure out was why Carlucci's goons were so anxious to talk to me.

There was one possibility I hadn't considered. What if Donovan knew who'd been causing the sabotage at the Bear Butte building site? If one of Big Joe's goons had seen me talking to Donovan, they might jump to the worst conclusion.

But I could jump to conclusions too. If they had seen me with Donovan, that meant they were responsible for shooting him.

As I approached my house, I noticed the Towncar wasn't parked in the driveway. Strange. Reggie and Tommy didn't seem the type to hoof it.

I slammed the car door and ran up the porch steps. My heart raced, blood rushed in my ears.

I pushed the front door open.

The familiar scent of my home, the lingering remnants of cigarette smoke, coffee, and vanilla candles didn't offer me the comfort it usually did.

Reggie was perched on the arm of my sofa, his gun dangling casually by his side as if he didn't find me a threat.

Kell wasn't a threat. They'd tied him to a kitchen chair, removed his sling and joined his hands together behind his back. With his sprained arm, he had to be in agony.

My gaze traveled down his body to his injured leg, also fastened to the chair with a length of twine. His swollen ankle had turned a hideous shade of purple, like he'd been kicked a time or two. His head hung to his chest.

Hot rage filled me. They'd fucking pay for this.

Reggie snapped out his wrist and frowned at his Rolex. "Twenty-four minutes. You're late, Ms. Collins."

His flat reptilian eyes locked to mine. "Tommy?"

Tommy grabbed Kell's hands and lifted them up behind his back until cartilage popped and Kell screamed.

My guts twisted like a dishrag. "I'm here now so you can untie him."

"Nah. Don't think I will. He's my insurance policy that you'll cooperate. But first," he angled his chin toward my purse, "toss it over. I'm interested to see what you're carrying."

In one quick move I whipped my purse at his chest hard enough the weight of it caught him off guard.

The big gun came up. Pointed at my head. "My patience is wearing thin, Ms. Collins."

"Yeah? So is mine. What do you want to talk to me about?"

"In due time. Now the jacket. Slowly."

Sweat trickled down my spine and pooled in the small of my back. I peeled off my rayon suit jacket with exaggerated slowness. For once it wasn't born out of sarcasm; I was afraid if I moved too fast the gun would slip out of my waistband and I'd be screwed.

Reggie passed my jacket to Tommy as he dumped the contents of my purse. Knife, wallet, lighter, lipstick, pens, perfume, and spare change clattered to the coffee

159

table. His eyes glinted, as if the contents had somehow disappointed him.

Tommy held out my jacket, reaching into the left pocket, coming up with a used tissue. He shoved his hand into the right pocket. Out came my cell phone, cigarettes, and another lighter.

"See?" he sneered. "Told you she wasn't carrying this morning."

Reggie asked, "Where is your gun?"

I didn't move. I didn't blink and I sure as hell didn't answer.

"At her office." The garbled response came from Kell. "I asked her to keep it there."

Kell finally looked at me. No mutinous expression distorted his face, nor did hatred darken his eyes. I almost wanted him to lash out at me because I could deal with bursts of temper. The sad, broken man staring back at me made me want to curl into a ball and hide my face in shame.

"Yeah? How come?"

Softly, Kell said, "Because I hate guns and the violence surrounding them."

Tommy and Reggie howled with laughter.

"That right?" Reggie said to me, amused.

I nodded, wishing he would disappear into the shag carpet like an orange juice stain.

"Let's get started." He gestured to the Lazy Boy recliner across from the entertainment center. "Have a seat."

"I'd rather stand." It burned my ass this dirtball was acting like the host in *my* house.

"Suit yourself." Reggie adjusted his slouch. "Saturday night you had a meeting with Rondelle Eagle Tail. Why?"

As my fear-coated mind tried to formulate a plausible reason, Tommy must've thought I was stalling, because he kicked Kell.

Again, Kell yelled out in pain.

Automatically I started toward him.

Reggie's gun sited at my heart stopped me.

"That'll happen every time you refuse to answer a question. So I ask you again: Why did you meet with Rondelle?"

"She had some information for a case I'm working on."

"What case?"

"Her daughter's."

Reggie's face registered interest. "What about her daughter?"

Stall stall stall. "Long story or short?"

"What do you think?"

"The girl's father snatched her. Rondelle wants the kid back."

"When did Rondelle hire you?"

My gaze fell to the tips of my red Candies sling backs. Talk about clashing with the carpet. I inhaled. Exhaled. Wondered what the hell was taking Jimmer so long.

Black loafers moved into my line of sight. I dragged my eyes up to Reggie's face now close enough to mine that I could count his long, black nose hairs.

"Tommy," he stated.

The crack of flesh hitting flesh bounced off the walls.

161

Kell didn't scream this time; he couldn't through the fist Tommy had plowed into his stomach.

"You'd better answer quickly, Ms. Collins. Pretty soon Tommy will get bored and move on to more persuasive methods. With you."

The leer on Tommy's squashed face as he made kissing noises made my skin crawl.

Instead of fear, a strange calm overtook me. Wrong move. I'd been raped once and I'd blow his brains out before he ever laid a finger on me.

"Rondelle hired me last Friday."

The back of Reggie's hand cracked into my face. Hard. Pain exploded in my head. I stumbled back in my heels, righting myself with the library table by the door before I fell on my ass.

"Don't lie."

I rubbed my jaw, blinked away the stars dancing in front of my eyes. "I'm not."

"You think we're stupid? Saturday night was the first time you met."

"Ever heard of the telephone?" *You dumb fuck.* "She called me."

Reggie made as if to slap me again.

I cringed and backed up. *Any time, Jimmer.*

Should I reach for my gun? Or would Reggie shoot me before I thumbed the safety?

"I'm asking the questions." He motioned to Tommy.

My stomach pitched as I watched Tommy backhand Kell.

Kell gasped, blood burst forth from his mouth, his

head flopped to his chest like a broken-necked doll.

Jesus. Just let him pass out.

"Rondelle couldn't give a shit about that kid," Reggie said, bulling his way toward me again. "So I know she ain't the one paying you to snoop around."

He turned his back on Tommy, planted his feet and aimed the gun at my neck. "Last chance. Who hired you?"

With my mouth waterless as a summer creekbed, I didn't know if I *could* answer.

"I hired her."

Reggie whipped his head toward the steely voice.

I didn't have to. I recognized it.

Tony Martinez.

CHAPTER 12

TOMMY'S EYES WERE LIQUID WITH FEAR AT THE ENORmous pistol Martinez had jammed against his temple.

In that split second Tony had Reggie's attention, I whipped out my gun and pointed it at Reggie's fat head.

Reggie swung his gun toward Kell.

"Well, Mr. Martinez," Reggie said, "this is a surprise."

I'd second that. What was he doing here? And where the hell was Jimmer?

"Appears we've got ourselves a—"

"If you say 'Mexican standoff'," Martinez interrupted coolly, "I'll blow a hole in you the size of Tijuana."

Reggie's lips curled with scorn. "My mistake."

Martinez said nothing.

What a fucked up mess. If I shot Reggie, Reggie would fire at Kell. Martinez in turn would shoot Tommy. Odds were in our favor but it didn't sustain my confidence.

"You here for business or personal reasons?"

Martinez leveled him with that cold-eyed stare.

Reggie sighed and looked at me, his disgusted perusal started at my toes, wandered up my body, landing on the hair plastered to my head by nervous sweat.

"Man. With you owning a strip joint and all I thought you'd have better taste in women."

Martinez merely shrugged.

"Didn't think you got your hands dirty anymore."

He fixed his gaze on Reggie without blinking for what seemed an hour.

My body oozed perspiration from that lethal glare.

Finally, he said, "That's your problem, Reggie. You don't think. You just do whatever Big Joe tells you to do."

"That's my job."

"Yeah? Thought your job was to wipe Little Joe's ass? Big Joe take you off babysitting duties?"

Reggie didn't answer.

"What were you doing at my place Saturday night?"

"We didn't actually set foot in the building, so technically we weren't there."

"Wrong. One little toe on my property means you broke the parameters agreed upon last year." Martinez pushed the gun hard enough into Tommy's temple I was amazed the barrel didn't go right through the skin and into his brain. "Why?"

Tommy stayed still but something in his eyes caused Reggie to talk.

"We had Rondelle followed. Didn't expect she'd show up at Fat Bob's."

"And when she did, you shoulda left immediately. But you didn't, did you? Why?"

"We wanted to ask her some questions. To find out how long she'd been working for you."

"Rondelle doesn't work for me," he said.

Reggie snorted. "What was she doing there?"

"It's a bar. You do the math."

"Which is what we thought, until Rondelle cornered her," he gestured with his head toward me, "in the parking lot. They were all kinds of chatty."

I shivered and my gun wavered slightly. Reggie and Tommy had been watching us? Creepy.

"So?" I asked.

"So," Reggie repeated, "Rondelle wrote something down and gave it to you. We wanna know what."

Great going, Reg. Way to blab to the man who'd hired me that I'd withheld information from him. It'd probably be less painful if Reggie shot me rather than turning me over to Tony.

"Answer the question, Ms. Collins," Martinez said.

"Okay." A weary little sigh escaped from me as my brain scrambled for a cover story. "But I can't give you specifics."

Reggie cocked his head.

"Rondelle gave me her secret family recipe for Indian tacos."

No one laughed.

In fact, no one said a word until Martinez intoned, "Well, there's your answer."

"Bullshit." To Martinez he said, "We figured you planted Rondelle to spy on Carlucci interests in Deadwood."

He laughed softly. Dangerously. "You figured wrong. I didn't know Rondelle was working for a dumb ass like Little Joe until a couple of days ago."

"Joe is gonna eat you for lunch," Reggie said.

The guy was stupid enough to taunt Martinez while he had a gun to his friend's head?

In response, Martinez ground the gun into Tommy's cheek, breaking the skin. "I don't need a spy inside your organization to know you've been messing with my distribution pyramid. The numbers don't lie."

"Take it up with management. That's not my job, remember?" Reggie retorted.

At that point, I thought Martinez would shoot him.

"Besides, that's not why we're here."

"Then why are you here?" I demanded.

Loud carnival music drifted in through the open window in the kitchen. A tinny megaphone blared, "Ice Cream! Frozen Treats!" A couple of cheerful honks of the clown horn and the merry-go-round music distorted as the truck drove away.

"Answer the question, Reggie," Martinez said.

"Rondelle has taken possession of something that don't belong to her. We want it back and we're done askin' nice."

No big stunner they wanted the disk. Everyone wanted that disk.

Reggie glared at me. "What did she do with it?"

"I don't know what you're talking about," I lied.

"Wrong."

"I already told you I'm trying to track down

Rondelle's daughter. That's it."

Reggie's eyes briefly flicked my direction then back to Tony. "Then explain, Mr. Martinez, why you hired her? We know you ain't the kid's father. What's your interest?"

Whoa. The Carluccis didn't know Harvey was Rondelle's brother? Maybe the thug network wasn't as tight as I'd imagined.

Martinez said, "We're like family. Rondelle needed help. I hired Ms. Collins."

Reggie nodded as if it made perfect sense.

My bicep spasmed from straight-arming the gun. My face hurt where Reggie smacked me, and we weren't any closer to laying down our guns and acting like responsible NRA members.

"The daughter really is missing?"

Tony shrugged.

"The father is involved? That's why Ms. Collins was up at the casino building site with Donovan Black Dog?"

How the hell did he know so much about where I'd spent my time?

My mouth opened to ask why someone had been shadowing me *before* I'd met with Rondelle, but Martinez beat me to it.

"Sounds like Rondelle isn't the only one you've been following."

"Not my call. I do what I'm ordered to do."

Had the Carluccis shot Donovan as a warning to Rondelle? Before I could wrap my brain around the question, Kell moaned, drawing our attention.

My throat closed at the sight of blood drying on his chin. The baseball sized bruise on his ankle didn't scare me as much as the lack of circulation in his hands.

I shifted closer to him. Reggie didn't try to stop me. Seemed we were all ready to lower our weapons.

Question was: who'd make the first move?

"Ms. Collins," Martinez drawled, "drop your gun."

I did, clicking the safety on before I hung it by my side.

"Now you, Reggie. Nice and easy. Slowly put it in your holster and I won't keep it. Good. Hands in front where I can see them."

Once Reggie's gun was out of sight, Martinez started to let his gun fall to his side, but at the last second, he spun it, held it by the barrel, and clocked Tommy in the face with the grip.

The plangent crack of metal on bone distorted the air.

Tommy winced, Reggie stepped forward, but Martinez jerked Tommy back by the hair, spinning the Ruger Super Blackhawk like some Mexican vaquero. He pointed it at Reggie's head. "Uh-huh. Stay put. You give Little Joe a message."

"Sure."

"I'm done playing nice."

My legs went watery at witnessing this stone cold side of Martinez.

"Done," Reggie said.

"Good." One handed, Martinez heaved Tommy to his knees in front of Reggie and waited until Tommy scrabbled to his feet before he said, "One other thing. If either of you ever leaves a mark on Ms. Collins again, I'll cut your fucking hands off at the wrist, understood?"

I might've missed Reggie's tiny scowl if I hadn't been so petrified this whole scene could still blow up in our faces.

"Get out," he said, motioning to my front door with the gun.

They exited so fast I figured I'd find scorch marks in the carpet.

My shoulders sagged from the strain. My vision swam, I tried to stay upright, but I swayed, landing on my hands and knees. The musky, putrid scent of Tommy's body odor permeated the room. I gagged and swallowed, hoping like hell I wouldn't throw up coffee and fear in my living room. As I fought the battle, I heard Martinez talking.

"They're gone. Follow them."

I looked up. Big mistake. Blood resonated in my ears; I was seconds away from an adrenaline crash. Before I dropped to the floor, I saw Martinez snap his cell phone shut and scramble toward me.

A sea of orange engulfed me before everything went dark.

"Oh no you don't, blondie. Get up."

A muscled arm circled my waist and I was vertical again. I blinked at him through the gray spots dancing in front of my eyes. "What?"

170

"You aren't gonna take the easy way and pass out."

"I feel sick."

"Tough shit. I'm not dealing with him."

I turned my head slowly until Kell came into view. Still slumped in his chair.

I shook off Martinez's arm. "Fine. Go."

"How do you plan on moving him?"

"I'll get Jimmer to help me. Where is he, anyway?"

"Following Reggie and Tommy."

"Is he coming back?"

"Doubtful."

The high-pitched whine of a Japanese motorcycle racing on the street echoed and faded.

"Why are you here?"

A baleful stare, then, "You know why."

Crap. "Where are your damn bodyguards?"

"Gave them the day off."

"Terrific timing."

Then it hit me: Jimmer had called Martinez for backup, not Kevin. Why? Had Martinez volunteered? Or had Kevin refused? Was I that low on Kevin's list of priorities? I pushed down the sour taste in my mouth that wasn't from blood.

I exchanged my gun for the knife, unsheathing it as I dropped into a crouch in front of Kell.

My hands swept down his bare leg. His skin was clammy. I angled across his knees, careful not to touch him as I placed the knife on the clothesline cord.

"I can't believe they did this. I didn't know . . ." The rush had burned off, and I shook like a junkie.

If I didn't get control I might accidentally cut him. Like he needed more injuries.

The tough girl in my head told me to suck it up, so I did.

Clear-eyed, I sawed away the last of his leg restraints, cringing at the bright red ligature marks bisecting his shins. I knew how much those type of marks hurt, how deep the scars went, regardless if they were visible on the outside.

I scooted around to cut the ties binding his arms.

"He'll fall off the chair if you cut those now," Martinez advised.

"Then you'd better hold on to him."

He braced Kell's shoulders. "Where you gonna put him once he's loose?"

"In my room."

Just like that, Martinez retreated, letting Kell flop. Annoyed, I looked up. "What?"

"I will not help you put another man in your bed."

Hell. This was the *last* thing I needed. His arrogance wasn't new, but the possessiveness in his gaze was.

I deliberately softened my voice. "Please, Tony, don't do this. Not now."

His eyes stayed flat black. "Soon," he said softly.

My reactions were as muddled as my thoughts so I refocused on the main issue: moving Kell. "Can we just put him on the couch?"

Martinez sighed.

I took that as a yes.

I hacked into the rope and kept up a running commentary. "He sprained his right arm and his left ankle yesterday hiking, so we need to make sure his right arm isn't wedged against the couch. We'll prop his left leg on a pillow once we get him prone." I bit my lip. "He probably should go to the hospital."

"How will you explain his injuries?"

"Good point. He doesn't have health insurance anyway."

Not sure, but I think Martinez sighed again.

When the cord broke free, Kell lurched forward.

Martinez caught him.

Somehow we half-dragged, half-carried Kell to the couch.

The medicinal scent of antibiotic soap and the tang of antiseptic chased the stench of Tommy and Reggie from the air. Martinez skulked about as I cleaned up Kell's bloody face. Then I wrapped a bag of frozen corn in a dishtowel and set it on Kell's ankle while Tony continued to pace. I hated when people paced. However, I said nothing.

As I gently slipped his arm back into the sling, Kell stirred.

"Julie?"

My fingers pushed the damp hair from his forehead. "I'm here. Don't try to move, okay?"

"Hurts," he mumbled through swollen lips.

"I know."

His eyes opened.

Martinez had placed his hand on my shoulder and leaned in to peer at him too.

Kell jerked then winced. "Who's that?"

"It's okay," I soothed, shrugging until Martinez removed his paw. "He's one of the good guys."

What the hell was I saying? Since when had Tony Martinez become one of the good guys?

Kell's eyes drifted shut. "Wanna sleep."

Burned my ass that this gentle man had been used to hurt me. And yeah, it doubled the amount of guilt for my brusque attitude yesterday.

I snagged the bottle of Tylenol with codeine from my medicine cabinet and shook out two pills. "Open up and swallow."

"Hey, that's supposed to be my line."

I bit back a smile. Kell did have a sense of humor at the oddest times.

Martinez didn't find it funny; his laser gaze seared a bald spot in the back of my head.

Kell's lips parted. I popped the pills in his mouth and gave him a drink of water, dribbled most of it down his bloodied Grateful Dead T-shirt. I mopped him up and said, "I'll be right here if you need anything."

As soon as his breathing deepened I fumbled for my cigarettes and headed for the kitchen.

Martinez followed a beat later but was smart enough not to speak.

With so many thoughts racing in my head I knew I had to focus on one thing or I'd go crazy.

Through all the harassment and pain inflicted on Kell on my behalf, I still wasn't any closer to my main objective for this case: finding Chloe Black Dog.

Did it matter? To who? Me? So I could convince myself I knew what the hell I was doing in the PI business? Or did it matter to Rondelle? Harvey? Martinez? Was it naïve to imagine she was safe? Maybe Chloe was better off if I *didn't* find her.

I smoked, staring out the ripped screen door. Weeds had popped up all over in my backyard again. I'd actually sprayed them this spring, more than once, at Mrs. Babbitt's urging. Seemed no matter how hard I tried to fix something, make it better, or make it right, somehow I always screwed it up.

A cupboard door banged. I stubbed out my cigarette in an empty can of garbanzo beans. Crossing to the sink, I pressed my butt against the counter and faced Martinez.

"Here." He handed me a glass of tequila.

I wanted to refuse. Truth was, I *needed* that shot.

I downed it before I did something noble and changed my mind.

Martinez's intense gaze focused on the spot where Reggie's fist had tested the strength of my jaw. "You should take care of that."

"I will."

And just like that, I wanted Kevin.

If he were here, he'd take care of it for me. Sure, he'd gripe about my tough girl act, pretend it was a pain to patch me up yet again, all the while his steady hands and serene eyes would soothe me.

But he wasn't here and Martinez wasn't the coddling type, not that I would have accepted it even if he'd offered.

Would I?

Martinez said, "What was on that piece of paper Rondelle gave you?"

"More ideas of where Chloe might be," I fibbed without an ounce of remorse.

"Had you planned on telling me?"

I tossed my head. Ouch. Damn, that hurt. "Of course. Things got a little hectic today, remember?"

His dark gaze made me feel like a bug under a microscope.

As usual, I bristled. "What?"

"Why didn't you call me this morning after these guys approached you at your office?"

"Because I'm not in the habit of running to my clients for protection, Martinez."

"Jesus, you are stubborn."

"So I'm told."

The refrigerator kicked on, filling the silence between us with white noise. Seemed we'd run out of things to say.

Martinez raked his fingers through his hair. Paced to the door. Circled my chrome dinette set. Studied the lack of fine china in my antique oak buffet. Ended up in the exact same spot he'd started.

His nerves surprised me so I cut him a break.

"Doesn't it seem strange to you that searching for one little girl has caused all this?"

"Rondelle's lies caused this, not Chloe."

"You still want me to find her?"

"More than ever."

"Do you think she's safe?"

"I hope so." His bootsteps were strangely quiet as he crossed the linoleum to stand in front of me.

I didn't budge when Martinez tentatively lifted his hand toward my face, his eyes riveted to the bump swelling on my jawbone.

My heart thumped. I wanted his touch as much as I feared it.

At the last second, he dropped his hand.

"You've got my number, blondie. Call me."

He slipped out the back door, and I was glad he was gone.

CHAPTER 13

KELL SLEPT IN FITS AND STARTS.

He had been a much better patient. Then again, I'd kept shoving painkillers down his throat and he hadn't stayed awake long enough to complain.

I sorted laundry. Washed sheets. Thought about making a pot roast. Was bored out of my skull by noon. Unfathomable, some women actually enjoyed this type of life. I sent a silent thanks to the feminist movement that had allowed me the choice.

TV sucked during the day. I could only schlep around in ratty sweats for so long. Much as I grumbled, I liked my job. Wearing nice clothes and makeup, conversing with real people instead of yelling at the idiots on the *Dr. Phil* show. Even filing was better than sitting around waiting for mold to reappear in the bathroom.

I smoked. I brooded. I called the sheriff to ask if Donovan's condition had changed. Nope. Still critical. Evidently the doctors were leaving him in a drug-induced coma, in an effort to prevent permanent brain damage from his head injury. What if he woke up with amnesia?

This whole scenario had changed from a simple parental custody dispute to one involving attempted murder and assault.

What would Kevin do with this case? No brainer. Turn it over to the cops.

Martinez expected me to handle it.

I had this bizarre need to live up to the faith he had in me.

Also, I needed to handle this case to prove I wasn't just wasting my time as an investigator.

Propped against the doorjamb, I watched Kell doze. Waking him seemed cruel, since he'd only just settled down.

I wrote a note, even signed my name with a happy face, and placed it on his chest.

Gun in my purse, I left quietly for the office.

In my absence, we'd had quite a few calls, crank ones included.

I'd come into Kevin's employment fulltime after a case in which my bow had been used to kill a man. A horrible man who'd done unspeakable acts and had deserved to die. A man I'd been credited with killing in self-defense—a lie I maintained to protect the person who'd actually made the kill shot.

My name and picture had appeared in the local

179

news, both in print and on TV. The notoriety disturbed me, especially the nickname I'd picked up, "Redneck Xena." Eventually the media attention had died down.

The good aspect of the publicity was the agency had acquired new clients. The bad aspect? Kevin hadn't been around to help me deal with the extra business. Or the assumption from some crazies that I'd liked killing so much I planned on making it a sideline.

Every once in a while I'd get a proposal to off someone's cheating spouse for a tidy sum of cash. Those contacts were forwarded to the RCPD. I'd even received several offers of marriage. Some strange, strange people inhabit the world.

Two brisk knocks sounded on the outer door.

Martinez?

Why did my heart beat faster?

I opened the door. No such luck. Three men stared back at me. Two young, lean, wiry types sandwiched a sausage-shaped man. "Can I help you guys?"

"You Julie Collins?"

"Got it on the first try. Who are you?"

The pot-bellied one shifted away from the other two. "I'm Bud Linderman."

My mouth made an "O" of surprise.

Not what I'd expected. Bud was in his early sixties. Thinning silver hair hung to his narrow shoulders, Elvis-like sideburns nearly reached the collar of his pearl snapped shirt. A bushy, gray mustache rode prominently below a crooked nose that'd been busted more than once.

He wore a dung-colored western cut suit with white

stitching, white piping, and white cowboy boots. A silver bolo tie, in the shape of a cow skull inlaid with alabaster, and matching belt buckle completed his ensemble. All he needed was a piece of straw in his mouth and he'd fit right in with the cast from *Hee Haw*.

When he smiled, capped teeth shone like he was auditioning for a toothpaste commercial.

"Can we come in?" he asked.

"Sure." I stepped aside and let them in, but left the door open. Didn't care if they thought I was paranoid. I was. With good reason.

"What can I do for you?"

Bud motioned to the chairs in the reception area and the guys flanking him plopped into the seats like well-trained heelers commanded to *sit*.

"I'd like to talk to you about a mutual friend."

"Who?"

"Rondelle Eagle Tail."

My expression stayed blank.

He exchanged a look with the gangly guy closest to him before he refocused on me. "Rondelle told me about your meeting with her Saturday night at Fat Bob's."

"Then you also know that I can't tell you what we talked about."

Frowning, he eyed the reception area. "Is there another place we can sit down and discuss this in private?"

"We've got nothing to discuss."

"I disagree."

My shrug said I didn't care.

"Did you consider maybe I'm not interested in what

you can tell me? But maybe you'd be interested in what I can tell you?"

Okay. I'll admit he'd captured my curiosity.

"How about my office?"

Again, his smile was a bit too slick and a bit too quick for my liking. "After you," he said, gallantly sweeping out his arm.

I settled in my chair and lit up while he not so subtly sized up the contents of my office. I let him. Gave me time to figure out how play this angle.

His gaze wandered back to me. "Got a nice collection of local artists."

"Thank you. But you'd didn't pop in uninvited to admire my taste in artwork."

My comment surprised him. He recovered quickly and drawled, "You're a straight shooter, aren't you? I like that."

"Cut the 'good old boy' crap, Linderman. I'm not in the mood. What do you want?"

One silver eyebrow winged up in a parody of censure. "We'll skip the pleasantries, then. I'm here because I'm worried about Rondelle."

"Why?"

"Various reasons."

I waited for him to expound on those reasons: her job with the Carluccis, Donovan's shooting, Chloe's abrupt absence from her life.

I inspected the tip of my cigarette and remembered what Donovan had said about Bud Linderman being a hard ass. Something reeked with this picture.

"Seems odd, that you're so worried about a former employee. Especially one who's now working for your competition."

"Rondelle has always been more than just an employee; we're practically family. She left my employ on good terms. The opportunity she was offered was too good to pass up."

A canned speech if I'd ever heard one.

My focus honed back in on him. His gaze stayed steady. Had Rondelle told him the same "I'm-a-ho" lie she'd told Harvey about her new job with the Carluccis?

"Was Rondelle's position at The Golden Boot similar to the one she'd taken at Trader Pete's?"

"Not even close. When she worked for me she was a cocktail waitress. Period."

I exhaled. "Wasn't she working the cage?"

"Come now, Ms. Collins," he chided with false humor, "I thought you were a straight shooter. Don't pretend you don't know what Rondelle was *really* doing upstairs in those private meeting rooms at Trader Pete's."

Bingo. He didn't have the real skinny. "I'm not in the business of conjecture, Mr. Linderman. What is it you're trying to tell me?"

"I'm concerned about what Rondelle might have told *you*. I don't know why she dragged you into this mess when I offered to help her"—he smiled tightly—"for free."

"Well, you get what you pay for. What were you going to help her with?"

"With the mess she's gotten into with the Carluccis."

"Mess? Thought this was too good an opportunity for her to pass up?"

"Might've started out that way. But I know the real truth about them now."

"Which is?"

"Big ambitions."

"So?"

"Ambitions don't seem like such a bad thing at first, do they?"

I blew smoke at him since he was blowing smoke at me. "Get to the fucking point or get out."

"Guys like Carlucci start out low profile. Acting like they want to be part of the community. Start out using local vendors. Sponsoring events. Hiring minorities. It's all a big lie." He huffed into his mustache. "Know why Big Joe Carlucci took an interest in Deadwood?"

I cocked my head. His opinion ought to be enlightening.

"He saw it as a laid-back hick town with huge potential. Before long they'll own everything, the casinos, the banks, the resorts. If we allow it, our lives will change. We won't be a quaint little western town with a notorious past, we'll be like Vegas and Atlantic City, with mob problems galore and no future."

"Unlike you, who only has the people of Deadwood's best interests at heart."

"See? Even you don't believe it. No one wants to believe it; they think *I'm* being paranoid. But I know they're breaking the law and thumbing their big Italian noses at us to get what they want."

"Is that your beef, Linderman? These guys don't fit the Waspish western South Dakota ideals?"

"No. You're getting off track. I'm here strictly because I'm worried about Rondelle. When she told me what she'd discovered at that place, I urged her to turn the evidence in to the FBI."

Evidence. Bud Linderman knew about the disk.

The pieces tumbled into place like three cherries on a slot machine. Linderman's concern wasn't for Rondelle; he wanted to use the disk as a business opportunity to run the competition out of Deadwood.

"Why didn't *you* turn them into the Deadwood Gaming Commission?"

"The evidence needs to come from an unbiased source, not from me."

After my conversation with Rondelle, I know she wouldn't have spilled her guts to this self-serving ass wipe, no matter how much he claimed she'd always been "more than just an employee." Now I knew why Rondelle had told me not to trust anyone.

I took my time extinguishing my cigarette. "If you're so buddy-buddy with Rondelle, why aren't you voicing these concerns to her? Why are you coming to me?"

"I haven't been able to get in touch with her. You saw her Saturday night. I wondered if she'd mentioned anything about her plans or where she'd be this week?"

I studied his impassive face. Owning a string of casinos probably contributed heavily to his ability to bluff.

My bluffing skills had improved, but I was nowhere near pro status. "We didn't discuss her schedule."

"What did you discuss?"

"That's between me and Rondelle," I said, with a toothy smile.

His eyelids dropped to half-slits. "She told you about the disk, didn't she?"

I didn't confirm or deny, although my unease with the situation grew when I thought about Rondelle telling anyone—especially this scumbag—what was on that recording.

"Rondelle was supposed to give that disk to me," he said.

"Yeah? Why?"

His shoulders slumped; his disillusioned sigh was almost believable. "So it didn't get into the wrong hands."

The change in his body language was a dead giveaway. He was lying and I was absolutely dying to hear whatever bullshit explanation he'd just concocted. I waited, knowing it wouldn't take long.

"See, we were supposed to meet on Sunday. She was going to hand the disk over to me for safekeeping but she didn't show up. I'm afraid the reason I haven't heard from her is because she's gone and done something stupid."

"Such as?"

"Such as using that disk to blackmail the people involved in it instead of turning it over to the proper authorities like we'd discussed. She could be in danger."

Danger? Blackmail? "Wow. I didn't realize you were working with law enforcement, Linderman."

From the hallway outside the offices I heard the squeak of the handcart as Ralph the UPS guy went about his daily routine.

"What?"

"You just said she was going to give the disk to you. Somehow I doubt that *you* qualify as the 'proper authorities', unless of course, you are working with the Feds."

Caught in his own lie, his hand rose to the black cords of his bolo tie.

I rested my forearms on my desk blotter. "Didn't you tell me about two minutes ago that in order for the contents of that disk to be taken seriously by the Deadwood Gaming Commission, it'd have to come from someone *other* than you? Now you're trying to convince me that Rondelle was willing to let you have it? For 'safekeeping'?"

I paused, enjoying his discomfort. "Wrong answer, Bud. I'm not that stupid and neither is Rondelle. I think you wanted that disk and she wouldn't give it to you because she knew you'd use the disk for blackmail yourself."

Bud Linderman's immediate good ol' boy grin was so strained his mustache had stretched out six additional inches. "Now, that's a downright fascinatin' theory."

I batted my lashes, coquettishly bowed my head. Scarlett O'Hara would've shed a proud tear.

"Except it's wrong," he said.

"Then why don't you tell me why you're all fired up to get your hands on that disk?"

"No. I don't think I will."

I hadn't been expecting that.

He stood. "When you talk to Rondelle again, tell her it'd be in her best interest to call me."

"And if she doesn't?"

"Remind her that I always get what I want. Always. And I want that damn disk."

Bud ambled to the door; his cowboy lackeys instantly materialized by his side like flies on horseshit.

He turned. "One other thing. Tell her she'd better hope you find her daughter before I do."

My belly plunged like I'd swallowed a spur. No mistaking his meaning that time. Before I found my voice to demand how the hell he knew about Chloe, he'd rounded up his posse and they'd rode off.

Had I really wanted to keep going with this case just to prove I could? I was in way over my head and sinking fast. Nothing made sense.

I focused my frustration with Rondelle and anger at Bud Linderman on something productive. Pulling up the emergency number Rondelle had given me, I called it, left a message, and smoked while I waited.

CHAPTER 14

MY PREDICTION RONDELLE'S FRIEND WOULDN'T CALL back was short-lived. My cell rang at noon. The caller ID read: Rapid City pay phone. Uneasiness prickled my skin like a sudden rash.

"Hello?"

"Julie Collins?"

No distorted computer voice.

"Yes, this is Julie Collins," I said.

"I got your message."

"Good. I'm, ah, a friend of Rondelle's."

"Yeah?"

Silence.

"You want proof?"

"Yes."

"Okay the word you're waiting for is *tiblo*." God. I felt like an idiot.

Pause. "I'll meet you at Storybook Island behind the Humpty Dumpty concession stand. Thirty minutes."

"How will I know you?"

"You won't. Tell me what you'll be wearing and I'll track you down."

Not exactly reassuring and plenty stupid on his part to think I'd blindly agree to his plan. "No dice. I need something more substantial to prove *you* really are a friend of Rondelle's."

Dead air.

Had he hung up? I'd had enough run-ins with Rondelle's "friends" for my trust issues to be completely justified.

"Rondelle trusts you because her brother, Harvey, doesn't."

Good enough for me.

"I'm blond and wearing a pink silk tank top." I punched the off button and clipped the phone to my waistband.

After closing down the office, I drove up Main Street until just before I reached the National Guard camp and turned left on to Sheridan Lake Road.

Storybook Island is exactly what the name implies; a kid's wonderland filled with life size characters from children's stories and rhymes. Kids can climb inside a giant concrete pumpkin like *Peter, Peter, Pumpkin Eater*, run through the crooked house built by the crooked man, see *The Three Little Pigs'* houses made of straw, twigs, and bricks, complete with a big, bad wolf huffing and puffing down the chimney.

My favorite display was Willie the Big Blue Whale, not for biblical similarities to Jonah, but because Willie had survived the 1972 flood.

That night in June, Rapid City had received over ten inches of rain in a few short hours. Rapid Creek had swelled, sending a wall of water crashing through Dark Canyon, and then roaring through town, destroying houses, bridges, cars, businesses, and over 200 lives.

I don't remember much about that tragic night, but I do remember riding in the car with my mom several days later when we'd ventured out to witness the damage. Seeing that concrete whale upside down near the Baken Park Shopping Center drove home the seriousness of the situation.

That broken image is the one that haunts me to this day.

The parking lot overflowed with family cars and campers. It was an odd place for this meeting. Adults didn't hang out here unless they had a kid or two in tow, so it'd make it easier to pick out a strange, single man.

I snuffed my cigarette and locked the Browning in the glove compartment. Hot wind blew off the pavement and ruffled my hair. The concrete path curved around waterways dotted with bright green moss, swimming ducks and swans, gurgling fountains, crossing under the stone castle and around the moat until it reached the main entrance—a fiberglass replica of the shoe in the *Old Woman Who Lived In The Shoe.*

Once I'd ducked inside, I tried to get my bearings. I took the left fork. The first concession booth was by the birthday house. "Custard's Last Stand" boasted frozen treats and cold drinks. Bet the Native American kids and their parents who visited didn't find humor in the pun.

I passed the mini-maze, and finally saw the concession stand with a cracked egg on top.

The bench behind it stood empty.

No suspicious types lurked behind Barney. I felt totally out of place in my mauve business suit. I crouched in front of the glass partition and ordered a Diet Pepsi from a red-haired, freckled teenaged girl, appropriately costumed as *Pippi Longstocking*.

The waxy cup nearly slipped from my hand as I dodged a gaggle of kids who'd cut me off. Parents pushing strollers apologized as they hurried after them.

I watched the byplay with a pang of envy. Did these children realize how lucky they were? Did they understand that love, laughter, and fun were not a guaranteed part of everyone's childhood?

Probably not.

Fortunately the bench was in the shade. Unfortunately, I couldn't smoke. Avoiding a white splat of bird poop, I plunked on the other end and slurped my drink.

Straight away a tall man slid into my peripheral vision.

"Julie Collins?" he asked.

I swiveled toward him. "Yes. Who are you?"

"Luther Ghost Bear." He offered me his hand. We shook.

He wasn't what I'd expected. I'd prepared myself for this mysterious friend of Rondelle's to be a total dirtball since Rondelle's life choices hadn't impressed me so far.

Not your job to judge her, a little voice reprimanded.

This man was in his late sixties. His sepia-toned face was pockmarked and scarred, but his brown eyes were clear, sharply focused. A braid—black threaded with silver—looped over his shoulder, reaching the waistband of his crisp jeans.

A group of kids trooped past, matching turquoise shirts proclaiming, "Camp Courageous!" One boy stumbled and scraped his knee. Luther rushed to help the youngster to his feet, patted him on his blond head and sent him on his merry way with an indulgent smile.

"Seems years ago I went away to camp," he mused as he reseated himself. "Do you have any children in your life?"

I shook my head, thinking of Kiyah.

Luther looked at me with unrestrained curiosity. Kevin looked at me like that—or at least he used to—as if my eyes were a conduit to my soul. I wasn't comfortable with anyone probing that deeply so I looked away.

My attention darted to a Skittles wrapper tumbling across the grass. "I suppose you wonder why I called you."

"Yes. If this is about Chloe—"

"It isn't. I mean it is." I blew out a frustrated breath. "Let me start over. Have you heard from Rondelle?"

"Have you?"

"No." I swished the soda around in the cup. "But I got a visit from Rondelle's old boss Bud Linderman today."

"In person, eh? What did you think of him?"

"Beneath that cornpone façade he's mean and slippery as an eel."

Luther chuckled. "*Shee.* How long 'fore he told you

193

what he really wanted?"

"Oh, he took his time. Started out full of concern for Rondelle, which I didn't buy. Got him to admit he wanted the disk."

He reached beside the bench and plucked up a cottonwood leaf wide as his palm. "What else he say?"

"That it'd be in Rondelle's best interest if I found Chloe before he did. I'm sure he'll deny it, but there was no mistaking what he'd meant." I paused, wondering how much this grandfatherly man knew about what'd been documented on that disk. "Have you seen the disk?"

"Yes."

Before I could wrap my brain around that, he added, "I told Rondelle she oughta turn it in. And not to the Deadwood Gaming Commission either, but to the Lawrence County States Attorney's Office."

I agreed.

Deft fingers pleated the green leaf while he spoke. "Everyone wants to place blame. Linderman shouldn't have sent Rondelle in there." His hand stilled. "He knew Little Joe was bad news. What that poor girl suffered through for his greed makes me sick."

Whoa. A bad feeling whipped the soda in my belly into foam. "Wait a sec. *Linderman* sent Rondelle to work for the Carluccis?"

"Yes." The fan-shaped leaf floated to the ground. "News to you, eh?"

I squeezed the cup until the plastic lid popped off. Rondelle's tearful explanation about not knowing who'd hired her had been complete and total bullshit.

Ah hell. I *so* didn't want to share this information with Martinez and Harvey. Now I didn't know what to believe.

"Well, Luther, since it appears Rondelle has lied to me about everything, maybe you oughta tell me what is going on."

Alarm passed through his eyes. "That she lied to *you* ain't the problem."

"Then what is the problem?"

"Not what. *Who.*" He paused, considering his response. "She lied to Bud Linderman."

My bad feeling mushroomed.

"Rondelle told me to tell you everything if you called. Don't think you're gonna like it much. But don't judge her too harshly until you hear it all, okay?"

I nodded.

His gaze tracked a tiny gray finch pecking at crumbs on the concrete. "Couple months back, when she was still workin' for him, Bud 'asked' Rondelle to apply for a job at Trader Pete's. Wanted her to spy on the Carluccis and report back on anything she saw that might interest the state gaming consortium. Was obsessed with provin' they were doin' something illegal.

"Rondelle refused. Said she wasn't gonna get mixed up with them for no amount of money. Linderman thought it was because of the Carluccis supposedly being one of them east coast crime families. But Rondelle wouldn't do it because of her connection to the Hombres."

"Bud didn't know Harvey was Rondelle's brother?"

"No. Bud, being the paranoid, controlling type, wouldn't let the idea go. He saw Rondelle as his chance. Ain't no secret Little Joe likes the ladies and Rondelle is a pretty girl. Bud figured that'd get her into the private places upstairs and give her access to private information. Rondelle still refused. Then it got nasty.

"Linderman 'found' meth in her employee locker. Enough to cause serious problems if he turned her in."

Meth is a big problem around these parts. Every law enforcement agency in the area has banded together to make an example of even the smallest user to get to the big dealers, so I knew Linderman would've followed through with the threat, if for no other reason than to make himself look like the upstanding citizen. "Did she use it? Or was she selling it?"

He shrugged. "Don't know. Didn't matter whether Linderman had planted it because he had proof. Said he'd 'overlook' it if she went to work for the Carluccis. She had no choice.

"When she wasn't getting him information as quickly as he wanted, Linderman switched tactics and threatened Chloe. Proved he could get to her any time he wanted by sendin' her pictures of Chloe with strange men comin' out of her daycare place. Rondelle lost it. She didn't have no one to trust and had to keep her mouth shut and hope she'd find out something to get Linderman off her back."

The pictures hadn't been a lie. I'd wondered. Linderman was more dangerous than I'd expected if he'd gone to that much trouble to threaten Rondelle. Even

Donovan had gotten a glimpse of those pictures as an extra insurance policy.

"But she didn't. After workin' the cage and some of those cocktail parties for a coupla weeks, Rondelle was frustrated 'cause she couldn't find a single thing illegal 'bout the Carlucci's operation. She also realized Bud was so obsessed with discrediting them that he wouldn't believe her until she *did* find something."

I braced myself.

"So she lied. She told Linderman she had a disk, showin' several high-rankin' members of the South Dakota Gaming Consortium in the meeting room upstairs with Little Joe, talkin' about how much it'd cost the Carlucci's to keep the Bear Butte Casino from opening."

Luther looked me dead in the eye. "I'm sure you're thinkin' maybe the security disk, the one showin' what horrid thing Little Joe done to her is jus' another lie. But it ain't a lie 'cause I've seen most of it. Made me mad. Made me want to help her in any way I could."

I found my voice. "Linderman still thinks the imaginary 'meeting' disk is out there and Rondelle is playing games with him?"

"Yeah."

"Holy shit. Does she have any idea how dangerous this is?"

"Yup. That's why she's stayin' out of sight."

A blood-curdling scream sliced through the lazy breeze.

We both froze.

A blond, pig-tailed girl of about four zipped past us,

shrieking at the top of her lungs as an older tow-headed boy chased her with a rubber snake. At least I hoped it was rubber. I shuddered. I hated snakes.

Luther and I seemed to have lost our momentum.

"You're wondering how I got mixed up with this," he said.

"It did cross my mind. You don't seem like Rondelle's type."

"Type? *Shee*. Love ain't something you can categorize."

At my bug-eyed expression, he chuckled.

"I'm not some dirty old man. I'm a spiritual leader for the Medicine Wheel Holy Society."

"Oh."

"Thanks for seein' beyond the wrinkles, even if I am too damn old to be foolin' with that kinda stuff." He frowned. "Too old to be foolin' with the other mess too."

"There's *another* mess?"

He stayed silent so long I didn't think he'd answer.

"Nothin' you should worry 'bout. Problems with the Medicine Wheel Society. Nothin' to do with Rondelle. Just politics. Same as usual. Be nice to say it'd never been that way, but it's always been like that. Even before the younger kids took over the operation and the meetings."

"That's where Rondelle met Frankie Ducheneaux."

"Frankie. How do you know him?"

"Met him briefly when I was talking to Rondelle. Acted like a total jerk."

"He is." Luther seemed to have gone into some kind of trance. "Though Frankie would argue he's full of 'principles.' Thinks old men like me are fools and oughta be put out to pasture. Wants to solve every problem with aggression."

I wondered how aggressive Frankie was.

He answered the question before I asked. "Frankie's a blowhard. Big ideas, but no follow through. I'm jus' sorry Rondelle got mixed up with him."

Donovan had mentioned the group as potential saboteurs. Had Rondelle recognized Frankie's voice in Trader Pete's when she overheard the conversation about sabotage? Had she given Donovan Frankie's name? Had Frankie shot Donovan to shut him up?

"Donovan used to be a member of the Medicine Wheel Society, right?"

"Yes. Helped us keep that shootin' range from getting built coupla years back. Then he got that job with Brush Creek." Luther shrugged. "Donovan had to choose a different direction."

"Doesn't sound like you approved of his choice."

"Not my place to approve or disapprove, jus' to accept. And to offer help to those who need it. Like Rondelle."

"Rondelle didn't strike me as the spiritual type."

"There you go with the 'types' again," he teased.

My cheeks burned.

"No doubt Rondelle has had a tough life. A lousy excuse for what she's been doin' 'cause most of us got bad stuff in our past. She's been driftin' along, makin' bad choices, lettin' her past control her future. Since she don't got nobody else, she looks to me for guidance. I'm jus' an old fool tryin' to set her on the right path."

Old fool my butt. I found myself drawn into the kindness and wisdom of his eyes.

"Are you helping her?"

"Yes." His gaze warmed. "And I can help you."

My breath stalled. "What do you mean?"

"You try to hide it, but it's there, the pain in your eyes."

I blinked, as if the action would hide or erase what he saw.

Calloused fingertips briefly touched the left side of his chest, and I felt it on my skin. "In your heart. Part of life is loss. It's time for you to let go of the past."

Instead of skepticism, I blurted out, "Literally? Just let it go?"

He nodded.

Let go of everything? My mom's death? Ben's murder? My broken marriage? My undefined relationship with Kevin? The resentment toward my father? How? Release it like a balloon?

I studied his weathered face, astute eyes, and the willingness to start me on the journey, even when he sensed I wasn't ready to take that first step.

Had this stranger seen so deeply inside me because of shaman magic? Or was this what normal people sought in their clergymen? A chance to find inner peace?

"Why are you hangin' on to this sorrow, child?"

I wanted to pull back, mull it over. My mouth and brain weren't on the same wavelength.

"Because pain is real. Sometimes I feel everything else in my life is an illusion but sorrow."

He contemplated the sky. "Sorrow isn't a place, nor

should it be a destination, but an end of one. My advice? Face your fear head on." He smiled. "Literally. The answers to your questions will make sense when you're not afraid to hear them."

Little too *woo-woo* for my taste. I managed to say, "Thank you."

Luther plucked a business card from his shirt pocket. Placed it in my palm. "Remember my door is always open." He touched the top of my head. "Be at peace, *kola*."

By the time I looked up, he'd vanished.

The corner of the business card jabbed my palm, proving this conversation wasn't a figment of my imagination. The folded leaf drifted past my pump. I snagged it and saved it between the checks in my checkbook, like a Lakota shamrock.

I was unnaturally subdued for the rest of the night.

Kell whined that I'd left him alone for a few hours, which I'd expected. Instead of telling him to quit sniveling, I slapped on a happy face.

I rubbed his sore neck. Cleaned his wounds. Remade the couch with clean sheets. Cooked dinner and hand fed him. Sat beside him and watched *Rock Star* on VH-1. Tried to shove a couple of codeine down his throat.

He wasn't too thrilled about the last one.

Mostly he dozed. When he wasn't dozing he wasn't talking. At least, not to me. T-Rex had called to check on him, ditto for his band mates. He wasn't inclined to chat freely with me in the room, which made me paranoid he was talking about me, so I graciously granted him privacy without being asked.

Besides, it gave me an excuse to sneak outside and have a smoke. Apparently cigarettes aggravated his injuries, so he (cough cough hack hack wheeze wheeze) suggested he'd feel better if I smoked outside.

When he got that "hey, baby" look in his eye around ten o'clock, for the first time in my life I used the old "not-tonight-dear-I-have-a-headache" excuse, and fled to my room.

Just to prove I could, I decided to stay home one more day.

About 2:00, I'd finished rearranging my Tupperware cupboard when the phone rang. I let Mr. Popularity answer it.

"Julie," he shouted a beat later from the couch, "telephone."

I took the handset from him. "Hello?"

"I might have a line on Chloe," Martinez said.

"How?"

"Don't worry about that now. Want to come along when I check it out?"

"Hell, yes, I want to come along."

"Be at Dusty's in fifteen minutes. Don't be late. You'd better bring your gun."

Click.

I changed out of my sweats and into jeans and a

T-shirt. Combed my hair. Applied some strawberry lip-gloss as make-up. Hid the gun in my purse. I thought about sneaking out the back door so I wouldn't have to face Kell.

Screw that. I'd grown tired of walking on eggshells around him. I grabbed my Doc Marten boots and practically stomped into the living room.

I'd finished tying my laces when he asked quietly, "Where you going?"

None of your damn business. "Following a lead for a case. Why? Do you need me to pick up something on the way back?"

"No." He paused. "Will you be gone long?"

"I don't know."

Another pause. "Are you taking the gun?"

Not *your* gun. Amazing how he'd still refused to give me ownership of it.

"You really want hear the answer to that, Kell?"

His eyes clouded, making me feel like I'd punted a bunny.

"Sorry. Look, can I do anything else for you before I leave?"

He shook his head, hiding behind his fall of golden hair as he sent his attention back to the show on Ovation.

Martinez roared in on a beat-up Harley with "ape-hanger" handlebars, wearing his plain leather jacket without all the patches, ripped up, faded jeans, and thick-soled boots. No helmet. He'd fashioned a bandana around his head "do-rag" style. Dark sunglasses. He epitomized badass biker.

Be still my heart.

He cut the engine.

"Nice bike," I said.

"It'll do. You ready?"

"In a minute." I leaned against my car. "Don't you want an update on the case first?"

"Why? Something else go wrong?"

I told him everything I'd kept from him. About Little Joe raping Rondelle and her stealing the disk documenting it. How she'd asked me not to look for Chloe. Then the visit and the threats from Linderman. I finished up with Luther Ghost Bear telling me how Linderman had forced Rondelle's cooperation in working for the Carluccis, and the other disk that didn't exist.

He stared at me for a full minute. Then he said, "Hop on."

"That's it?" I threw my hands up in the air. "Jesus, Martinez, don't you want to yell at me, fire me, tell me how badly I fucked up?"

"Not especially."

"So I don't get to see the wrath of El Presidente first hand?"

Martinez slid his glasses down his nose. "Trust me. That's something you don't *ever* want to experience."

"But—"

"Get your butt on the bike, blondie. Now."

I got on the bike.

CHAPTER 15

MARTINEZ AND I HAD BEEN CROUCHED IN A FOUL smelling drainage ditch for thirty minutes. Watching nothing through a shared pair of binoculars. Not talking. Waiting for anything to happen besides bug bites and sunstroke.

The abandoned cabin was straight out of a teen horror flick: moldy pine siding, faded gray in spots, stained black in others, a sagging roof, shattered windows that had been boarded up. The whole structure listed to the right. A strong breeze would reduce it to ancient lumber.

I studied the surrounding landscape. Dead trees served as sentinels, the bleached branches dissonantly reminiscent of gigantic bones.

No cars. No sign of life. The tall grass in front of the door had been trampled, indicating there'd been activity of some kind recently.

I expected Donovan would've picked a better place to hide Chloe.

There was something seriously wrong here. What were we waiting for? I might be impatient, but Martinez was flat-out stalling.

Why?

Like he'd tell me. And it didn't help my mood he didn't trust my gut feeling the same way Kevin always did. He sure as hell wasn't Kevin.

Doesn't mean that's a bad thing.

I sighed.

"Will you stop with the heavy sighs?" Martinez hissed.

I slapped a fat black fly on my forearm, wishing I could've smacked it off him.

"Stop fidgeting."

I shifted forward on the balls of my feet. "I'm sick of hiding in this stinky goddamn ditch. We either go in or we leave."

He muttered something.

"Who gave you the tip about this place, anyway?"

"It was anonymous," he replied tersely.

I snorted. "And you trusted it? Shit, Martinez—"

"Don't see that *you've* turned up any new leads, blondie."

The half-empty water bottle clutched in my hand hit the ground. I leapt to my feet like a rattlesnake had crawled in my pants.

"Kiss my ass. You can sit here for another hour, but I'm going in."

I'd stomped about fifteen feet before he spun me around.

"Don't get pissy with me. Just make sure you're ready

for whatever we find in there."

He palmed my shoulders and peered into my face.

I hated that his eyes were obscured. Not that it mattered. Martinez was a master at hiding his emotions, even without mirrored sunglasses.

"Ready for what? A room full of dead mice and birds? A goose, maybe, since this anonymous source of yours has sent us on a wild damn goose chase?"

With forced patience, he turned me back toward the building. Stood behind me, circling his arms around me, and raised the binoculars to my eyes, pointing the lenses at the door.

"What do you see?"

"Besides a broken down shack?"

"Look closer."

I trained the binoculars on the vegetation growing out of the roof, then down past the black splotches on the warped siding, to the dark stains on the door. I squinted, straining to see whatever Martinez had seen.

The spots on the door wavered.

I blinked several times. Had to be an illusion. I held perfectly still. Waited. The spots swirled, creating a different pattern. I bobbled the binoculars, but Martinez's steady hand caught them.

"What the hell is that?"

"Flies. Hundreds of them, by my guess."

He didn't have to explain what all those flies meant. I'd read Patricia Cornwell novels. Something had died in there.

Or someone.

"Oh shit," I said.

His breath grazed my cheek. "If you're not ready, stay here and I'll go check it out."

Now I knew why he'd been stalling. He didn't want to go in there any more than I did.

Sweat prickled my scalp, and then slowly slid down my hairline, past my ear to where my jaw rested against the stubble on his.

Martinez backed up, removed the red bandana from his head and passed it over my shoulder.

Wordlessly, I mopped my face and neck, my gaze glued to the shifting swarms of flies.

"Julie?" he murmured.

"I'm going with you."

Before I chickened out and crawled back into the culvert, I headed toward the cabin. I shoved the bandana in my back pocket and unclipped my gun from the holster.

Martinez walked beside me. My boot crunched the dry grasses and parched soil; his heavy boots made no sound at all. I counted each plodding footfall, *seventy-six, seventy-seven*.

Insistent buzzing broke my concentration. I looked up.

Martinez had shoved his sunglasses on top of his head and had drawn his pistol. My heart rate increased with each inch we moved to the dilapidated building. The constant drone of the flies made the hair on my arms and neck stand at attention. Made my stomach lurch to imagine what we'd find.

He ran up the steps.

The stench hit me even as I scrambled to follow

Martinez inside.

Holy fuck. It was the worst thing I'd ever smelled. A thousand times worse than the trucks that picked up rotting animal carcasses off the roads, or a meat processing plant during hunting season.

My eyes watered even as they adjusted to the dimness. I tried to breathe through my mouth. Didn't help. The heat was unbearable. Revulsion leaked from every pore in my body.

Martinez stopped abruptly.

I'd stuck so close to him upon entering this hellhole that I ran directly into his back. His leather vest brushed my forehead. For a second, I closed my eyes and buried my nose between his shoulder blades hoping to catch a whiff of his familiar scent to block out the fetid smells of death.

"Oh no," he said. "Oh shit. Oh fuck. No. For Christ's sake, *no.*"

His bootheels thumped across the planked floor as fast as my heart thudded in my chest.

My protective barrier gone, the rank odor assaulted me again. Worse than ever. God. I didn't want to see what atrocity had made Tony Martinez whimper. What had made him run.

I made myself look.

I saw the shoes first; bright pink with glittery silver bows. Then the compact body. Slender bare legs. Small torso. Long black hair tangled around slight shoulders and a slim neck. Nothing registered above that; her face had been blown off. She'd be difficult to ID.

But I knew her.

Rondelle.

Black puddles had congealed beneath what was left of her head. Dark spatters dotted her clothing, her skin. Strangely enough, her pink velvet purse had stayed pristine. The wall behind her was sprayed with rusty blood spots and chunks of gray matter that had dried into hard strings.

Hunched over Rondelle, Martinez whispered in Spanish. He formed the sign of the cross in the air above her body with the hand holding his gun. Picked up the bandana lying next to her and slipped it in his pocket.

The flies buzzed around her, in her, oblivious to us.

My gag reflex kicked in. Stomach, spleen, kidneys, lungs; everything inside me crawled up my throat and wanted out.

I bent forward, holding my breath, fingers curled tight around the plastic grip of the gun. The muscles in my throat constricted against the rising bile even as my belly rippled to expel the roiling remnants of my lunch.

Tears stung my eyes; my jaw ached from the effort of clamping my teeth together.

Next thing I knew Martinez had clapped his hand over my mouth and hauled me tightly against his body.

"Goddammit, Julie, get control of it. Now. You *will not* leave any sign we were ever here." His ragged words wormed past the blood pounding in my ears. "Come on. Breathe through it. You're stronger than this, I know you are."

I closed my eyes against the carnage. Focused on

matching my breathing to the labored puffs of air coming from his lungs. Didn't take long to realize that he was just as disturbed as I was. We even shook in tandem. When I felt like my innards might stay in place, I slumped against him.

Briefly, he squeezed me tightly. "Can you deal with it?" he asked in a hushed tone.

I nodded.

He let go and sidestepped me.

I opened my eyes. My gaze slid to Rondelle before my brain screamed *no*. Her arm was outstretched, reaching for something.

Then I noticed what I'd missed before. Another body.

My breath caught.

Martinez whirled around. Glared at me to make sure I wasn't going to hurl, then advanced to the second form sprawled on the floor.

Wearing cowboy boots, jeans, and a T-shirt, the man could've been anybody.

"What the hell happened here?"

"Looks like an execution."

"When?"

"I'm guessing yesterday." He crouched over the man. With the barrel of his gun, he poked an object on the floor that resembled a piece of rope.

Not a rope. A long, black braid shot through with silver.

"Omigod." I slapped my left hand over my mouth.

He glanced up at me sharply. "You know him? Who is he?"

I swallowed. Increased the grip on my gun before I lowered my trembling hand from my equally trembling lips.

"Remember I told you about Luther Ghost Bear. Spiritual leader of the Medicine Wheel Society? That's him. He's the one who saw the security tape."

He's the one who saw the sorrow in my soul and offered me solace.

What if I'd led whoever was looking for Rondelle straight to him?

Vertigo seized me again.

Martinez stood. Wiped his forehead with the heel of his hand. Waved that same hand through the flies buzzing above the hole in Luther's chest. Strangely enough, there were no flies buzzing where his head had been blown apart. "Jesus Christ. There's another one."

"You gotta be fucking kidding me."

"Nope. Behind the door."

I stared straight ahead as he bypassed me. No doubt we'd both know the identity of the third victim, but I was scared shitless to find out who it was.

"I don't believe this," he said.

My heart jumped. *Please, please don't let it be Chloe.* "Who is it?"

"Tommy."

"Tommy who?"

"Tommy, as in the Carlucci's bodyguard, Tommy."

I tiptoed to where Martinez had squatted beside yet another corpse.

It was Tommy all right. Someone had shot him a

bunch of times. However, they'd shown him mercy they hadn't shown Rondelle and Luther: Tommy's head was still intact.

If a Carlucci bodyguard was dead, then who the hell had done this?

"I don't get it," I said.

"Me either. And I've seen enough."

He pushed up off the dirty floor. Scanned the cabin one last time. Lingered sorrowfully on Rondelle before the look hardened and he slid his sunglasses back in place. "Let's get the hell out of here."

A gust of wind blew inside, stirring the putrid smells of human waste, dried blood, and rotted flesh.

My stomach heaved. This time I couldn't hold it. I ran out the door, through the ditch and up the small, rocky hill. I ran until my lungs burned. When I finally stopped, I fell to my knees on the hard-packed ground and threw up through my tears.

After I'd finished retching my guts out, I wiped my mouth with the soggy bandana. I grabbed my gun—how I'd managed not to barf on it was a mystery—and wobbled to my feet. A wave of dizziness struck. I rested my forearms on my thighs before I stood; fainting in my own sickness would completely send me over the edge.

God. I'd never be able to block those images from my nightmares. Never.

Grass crunched behind me. A water bottle materialized. I took it without comment. Swished a mouthful and spit it out. Watched the water disappear as the cracked, red earth sucked it up like a greedy sponge. I wiped another stream of sweat from my brow.

Martinez said: "You okay to ride?"

I eyed the motorcycle propped in the ditch and held a hand to my queasy stomach. We should probably stick around and call the sheriff, but for now I couldn't wait to get away. "I guess."

He rolled the Harley uphill to the road. Swung a leg over the seat as I holstered my Browning. I climbed on behind him, wrapped my arms around his waist, and we roared off.

I closed my eyes and pressed my cheek into the middle of his back. Didn't matter where we were going as long as it was far, far, away from where we'd just been.

We must've crisscrossed half a dozen country roads. Gravel spewed behind the fat back tire. Rock chips pelted my legs. Dust clogged my nose, layered on my hair and skin like talcum powder. The sun beat down on my head. I was dirty, bruised, sunburned, and I didn't care.

When Martinez slowed, I opened my eyes and scooted back in the seat. I had no idea where he'd taken us.

We hung a sharp right between two crooked wooden fenceposts, bumped over a rusted cattleguard and motored through a field until we reached a cluster of half-dead elm trees.

He cut the engine.

I scrambled off while he steadied the bike.

Kickstand in place, he rummaged in the left rear

saddlebag.

He turned toward me. His sunglasses were gone.

At the look on his face I automatically took a step back.

Without saying a word, he cracked the seal on a bottle of Bacardi. Still watching me, he tipped his head back and drank. And drank until the bottle was half empty.

Martinez wiped his mouth with the back of his hand, then jiggled the elixir. "Want some?"

Despite my nausea, I nodded and bridged the distance between us. My fingers brushed his as I latched onto the bottle. I brought it to my mouth and gulped the sweet liquid until my throat caught fire. Took a breath, took another long, long drink. Then another.

Eyes watering, I passed it back.

He killed the remainder.

In less than two minutes we'd sucked down a bottle of rum. It should have bothered me. It didn't. Yet, I'd never seen Martinez so close to losing control.

He'd perched his backside on the motorcycle seat. He reached down, picked up a big dirt clod and chucked it at the closest tree trunk. It exploded, leaving fine red dust in its wake.

His voice was nearly unrecognizable.

"How am I supposed to tell Harvey about Rondelle?"

I rounded the back end of the bike and wrapped my arms around his neck. Laid my cheek on the top of his head. Inhaled the sun-warmed scent of his shampoo. "I don't know."

The air didn't stir. Normal outdoor noises were

curiously absent. Evidently the brutal heat had sent birds and other wildlife seeking shelter. No breeze, but I was grateful for the shade.

Martinez sighed and angled his neck to rub his jaw over my knuckles.

"He'll go ballistic," he said. "This will tip him right over the edge."

Was that Martinez's way of admitting Harvey wasn't stable under normal circumstances?

"So what do we do now? You want me to call the sheriff?"

"No. No cops."

I lifted my head. "What do you mean 'no cops'?"

"Just what I said. No cops."

I waited for him to explain. Of course, he didn't.

"We just saw three mutilated bodies. We can't leave them lying there. The families need to know what happened. God. Whoever did this can't get away with it."

"They won't."

I'd crossed the line into gray areas a couple of times in my PI work. Yeah, I'd defended my actions because the end had always justified the means. But there wasn't any justification for purposely concealing a crime of this magnitude. Those victims were dead, bloated, and worm food. That went beyond the gray area into pure black and I wouldn't have any part of it.

I pushed him. "Just because you hired me does *not* mean you get to make that decision."

Before I could stomp off, he'd vaulted the bike and spun me about. His body blocked mine; his hands cradled my head, forcing me to drown into the icy blackness of his eyes.

"Yes, I do, because you aren't thinking rationally."

I froze.

"Stop looking at me like I'm the Boston Strangler," he snapped.

"Then get your goddamn hands off my neck and quit acting like you're going to strangle me."

He kept his hands right where they were. "You've got to listen."

"Fine. I'm listening."

"I'm not stupid. You think I didn't know something was up? An anonymous tip? About Chloe? Come on. It's obvious someone wanted me to find the bodies before the cops did. Why? And is it a coincidence all their personal belongings were left so the cops could ID them? I don't think so."

Since I couldn't shake my head with the vice grip he had on it, I blinked.

"We are in deep shit here, blondie, since in one form or another we've dealt with every one of those dead people in the last week. Neither of us can afford to get involved in this investigation right now.

"Once they connect Rondelle to Donovan, they'll come to you. They'll already be looking hard at the Hombres with Tommy being one of the victims. Our beef with the Carluccis isn't exactly a secret. Add Harvey and Rondelle into the equation and we're seriously fucked. No one can know what we've seen. Someone else has to discover the bodies."

"How long are you going to let them rot there?" I demanded.

"You think I'm the only person who's been tipped off? I'm surprised we got out of there before the cops showed."

His grip gentled. Shaking fingers caressed my cheekbones.

"Trust me on *this*, if nothing else. Doing nothing is the only way we can handle it."

Part of me knew he was right. Part of me feared if I took this one wrong turn, would anything in my life ever be right again?

I stared at him, looking for guilt, or conceit. I only saw anguish he didn't mask.

"Okay," I said.

And in that moment everything between us changed.

He closed his eyes and exhaled. Pressed his warm, soft lips to my forehead. "Thank you."

"What about Chloe?"

"Now you've got a bigger reason to find her."

Martinez held on to me, like I was the only thing keeping him up. I didn't question my reaction and I sure as hell didn't try to squirm away.

Finally he withdrew. "Let's go."

"You okay to ride?" I asked.

"Yeah. Be better if we could stay here and get drunk."

That numbness had settled inside me, like I'd seen the whole thing on TV. The grisly images replaying in my mind would haunt me for the rest of my life. Alcohol wouldn't blur them, yet I figured it was worth a try.

"That was the worst thing I've ever seen."

His eyes closed. "Wish I could say the same."

"You've seen worse?"

No particulars. No surprise.

He climbed on the bike.

I placed my foot on the peg and threw my leg over, huddling behind him. We didn't speak during the ride, or even after he'd dropped me off at my car.

There was nothing left to say.

CHAPTER 16

I DIDN'T KNOW IF I COULD DEAL WITH KELL AFTER THE horror I'd seen. Hell, I didn't know how to deal with myself. I sat in my car and let the heat of the day bake me. Maybe I could sweat those images out.

Didn't work.

The Babbitt's garage door opened. Before Mrs. Babbitt came over to see why I'd been basting for twenty minutes, I dragged my butt up the steps and inside the house.

Kell sat on my couch, foot propped on the coffee table.

Without a word I kicked off my shoes, stripped, and crawled into the shower. The water washed away the smell of death, but didn't seep into my brain to erase the mental pictures. I stayed under the deluge until the water turned icy. Sad that this was becoming a habit with me.

Robe on, hair combed, I bypassed the niceties with Kell and went straight for the Don Julio in the kitchen.

Three slugs later, I began to breathe again.

Bottle in one hand, empty Flintstones Village mug in the other, I shuffled into the living room and sat down.

"How are you feeling?" I asked, hoping it sounded more sincere than it felt.

"Better."

"Good." Tequila splashed my hand as I poured another shot. I lit a Marlboro, grateful the smoke seeped to my lungs through the tightness in my throat.

The air in the room was noxious, but not from the cloud of tar and nicotine.

"What happened today, Julie?"

Death. Distrust. Disloyalty. Pick one. I couldn't muster up the guts to admit the truth. "Just another day at the office."

"No. Doing paperwork doesn't put that haunted look in your eyes."

I traced a shaky fingertip around the lip of the cup.

"Can you talk about it?"

Not like Kell to press.

I realized he normally didn't ask me anything about my job because he didn't care. I shook my head.

"Then we'll just have to talk about what happened the other day. It won't go away no matter how much you try to ignore it." He patted the cushion. "Come sit by me."

I knocked back the tequila and moved next to him, bringing the bottle along. My cigarette burned untouched in the ashtray.

"You're hitting that stuff pretty hard." Kell reached for my hand. I moved it away. "Booze isn't the answer."

221

"Depends on the question."

As usual he gave me time to consider my smart-ass response. Resentment welled up. Who was he to sit back and pass judgment on me? Or my choices? Better to blurt out the first thing that popped into my head than pretend everything was sunshine and fucking roses.

Dramatic pause. Dramatic sigh. "Julie, you have to know this isn't working."

I didn't argue. But I didn't want to hear his theory on why it wasn't working. Was it too much to hope for he'd keep his wisdom to himself? Probably.

"I know," I said.

"Do you know why?"

"Because we're too different?"

"Partially." He flipped his hair over his shoulder. The move I'd considered so sexy now seemed so . . . staged.

"Partially?"

"You want specifics? Okay. I thought I could accept the parts of you that are so different from me."

Ah. The old "It's not you, it's me" line.

"And now?"

"I realize I can't."

I swallowed the shot and faced him. "I've never hidden who I am from you, Kell."

"That's the problem. Maybe I didn't want to see the real you."

"The real me," I repeated. "What the hell is that supposed to mean?"

"That there are parts of your life, your job for one thing, that I don't understand. That I don't *want* to understand."

The pity in his eyes was my undoing. "Yeah, good, because I don't feel like explaining them." I scooted away and attempted to get up, get away from him and his stupid amateur psychobabble.

Kell grabbed my wrist, with more force than I'd believed him capable of and yanked me back. For a second I panicked. Could Kell have a violent streak like Ray? Like my father?

"You will sit here and listen to me if for no other reason than you owe me for the pain I endured."

Shit. Kevin had been wrong. Kell did have a backbone. Why had he waited until now to show it? My stomach protested the tequila. I wanted to slink away and drink until it didn't.

"Do you know what I see when I look at you?"

I didn't move; this ought to be stunning.

"A beautiful, strong, capable woman with a rock and roll heart and a warrior's soul."

I sensed a "but" coming. There always was.

"But, other times, I see darkness. A woman whose secrets, fears, and scars run so deep I'm afraid I'll get sucked into that black hole. I've clawed my way out of those depths once, Julie, and I swore I'd never be dragged down again."

My fragile hold on my emotions started to slip.

"I've spent years distancing myself from my violent childhood. I thought I could overlook the differences between us because I like being with you."

"But only when I'm 'happy-go-lucky-Julie-the-party-girl.'"

"You've never acted like you wanted more from me than a good time, Julie."

"You didn't seem to mind when you were fucking my brains out, Kell."

He winced.

Infuriated, I snapped, "And don't give me that bullshit line about using sex as a way to get closer to me."

"I could slice you open, crawl inside you, and I still wouldn't get any closer to you," he snapped back. He closed his eyes and shuddered. "Shit. Do you see what's happening? I'm not like this. Not any more."

All the righteous anger left me. Kell was right. He didn't have to stick around and put up with the life I'd chosen. Especially when it was diametrically opposed to the life he wanted.

He inhaled and exhaled slowly. "There's something else you need to know."

My laugh left a bitter taste in my mouth. "I don't think I can stand more honesty today."

"When those guys were here? I didn't pass out."

I gaped at him. "Yes, you did."

"No. I heard every word. I pretended to pass out. I knew the fun would disappear for them once I stopped screaming," he said with resentment. "I was awake until the codeine kicked in."

"So you heard everything."

"Yes."

"That's pretty dangerous knowledge."

"I know. That's why I'm leaving town."

I wanted to ask where, but it was probably better if I

didn't know. I already knew the why.

"The band got a six-week road gig. I can't play for another week, but I'm going anyway. We'll see what happens from there."

"You won't be coming back?"

"No."

I turned my head toward the living room window so he couldn't see my guilty relief. "When are you going?"

"T-Rex will pick me up when I call him."

My gaze zeroed in on the overstuffed army green duffle bag and grungy guitar case by the front door. How had I missed it?

Right, I'd been thinking about the fly-covered bodies rotting in an abandoned shack. Could my life get any more screwed up? Why had I assumed any man would willingly want to be part of it?

"I'm sorry," I said. "I know I should've . . ." What? Done more to try and make him happy so he'd stay? Change my whole life for him so I didn't have to be alone?

Kell reached for my hand. "Hey."

"Don't be nice to me, Kell. Not now."

"I can't help it. You think this is easy for me?"

My eyes finally met his and wished they hadn't.

"I liked being with you, Julie. But the price of being with you is just too high a price to pay."

Excellent parting shot.

"Good luck with the band thing," I said lamely.

Snagging the bottle of tequila, I sought the sanctity of my room.

Curled up in my bed, I heard T-Rex's monstrous rig pull up, the low murmur of masculine voices in the living room, then quiet.

With the mug forgotten on the coffee table, I swigged directly from the bottle. I had better than a buzz on. If I kept it up, I'd pass out.

Who'd care if I fell face first in my flannel sheets?

I thought about calling Kim. Weren't girlfriends supposed to share break-up stories?

I debated on calling Kevin. But he'd always been less than impressed with the men I chose, and consequently, less than sympathetic when the relationship ended. He might even think I'd finally gotten my comeuppance, since I was usually the dumper, not the dumpee.

I swallowed another mouthful, but the liquid burning down my throat didn't wash away the self-reproach.

Who was I to feel sorry for myself, anyway? Rondelle was dead. Harvey would be devastated. Chloe's life would be forever changed. Losing a lover because of my own bad choices paled in comparison.

Dizzy, I let my head thunk back into the headboard. My eyes closed. I'd sleep. Forget about everything. Just a little while.

Peaceful sleep was elusive.

I dreamed. Not about Rondelle, or Chloe, or Kell,

226

but Lilly.

I swept back the beaded curtain leading to her domain, and cool, dewy grass tickled my bare feet. The nauseating scent of Easter lily was in the air, and I couldn't breathe.

Lilly sat in the center of a pillow-covered bed, holding court, her white gossamer gown cascading into a bridal train. Muted sunlight backlit her into an angel.

I shuddered and told myself it was an illusion.

She beckoned me to a marshmallow chair beside her. "We need to talk about Kevin."

Callous Lilly and I never talked. We sniped, argued, and glared. Chatting like old chums was as far out of our realm as this dream. I willed myself to wake up.

Why had my subconscious created a deathbed scene, reminiscent of the one in *Gone With the Wind* where Melanie begs Scarlett to look after Ashley when she's gone?

Lilly stared across the field, the yellow sunflowers turned toward her, anxious to bask in her golden glow. "I know you don't like me."

I said nothing. Lying to a dying woman served no purpose.

"I don't like you either." Her limpid brown eyes met mine. "That's why I'm taking Kevin with me when I go."

"No!"

I reached for her; she disintegrated before my eyes. An ear plopped on her lap. Parts of her body began to drop away like chicken from the bone, until nothing remained but a pile of shriveled black chunks.

Then Kevin shuffled into the room, catatonic,

wearing shackles and a navy Brooks Brothers straitjacket, his gaze stuck on his blue paper shoes.

I tried to get up. To help him. To save him. My chair distorted. Iron clamps snapped across my arms, around my ankles. A crowd gathered, my dad, a priest, my ex-husband, Ray, Harvey. They eyed me through bulletproof glass.

A metal cap covered my head.

Bud Linderman entered the room, tipped his cowboy hat at me, grinned, and flipped the death switch.

In the next second I was standing at the door of the deserted shack. I had a gun in my hand and blood on my clothes.

Dark shapes littered the space like piles of dirty laundry.

Kell was on the floor, dead. Ben was on the floor, dead. Martinez was on the floor, dead. Flies buzzed everywhere.

"See? I told you she'd do it."

I whirled to face Lilly.

All that remained was her voice.

I stared in horror at the carnage before me.

"You've killed them all," Lilly said.

"I didn't kill anyone."

"Wrong. If they're with you, they are as good as dead."

The bloody heaps had multiplied.

Kevin appeared, dazed.

His white tuxedo pants absorbed the pools of blood, red raced from the hem, faded into watery pink when it reached the waistband.

"Make him pay the high price. Shoot him," Lilly urged sweetly. "Pull the trigger."

"No!"

But my arm lifted anyway.

I cried as my thumb released the safety. Screamed as I cocked the slide. Felt the devil snatch my soul as I sited my target.

Kevin came out of his stupor. His eyes went wide with terror.

"Julie, don't—" he yelled as I squeezed the trigger and killed him.

CHAPTER 17

AFTER THE HORRIFIC DREAM, I STARED AT THE POP-corn-texture of my ceiling trying to make sense of it. When the phone rang, I shot straight up like a firecracker had exploded beneath my bed.

I squinted at the clock.

Nothing good comes from a 2:49 a.m. wake up call.

"Hello?"

No answer.

A hang-up? I was about to slam the phone back down when I heard soft breathing, followed by the chink of a bottle against the receiver on the other end.

"Who's there?"

"It's me, Jules."

My strained muscles relaxed. "You scared the crap out of me, Kevin." I shoved pillows aside until my spine connected with the headboard. "Where are you?"

"Home."

"You okay?"

"No, not really. Lilly . . ." He cleared the hoarseness from his throat. "She's gone."

I closed my eyes at the sharp pain in his voice. "When?"

"This afternoon. I came home after. Nodded off. When I woke up, I wondered if maybe it'd all been a bad dream." His labored breathing hummed in the earpiece. The bottle of whatever he was drinking clunked against his phone again. "Has it all been a bad dream? The last few months?"

The bedcovers flew as I hopped up and frantically searched in the darkness for my clothes. "Shit. Hang on, I'll be right there."

"No. Not necessary. I don't need you."

The room spun. My toes dug for purchase in the carpet after my heart dropped to my feet. "What?"

"What I meant was, I don't need you right now. I didn't call you so you could rush over here and hold my hand, Julie."

"What if I want to come over and hold your hand?"

He sighed.

I wanted to scream.

Instead, I asked softly, "Then why did you call me?"

When Kevin didn't answer, my mind supplied wild reasons, all of them selfishly about me, none probably even close to the truth.

"I just wanted to let you know about Lilly."

Was I supposed to say thanks? I bit my tongue.

"It'll be at least another week before I'm back in the office full-time," he continued. "Her parents have asked me to help tie up loose ends and I . . ."

Couldn't refuse. Kevin wasn't a doormat; he was pragmatic. He'd also need to tie up loose ends before he could move on with his own life. I hoped Lilly's parents were the type to *let* him move on.

"Is there anything I can do?" I was so used to being on the other end of dealing with grief that my consoling skills weren't rusty; they were completely corroded.

"Would you call Jimmer in the morning? I've hit my limit in being the bearer of bad news."

"Sure."

Sounded like he took another swig. "Death messes you up, doesn't it?"

Kevin's news added another nasty layer to the gruesome deaths I'd seen today. I shuddered. "Yeah, it does. Are you sure you don't want me to come over?"

"No. I'm not sure of anything except I'm relieved it's done."

From twenty miles away I actually felt him wince through the phone lines.

"Shit, I'm such a bastard for even thinking it, let alone saying it. But, God, she was in such pain. And I couldn't help her." His sure, strong voice wobbled. "Maybe it's clichéd, but at least she's not suffering any more."

"You've done more than anyone could have expected."

"It wasn't enough though, was it?"

"Don't—"

"Sorry. Look. I'll talk to you soon."

"Kev—"

Too late. He'd hung up.

Half an hour later I sat in my car at Kevin's condo, smoking the tail end of my Marlboro Light. The lights were off. Chances were slim he'd fallen asleep.

I'd almost bought his bullshit story about not needing me. Almost. But if it'd been me making the muddled late night phone call, Kevin wouldn't have asked, he just would've shown up on my doorstep.

So here I was. I made space in the overflowing ashtray to stub out my cigarette and shouldered my purse.

As I crept up the redwood steps, I separated his shiny key from the others on my key ring. I shoved it in the lock and quietly swung the door open. Inside, I punched in the code, and waited for the amber light.

I could've knocked, but it would've been too easy for him to ignore me. I reset the alarm and reluctantly hauled myself up another flight of stairs.

The house was absolutely quiet. Completely void of any light, normal household noises, or the lingering scent of food. Totally creeped me out.

Where was Kevin?

I headed down the narrow, dark hallway toward his bedroom, my fingers trailing along the pebbled texture of the wall as a guide.

Behind me I heard a gun slide snapping back as the cocking mechanism clicked in place.

"Don't move," Kevin said, "or I'll blow your fucking head off."

I froze. My mouth didn't.

"Goddammit, Kevin, that isn't even funny."

"Julie?"

I heard the surprise in his voice, but didn't see him, which sent chills up my spine. It was like talking to a ghost. I spun around and glared at nothing.

"Who the fuck were you expecting? The Easter Bunny?"

He revealed his hiding place to be the bathroom, but I still couldn't see his face. "I wasn't expecting you."

"No shit."

"Sorry."

Nerves made me babble, "How many people have the security access code to your house, anyway?"

"Just you and Lilly." He dropped the gun by his thigh. "With all the other things on my mind tonight I wasn't sure I'd reset the alarm."

"Well, you did."

"I thought you were . . . hell, I don't know what I thought."

"I think you almost shot me. No wonder. This place is like a goddamn cave."

Kevin walked to the kitchen. Flipped on the under counter lights and set his gun next to the coffee maker. The yellow glow highlighted the deflated set of his shoulders. He didn't turn around.

"I can't believe you came," he said.

"Yeah? I can't believe you thought I'd stay away."

Silence.

Berating him didn't qualify as comfort.

Oh God. My heart hurt just looking at him.

I slipped behind him and wrapped my arms tightly around his waist, burying my face in the warm cotton shirt covering his back.

His hands rested on my forearms. He leaned into me. I leaned into him. I didn't cry. He didn't cry. Neither of us said a word.

We stayed locked together in silence for a long, long time.

Finally Kevin squeezed my elbows and untangled my arms from his stomach. "Coffee?"

"No. But I will have whatever you were drinking when you called me."

"Peach brandy."

I made a face. "Didn't know you were a peach brandy fan."

"I hate the stuff," he said. "Lilly loved it. Since she won't be around to drink it . . ."

"Peach brandy is fine."

He turned slowly and pressed his backside into the marble countertop.

No wonder he hadn't wanted me to come over; his zombie impression was stellar. Bloodshot eyes, two days worth of stubble, deep lines accentuating his lean face. A ratty baby-blue oxford shirt flapped open, leaving his broad chest bare. A pair of faded Hawaiian surfer shorts hung dangerously low on his hips.

I hadn't seen him in such a state of undress lately. He had to have dropped fifteen pounds in the last month.

My concern gave way to fury. He hadn't bothered to

take care of his own health while he'd been taking care of Lilly. It further incensed me Lilly's family hadn't noticed the toll that round-the-clock care had taken on him.

"Bottle is in there on the coffee table."

Without comment, I followed him. He turned on a metal floor lamp. Cool purple light illuminated his ultra mod living room, the ultimate in bachelor digs. Industrial gray carpet, snow-white walls. Sleek black leather furniture faced an entertainment center that took up one entire side of the room. No knickknacks, artwork, or family pictures cluttered the clean lines of the ebony end tables. So the worn denim comforter and pillow from his bed looked peculiarly out of place in such stark surroundings.

I spied the half-empty brandy bottle and picked it up before dropping on the couch.

Oddly enough, Kevin didn't settle on the opposite end. He plopped right beside me.

I swallowed a hit of the sickly sweet liquid, shuddered, and passed the bottle to him. He knocked back a slug.

"Actually, this stuff's not half bad," he said, handing me the almost empty container.

"An illusion. Downing half a bottle numbs the taste buds." I sipped, then decided the hell with it and gulped a mouthful.

Kevin tipped his head back and drained it. Handed me the empty and kept his neck wedged between the cushions. He stared at the shadows on the ceiling.

I stared at the shadows on his face.

Was I supposed to press him to talk about Lilly? Find another bottle and encourage him to drink until he blacked out? The last time we'd gotten liquored up together, we'd nearly ended up naked.

Not surprisingly, Lilly had been between us that night too.

"What am I supposed to say, Kev? What am I supposed to do?"

"Weird being on the other end, huh?" He rubbed his forehead with the heel of his hand and sighed. "Talk to me. Tell me about how things are going with Kell. Update me on the Black Dog case. Bitch about what happened with your dad on Sunday. Anything. Just don't ask me any questions, okay? I don't think I can stand to answer another fucking question today."

"I've been a bad influence on you," I said. "You never used to swear this much."

"Learned from the best. If you're good at something you should stick with it."

"Fuckin' A."

A tiny smile from him. "So what's up with guitar boy?"

"Old news, my friend. He hit the road with the band."

Kevin lifted his head and frowned. "When?"

"About four this afternoon."

He paled and I knew he'd been mourning a loss around that same time, but a much deeper one than mine.

"Can you believe he dumped me?" I said hastily. "Couldn't deal with the 'darker' aspects of my life."

"Such as?"

237

Kevin didn't know about the visit from Bud Linderman and his posse. Or Carlucci's goons. I couldn't tell him about the bodies Martinez and I had found, not that I wanted to recount that horror. Ever. I had nothing to report on Chloe since I still hadn't found her. Oh, my life was one happy event after another. Maybe Kell had been right.

"Julie?"

"He said the negative energy surrounding my job put a blot on my soul. Like spending his life chasing a record deal made his soul somehow more pure than mine. What a load of crap."

Kevin studied me. Saw right through my bullshit. "I'm not surprised. The only reason you hooked up with him in the first place was because he was the exact opposite of Ray."

I snagged the pillow and squeezed it. "Probably." Without a hint of subtlety, I changed the subject. "Thanks for having Kim rescue me last Sunday."

"No problem. What's new at the ranch?"

"Dad was bitching about the dust from the casino construction. Guess the Sihasapa Tribal Council and the county is blowing off the ranchers' concerns. You know how well that sits with those old boys. He acted all tough, like they'd round up an angry mob and handle it themselves with pitchforks and torches."

"Think his blustering has any merit?"

"No, he's all talk."

Those cool green eyes stayed steady on mine, patient as a cat's. "Not always."

Neither of us said anything for a while. The buzz I'd anticipated from the brandy morphed into sleepiness. I yawned and glanced over at Kevin, who was once again rubbing his temples.

"You okay?"

"Feels like my eyeballs are going to burst."

The clock on the DVD player read 4:02. "I'll go so you can get some rest."

His hand dropped and gripped my thigh. "Stay."

One little word with so much power.

I stayed.

Before I was aware of his intentions, he'd nestled his head in the plumped pillow on my lap and stretched out.

I brushed back the hair from his cool brow. Massaged the tension from his head until his breathing slowed.

Before Kevin drifted off, he murmured, "I'm really glad you came."

Strange, how the simple touches and simple words had healing powers for me too.

I closed my eyes and floated away.

Several staccato knocks echoed and jolted me awake. Sun shone through the blinds, casting barred shadows on the gray carpet. Not orange carpet. I wasn't at home.

Someone grunted.

Kevin.

At some point last night Kevin and I had fallen asleep, me on the floor, and him on the couch. "Kev?

239

Someone's at the door."

"I'm hoping they'll go away."

The banging became decidedly louder.

He pushed up from the cushions. Dragged a hand through his hair. Untangled his legs from the blanket. Stumbled to his feet.

"All right, all right," he grumbled. "I'm coming."

Kevin made his way down the stairs to the front door.

I yawned and scooted up on the couch. With the amount of booze I'd poured into my body yesterday I'd anticipated the world's worst hangover. But the throbbing was minimal. Until the door opened and an arc of light stabbed my eyes. Oh, yeah. There it was.

A lilting female voice exclaimed, "Kevin, it's about time! You had me so worried."

"Hello, Rose," Kevin said. "What are you doing here?"

Rose? Who the hell was Rose?

"You left so quickly yesterday, and we didn't hear from you last night. Mom and Dad sent me to check on you. Are you sure you're all right?"

"I'm fine."

Stairs creaked. At the top, a petite woman with a glossy cap of brown hair stopped and stared at me with something akin to horror.

I resisted the urge to practice my beauty contestant wave.

"Who are you?" She eyed the empty brandy bottle, the twisted bedcovers, my disheveled appearance.

Hoo-fucking-ray. Her resemblance to Lilly was

uncanny.

Before I could answer, Kevin interjected, "This is my partner, Julie Collins. Julie, this is Lilly's younger sister, Rose Howard."

She folded her arms over her chest. A move rife with hostility, but not as grating as the way her impertinent little nose flared repulsion. "Lilly told me all about you."

"Yeah?" No doubt Lilly had made me out to be the anti-Christ. Rose had just lost her sister; her antagonism didn't surprise me. I chalked up her attitude to grief and let it slide. I inched my toes into my Birkenstocks.

"I'm sorry for your loss," I said automatically.

"I was just about to make coffee," Kevin said. "Be right back."

Then the deserter snuck into the kitchen, leaving me alone with the prickly Rose.

Cupboard doors banged, water ran, coffee beans crunched in the grinder. How the hell long did it take to make coffee?

Evidently Rose was far unhappier with me being here than I had suspected and she wanted to make sure I knew it.

"Didn't take you long, did it?" she sneered. "My sister's been dead less than twenty-four hours and yet, here you are, cozied up to Kevin."

When Kevin returned, she spewed her venom on him. "Lilly warned me this would happen. But I'd expected better from you."

I shot to my feet. Had to be a new record for me: from conciliatory to confrontational in 2.3 seconds.

"Shut up. You don't come here and treat him like some goddamn delinquent after he's spent the last three months at Lilly's bedside."

"Julie—"

"No. She wants to think the worst of me, fine. But I will not stand here and watch her treat you this way."

I glared at her until color bloomed on her cheeks.

"Why the hell are you here at 7:30 in the morning? Give the man a little time. It's not like he hasn't spent every waking hour with your family. Or is his grief a group activity too?"

My cynical side wondered if Rose was hoping Kevin would turn to her so they could share their sorrow. That thought made my skin crawl.

But not as much the horrid thought that immediately followed.

Is that what everyone assumed about me? That I'd been biding my time until Lilly died and then I'd make a move on him?

My God. Is that what *Kevin* thought?

I felt all kinds of ill that owed nothing to alcohol.

Kevin sighed.

Rose shot me a dirty look that would've done Callous Lilly proud. "It's none of your business why I'm here."

"Rose, why don't you go into the kitchen. I'll be right there," Kevin said.

She gave him a tremulous smile. "Of course. I'm sorry. It's just . . . so hard." A tiny sniff of distress escaped. Shit-brown eyes glistened with tears. She dropped her waiflike chin, too distraught to continue.

And I thought Lilly had been bad.

Kevin reached out to her, touching her shoulder, offering reassurance. "Don't worry about it. I'll just see Julie out."

Since he was facing me, he didn't see her triumphant look before sashaying into the kitchen.

I *so* didn't need this crap. I snagged my purse, and gave Kevin a wide berth on my way downstairs.

He caught me at the door and pulled me next to the coat closet and out of earshot. "Hey. I didn't know she was coming."

"Pity you didn't pull the gun on *her*."

Kevin smiled. "Always the tough girl. Thanks for showing up last night and kicking my ass. I wasn't thinking straight when I said I didn't need you."

"I know that, doofus." I smoothed the wrinkles on his shirt. "And you're welcome."

"Doofus. Haven't heard that one in a long time."

"I meant it in the most affectionate way, you dork."

He covered my hand with his. Leaned down and rested his forehead to mine. "I know."

The coffee pot beeped twice.

I gave him a small headbutt and backed away. "Call me if you need anything."

He nodded, but I wouldn't hold my breath waiting for the phone to ring.

CHAPTER 18

I'D MANAGED TO SCORCH MY LUNGS WITH A FEW CIGA-
rettes on the way home from Kevin's.

The soft, sweet air exclusive to summer mornings
breezed through my car window. On this glorious day,
I drank in the sights and sounds of the season that I'd
been too busy to notice.

A rocky meadow stretched alongside the road. The
rolling ground dipped and spread out until it butted up
against a steep pine-covered hill. Sumac grew in spots
along the fence line, the rosy-magenta blooms of fire-
weed played peek-a-boo with the tall stands of grass.
This time of year the grasses ranged in color from a ro-
bust green to mustard yellow to a toasted brown.

My imagination, or was everything covered in a fine
layer of dust?

In the pen of the riding range that ran perpendicu-
lar to the highway, two colts frolicked while the rancher
loaded hay bales into the back of a beat-up Ford truck.

I stuck my arm out the window and waved. He waved back.

We're all neighbors in friendly South Dakota.

A few early risers on my street, who cared about their homes, were out watering lawns, flowers, and vegetable gardens in hopes of combating the impending heat.

Life didn't stop for death. While the gardeners were fretting about dry rot and fertilization, people like Kevin, and Lilly's family, were mired in grief.

I passed Kiyah's run-down house; chipped gray paint, busted screen door, garbage scattered throughout the front yard. My feeling of peace dissipated.

The periodic visits from Social Services hadn't changed her situation. Strange men still paraded through her mother's house and bed. Because of the restraining order, Kiyah could no longer seek refuge with me.

Without me as a crutch had Kiyah finally made friends her own age in our neighborhood?

I gave myself a mental slap. I had to let go, no matter how much I hated it. No matter how many nights I'd lain in bed listening to the loud party next door, worrying about one scrawny seven-year old girl.

Hopefully Chloe Black Dog was in a better situation.

I parked and headed toward the house when I noticed Mrs. Babbitt on her knees, pulling weeds by the chain link fence that separated her property from the Crendahl's. A tattered straw hat was perched on her head, the lemon yellow ribbons flapped merrily in the wind. Next thing I knew, the hat was cartwheeling toward me.

I snagged it before it became a kite.

Mrs. Babbitt scampered over. "Oh, thank you!"

"No problem." I twirled the hat on my finger before passing it back.

For most of my neighbors money was tight. The Babbitt household was no exception, but Eleanor always looked neat as a pin, whether in worn gardening togs or Sunday-goin'-to-meetin' clothes.

Today she seemed frayed around the edges.

Her gardening gloves were caked with dirt, as were her navy polyester pants, pilled in places, patched in others. The long, loose-sleeved blouse, dotted with blue cabbage roses, hung past her ample hips.

No chi-chi neon-colored rubber gardening clogs for her. She wore plain white canvas lace-up tennis shoes, covered with grass stains that matched the gloves.

"Beautiful morning," I said.

"Yes, yes, it is." She made a big show of securing the hat, tying the ribbons, avoiding my gaze.

Normally I steered clear of her. Instead of counting myself lucky, I perversely dug in my heels for a long overdue neighborly chat.

"Your petunias have really taken off in the last week." I pointed to the pale lilac blooms she'd called *Sugar Daddy*, that were cascading from the whiskey barrels lining the sidewalk.

"They love this heat much more than I do." She fidgeted with her gloves, eyes fixed on my spotty lawn. "I'd better get back at it before it gets too hot."

"Is everything all right?" I placed a tentative hand

on her shoulder.

She flinched and glanced up at me.

And I saw it. The wide brim of her hat couldn't quite shade the purple bruising around her right eye.

"Jesus. What happened to you?"

Her gloved fingers automatically touched the mark, leaving a dirt smudge on her pallid cheek.

"Oh, that." She laughed feebly and jerked off the gloves. "I jabbed myself with the shovel handle separating iris in the backyard. Sometimes I'm so clumsy."

At least she'd come up with an original lie, not the old standby she'd "run into a door."

My first impulse was to demand to know why she stayed with a man who hit her. Didn't she have an ounce of self-worth? But I bit my tongue. She probably would've left if she'd had the choice. Making her feel like an idiot for staying wouldn't help. It'd just make her feel small. I figured Mr. Babbitt had done that enough.

A hollow feeling settled in the pit of my stomach. Eleanor Babbitt was another person I couldn't help. I'd try, I'd worry, but in the end it wouldn't matter. Seemed to be the story of my life. No wonder I drank so much. No wonder I ended up spending so much time alone. I was a magnet for broken souls.

On impulse I said, "I was just about to make a pot of coffee. Would you like to come in and have a cup?"

Her fingers stopped making nervous knots with her gloves. "You're inviting me in?"

"Uh, yeah. Unless you've got other plans."

"No, no," she assured me quickly, "its just . . .

unexpected."

Unexpected that I could act sociable? Hey, I *chose* not to hang with my neighbors. My aloofness was totally justified; they'd shunned me first when I worked for the sheriff.

After the turmoil I'd suffered with Kiyah, I didn't think I'd had the guts to go through that again. Yet, here I was, opening myself up to it. Would I ever learn?

The front door banged on the Babbitt house. Mr. Babbitt bustled out—reminding me more of a Weebol than a man—and blocked the sun with his hand as he peered over the railing. "Eleanor?"

"I'm sorry, I can't today. But maybe another time?" Her brown eyes pleaded, clearly fearful I'd rescind the invitation. "I could bring a zucchini cake?"

"Sure." I smiled, because I knew that's what she wanted. But for me, the moment had passed.

Nothing was splashed across the front page of the Rapid City Journal about a triple homicide. Calling Martinez to see how Harvey had taken the news about Rondelle made my head hurt worse.

I needed a way to release this pent-up energy. An escape, if only for a few hours.

I wandered into the spare bedroom. From under the bed I pulled out my new bow, nestled in its soft-sided case. My hands brushed the camouflage cover. Like my gun, I'd kept my bow out of sight, at Kell's insistence.

Why had I ever agreed? For being of the "make love-not war" mentality, Kell had redefined passive/aggressive behavior.

The anger I'd suppressed yesterday bloomed full force. As for Kell's claim he hadn't known the *real* me? How was that my fault? It was at *his* request that I'd kept those parts of myself that he didn't like hidden away like some dirty little secret.

Was I so desperate for affection I'd take any man who paid attention to me? Even if he was so obviously wrong for me?

Tony Martinez popped up in my mind's eye.

Talk about wrong for me.

Yet, he'd seen me at my worst: angry, violent, and heartsick. He'd accepted those parts of me without question. Without judging. Was that the pull between us? We'd shown our true, our *real* selves to each other?

How much more would things change between us before we wrapped up this case? How much more were we willing to reveal?

Pointless to think about now. Whatever happened, happened. I'd deal with it when and if it did, not before.

I snagged the bow case with one hand and my gun case with the other.

Usually I double-checked everything before I left the house, but I knew Jimmer had made sure the case was fully loaded with all the supplies I'd ever need. Including a new ball cap embroidered with the phrase:

YOU GONNA COWBOY UP OR YOU GONNA LAY THERE AND BLEED?

Jimmer had known I'd cowboy up eventually.

Yee hah. I sent him a silent thanks and made tracks for the ranch.

I didn't stop at the house. Dad would be out in the field. Practicing shooting my bow was a solitary pursuit, anyway. I hated an audience, especially a critical one.

My mother hadn't been critical. In fact, she was the one who'd urged me to try the sport through the city's "Summer Enrichment Program" the year I'd turned twelve. I don't know if I fell in love with bows and arrows because I (childishly) believed it might be an activity I could share with my brother. Even after Ben had laughed at me for falling prey to Indian stereotypes, I hadn't cared.

I'd spent hours in my backyard practicing with that first beloved bow, a cheap, recurve model Mom had bought at a sporting goods store.

My dad had never said a word.

Mom, however, had cheered me on. She'd decided with my natural aptitude, we had to be descended from the Valkryies.

I smiled. Been a long time since I'd dredged up a memory of my mother. My father had been determined to erase all traces of her. Sad thing was, he'd mostly succeeded.

About a mile from the turnoff to the ranch, I hung a right through a break in the fence line that allowed access to the south pasture. The dust from the gravel road was thick as fog. When I could see again, I swerved around rotted tree stumps, boulders, and sinkholes.

Even the weeds—buck brush and leafy spurge, were half-dead and suffering the effects from the excessive dirt. I couldn't imagine how the grazing areas looked. No wonder Dad and the other ranchers were distressed.

I found a relatively flat spot and parked. Placed the hat on my head and tucked my hair inside. I hauled my beanbag practice target from the pickup bed. It'd been a while since I'd shot so I opted for short range—twenty yards. Gauging the correct distance, I marked off my spot and then retrieved my case from the truck.

I slipped on my chest protector and adjusted the plastic shield over my left breast and the straps under my shoulder blade. Next came the arm guard, which protected my left forearm and wrist from string burns and string slaps after the arrow is released.

My fingers traced the aluminum arrows loaded with blunt rubber tips. With screaming orange urethane vanes, these suckers wouldn't be hard to find if I shot wide or high and missed the beanbag entirely. I hooked the quiver around my hip, removed one arrow and picked up my bow.

It was lighter than my last one, a bit smaller, same camouflage color with two cams and a reflexed riser. I'd opted to forgo the stabilizer, since I didn't shoot game, strictly targets.

I'd missed the fresh air, sun on my face, long-forgotten muscles primed and ready. No distractions, no demands besides my own. Just the challenge of consistently hitting the bulls-eye.

After I got the arrow settled in the pass-through rest, I had to twist the nock so the fletching would clear the rest cleanly. When I'd figured out the best adjustment, I clipped the caliper to the string.

I turned my hips sideways. Raised the bow. Leveled my breathing. Relaxed my shoulders. Pulled back, curled my hand around the index finger release as the rubber tubing of the peep site stretched tight. I eyed the targets, allowing them to fade into the background as I focused on the top pin site and let go.

Thunk.

The arrow hit the target, but not the spot I'd been aiming for. I adjusted the pin site slightly to the left and tried again. And again. And kept trying until all eight arrows were spent and I had a better feel for the limits.

By the second round of arrows, I'd fallen completely in love with the bow's performance. Giddy, I kept shooting, my mind cleared of all thoughts except nailing that little blue dot.

I'd shot so many times my arms sang from the strain. Rocks crunching and the sound of an engine gunning broke my concentration. Dust eddied around me. I blinked the grit from my eyes and coughed.

An old Chevy truck bumped into the pasture like a prairie fire was licking at its tires. I lowered my bow to my side, wishing I had time to grab the Browning.

I squinted against the sun's blinding rays and hacked again.

Three men hopped out. Didn't have to squint to see

the metal glare of three rifle barrels pointed at my head.

"Drop the bow or we'll shoot," a harsh voice said.

"But—"

"Do it and don't argue. You're trespassin' on private property."

"I think my father would disagree."

Silence.

"Julie Collins? That you girl, underneath that smart-aleck cap?"

I recognized the raspy voice on the right. "Don Anderson?"

"Yeah."

Relief washed through me. I liked Don. Mostly for the reason he'd never seemed too crazy about my dad.

Apparently finding me no threat, they closed in so I could see who they were.

The stocky man on the left with the beer gut was Dad's crony, Maurice Ashcroft.

When he kept the gun aimed at me, I said, "Mind putting that thing away, Maurice?"

He did so, reluctantly. "Doug didn't say nothin' to me about you being out here today."

"That's because he doesn't know."

They moved together as one unit. Maybe there *was* a Bear Butte County militia.

"Not the smartest thing in the world, for a woman to be out in these parts alone with all the stuff's that's been happenin' round here."

The third man, Dale Pendergrast, a short, bow-legged, scrappy, former rodeo clown in his late sixties, dropped his rifle to his side and spit out a brown wad of tobacco.

Yuck. And people complained about smoking being gross.

"What things?" I asked, as if I didn't know.

Dale pulled out a can of Copenhagen and took another dip before saying, "TV stations ain't got wind of it yet, neither have the papers, but when they do—"

"You-know-what's gonna hit the fan," Don finished.

Martinez had been right. It hadn't taken long.

Maurice said, "We heard 'bout it on the scanner. Appears they found three dead bodies in that old settler's cabin on Bill Tompkin's property."

"*Three* dead bodies?" I aped. "Who found them?"

"Sheriff's department."

I didn't envy Sheriff Richards. Talk about having a bad week. "The bodies been identified yet?"

"Prolly. But ain't nobody sayin' nothin' 'bout who it is."

"'Course, we all got our own theories," Don said.

He didn't freely expound on those theories, which was odd for him.

The air stayed silent as a grave. "You think they're locals? Kids in trouble? Drug related?"

Dale snorted. "No. Plenty 'o other places them hooligans like the Baker boys can get inta trouble. I'm bettin' that's *why* whoever done this picked the Tompkin's place."

His rheumy-blue eyes caught mine. "You see what's happenin', don't you?"

Hello, conspiracy theories. "What, Dale?"

"They're tryin' to force us to change. Look around." His hand swept in an arc. "With this construction, all them cars and trucks kickin' up dust, dust that's killin' our grazin' land. Where are them environmentalists now? Stayin' mighty quiet. Makin' matters worse, the officials *we* elected ain't listenin' to us. Nobody cares that the people who've lived in this county don't got no say in nothin'."

The dust issue did need to be addressed, preferably not by a bunch of vigilante ranchers.

"Ain't nobody happy 'bout that. Stepped in fast enough when we wanted to put up a shootin' range, but it's okay for *them* to put up a damn Indian casino? How's that fair?"

I wanted to point out the (popular) county commissioner who had played a shell game with federal funds shared equal responsibility for the demise of the range along with the Medicine Wheel Holy Society.

"Now they're findin' dead bodies." He spit again. "Heard you were up at Bear Butte with that Indian guy when he was shot."

I nodded.

"Why?"

"For a case I'm working on."

As one, their hard gazes zoomed in and fried me like a bug in a zapper.

Dale asked, "Who're you workin' for? The tribe? Or that greedy contractor from the rez?"

His vehemence didn't surprise me.

255

"Can't imagine your daddy'd be happy about either one of them payin' your bills," Maurice added slyly.

"My *Daddy*," I emphasized through clenched teeth, "doesn't have a damn thing to say about how I make my living."

"Maybe he should. Maybe you oughta listen to him, instead of messin' in something that ain't none of your business."

Stung, I retorted, "But the Sihasapa tribe legally putting a casino on their property is somehow *your* business?"

Dale got right in my face. "Damn right it is. We ain't gonna sit back and do nothin' while this county goes to hell in a hand basket. We'll show 'em we're more than just a bunch of dumb ranchers that they can push around."

A strange sense of déjà vu crept over me. "Show who?"

They didn't exchange a smug look. In fact, they didn't look at each other at all, just glared at me.

"Are you guys planning something?"

I swear crickets chirped in the immediate silence.

"Is my father in on this?" I said to Don.

"Why don't you ask him?" Dale sneered.

"Because I'm asking Don."

Don seemed torn, but Maurice wasn't. "See? That's why Doug don't tell her nothin'. He's got no idea where her loyalties lie."

My bow nearly crashed from the amount of angry sweat covering my palm. "True. But Sheriff Richards knows exactly where my loyalties lie. Maybe I should talk to him?"

No one moved or answered, so naturally I felt perfectly entitled to goad them some more.

"Or Red Granger? He might be real interested."

Maurice laughed. "You do that. Maybe when they spout their same tired lines then you'll figure out you're on the wrong side."

Side? What side? When had I time-traveled to the late 1800's where grazing rights, water rights and land disputes had turned neighbors into enemies?

"I'd watch my step, if I was you," Dale warned. "Better yet, since you don't seem to have a problem stayin' away from your dad, maybe ya oughta keep away 'til this is settled."

God. Were these guys, my father's friends, threatening me?

"Let's go," Maurice said.

Dale trotted after him like an eager pup.

Don hung back for a second.

"What the hell is going on, Don? Talk to me."

"I can't. For your own good, Julie, drop this case and stay away," he said quietly before he climbed in the truck.

I watched the dust plumes chase the fence line until they evaporated into the atmosphere, leaving clear blue skies, but no sense of peace.

So much for releasing my pent-up energy. I was more frustrated now than before.

CHAPTER 19

AFTER I UNLOADED MY EQUIPMENT I DEBATED ABOUT what to do.

Hiding out at the office had potential. But Kevin would use it as his escape pod. He needed a break from reality much worse than I did.

Kevin. Was he overwhelmed with the demands of Lilly's grieving family? Same story for Martinez dealing with Harvey?

I drove past the ranch. Dad wouldn't talk to me if I stopped at the house, especially if Maurice, Don, and Dale had alerted him to my presence. He'd be spitting mad. I was not in the frame of mind to handle his temper. Plus, with the Browning in my possession I might be tempted to use it on him.

At home, I changed clothes and cars. Successfully avoided Mrs. Babbitt. I drove aimlessly for several miles. On a whim I headed to Sturgis. T-shirt vendors had already set up tents along Lazelle Street. Vultures. The motorcycle rally was still weeks away.

If they were locals I'd cut them some slack. If anyone deserved to make a few bucks from the doctors, lawyers, and stockbrokers who rolled into town posing as "bikers", it was Sturgis residents who put up with two weeks of hell.

These vendors were from California—according to the plates on their Haulmark trailer. They'd take their profits out of state.

I followed 385 until I hit Boulder Canyon. Don't know what I hoped to accomplish in Deadwood, but it beat sitting around twiddling my thumbs.

Rock cliffs lined the twisting road. The DOT had broadened the goatpath into a real road a few years back. Some Black Hills residents had cried foul, arguing widening the road would make the historic drive lose its charm. Evidently those naysayers hadn't followed a fifty-foot motor home driving 25 mph up the canyon, with no chance to pass, stretching what should've been a twenty-minute drive into forty.

One thing the new improved road hadn't done was decrease the amount of fatal accidents, especially during the Rally. Diamond shaped signs asking, "Why Die?" were staked along the embankments, marking where some motorist had crashed.

A main draw to the Sturgis Rally was South Dakota does not have a motorcycle helmet law—great for feeling the wind on your face as you take in the breathtaking vistas of the Black Hills—bad when your bike skids out of control, throws you over the handlebars and head first into a rock the size of Mt. Rushmore.

Mottled patches of sunlight filtered through the pine trees. I caught a glimpse of the creekbed running along the left side of the road. Dry as a bone. Even at this higher elevation we hadn't had much snow in the last few years. Not only do the farmers and ranchers suffer during a drought, winter sports—skiing, and snowmobiling—do too.

With the windows rolled down, and the cool darkness of the canyon soothing my mind, time zipped by and soon I was climbing the last, steep craggy hill into Deadwood.

Deadwood. Notorious Old West town, home to Calamity Jane, Seth Bullock, Poker Alice, Potato Creek Johnny, and William Butler Hickock—otherwise known as Wild Bill.

Thank God Deadwood doesn't look anything like it did during its heyday in the late 1870s. No rickety-ass boardwalks leading to cheaply constructed saloons and whorehouses. The street, which in the goldrush days was ankle deep mud mixed with animal shit, had been repaved, cobblestone style, thanks to historic preservation funds.

A few buildings, the brick ones lucky enough to survive the various fires over the last 130 years, are still standing. The Old Style Saloon #10 where Wild Bill played the infamous dead man's hand. The Adams House, now a museum, and The Bullock and The Franklin hotels. The unique underground tunnels, dug by Chinese immigrants and used as opium dens, were closed to public tours because of the dangers of cave-ins.

In the early 1980s Deadwood was practically . . . dead. The push for legalized gambling brought it back from the brink of extinction. Back then, Lead, Deadwood's sister city, was the economic center. Then Homestake Mine pulled up stakes in 2001, abandoning the formerly lucrative gold mine and the hundreds of workers who'd been dependent on it.

Although gambling had saved Deadwood, in some ways it'd destroyed it. The quaint corner drugstore, the family owned grocery market, the clothing boutique, and the barbershop all vanished. The only businesses you'll find on Main Street Deadwood are gaming halls, a souvenir shop or two, restaurants and bars supporting gaming, and hotels—new and old—catering to bus tours and low stakes gamblers.

I'm not a gambler. I work too damn hard for my money. So I wasn't familiar with the location of the casinos unless they had a restaurant.

I drove slowly to avoid hitting tourists who apparently didn't realize Main Street was actually a *through* street.

Bingo. The Golden Boot. I kept driving until I found Trader Pete's. They were on opposite ends of town. I pulled into the parking garage halfway between.

A nasty metal machine spit out a parking stub. Like most Midwesterners, I hated to pay to park.

I emerged from the dungeon into the sunshine.

As I waited at the intersection, I surveyed the jagged fire escapes bumping out of the bowed backs of the buildings, like ugly scars on old skin. Some were made of metal, some of wood. A wide alley, walled off from the street, ran parallel to the road. I debated on ducking in the back door of Trader Pete's, but with various delivery trucks clogging the passage, I walked until I hit Main Street.

Muzak blared from loudspeakers, so no matter where you went you were subjected to yet another crappy instrumental rendition of "The Girl from Ipanema."

Trader Pete's didn't impress me. Decorated in the standard bordello fare: heavy red velvet curtains, flocked wallpaper, gargantuan chandeliers, gold painted molding, fake tropical plants, vibrantly jewel-toned carpet. And the main focus: dozens of slot and video poker machines.

I meandered up to the cashier's cage. Didn't have a lick of cash to my name so I wrote a check for a whopping twenty bucks. The gum-snapping granny gave me an odd look at the small amount, half pity/half curiosity.

Tempting to ask if she was Rondelle's friend Robin, or if she'd known Rondelle. But the cops would start canvassing soon and I didn't want her remembering I'd been here nosing around before they'd released Rondelle's name. The row of cameras sporadically blinked, the red light reminding me Big Brother was watching.

I grinned and blew it a kiss.

With my tube of quarters and five rolls of nickels, I hunkered down in the nickel slot area in the far corner away from the more lucrative Blackjack and Poker tables. One thing I did like about casinos; I could smoke and no one could bitch about it.

I'd made a tidy profit of fifty-five cents, was enjoying my cup of warm Coors and my fifth cigarette when the chair beside me screeched. I didn't glance up from the blue glow of the video screen, it'd just encourage the intruder to talk to me. I was feeling highly antisocial, because, hey, I *was* winning.

A couple of bad hands sent me back to my starting point of two bucks. I cashed out, figuring I'd give another machine a chance at making me rich before trying to sneak upstairs.

Don't know what I expected to discover. With the amount of security cameras I'd probably get caught, but it was worth a shot. My situation with the Carluccis couldn't get worse, could it?

I heard Kevin groan in my head.

Better to cross paths with them in a public place than to wait for them to come at me again when I didn't have control of the situation. Since Martinez and Kevin were unavailable, like it or not, I was on my own.

I scooped my nickels into a cardboard cup. I'd drained the last of the beer when a person behind me said, "If all our customers quit while they were ahead, we'd go out of business."

My stomach plunged. I lowered the beer cup to the ledge near the ashtray and spun in my chair toward the voice I'd immediately recognized.

Reggie.

I stood and jiggled the container of nickels. "Well, I don't expect that my paltry donation to the Carlucci coffers will add much to your retirement account, Reg."

"You always such a wise ass?"

"Yep."

"What're you doin' here?"

"Gambling. Drinking. Admiring the décor." I pointed to a sparkling chandelier, which would've made Liberace weep with jealousy. "Think that's too formal for my dining room?"

He towered over me. Damn, if it didn't send my heart galloping like a Pony Express rider.

"Cut the shit," he said. "Who sent you?"

I peered around him. "Where's your buddy? Tommy, right? How come he's not helping you harass me? Thought you goombahs were joined at the hip?"

Reggie's eyes burned fury. "Answer the question, Ms. Collins."

I couldn't tell if he knew Tommy was dead. He sure as hell didn't act like he was in mourning.

"I'm up here because I was curious, okay? Rondelle told me about this place. I was in the neighborhood and wanted to check it out for myself."

His shark grin chilled me to the bone.

"You're in luck then, because Big Joe wants to see you in the office. Right now." He pressed his big beak to mine. "Maybe if your luck holds, he won't give you a personally guided tour."

Oh double crap.

"Come on." He grabbed my right elbow.

Big mistake.

Intuitively I dropped my arm, brought it around the

outside of his forearm and knocked it away.

The change bucket went flying; nickels pinged against the metal machines and bounced on the carpet like silver raindrops.

I shoved the swivel chair between us.

"Don't you ever fucking touch me again, Reggie. I'll talk to Big Joe. But if you lay one fat finger on me I will hurt you bad."

Reggie adjusted the sleeve of his ugly silk suit, glaring like I'd somehow soiled it. "*You* gonna hurt me bad? Or you talking 'bout that fuckin' slimeball spic Martinez?"

"Me."

"Try it and I'll show you the meaning of hurt. That little tap I gave you coupla days ago will feel like a love pat, compared to the pain I can cause you."

"Make you feel all macho, threatening me?"

"We'll see how tough you are when Big Joe gets through with you." He frowned and shoved his hand in his jacket pocket, pulling out a slim cell phone. "Shame you'll probably disappoint him."

Stall, stall, stall, my brain insisted. "What about my nickels?"

"Forget them." His pencil thin lips twisted; he allotted me an insulting once over and an Elvis-worthy sneer. "Unless you need them to make the monster truck payment this month?"

"Oh ho. That was a real knee slapper, Reg. Maybe you oughta ask Mr. C. to put in a comedy club so he could buy you a sense of humor."

Since I'd tagged his punchline, he snarled, "Get

movin'. He don't like waiting."

I shouldered my purse. I'd half expected he'd breathe down my neck, poking my spine with the big gun bulging beneath his suit jacket. Again, he mustn't have found me much of a threat, as he kept his back to me. Hadn't he learned anything from what'd happened to Wild Bill?

We marched single file around the cashier's cage, past the empty card tables with the empty-eyed dealers, and up the narrow wooden staircase marked "Employees Only."

I sauntered past several closed doors, trying like hell not to think about what had happened to Rondelle up here.

Reggie paused at the end of a long carpeted hallway and waited. Knocked on a door with knuckles deeply scarred from multiple rounds with a heavy bag.

How had I missed that little detail?

The door swung inward; a bony, bespectacled chap clutching a briefcase hustled out, then another beefy man resembling Reggie.

Yikes.

Except at second glance, this guy was about twenty years younger, two inches taller, and a hundred times better looking. The clincher? He had excellent taste in clothes.

He stopped, did a double take. "Whoa. You here to see me, dollface?"

And . . . he blew it. Men never failed to disillusion me.

Reggie not so subtly maneuvered Mr. Charming away. "Go play in the sandbox, Junior. She's here to see your pops."

My turn to do a double take. *This* was Little Joe Carlucci? Holy crap. Beads of sweat popped out on my forehead.

Big Joe couldn't possibly be bigger than this grape ape—could he?

"Have fun," Little Joe said to Reggie. "He's in a lousy fuckin' mood. Let you get your flabby ass chewed for a change." He allowed me one last creepy leer. "I'll be in the bar if you need me."

"Big fuckin' surprise." Reggie warned, "Stay outta Big Joe's private stock."

"Or what?"

Reggie's glare could've peeled off the top layer of skin. I shuddered. Little Joe laughed.

"Right. That's what I thought you'd say." Little Joe strutted off.

"Douche bag," Reggie muttered before he ushered me inside the space that smelled like boiled corn and old newspapers.

Not an impressive office for a mob Don. Unlike the attempt at elegance downstairs, cramped was the decorating style up here. A window air conditioner dripped water on one of the five gray filing cabinets ringing the room. An oversized black chair behind the colossal desk faced the bank of windows covered with condensation.

I slid into the wingback chair opposite the desk and waited for my first glimpse of Big Joe.

Wheels scraped plastic as he revolved, giving me a second to brace myself.

Again, my imagination—helped along with years of TV stereotypes—had led me astray. I'd expected Big Joe to look like . . . well, Brando in *The Godfather*. Or Gandolfini, from *The Sopranos*. Or Sinatra.

Wrong on all accounts. This wisp of a man was a ringer for the guy who played Arvin Sloan on *Alias*, from the grayish-black stubble on his chin to the wire-rimmed glasses sliding down his patrician nose. He looked about as Italian as I did.

He snapped his cuffs before he set his elbows on the desk. Smiled wanly. "Ah. Ms. Collins. So nice to finally meet you."

I noticed he didn't offer his hand for me to shake. Chauvinistic? Or a germ phobic?

"Likewise." I managed not to make it a smart retort.

"You're a private investigator?"

I nodded.

"I've got a couple companies on my payroll back east. Very handy. Of course, I could always use a local company."

I wanted to say, *I can recommend a couple*, but I refrained, lest he cut my tongue out.

"Naturally, you'd have to prove your investigative skills are adequate."

"Naturally."

"How is your latest case coming along? Any luck in locating Ms. Eagle Tail's daughter?"

At least he didn't mince words.

I offered a polite smile. "As I'm sure you're aware, with your extensive experience with private investigators,

Mr. Carlucci, that is privileged, confidential client information that I cannot share with you."

"True. But as I'm sure you're aware, Ms. Collins, we've got a particular interest in this case. When was the last time you saw Ms. Eagle Tail?"

"Why don't you tell me? Since we both know you were having Rondelle followed." Dammit. So much for keeping smart comments to myself.

Big Joe studied me, probably devising new torture techniques.

Reggie shifted in the chair next to mine, probably in anticipation of executing those techniques.

Or was it from nerves?

And then it hit me: Reggie hadn't actually been following Rondelle, someone else had. And she'd given them the slip.

That was a possible explanation on why Tommy had been in that cabin. He'd been following her and had been in the wrong place at the wrong time and wound up dead.

If they didn't know about Tommy's murder, then they didn't know about hers either. Which put me at a slight—albeit unwanted—advantage in this situation.

"Answer the question," Reggie said.

"Last time I saw Rondelle was in Fat Bob's parking lot."

Reggie snorted disbelief.

"So, she hasn't contacted you since?"

"No."

"Have you contacted her?"

I shook my head.

Big Joe sighed, and reclined back in his chair, tapping his fingers on the armrest. "Then we've got a bit of a dilemma, Ms. Collins."

"I fail to see how your dilemma concerns me."

His benign smile sent shivers from my nape to my tailbone. "Surely, you don't believe that."

I shrugged.

"I can ensure your cooperation, but I'd much rather have it willingly. You choose."

Painful, talking around the sudden fear lumped in my throat. "I honestly don't know how I can help."

"I do. When you find her daughter, you'll call me."

Imagining Chloe Black Dog in this guy's hands kicked my gag reflex. "And what are you going to do with her?"

"Propose a trade. I'll have something Rondelle wants; she has something I want."

"Which is?"

Those squinty black eyes zeroed in on me again. I didn't look away. However, I think my eyeballs were actually sweating from the effort it took.

"Fine, Ms. Collins, we'll play it your way. I want the hundred and fifty thousand dollars she stole from me."

CHAPTER 20

ROGER RABBIT HAD NOTHING ON ME; MY EYES BULGED out of the sockets. "What?"

"Rondelle managed to walk out of here with one hundred and fifty thousand dollars in cash."

"When?"

"We're guessing a week ago."

Bull. What kind of businessman didn't know exactly when he'd been ripped off?

Unless he hadn't been ripped off at all.

"Mmm," he said over the rolling *tap tap tap* of his fingers on the plastic arm of his chair. "Appears you don't believe it."

"It's not that. I just don't get why you're telling *me*."

"Isn't she your client?"

"In a manner of speaking." I angled my head toward Reggie. "Didn't your goombah tell you Tony Martinez is footing the bill?"

He didn't spare Reggie a glance.

Hah. Take that Reggie.

Furrowing my brow in confusion added a nice dramatic touch. "So how did Rondelle get her hands on so much money? Especially when she claimed she didn't have enough to hire me? Did she take it from the cage?"

Big Joe watched me closely before he shook his head. "There's another vault upstairs. Which was opened at the end of Rondelle's shift."

"Who opened the vault?"

"The bookkeeper."

"So ask her."

"We did."

"Then what's the problem?"

"She wasn't the only one involved. An upper level manager has to be present whenever the safe is unlocked and the money from downstairs is transferred."

"Who was supposed to be overseeing the money transfer that day?" I asked, even when I suspected the answer.

"My son. Little Joe."

"Who else besides the bookkeeper has the combination to the vault?"

"No one." At my puzzlement, he clarified, "The upstairs vault is on a random time release. There is no set schedule for it to be opened."

This time I didn't have to feign confusion. "Why? Don't you need access to that money for change for the cage or whatever?"

When he didn't answer, I realized if he did, he'd be giving away too much information on the amount of cash on hand. In all likelihood, the upstairs safe held the big bills, but I found it hard to swallow that only one person had control over that much money.

Unless that money wasn't even supposed to be there.

As a South Dakota girl I didn't know the first thing about money laundering. Skimming didn't make sense because I doubted there'd be any benefit in the Carluccis skimming from themselves.

Big Joe continued, "He did handle the transfer, according to Betty. But before she made sure he reset the safe, Rondelle showed up half naked, caused a ruckus, and he kicked Betty back downstairs."

Yeah, so he could drag Rondelle into another room and rape her, the bastard.

My blood boiled. "So it's his word against hers."

"I'm fully aware my son neglected his responsibilities for a quick tumble, Ms. Collins. Little Joe made a mistake."

"Doesn't sound like you blame him for the missing money."

Those long, thin fingers rolled a slow, steady drumbeat. "Should I? Especially since in the interim Rondelle has vanished?"

"That automatically makes her guilty?"

"In my experience, yes."

I chewed on that for a second. "Okay, let's assume you're right. Tell me: How did Rondelle manage to sneak away from Little Joe? If they were doing the nasty, wouldn't he notice if she'd disappeared?"

A pained expression creased Big Joe's forehead.

"You'd think so. Unfortunately my son has . . . shall we say, *eclectic* appetites when it comes to sex? Apparently Rondelle has taken advantage of these appetites on many occasions, none more so than that afternoon."

What lie had Little Joe created for his father to cover up the truth that he'd raped Rondelle? In the next room? While he'd left the damn safe open? It had to be something that would paint Rondelle as a sneaky, controlling, money-grubbing bitch.

"How?"

"Evidently Rondelle rendered him incapable of escape."

I made my eyes widen. I even let out a little shocked gasp—mostly because I knew it was total bullshit.

"Little Joe *let* her tie him up?"

Reggie snickered.

Venom shot from Big Joe's eyes, ending Reggie's hilarity.

"Her idea, according to my son. He swears she left him alone for at least ten minutes. Plenty of time for her to skulk back into the office and grab money out of the safe, don't you think?"

The indignation I'd been holding back exploded.

"Let me see if I've got this scenario right: Rondelle, half naked, ties up poor, helpless, horny Little Joe. She would've had to gag him to keep him from hollering since the tying up was *her* idea, right? Leaving him with his dick flapping in the wind, she manages to run down the hallway—again, half naked, and sneaks into the office unseen, spies the open safe and starts grabbing piles of cash?

"Where does she put the money? Couldn't stuff it in her bra. Could she even fit 150K in her purse? I'm assuming the safe holds big bills, let's say hundred dollar bills, and supposing they'd been bundled into stacks equaling 5000 bucks each, she would've had thirty stacks to hide.

"So, she would've had to stash them in a backpack or briefcase that would've been conveniently located nearby. Oh, on a *random* day the safe is opened. Wouldn't Little Joe be curious if she sauntered back in with a briefcase? Sure, she might've told him it contained sex toys to throw him off, but, being a man of 'eclectic' appetites, he'd want her to open it. If she didn't? Well, we're back to him getting suspicious.

"The other alternative is she put the bag containing the money someplace else. You really think she'd take a chance and leave it unattended in the hallway after going to all that trouble to steal it?

"Then once she's had her wicked, wicked way with him, she unties him, kisses his cheek, grabs the money and skips off into the sunset?"

I didn't bother to hide my revulsion.

"Wrong. I'm not that stupid. I'll give it to Little Joe for his imagination. But no way in hell did that happen. Someone else took the money."

If there even was any money missing. This might've all been an elaborate lie on the Carlucci's behalf to justify tracking down Rondelle because of the disk.

Tension soaked the air.

Big Joe stared at me inscrutably. Was he figuring

out where to dig the hole to have me buried in?

Reggie huffed, hands curled into fists. All Big Joe had to do was give the word and Reggie would feed me lunch in the form of a knuckle sandwich.

"Is there something else you'd like to share?"

I glanced up at Big Joe. "Of course, I could be wrong."

I lifted my hand and pointed to the camera in the corner.

"What about security cameras? From what I've seen you've got every inch of this place covered. Does the disk from that day show her actually stealing the money?"

More sticky silence.

"Interestingly enough, the disk from that day is missing."

"Don't you have copies archived within your security system?"

Reggie cleared his throat.

Big Joe's mouth turned dark, prune-like. "When Little Joe took over this casino, I urged him to update the surveillance system. He did. By upgrading to encoded disks."

"That's it?"

"To say the current system is antiquated is putting it mildly. Since we don't often use the rooms up here, these cameras are on a separate feed from the ones in the main casino."

Hence, the separate, lone disk. "Why didn't you call the cops?"

"Why bother without the evidence?"

Point taken. Then again, missing disk and missing money gave them a great motive for wanting her dead.

Yes, Rondelle had taken the disk, but not because she'd stolen the money.

But in reviewing that disk, she saw who did.

His fingers stopped moving. "Can you see our dilemma now?"

An intercom on the desk buzzed.

He scooted forward and punched a button. "Yes?"

"Sir, I hate to bother you, but your son insists on opening the Jack Daniels reserve. He's, umm, very insistent and several customers have already left—"

"Say no more, Henry. Reggie will be down immediately."

Reggie stood.

I couldn't help but prod him. I dug out the yellow ticket. "Hey, while you're down there, Reg, could you validate my parking? Then have the valet bring it around? It's a blue Nissan Sentra. Big dent on the roof. Can't miss it."

His neck bulged. He scowled so hard his eyebrows almost covered his big nose.

All Big Joe said was, "See to Little Joe," and Reggie was gone.

Dammit. I'd still have to pay for parking. If I was allowed to leave.

Big Joe sighed. Pressed back in his office chair and gazed up. "Do you have any children, Ms. Collins?"

Huh? "No."

Time dragged on. I didn't dare break his reign of silence.

Finally, he said, "Children are a curious thing. They

can grow up in the same house, with the same mother and father, same financial circumstances, same education, same priest, same set of expectations.

"So how is it I've got three sons who never have caused me a minute's worry, but the fourth one is a complete and total fuck-up?"

"Was that a rhetorical question?"

Head back, he continued to stare at the dingy ceiling tiles. "I could make excuses for him. Or I should say, I *have* made excuses for him."

"All that makes is a sorry excuse for a human being."

He chuckled. "Know what's ironic? I bought this casino to keep my son from further screwing up my other businesses in New Jersey. I'd thought without his brothers or me interfering he'd find his own way. Find success. Within one month, I had to send in a fulltime babysitter."

Reggie. Wondered how he felt about being a highly paid *Mary Poppins*.

"Bud Linderman claims you want to own Deadwood," I said.

"Bud Linderman is a red-necked idiot. I don't want to own the casino I've already got, say nothing of more. There's no money to be made here."

Maybe Linderman was paranoid, seeing problems where there weren't any. Would that make him dangerous? And careless?

"My businesses that are profitable are suffering because, once again, I'm here putting out my son's fires." Big Joe sat up and swiveled so quickly it made me dizzy. "Do you know for sure Rondelle didn't take the money?"

That question shocked me almost as much as his confession about his disappointment of his son.

"Please don't bullshit me or think you have to tiptoe around the truth, though, God knows, you've had no trouble telling me exactly what you think so far."

Me and my big mouth. But maybe for once my mouth had kept me from wearing cement shoes.

"Yes, Rondelle told me she took the security disk. But it was a little hard for her to grab the money while your son was raping her in the next room."

Not a single change in his facial expression.

"And you believe her?"

"About the rape? Without question."

"Have you seen the disk?"

"No." I exhaled, slowly. "I'm not going to sit here and tell you Rondelle was the most virtuous woman on the planet. But the fact remains your son raped and sodomized her. That is not her fault. And she has the evidence to prove it.

"It sickens me, the 'she-tied-me-up' version he fed you. It's beyond ridiculous. You know it is, or else you wouldn't be talking to me, would you?"

Drum drum drum, interspersed with a probing stare.

"I had my suspicions." He removed his glasses, pressed his thumb above his right eye socket and sighed wearily. "Did Rondelle tell you what she'd planned on doing with that disk?"

"Not specifically. She'd mentioned taking it to the Lawrence County States Attorney's office. Whether or not she did . . ."

"It's possible she hasn't done anything with the disk and might still use it to blackmail my son."

I debated on telling him Rondelle wouldn't be blackmailing anyone. I held back. "Someone ripped you off, Mr. Carlucci. That someone was not Rondelle."

Again, he tortured me with silence.

"I wish it had been her."

Briefly, I felt sorry for him. Difficult to swallow that someone you love is capable of betrayal. Then I remembered how the men in his employ had threatened me, broken into my house, smacked me around and beaten an innocent man.

The tiny bit of sympathy evaporated.

I cleared my throat to garner his attention. "Is there anything else?"

"No." His blank eyes met mine. "If you do hear from Rondelle, contact me."

"Why should I?"

"My patience only stretches so far, Ms. Collins."

Yikes. I think I actually heard the thin thread snap in the abrupt stillness of the room.

"I will get answers. Having to track you down for them? Not fun for me, definitely not fun for you."

"Ah, sure, I'll call you."

"Wise decision." He spun back toward the windows. "You know the way out."

I successfully avoided Reggie and Little Joe as I escaped to the parking garage and out of town.

But I knew I hadn't seen the last of them.

CHAPTER 21

THE STUPID SON OF A BITCH WOULD BE DEAD INSIDE two minutes.

No close range shots this time. No chance to see the look of surprise. Or feel the vibration of fear as his life was snuffed.

With his left hand he yanked the red bandana out of his pocket and mopped the sweat from his forehead.

Through the scope, he saw the man fumble the wire cutters.

Frustrated, the man swore and grabbed the replacement section of 10-gauge wire that had fallen to the ground. He began to twist it around the fencepost. Dropped his glove. Took his own sweet time standing up and getting back to work.

Get moving, old man, I ain't got all day.

He lifted the rifle slightly, and squinted through the scope again. About 150 yards out. Ideal range.

The man turned around.

A clear shot.

Oh yeah. The pocket on his yellow polo shirt made a perfect bulls-eye.

Not a breath of wind whispered his murderous intentions.

He pulled the trigger. Pulled it twice more before the body crumpled to the ground, amid broken barbed wire, milkweed, and dirt.

He waited, keeping the scope trained on the form in case he'd missed.

But he never missed.

Gun down; he studied the blazing midday sky. With any luck no one would come looking until dusk.

By then he'd already have served as a buzzard's afternoon snack.

CHAPTER 22

THE MAIN DOORS WERE OPEN AT FAT BOB'S AND STILL the sour scent of booze, unwashed bodies, and mildew lingered.

Whew. This place could benefit from an industrial-sized air freshener.

A bartender with the mass of a John Deere tractor was parked behind the bar. He eyed me like he knew me but couldn't quite place my face.

"What can I get for ya?"

"What's on tap?"

"Bud, Bud Light, Coors, Coors Light, Miller, Miller Light, and Leinenkugel Red."

"I'll take the Leinenkugel."

The pilsner glass he slid in front of me had a substantial head of foam. No wonder he worked the day shift. Even I could pour a better glass of beer. I tossed a five on the counter.

He snatched the money and brought my change. A

blue flame flickered as he struck a match and held it to my cigarette.

"Thanks," I said, blowing out the flare with my first exhalation. I sipped the amber-colored brew and my mouth, tongue, and teeth hummed "Ode to Joy." On a hot summer day, a sip of cold, crisp beer is close to a holy experience for me.

"Haven't seen you in here before," he said.

I shrugged. "Mostly I've been in at night."

"Ah." Sensing I wasn't in the mood for conversation, he busied himself, arranging liquor bottles, removing empties and lining them up on the far side of the bar. Breaking open the stacked cases of bottled beer and loading the individual bottles back into the glass coolers.

I stole a quick glance around. Kind of unnatural with no shitty music blasting or people getting drunk and acting like total jackasses.

With nothing else to do except enjoy my beer, I watched the bartender, namely the bloody dagger inked on his forearm. Since Martinez and Harvey had the same tattoo, I figured it must be a Hombres thing.

He got close enough that I didn't have to shout over clanking bottles. Casually, I said, "Martinez around today?"

Any pretense of his earlier friendliness fled. "Depends on who's asking."

"Me."

"And you'd be?"

I crushed out my cigarette. "Julie Collins."

His eyes took on a harder edge. "You're not supposed

to be in here."

"Yeah, I know." I braved a smile. "I won't tell if you don't."

"Harvey don't need anyone to tell him. He knows every little thing that goes on in this bar."

"Is he here?"

As an answer, he picked up a phone and dialed. Angrily. Fixed his evil eye on me as he listened to the person on the other end of the receiver.

I wasn't surprised he'd reported a Julie Collins sighting. I'd actually expected my butt to meet the pavement much sooner than this.

"Mr. Martinez wants you to meet him in his private office."

More time in close quarters with Martinez? Not wise. I needed to keep this relationship professional, though I wondered if I was the only one deluding myself about the status of that relationship.

I shook my head. "Tell Martinez if he wants to talk to me I'll be sitting right here, finishing my very tasty beer."

The bartender seemed reluctant to relay the message but he did so anyway.

"He'll be right out," he said, and dumped my spent cigarette butt. "Get you anything else?"

"Just your name. You know, so when Harvey kicks my ass I can tell him I tricked you into serving me. At least *you'll* be in the clear."

He grinned and it was a beautiful thing. Obviously he wasn't a former hockey player; his perfect smile rivaled Martinez's. "Name's Big Mike."

Oh. I'd heard the name before. No wonder he was so lousy at tending bar; he wasn't a bartender at all, but one of Martinez's bodyguards.

I held out my hand. "Nice to meetcha, Big Mike."

"Same here."

Big Mike yanked his back like I'd shocked him with a joy-buzzer.

When Martinez sidled in behind me I knew why.

"Ms. Collins. Haven't you been warned about trying to charm my bartenders into serving you?"

Glad to see he was capable of lazy amusement after what we'd seen yesterday. "Big Mike here doesn't count, seeing that he's a bodyguard, not a bartender."

"Smart girl."

I rolled my eyes at the "girl" comment.

He purposely layered his body against mine as he leaned over and instructed Mike. "Bring us a pitcher of whatever she's drinking and two glasses. We'll be in the back. Hold my calls."

"Yes, sir."

I gathered my stuff, leaving the money for a tip.

When Martinez took my elbow, I didn't respond with a forearm strike, as I had with Reggie.

He directed me to the first of two circular booths where the bars separated, where it was really dark.

I slid in. He slid in next to me. Right next to me. A bar napkin wouldn't have fit between us.

Nervous, I pulled a cigarette from the pack and he had my lighter out before I'd brought the filter to my lips.

He flicked it. I inhaled. "Thanks," I said, blowing

smoke away from him.

His fingertips skimmed my neck. He brushed my hair from my face. "Are you okay?" he murmured.

"I'm fine," I lied.

"Bet you didn't sleep any better than I did last night."

The nightmare reemerged and I suppressed a shudder. "No. I didn't. Did you tell Harvey?"

His hand fell to the table like a sail without a breeze.

Big Mike dropped off the pitcher. Martinez poured the beer. No foamy head this time. I drank deeply, using the lull to organize my thoughts.

"Yeah, I told him. Last night after we closed and everyone had left."

I didn't ask him how Harvey had taken it. I knew. I took another tentative sip.

"I really think . . ." He sighed. "Fuck it. I *know* he's lost it. I've never seen him like this."

"Why did you tell him?"

"Because I realized it might be days before the cops contacted him as Rondelle's next of kin. He needed to know. He needed to hear it from me."

That reminded me I'd forgotten to call Jimmer this morning about Lilly. The one thing I'd told Kevin I'd do I hadn't. Yeah. I was some reliable friend.

"What's wrong?"

Normally, I would've hedged the personal garbage and stuck strictly to the facts of the case. But Martinez and I had gone beyond our previous boundaries in the last few days, and frankly I needed someone to unload on.

Cynical laughter trickled out as I exhaled. "Sure

you wanna hear this, Martinez? Cause it doesn't show me in the best light. And I know you've put me up on some kind of marble pedestal."

"Tell me."

"When I got home yesterday, after what we saw . . ." I took a fortifying sip of beer as those gruesome images danced in my head. "Needless to say, I was a wreck. Kell used the opportunity to point out everything that's wrong with me before he hightailed it out the door. Not that I'm sorry he's gone."

Thinking about it made me so angry I smashed my cigarette butt until the filter unraveled. "With the help of my old friend Don Julio, I numbed myself enough to fall asleep until this epic nightmare woke me up.

"Then, I got a phone call from Kevin telling me Lilly had died. So I raced over there in the middle of the night to make sure he wasn't suicidal, even though I suck at the sympathy thing. But I couldn't tell him anything about what's going on with this case, which is so not the norm with us because we *are* partners.

"After I got home this morning, I drove out to the ranch to shoot my bow and clear my head. This pickup load of men comes barreling up with their goddamn rifles. They threaten *me*. On my dad's land. God. Ends up these old guys are my dad's friends and are patrolling the whole damn county. Acting like they'd shoot anyone who mouthed off to them."

His lips twitched. "Did you mouth off to them?"

"What do you think? Anyway, they recommended I mind my own business. Suggested I drop this case.

Flat out told me I'm embarrassing myself and my father, yada, yada, yada."

Martinez just stared at me.

"What?"

"I've never seen you run off at the mouth like that."

Embarrassment stained my cheeks. "Well, we haven't exactly had much time to socialize."

"Would you like us to socialize, blondie?"

My non-response was more telling than all the denials in the world.

"Why do I have the feeling you're not done with this story?" He'd reclined, beer in one hand, muscled arm propped on the booth behind me.

"Because I saved the best for last. Figured with the way my luck was going, I oughta be up in Deadwood."

He actually cringed. "You didn't."

"Yes, I did. Paid a visit to Trader Pete's. My bad luck continued because I'd been enjoying my free beer for about half an hour before our pal Reggie dragged me upstairs. Seemed Big Joe wanted a word with me."

Martinez became deadly still. "About?"

And there was the lethal look that curled my innards. Mouth parched as the Badlands, I slurped the last of my beer.

"Here's where it gets interesting. The Carluccis claim Rondelle stole 150K from them. That's why they've been looking for her."

"They have proof?"

I shook my head. "Remember the disk I told you about? The one Rondelle stole because it showed Little Joe . . ."

His black eyes pierced my soul, but I breezed on, "Evidently that's the same disk. But they claim she took it because the security feed showed her grabbing the cash from the safe."

Martinez made no move to refill my beer. Nor did he whip out the lighter when I snagged a Marlboro Light from the half-empty pack. Jaw tight, he stared into space, digesting the possibilities, none of which I needed to point out to him.

Rondelle had lied more than she'd told the truth.

If she'd stolen a big pile of money and disappeared, it gave credibility to why the Carluccis had been so anxious to track her down.

But I'd seen her face. Her shame and fear had been real. No way in hell had she faked it. No way did she take that disk for any other reason than Little Joe Carlucci needed to pay for what he'd done to her.

Question was: Had they tracked her down and made *her* pay the ultimate price for attempting to cross them?

Dread turned the contents of my stomach sour.

One other angle I hadn't considered. Could Bud Linderman have been involved? With the rumors surrounding the Carlucci's ties to organized crime, they would be high on the cops' list of suspects for killing Rondelle.

Bud probably hadn't been aware Rondelle was under suspicion for ripping off the Carluccis. But he'd wanted the disk and Rondelle had double-crossed him. Was it enough to get her executed? And conveniently point the finger at the Carluccis?

And where the hell was the disk anyway? Had the murderer gotten a hold of it after killing everyone in the cabin?

Christ. My head could pop off my shoulders and fly around the room with all the crazy theories spinning in my brain.

Martinez reached for the pitcher, absentmindedly replenishing our glasses. "What else?"

"*Else*? This is majorly fucked up. But know the one thing I don't get?"

He swigged his beer and made an on-with-it gesture.

"Where's Chloe? We've uncovered all this bullshit that no one wanted to know and I still haven't found one five-year old girl. How can the people who are taking care of her *not* know Donovan was shot?"

"If she's on Pine Ridge, she might be staying with someone who doesn't have access to—"

"TV, radio, or newspapers? Wrong. Try again."

"Am I supposed to be playing your partner's role as devil's advocate?"

My gaze homed in on him. I couldn't tell if his tone was condescending. "You pissing with me, Martinez?"

"No. Not used to you bringing me in the loop. Don't want you giving away trade secrets."

"No secrets. I'd like to think I'll find Chloe through good old-fashioned detective work."

Those dark, thoughtful eyes examined me over the beer mug. "Does that mean you can track down the person who murdered Rondelle?"

I'd been afraid this would come up. "I can't do that."

"Can't? Or won't?"

"Can't. That fun job belongs to the law enforcement agencies." I recited, "'A PI can't investigate homicide, or work on a current case while the PD is pursuing it.' Period. I imagine the Feds are involved because the sheriff doesn't have the expertise or the resources to handle a case like this." When he frowned I rushed to assure him, "Not that they're inept, but multiple murders do not happen in Bear Butte County."

"Give me your best educated guess. Who do you think killed Rondelle?"

I paused.

"Yeah," Harvey's raspy voice drifted from the booth behind us, surprising a girlish yelp from me. "Tell me which one of those fuckers murdered my little sister."

I swallowed to dislodge my heart from where he'd scared it into my throat.

Martinez leaned over the booth ledge and growled, "Jesus Christ, you been laying there the whole time?"

"What's it to you?"

Belligerence instead of deference? From Harvey?

"Get up."

A head popped up. Whoa. Scarier than usual appearance for Harvey.

His waist-length black hair was in snarls. Stubble dotted his chin and it looked like he was trying to grow a porcupine on the shaved portion of his head. His skin had a sallow yellowish tinge, a sign he'd spent the night drinking, throwing up, and drinking some more. He could've packed a dime bag in the folds of flesh hanging beneath his bloodshot eyes.

When my gaze snagged his, my guts tightened into knots rivaling those in his hair. If I'd imagined his eyes were cold and flat before, they were downright full of love and compassion compared to what I witnessed in those same eyes now.

Not a flicker of humanity remained.

My mother and Ben's deaths had devastated me, but that hollow nothingness had never stared back at me in the mirror, not even on my worst days.

Harvey reached for the pitcher of beer, threw his head back and poured a stream into his open mouth. Swallowed noisily. Wouldn't have shocked me if he'd have gargled, then spewed like a fountain.

Tipping his face toward us, liquid dribbled down his chin leaving wet splotches on his FREE LEONARD PELTIER T-shirt.

Martinez uttered not one word.

No doubt about it; Harvey had gone completely round the bend.

This was not good. I took a deep breath and let it out slowly, afraid what would happen next.

He belched. "That uppity little sniff mean you ain't gonna tell me, don't it?"

"Tell you what, Harvey? Who might have done it? We all know who's on that list because Martinez has told you everything. But I'm not going to sentence any one of those persons to a certain death at your hands just because they *might* have a reason for wanting Rondelle dead."

My breath sawed in and out of my lungs in an effort to stay calm.

"I will find who did this, with or without your help." He smiled pure meanness mixed with insanity. "Don't pretend, *blondie*," he snickered in self-satisfaction at using Martinez's nickname, "that you wouldn't do the exact same thing if you ever find out who sliced and diced your brother."

"Shut up," Martinez said. "You aren't making any sense." He screwed up his nose. "Jesus. You reek. Go take a shower. We'll talk about this later."

My eyes stayed locked with Harvey's. In that instant, he recognized the black smudge on my soul. The infected part I'd kept hidden, the mark of my own inhumanity that would destroy—without remorse—the person who'd taken Ben's life.

For that brief moment, we connected on a hellish level no one should descend to.

"Find Chloe," Harvey whispered. "She's all I've got left."

I blinked.

He was gone.

Martinez sighed. "See what I mean?"

"He's right, though. I can't do anything for Rondelle, but I can find Chloe. I should go."

The small of my back stuck to the Naugahyde as I slid from the booth.

I tugged my shirt back in place, aware of Martinez's hot gaze searing my skin. "I'll stop by the sheriff's office tomorrow. See if he can tell me anything. I'll try to get in to see Donovan. Maybe he's got family members holding vigil and they can offer some suggestions."

"Need any help?"

He hadn't moved, but I sensed renewed tension as he waited for my answer.

"I don't know."

Evidently it was the right one because the breath-catching smile I hadn't seen in days lit his face. He grabbed my cell phone and started punching buttons.

"Hey! What are you doing?"

"Giving you my private cell number. About ten people have it. I'd appreciate it if—"

"If I didn't write the number and 'For a good time call Tony' on the bathroom stall?"

His calloused knuckles abraded the bared skin of my belly, sending a shiver through me as he clipped the phone to my waistband. "You are such a smart ass."

"Uh-huh. I prefer to call it my 'redneck charm'."

Much easier to toss out quips than to admit Martinez's sudden trust scared me to the bone.

"Keep me in the loop."

"I'll call you tomorrow as soon as I know anything."

CHAPTER 23

I MADE GOOD ON MY PROMISE TO KEVIN AND CALLED Jimmer. He was more interested in the news reports and rumors surrounding the bodies discovered in Bear Butte County than in Lilly's demise.

Since the victims' names hadn't been officially released, I had to feign shock, but not my anger. That was real.

I tried calling Kevin. Big fat zero on all three of his numbers. How long had it been since I'd talked to him?

Man. One day was bleeding into the next in my life.

On impulse, I called Kim and asked her to meet me for supper. Female camaraderie, I needed a dose.

We met at Casa Del Rey, a Mexican restaurant with decent food and even better drinks. With two frosty lime margaritas lined up, I jumped into the conversation head first.

"Kell dumped me."

Kim crunched a tortilla chip and wiped the salt from

her mouth as she chewed and swallowed. "Well, sugar, you don't look too busted up about it."

I frowned. "I'm not. I mean, I knew it'd end at some point, but—"

"But you're used to ending things on your terms."

"Yeah. I'm not upset because he beat me to the punch, if that's what you're thinking." I fiddled with the red and white striped straw floating in my glass.

Kim placed her cool hand on mine. Her gold fingernail polish glowed bronze in the candlelight, making her nails creepily talon-like. Suddenly I felt like a cornered mouse with a hungry hawk circling me. "What did he say that's got you all fidgety and unsure of yourself?"

I squirmed, unobtrusively removed my hand and wished I hadn't brought it up. Swapping confidences ranked right up there with a bikini wax on my pain threshold.

When I downed my margarita instead of responding, she sighed.

"Should I point out *you* asked *me* here? You shouldn't hafta get drunk to be able to talk to me, Julie."

"I know."

"I *know* you know. Honestly, you can't tell me anything that'll make me think you're some kind of freak."

The first night Kim and I had hit the bars, after a couple of beers I'd told her what'd happened to my mother and to Ben. Gradually, as we'd spent more time together, other things had tumbled out. But so far, I hadn't purposely sought her out and blathered on about my problems.

Not surprisingly she'd hit my fears right on the head. Maybe if she learned too much about me, she'd realize I *was* a freak. Conversely, if she accepted my quirks, we'd have a shift in our friendship. Right now those scales were pretty evenly balanced.

"Feeling up for a little truth or dare?" she asked.

Nice segue, Kim. "Always."

"You start with truth. Then you can do the same, or challenge me to a dare." Her voice lowered to a husky whisper. "I'm hoping your dare involves me askin' that hottie in the corner for his phone number."

I snuck a glance at the hottie in question. "He's practically jailbait."

But Kim wasn't about to let me get sidetracked.

She leaned forward. "Truth."

And the words rushed out as if my mouth was anxious to get rid of the toxins.

After I'd finished spewing my confusion about why I'd been eager to change for Kell, she tapped a manicured nail on the edge of the table. She looked skyward, her glass eye rolled like the olive in her martini.

"I'm not surprised. No offense, Jules, but he always did seem a little holier-than-thou."

"Still, it smarts getting the old heave-ho."

"True. But he was prettier than you, too. My Aunt Tillie—God rest her soul—claimed a pretty man was the devil in disguise."

No surprise I thought of Martinez.

"No matter how good he rocked the bed, musicians are always broke," she added. "A poor man is never a good bet."

"But a rich man isn't much better, trust me. I'll take a dynamo in the sack over a big bank account and a big ego any day."

She didn't give me time to regret my statement.

"The mysterious ex you don't talk about. I take it he had money?"

"Some. He'd made a killing in the stock market before it crashed. Gave him a God complex."

"You said it's been, what? Almost four years since your divorce?"

I nodded, increasingly unnerved with the conversation.

She laughed softly.

My face burned. "What's so goddamned funny?"

"You. For all your trash-talking you aren't out there hopping from one bed to the next, are you?"

I shook my head. That had been my ex-husband's flaw, not mine.

"None of the men you've been with were anything like him, were they?"

"No." I made wet rings in the cocktail napkin with the bottom of my glass. Fajita meat sizzled and the scent of onions and green peppers wafted past. "Maybe Kev was right when he said I only hooked up with Kell because he was the exact opposite of Ray."

"I've got my own theory on that." She chivied the olive from her empty glass and chomped on it. "How is Kevin?"

"Either efficiently robotic or a total scatterbrain. He's dealing with the grief and the details all by himself, as usual."

"And dare I ask about the case you're working on all by yourself?"

"It just keeps getting more complicated. Martinez, he's been . . . I don't know, *there* every step of the way."

"Hmm."

I glanced up at her. "What?"

"Sugar, you really haven't had enough to drink to hear my opinion on the powder keg situation between you and Martinez."

I opened my mouth to regurgitate the automatic denial that Martinez was just a client, when our perky red-headed waitress brought another round. Big tip for her for her excellent timing.

Kim tapped her glass against mine in a toast. "To men. A necessary evil."

"I'll drink to that."

She upended her martini.

Definitely a novelty that Kim was knocking drinks back faster than me. "Those must be some tasty martinis, girlfriend."

"Not especially. Just getting ready to answer your question."

"How do you know what I'm going to ask?"

"'Cause it's as plain as the nose on my face." She adjusted the satin straps of her lace camisole. "Maybe I should say, it's as plain as the glass eye on my face."

Heat crept up my cheeks again.

Kim stirred her dirty martini. With her head tilted forward I couldn't see anything behind her cloud of hair.

"My horse kicked me in the head when I was thirteen," she said without preamble. "Freak accident. Besides losing my eye, I wasn't even seriously injured."

I reached for my cigarettes.

"When people ask, and trust me, they do feel perfectly entitled to ask, that's what I tell them, because it is the truth. But it's not the whole truth."

My gut feeling? This was bad. "Kim, you don't have to tell me this."

She looked up at me, uneasily, then away to the rainbow fringed sombrero on the wall beside us. "You're the first person I've wanted to tell in a long time."

For all her bold talk, Kim had just as many trust issues as I did.

Whatever I expected was blown to hell the minute she said, "My father sexually abused me.

"I didn't grow up in the backwoods of Appalachia where incest is just accepted. My parents are pillars of the community. Very well off. But the one thing they couldn't have in their perfect life was kids, which forced them to adopt. Lucky me, huh?"

Did she realize she'd referred to herself as a *thing*?

"For as long as I can remember my dad came into my room at night. I threw a screamin' fit at bedtime. Eventually I understood it made him happier if I fought back."

She paused, sucked down a tiny sip of courage. "I'm not gonna go into the sordid details, but I will say when I finally told Momma what'd been happenin', she didn't act all that shocked. And it didn't stop after that, either."

The air between us tightened into an invisible noose.

"I was twelve years old when I tried to kill myself."

Tears snuck out the corners of my eyes and added extra salt to my margarita. I couldn't breathe.

"When I was in the psych ward at the hospital, my Aunt Tillie, my mom's aunt, managed to worm out of me what no one else could, even though I was so embarrassed I'd like to have died. Thought it was all my fault. If I'd been a better daughter it wouldn't have happened."

Her voice had taken on that thick, hard-to-understand southern drawl. "She confronted them and said if he touched me again, she'd sue for custody of me. And wouldn't that send the tongues waggin' at the country club?

"Don't know if it was her threat that worked or that I'd started my monthly. I jes' know he never came into my room again."

Kim sniffed and wiped her nose with a napkin. "Asshole must've felt some kind of guilt because he finally bought me the damn horse I'd been beggin' for."

A sharp sob escaped; I don't think Kim noticed.

"So instead of buyin' his own forgiveness and mine, every time he looks at me, and sees this ugly glass eye starin' back at him, he's reminded of the ugly things he did to me."

I downed my margarita. Welcomed the brain freeze. Still, even the loud mariachi music couldn't drown the void between us.

Perky waitress brought our food. I stared at the enchilada smothered in red sauce and the mound of cheese-covered refried beans. The spicy scent of salsa and guacamole only increased my desire to throw up.

"Come on, sugar, aren't you gonna say something?"

Only a trace of the young victim she'd been was reflected back at me in her bright blue eye. She'd survived. Telling her how sorry I was would've been the politically correct response.

I went with option B.

"Well, I guess we can cross 'shopping for Father's Day gifts' off the list of activities we can do together."

Her eye widened before she laughed until she cried.

I could breathe again.

She reached across the table and squeezed my hand. "Thanks."

"For what?"

"For listening. For trusting me. For not thinking I'm a freak."

"You're taking your chances getting stuck with that label if you hang around with me for too long."

"What's that supposed to mean?"

"I am a conduit for cosmic negativity. Most people are drawn to the vivacious, fun, lucky people. The type of person everyone adores.

"I, on the other hand, seem to attract people who've been chewed up by life and spit out. Who are more broken than whole."

"Does that bother you?"

"Sometimes. I wonder if I'll ever meet someone who doesn't have baggage or trauma or permanent damage from life events they either wouldn't or couldn't control."

Didn't seem to bother Kim that I'd included her in

that group.

"People are drawn to you, Jules, not because you've been beat up by life, but because you've survived it." She added softly, "Not everyone does, sugar."

"You did," I pointed out.

"Accepting who I was then isn't who I am now. That was survival. Some people can't get past that part of my past."

"People are stupid."

"Amen to that, sister."

She wrinkled her nose and shoved aside her plate of nachos. "I'm not really hungry."

I wasn't either.

The hug I gave her in the parking lot before we parted ways didn't feel as clumsy as I'd feared.

Instead of mulling over the info I'd uncovered on the Black Dog case, or dwelling on the nasty secrets of Kim's childhood, I popped in an Audioslave CD and let the distorted guitars and Chris Cornell's haunting vocals numb my overactive brain cells.

Thankfully Mrs. Babbitt didn't come scurrying out when I got home. Didn't think I could handle more emotional distress today.

I stripped in the living room and walked buck-ass naked into the kitchen. My house. I could do whatever the hell I wanted. Diet Pepsi in hand, I cranked the window air conditioner on full blast, and plopped in front of the TV.

Usually I skipped the local news, but I was curious to see how much information the sheriff's department had given the media on the murders. The story did get top billing on both stations but the details were vague.

It wasn't the only death reported in Bear Butte County in the last twenty-four hours.

My jaw nearly hit my knee when the newscaster announced county commissioner Red Granger had been found dead in a field a mile from his house. No details on whether foul play was suspected, which led me to assume old Red had suffered a heart attack or stroke. Poor guy. I'd always liked him.

I watched *The Philadelphia Story* for the millionth time before I drifted off into dreamless sleep.

Next morning at the office, I typed a chain of events relating to the Black Dog case. Interesting reading, but it didn't help me one bit on discovering Chloe's whereabouts.

Frustrated, I scribbled a second list, one I'd intended to give to Martinez detailing my reasons on why the cops needed information on Chloe's disappearance. Especially now that Rondelle was dead.

The outer door slammed. Damn. I'd forgotten to lock it again. I scooted back, expecting to see Kevin.

My office door banged open.

I gaped at the angry man careening toward me.

305

What the hell was my father doing here?

"I want to hire you," he said.

"For what?" I said calmly, as if he burst in like an angry bull every day. Truth was, this was the first time he'd ever graced the offices of Wells/Collins Investigations.

"I want you to find the son of a bitch who killed Red Granger."

CHAPTER 24

"Is this some kind of joke?"

"No." He pulled a creased leather checkbook from the back pocket of his faded Wranglers and clutched it in his right hand, stopping in front of my desk.

"How much?"

Just breathe. "Dad, listen—"

"No, girly, *you* just listen for a change. Don't know if you heard me, so let me repeat it. Red Granger is dead. Somebody shot him. Right through the heart. Right on his own damn land while he was mindin' his own damn business and fixin' his own damn fence. And I wanna know who did it."

That news jarred me. Not a heart attack or a stroke but another murder?

"Sit down," I said.

That belligerent look I knew so well settled on his weathered face and I prepared myself for the inevitable argument. Shocked the hell out of me when he clamped his teeth together and his butt dropped to the chair.

It wouldn't last; it never did.

"First, I heard about Red on the news last night and I'm sorry. I know you guys were friends." Or as close to it as my dad got.

He scowled.

"Second, put away your money."

"Why?"

"Because I can't work on the case."

Those mean, mean eyes focused on me. His whipcord lean body remained still as a rattler ready to strike. For an instant I morphed back into my younger self and steeled myself against the blow.

"Can't, or won't?"

Hadn't Martinez taunted me with the same response yesterday? Before I formulated my answer, he did for me.

"Oh, I see." He tossed the checkbook on the desk. "My money ain't good enough for ya?"

"It's not that—"

"Then what? Why is it you'll bend over for those Injuns, but when I ask you to do one thing for me—and I even offer to pay you—not only won't you do it, you won't listen to me?

"As if it ain't bad enough you're runnin' all over the damn county, tellin' people, men, good men, that've lived their whole lives on that land, that they're idiots for not just acceptin' the changes we got no say in? But now I gotta tell them you ignore your own kin? What? I gotta dye my skin red to get you to help me?"

"Shut the fuck up." Anger burned in me so hotly I

suspected my eyes were bleeding.

"Watch your mouth," he snapped.

"Then stop interrupting me, goddamn it, and let me explain, instead of spouting your usual racist bullshit!"

The ensuing silence was more deafening than my outburst.

He'd made me lose my temper, which pissed me off, but not as much as his self-satisfied expression that I'd behaved exactly as he'd wanted.

Fuck.

I reached for my cigarettes. Wished I could drag out a bottle of tequila. I told myself his disapproval against my favorite vices held no weight in my office or in my life. I lit up, and blew the smoke in his face.

Any second he'd tell me to put out my cigarette. Or, he'd try to prove he had more control than me by not rising to my bait. Little did he realize either one served my purpose. I got to tell him I could do whatever the hell I wanted in here, or I got to smoke without him bitching about it.

Oh yeah. The Collins clan redefined *dysfunctional*.

"Here's the deal, Dad. I cannot, I repeat, cannot work on an ongoing police investigation. Nor can I run a parallel investigation that interferes in any way with any agency, including the Sheriff's Department, the FBI, the CIA, the BIA or the Mickey Mouse Club." I smiled—all teeth. "So see, legally, my hands are tied and it has nothing to do with you personally."

His brow furrowed with skepticism. He sunk a bit lower in the chair.

"But as long as you're here, why don't you tell me how you found out that someone shot Red, when it isn't common knowledge."

"Maurice, Don, and Dale stopped by soon as they heard it on the scanner."

"I hate those damn scanners," I said.

"Don't matter. Keeps the cops in line if they think someone's listenin' to whatever they're doing."

After working in the sheriff's office, I disagreed. He knew how I felt, but I wasn't about to start another argument I couldn't win.

"At least they'll be earning the money we're payin' them tomorrow," he grumbled.

"Why? What's going on?"

"There's gonna be a big protest in the afternoon where they're buildin' the casino. Lot of people showin' up."

"Who?"

"Citizens worried 'bout all these murders. Members from the other tribes organized it. Maurice said those fellas from the casinos up'n Deadwood will be there. Dale thinks the TV stations will show up."

"Just what they need. More attention."

He shook his finger at me. "Even you can't deny none of this bad stuff happened before they broke ground."

"Will you be there?"

"No. I'm helpin' Red's wife finish patchin' the holes in the fence. The cows don't know that Red's dead and they're still gettin' out."

For a fleeting moment I pitied him more than I hated him.

Then his accusing gaze narrowed on me. "What about you?"

I shrugged. "What's it matter to you? Afraid I'll somehow embarrass you?"

"Wouldn't be the first time."

"Yeah?" I set my elbows on my desk, refusing to back away from him. "Maybe I'd give a shit *what* you thought if you hadn't embarrassed *me* by smacking me around."

"Maybe if I would've taken the strap to you more often you wouldn't have such a smart mouth."

"Like to see you try it now."

"Don't tempt me, girly."

From my peripheral vision I watched his fist clench. Unclench.

Come on you son of a bitch, do it.

"I wouldn't, if I were you."

Kevin shadowed the doorway.

Dad scowled over his shoulder at him.

"Get out," Kevin said. "I don't give a flying fuck why you're here, Doug, but no one comes into these offices and tosses around threats."

Part of me bristled that Kevin had decided to come in and save me. I'd been doing fine on my own. I'd had it under control. I didn't need his help.

My dad stood. Reached over and picked up his checkbook from the desk.

I flinched.

After he'd walked out I breathed again.

"You all right?" Kevin asked.

No. "Yeah."

"What was he doing here?"

"He wanted to hire me to find out who shot Red Granger. Pissed him off when I told him I couldn't."

Kevin frowned. "The news reports didn't say anything about Granger being killed. They said he died unexpectedly."

"The reporters didn't talk to the Bear Butte County Militia. With their trusty scanners—no detail gets past them."

"Speaking of murders in Bear Butte County . . . did you read the paper this morning?"

I shook my head.

"They released the victims' names from the other shooting."

His eyes caught the guilt in mine and he swore.

"You knew. You fucking knew and you didn't tell me. Why?"

"You had other things on your mind, Kev."

He was looming over my desk before I blinked.

"Don't give me that bullshit, Julie. How did you find out?"

I had no choice but to tell him everything. I was tired of keeping secrets. Tired of running the damn business without his help.

"Martinez put the word out he was looking for Chloe. An anonymous tip came in on where he could find her, so we went."

My fingernails dug into the foam armrests on my chair for support. Still made me dizzy and sick to think about it. "We got there and it wasn't Chloe, but Rondelle. Dead. We saw her, saw the other bodies, before the cops did. Then we got out as fast as we could."

"And while you were busy making your escape from a crime scene, you didn't think to contact the cops on what you'd discovered?"

"That was my first instinct until we realized someone had set us up to find them. We'd probably still be at the sheriff's department answering questions and it wouldn't get us any closer to finding Chloe."

"*We* meaning you and Martinez?"

I nodded.

"How do you know Martinez didn't have something to do with it?"

"Because I was there. I saw the look on his face when he figured out it was Rondelle lying on the dirty floor with half her head blown off."

He winced, but wasn't finished conveying his scorn. "Don't you think it's pretty convenient he knew exactly where to find the bodies?"

I was as sick of defending Martinez as I was of defending myself. My temper flared. "Anyone who's lived in the county knows where that shack is, or can tell someone who doesn't know where it is how to get there, so I'm failing to see your point."

Kevin stared at me as if I'd spoken Swahili. "He's got you completely snowed, doesn't he?"

"Who? Martinez?"

"No. The fucking tooth fairy. Yes, I'm talking about Martinez. How in the hell can you possibly justify trusting him?"

Because I needed to trust someone and you weren't around.

Even as the words surfaced, I knew it was a cop out. I trusted Martinez. Period. In some ways I trusted him more than I trusted Kevin, which shocked the hell out of me.

"Back off." I leveled my rapid breathing. "You told me you trusted my judgment with the agency. I did what I thought was right."

"Well, it wasn't." He jammed a hand through his hair. Acted like he wanted to pull it out. "Anything else you want to tell me?"

The information burst from me like a dam breach. "Rondelle supposedly ripped off the Carluccis, suspected members of an east coast crime family for a tidy sum of money. She double-crossed her old boss, Bud Linderman, by lying to him. Her association with Luther Ghost Bear of the Medicine Wheel Society got him killed, probably her ties with any one of those groups got Donovan shot. Oh. And grief has sent Harvey off his rocker. I suspect he'll go on a rampage if he ever finds out who killed his sister.

"I've been followed, threatened, assaulted. I've had to deal with pissed off bikers, angry ranchers, my father, the sheriff, mob bodyguards, and a cowboy posse. Not to mention witnessing a man getting shot right in front of me and stumbling onto a gruesome murder scene that will haunt me for the rest of my life."

I took a breath.

"This case has been an absolute fucking nightmare from day one. And I still haven't been able to do the one thing I was hired to do: find Chloe Black Dog."

That shut him up.

Silence stretched until I wanted to scream.

"But the good news is I saved fifteen percent on my car insurance by switching to Geico."

He didn't even crack a smile.

I sighed. Screw it. Screw *him*. I collected my cigarettes and stashed them in my purse as I rose to my feet.

"The bottom line? I'm in way over my head. I'm not exactly an old pro at this PI stuff, Kev, and you haven't been around to mentor me. So, I apologize if I've made bad decisions. Write me an official reprimand and stick it in my employee file. But I will not sit here and let you berate me as an outlet for your grief over Lilly."

By his look of incredulity, followed by the hard glint in his eyes, I knew I'd overstepped my bounds.

"Like you've never taken your grief out on me? How many times, no, how many *years* have I suffered alongside you? Am I even allowed to grieve, or is that strictly your milieu?"

The fact he was right didn't make the truth easier to swallow.

"Dirty pool, Kevin. While it won't do any good to defend myself, I will say that I didn't 'take out' my grief on you. I let you in, which is a helluva lot more than you've let me do for you in the last few months."

He closed his eyes. "Shit."

I swept by him.

"Julie, wait—"

"No. I'm done waiting. Lock the door and set the alarm when you leave. I won't be back today."

My mantra of *don't cry, don't cry* didn't work. Tears leaked past my defenses anyway. At least when Kevin wasn't around we didn't fight and I could pretend everything was lollipops and rainbows. Whatever ground we'd gained in getting our partnership back on track, we'd lost in the last half hour.

If this was another issue we'd sweep aside, pretty soon the bumps under the proverbial rug would trip us both.

After I'd calmed down I stopped in the sheriff's office. Missy and I chatted amiably, more so than when we'd worked together. Without questioning why I was there, she ushered me into Sheriff Richard's office and closed the door.

"I'm surprised to see you." His gaze zeroed in on the Styrofoam box in my hand. "Whatcha got there?"

"A piece of heaven." I opened the lid. Sugar, yeast, and cinnamon scented the air.

He licked his lips. "Must be a pretty important favor if you're bribing me with a warm cinnamon roll."

"It is." I pointed to his coffee cup. "Need a refill?"

"Now you've got me scared. Julie Collins offering to wait on me? Snowing in hell for sure."

"Ha ha."

He held out his mug.

I poured us each a fresh cup. As he ate, I sat in the visitor's chair and watched him.

Clean-shaven, hair slicked back, tan uniform pressed. Only the luggage beneath his eyes gave credence to my theory he hadn't had much sleep in the last three days.

"Sounds like things have been pretty interesting around here."

He grunted and shoved the last heavily frosted piece in his mouth. "Understatement of the year. Don't even have time to open my damn mail."

I eyed the stack in his "In" box. "Any change in Donovan Black Dog's condition?"

"He's stabilized. Swelling around his brain is down. Tomorrow they're gonna take him off the meds that've kept him in a coma." He sipped his coffee. "Course, you didn't hear any of that from me."

"Does he have any family staying with him up at the hospital?"

"You looking for someone in particular?"

"Yes."

"Who?"

"His five-year old daughter, Chloe."

Glaciers formed in his eyes. "Why?"

I wouldn't get another lick of information until I explained.

"Okay, here's my case in a nutshell: Donovan

snatched her in a child custody dispute. I was hired to find out where he'd hidden her."

"Dammit, Collins. Were any of the proper agencies made aware of this situation?"

My cheeks flushed with guilt.

"The mother hired you?"

"No. I was hired through the girl's uncle."

The Sheriff scowled. "Well? Spit it out."

"That day up at Bear Butte I was trying to convince Donovan to turn Chloe over to me so we didn't have to involve the 'proper authorities'. Then before he told me where she was, someone shot him."

"Where is the mother? Why hasn't she come forward?"

"See, that's the interesting part. Her name is Rondelle Eagle Tail and she's the woman you found dead in the cabin."

He lowered his cup very slowly. "Run that by me one more time."

Felt like a high schooler in the principal's office explaining why I'd skipped geometry. "Umm. Rondelle is Chloe's mother."

"And you're just coming to me with the information now?"

"Honestly, I didn't think it mattered before. But as I've been trying to find this girl, I found out a bunch of stuff I didn't want to know."

"Start talking, Collins. Don't leave anything out or you'll be cuffed and in FBI custody just for my amusement."

318

"But—"

"Talk!"

Crap. "Okay. One of the dead guys worked for Rondelle's boss up in Deadwood."

"Tommy Defiglio. Worked security at Trader Pete's for the Carluccis. That's not new information. Keep going."

"You also know that Rondelle was employed by Bud Linderman right before she went to work for the Carluccis?"

He nodded. Glowered. His nostrils flared.

"Then you know Harvey Vai—Tony Martinez's right hand man with the Hombres—is Rondelle's brother."

"Which means Harvey hired you."

"Umm. No." For something to do with my restless hands, I broke off a piece of Styrofoam and dropped it in the empty cup. "Martinez hired me on Harvey's behalf."

The sheriff didn't utter a peep.

To pass the time I watched the jagged white chunk floating in my cold coffee. Considered breaking off another piece and having a race.

"With all the personal stuff he's been going through, is your partner aware you're working for the Hombres?"

"Yeah. I mean no. I'm working for Martinez, not the Hombres."

"Same damn thing."

Not a good idea to argue the differences, especially when I wasn't precisely sure there were any.

"Tread lightly here, Collins. Dave Tschetter with the Lawrence County Sheriff's Department hinted there's been some trouble brewing between the Carluccis and the Hombres the last few months. It could get nasty."

"I know nothing about that." I took a chance. "But I would like to know if Red Granger's murder is somehow tied to all of this?"

"While I've always appreciated your insight and instincts, I don't need your speculation now. Stay out of this mess or I'll have you arrested for obstruction."

I nodded. Sheriff Richards didn't bother with idle threats.

"Besides. I can't tell you anything about an ongoing investigation." His relentless gaze pinned me to my chair. "But you already knew that, so why are you really here?"

Might be petty, but I'd keep the info about the security disk and the missing money to myself for now. I doubted either the Carluccis or Linderman would bring it up. Talk about providing perfect motives for murder.

"I'm here because I've failed to find Chloe Black Dog. The favor I need is simple: call me when Donovan regains consciousness. If I can find Chloe, it'll go a long way in easing Harvey's grief and closing my case."

"That I can do."

"Thanks. Then I'll be out of your hair." I tried to ease the tension. "What little hair you've got left."

"Funny. Who'd have thought I'd miss your bizarre sense of humor?"

Flustered by the remark, I stood and pitched my cup in the garbage.

"God knows I could use a good laugh." He drained

his coffee and stretched, his head nearly touched the water-stained ceiling. "You've got no idea the crap I'm putting up with this week."

"How many deputies are working the protest tomorrow?"

"A couple. I don't expect much will happen."

"I hope you're right."

"You going?"

"Probably. I haven't decided for sure."

"Hmm." He rocked back on his heels. "Maybe I oughta send in extra men if there's a chance you'll be there."

"Why would that make a difference?"

"Because, Collins, trouble seems to follow you everywhere."

No use denying it. I just hoped he was wrong for a change.

CHAPTER 25

SINCE I WASN'T GOING BACK TO THE OFFICE, I REMEMbered I hadn't checked out the Smart Start daycare angle. In my notebook, alongside where I'd written *Cindy*, I'd jotted the phone number. I dialed. Luck be my name. Cindy was working.

Don't know what I'd hoped to find. Because of confidentiality laws I doubted Cindy could tell me much. Still, it'd bothered me that Donovan's version of how Chloe had come to be in his custody didn't match Rondelle's, particularly when they'd eventually worked together to hide her.

Donovan said Smart Start had kicked Chloe out.

Rondelle had claimed she'd gone to pick Chloe up and Chloe wasn't there.

Who'd been telling me the truth?

Did it matter?

Yes. If it got me closer to finding the child.

It really bugged me to know how Linderman had

gotten pictures of Chloe with strange men. And close-ups? Most daycare places had safety parameters in place to keep strangers away. How had Linderman circumvented that?

Did he have grandkids there?

Nah. Smart Start was for low-income families. Linderman's privileged kids wouldn't have qualified.

Only one way: someone on the inside. Question was, had it been willingly? I'd seen the lengths he'd gone to, to ensure Rondelle's cooperation. Couldn't have been the first time he'd used threats to get his way, wouldn't be the last.

The Smart Start building had more in common with a welding shop than a school. Prefabricated metal. Zero windows in the front. A steel door with a sun-faded blue and white striped awning and a cartoonish sign propped above it. Two cars in the weed-covered parking lot.

The door was unlocked. Inside the entryway was another door next to a glassed-in reception desk.

It smelled like an elementary school. Dirty socks, ripe bananas, sour milk, and the underlying hint of cleaning products trying to mask those scents.

A young brunette with rodeo queen hair glanced up from the computer keyboard. God. Her boobs were so huge I wondered how she could see over them to type. "We're closed for the day," she said.

"Good. I'm here to see Cindy."

Her cherry-colored lips pursed. Made her mouth look like a piece of red licorice. "I'm Cindy. Who are you?"

I pushed a business card under the partition.

She snagged the card with a crimson claw. "What do you want?"

"Information on Chloe Black Dog."

"Sorry. All our information is confidential." She set her hands on the keyboard again, but her fingers didn't type. Pretty sure she'd stopped breathing, too.

"You do know that her father, Donovan, was shot recently?"

She didn't move.

"And her mother Rondelle is dead?"

Her gaze reluctantly slid to mine.

"I was hired to find Chloe before any of this happened. She's still missing and there are some really bad men after her, hoping to find her before I do."

"I don't know how I can help you."

"Okay." I plucked the guilt card from midair and played it. "Then why did you help *them*? For money? How much did Bud Linderman pay you to get those pictures of Chloe?"

She recoiled and sent a petrified look behind her. "Nothing! Omigod. You *know* about that?"

"Yeah. But I'll bet your boss doesn't."

Horror twisted her face, virtually cracking the caked on makeup.

"Your choice. You talk to me or I talk to your boss."

Five seconds later she angled back in her chair and yelled through the open office door, "Charmaine? I'm going out for a quick smoke break."

"Okay," echoed back.

Cindy grabbed a set of keys and a saddle-shaped purse.

I followed her outside, prepared to tackle her if she attempted to run.

At the corner of the building she plucked out a pack of Salem's and lit up. Tipped her head back and exhaled.

I performed the same ritual. Let the silence slide for about a minute. Then I said, "Talk."

"I didn't do it for the money."

"Why, then? How did you get involved with a scum bucket like Linderman?"

She coughed. "Not by choice."

Blackmail. No surprise.

"About six months ago I started seeing PeeWee, guy that works on his security team."

I frowned. PeeWee? Didn't fit the description of either of the guys I'd seen with Linderman. "He a cowboy?"

"Bullrider." She puffed. "*Ex*-bullrider. Got injured and couldn't compete any more. Linderman was his sponsor and made him his personal security. Been doing it about a year."

"You still with, umm . . . PeeWee?" The name sounded strange tripping off my tongue, dirty somehow.

Cindy chuckled. "Trust me. The name don't fit. See, 'PeeWee' is a joke from other cowboys because the man is hung like a bull. Nickname stuck."

More information than I needed.

"Son of a bitch is mean as an old bull too." She crossed her purple ropers at the ankle. "Being with a bullrider wasn't as exciting as I thought. He was all kinds of jealous. Would start a fight with any guy who so much as looked at me."

325

Sounded like Martinez.

"And he drank like a fish too. We broke up. End of it, right? Wrong.

"Month or so ago, PeeWee calls me, all sweet-like, and says he needs a favor. When he tells me what it was, letting him take those pictures of Chloe, I said no way. Told him to go to hell.

"The next day, old Linderman himself shows up. Said if I didn't do exactly what he wanted, he'd evict my granny from the nursing home."

Martinez had told me about Linderman's various businesses. Tossing out an old lady went beyond cold. I'd think Cindy was telling a big fat lie if I hadn't met Linderman first. Nothing was beyond the scope of possibilities with him.

"Sounds like a buncha shit, I know, but it's true. My great-granny is ninety. She lives on subsidies. She's lived in Meade County her whole life. Stuck in a wheelchair she ain't got no place else to go."

"So you agreed."

"Not proud of it, but yeah."

She took the last drag and flicked the smoking cigarette butt into the gravel. "Three men showed up one day when Charmaine was at lunch. Made me tell Chloe we were gonna play a secret, special game. She was supposed to act scared. Then happy, then scared again. They snapped pictures of her with all three guys. Made me want to vomit when I watched, but I wouldn't leave her alone with them for a second."

"Didn't she think it was weird?"

"No." Her chin trembled. "Chloe trusted me because I was her teacher. God. I never felt so low in my life.

"I kept waiting for Linderman to come back and make me do something else. He didn't. Thought he'd be an asshole and call Charmaine and I'd lose my job anyway. About two weeks later Rondelle lit into me when she picked up Chloe. She'd gotten those damn pictures the SOB had taken. She knew it was Linderman and was scared I was helping him."

I ground out my cigarette.

"So, I told her everything."

"What'd she say?"

"What could she say? We were both fucked." Her eyes gleamed. "Until we figured out a way to fuck that bastard over."

"How?"

"Rondelle left Chloe here. I waited until the end of the day to call Donovan. Told him Rondelle hadn't shown up, knowing he'd blow a gasket. They always fought about custody stuff. Anyway, when he got here, I acted all pissed off. Showed him fake records of how many times Rondelle had been late, how she'd given all these other people access to Chloe. I threatened to call Social Services. I let Donovan convince me not to contact them by telling him Chloe couldn't come back. Ever. That was the best way to keep her safe, because she sure as hell wasn't safe here."

Her risk, her bluff had paid off. "Has Linderman been back?"

Cindy nodded. "But by that time Chloe was long

gone and I wasn't of any further use to him. Been wondering if I ought to go to the police with it, now that Rondelle is dead. Even if it means I gotta find Granny another place to live. Even if it means my job."

I didn't say anything. I couldn't make that decision for her.

"You really don't know where Chloe is?" she asked.

"No." I faced her. "You wouldn't happen to know, would you?"

Her hairdo didn't move when she shook her head, but the turquoise chandelier earrings swung into her cheek. "She's a great kid. Rondelle may've acted as if she didn't care, but she wasn't a bad mother. Not like some I've seen around here. She'd have chewed through glass to keep her kid safe."

Or taken a gun blast to the head. The horror of it hung on the fringes of my subconscious every damn day.

"Since I talked to you will you do me a favor?"

"Depends."

"When you find Chloe call me and let me know she's okay."

"I can do that."

Cindy had made it halfway to the door. The lace petticoats beneath her denim skirt swished when she turned. "Linderman will get away with this, won't he?"

I couldn't lie. I said nothing.

Without another word, she went back to work.

CHAPTER 26

GREASY EGGS, FATTY BACON, WHITE TOAST SOAKED IN butter, hash browns fried in lard. When I craved the breakfast of cardiac patients, I went to The Road Kill Café.

I'd arrived late, in hopes of avoiding the ranchers' morning coffee klatch. No such luck. Several guys who knew my dad gave me that imperceptible nod, which meant they'd seen me, but didn't want to talk to me.

Maurice, Dale, and Don didn't bother with the ol' tip of the Stetson.

I caught snippets of conversation regarding the protest. However, the main topic of discussion was Red Granger's murder.

I'd left Martinez a message on his cell. He phoned back, but I could scarcely hear him over the din in the café. The call lasted a minute, at best.

Misty, a gorilla of a woman with five kids and no dental plan, lingered while she reheated my coffee. Chattered about her second cousin Hal, who'd hired a

PI in the early 1980s to track down his good-for-nothing wife.

Evidently the wife had skipped town with his Chevy truck. Good riddance, according to Misty. The one-sided dialogue stretched into a detailed dispute about a doublewide trailer, seersucker curtains, and ended with an anecdote about an incontinent Pekinese named Mumbles.

I listened, mostly because I doubted anyone else ever did.

Plus, I didn't have anywhere else to go.

Someone hollered for more coffee.

The salt and pepper shakers rattled on the Formica counter as Misty sashayed away.

A steady flow of men entered and joined the group in the back room. Ranchers, business owners from Butte City, the Lutheran minister from up in the northern corner of the county.

When Bud Linderman and his gang loped in, I knew I'd stayed too long. What was he doing here? He didn't live in the county and this café wasn't renowned for culinary delights.

I lit up, fascinated with how he'd shouldered his way into the close-knit group. Within minutes he'd tried to wrest control. He hadn't seemed compelling enough to pull it off, judging from our only meeting. Then again, he did own a boatload of businesses. Somewhere along the line he had to have perfected the art of the schmooze.

What did he want from these guys? To prove he was just another simple working class man, who shared their concerns about problems surrounding the new casino? Offering his support? Financial, perhaps?

Made me want to puke. Bud's only interest was self-interest.

Apparently my fellow Bear Butte County neighbors agreed. Pretty soon after he'd arrived, cowboy hats went back on, boot steps thumped and shuffled out the door.

I'd decided to wait to leave until Bud and his lackeys were gone. Not that I was avoiding him. Okay, maybe I was. I'd wanted a quiet, uneventful morning for a change. Locking horns with Linderman would guarantee my day would get off to a crappy, possibly violent start.

Lackey #1 elbowed Bud. Murmured something. Bud's gaze traveled to me in the last booth.

The eggs in my stomach scrambled, but I merely stared at him over the chip in my coffee mug.

He moseyed toward me. The cowboy Bobbsey twins took up defensive positions at the counter by the door.

Everyone else in the diner had disappeared. We were essentially alone.

Shit.

"Ms. Collins," he said. "Mind if I join you?"

"Yes."

He laughed and slithered in the booth anyway. "Been meaning to stop in and talk to you."

"Yeah? I've been meaning to stop into the sheriff's office and talk to him about *you*."

The carpet above his lip didn't move one whit. Staring in his brown eyes reminded me of gazing into a mud puddle.

"Pity about Rondelle, isn't it?" Linderman sighed. "As you know, the last time we spoke I was afraid this might happen to her."

He had come to my office to express his "concern" about Rondelle, in an underhanded attempt to get info on the disk. Then it hit me. If I ratted on him to Sheriff Richards about the visit, the sheriff would see it exactly the way Bud had intended for anyone to see it: Rondelle had become involved in something sketchy with her new employers.

Slimy toad.

If I stupidly got insistent with the sheriff about Linderman's true motive, wanting the disk, it'd play right into Linderman's hands too. Then he could point the finger of blame for Rondelle's murder right back toward the Carluccis. It *proved* she'd seen something. She'd had evidence. She'd paid the price.

Linderman wasn't aware Rondelle had been leading him around by the nose ring like a prize-winning steer. He didn't care what was really on the disk. In the end he'd get exactly what he'd wanted: the Carluccis gone, just like he warned me he would.

Which made him one of those toxic kinds of toads.

I felt warts popping up all over my body.

"How is that little girl dealing with her mother's brutal death?" he asked.

Bud didn't know I hadn't found Chloe.

On the other hand, he hadn't found her either.

Color me ten shades of relieved.

"What were you doing back there, Linderman?

Inciting them to riot?"

He caught my abrupt subject change. It didn't faze him. "They don't need me for help on that. Seem pretty riled up already." He stretched his arm along the table next to mine. "Why are *you* here? You protesting the casino too?"

"Hardly. What the Sihasapa tribe does with their land is their business, not mine."

"Bet that doesn't make you popular around these parts."

This pseudo-friendly chitchat set my teeth on edge. "Unlike you, I don't care. But if you're here in the interest of community service, where's your camera?"

"What camera?"

"The one you used at Smart Start." I lowered my coffee cup. "Or do you just use it to take pictures of little girls?"

Linderman's body went board stiff; I could've ironed on him.

"Those pictures you showed to Rondelle and Donovan? Skating awfully damn close to kiddie porn, Uncle Perv."

"I've no idea what you're talking about."

I stirred cream in my coffee, though I drink it black, for something to do with my hands besides wrap them around his red neck.

"Thought you were a straight-shooter, Bud. I know you sent Rondelle to work at Trader Pete's. I've gotta tell you, I saw firsthand how the Carluccis reacted when they thought Rondelle was spying for the Hombres. Not pretty."

"What do the Hombres have to do with anything?"

My brows lifted. "You mean you don't know?"

Irritation splashed in those muddy pools. "I've no intention of playing twenty questions with you."

"Me either, 'cause it'll only take one answer. Rondelle's brother Harvey is the chief enforcer with the Hombres." I paused to let the reality sink in. "For being practically *family*, you sure as hell didn't know much about hers, did you?"

Black hairs poked through the fish white skin covering his hand. His fingers adjusted his bolo tie. "Your point being?"

"If I bring up the photos with the sheriff, he'll feel compelled to investigate. When he connects them to you and that poor girl, Cindy, that you browbeat into helping you . . . well, you'll probably be safer in jail than in Harvey's hands."

"What photos?"

"The ones your rodeo clowns rammed in Donovan's face after they beat the living hell out of him."

Linderman smirked. I fought the urge to bean him in the head with the steel napkin dispenser.

I continued winging my way through the conversation. "You know, I thought you were a smart guy. But having a set delivered to Rondelle at Trader Pete's? There was your mistake. Shouldn't have let her keep them." I blew on my cold coffee. "Maybe I oughta burn the whole damn box of stuff she sent me. I can't prove you snapped those pics anyway."

"You are a very bad liar, Ms. Collins. You've got

nothing."

I smiled, slightly sheepishly. "Okay. You caught me. I'm a habitual liar. I don't have the pictures. I don't know where Chloe is. I don't have the security disk with Little Joe Carlucci meeting with, gosh, was it two or three members of the South Dakota Gaming Consortium? In the upstairs meeting rooms at Trader Pete's." I sighed with disgust. "Sometimes I lie so much it even makes *me* sick."

His right hand manacled my left wrist so fast I gasped. A heavy boot slammed on each instep, immobilizing my feet.

"Tell me where the goddamned disk is."

Jesus. My arm stung. "Fuck you," I said through clenched teeth. "Let me go."

He twisted harder. "Stop pissing with me."

The fingers on my right hand inched toward the fork by his left elbow. "Let go of me right fucking now."

"Answer me."

My middle finger brushed the tines.

The bell above the entrance jangled.

I didn't look away. Neither did Linderman.

Boots scuffled. Before the commotion registered, a shadow fell across the table.

"I'd advise you to let go of her if you ever plan to use that hand again, Linderman."

Bud peeled his fingers off my flesh and glanced up. Relaxed back in the booth, removed his feet and the snake oil salesman reappeared.

I snagged the fork anyway.

"Mr. Martinez. You're looking good. Didn't see you at the Deadwood Blues Festival. Missed a great show. Sorry about your, ah, *employees* losing the security contract to Little Joe Carlucci's team this year." He shrugged. "Just business, you understand, nothing personal."

In the sliver of space between Martinez's lean hip and Bud's bloated body, I saw No-neck had both of Linderman's guys corralled.

"Your understanding touches me," Tony said.

He leaned over.

Linderman had to crane his neck to see him.

"However, you touch *her* again? That ridiculous mustache will be the biggest piece of you they'll ever find."

The menace in his tone made my bones quiver.

Martinez stepped aside. His body language said, *Get the fuck out of here.*

No-neck dragged the lackeys outside, one in each hand.

Linderman scooted from the booth and glared at me before he clomped off.

Misty waddled up to the booth and said to Martinez, "Coffee, sir?"

"Yes. Please."

He glided in across from me. Watched as Misty poured him a cup and reheated mine. He smiled at her. "Thanks."

She was totally flustered by that smile.

I knew exactly how she felt.

My vocal cords had grown polyps.

Martinez ripped open five packets of sugar and two creamers and dumped it in. He snagged my spoon and

336

stirred.

"You already eat?" he asked.

Was he serious? He wanted to act like he'd just been delayed for brunch? Not that he'd threatened to kill someone in front of me? *For* me?

No way. I'd suffered through enough avoidance in my life, especially with men. "Why are you here, Martinez?"

"I was in the neighborhood."

He sprinkled in another packet.

"Think you've got enough sugar in there?"

"No. Stuff tastes like shit without it."

I growled and angled across the table so he couldn't ignore me. "Tell. Me. Why. You're. Here."

He brooded and I wondered if he'd answer.

"Didn't like what I heard in the background when I called you. Came to check it out."

"Yeah? Well, I was doing fine on my own."

His gaze flicked to the fork clutched in my fist. "Looked like it."

The clever retort dancing on the tip of my tongue was forgotten the minute his fingers gently traced the red finger-shaped welts where Linderman had given me a snakebite.

"It hurt?" he murmured.

"A little."

Martinez's eyes caught mine. He slowly lifted my wrist to his mouth and gently, thoroughly kissed those marks on the inside of my forearm before he set it back down.

I was freefalling. I'd stepped off the edge of a cliff.

I think I whispered, "Omigod," before I hit bottom. I even dropped the damn fork.

"What?"

I blurted, "You scare the hell out of me, Martinez."

He waited a beat. Sipped coffee as murky as his eyes. "Same goes, blondie."

No-neck came back inside, muttered in Tony's ear and then parked himself at the front door, even though we were the only ones in the joint.

"Only one shadow today?"

"Yep."

"You should buy a black T-shirt that says, 'My bodyguard can beat up your bodyguard.'"

"You're the one who needs a damn bodyguard."

"Where's the other guy? Don't you usually have two?"

"He's watching Harvey."

"Why?"

Martinez frowned.

When he didn't answer, I reminded him, "You make me tell you everything."

"True." He sighed. "Honestly? Because he's freaking me out. He's beyond grief. It's not like him *not* to talk to me, about Rondelle or anything else. Just keeps getting worse."

I'd been living with the same situation for the last few months. I waited to see if Martinez would confide in me or if he'd clam up, like Kevin.

"The thing is," he continued, "I know what he's going through. He won't let me help him and it drives me—how did you put it—bat shit."

I threaded my fingers through his.

The move surprised him. He glanced up before he tightened his hold on our joined hands.

"I know. Kevin hasn't been talking to me about Lilly. When she was first diagnosed and he knew she was going to die I thought I'd be able to help him. He didn't want my help. Then or now."

The understanding of that kind of loss, the experience of grief passed between us.

Another shift pulled us, this one no more subtle than the first.

"Do you realize that this is the first time we've been together outside of a bar? Or some kind of fight? Or stumbling across . . ."

Dead bodies.

I shuddered.

Martinez swept his thumb across my knuckles.

My stomach swooped again. "Weird, huh?"

"It doesn't have to be," he said, watching me with lazy intent. A predator who'd finally cornered his prey.

How much longer would he wait before he pounced?

Why wasn't I panicked and running for my life?

I stared at him for a couple of seconds, then dropped my gaze to the black scuffmarks on the chrome barstools beside us.

"Think about it, okay?" he said.

"I have been," I admitted.

"Good."

He released my hand.

"Watch your back at the protest. Steer clear of

Linderman if he's there."

"No problem. What will you be doing?"

"Checking on a couple of things in Spearfish."

A lead on this case he wasn't sharing? "Regarding Chloe?" I asked a little sharply.

"No." He stood, withdrew a crumpled twenty from the pocket of his Levis and tossed it next to my bill. "Hombres business."

He walked out the door flanked by No-neck.

What had I gotten myself into? Where was that gut reaction that I'd made a huge mistake?

CHAPTER 27

My Sentra chugged as I drove to the Bear Butte Casino construction site to see who'd shown up for the protest. Despite my father's claims, I doubted many people would bother.

Was I wrong.

All types of vehicles, family cars, pickups, motorcycles, shiny new SUVs, beat-up vans, even a couple of old blue school busses lined the gravel road. I had to walk two miles to reach the outer edges of the crowd. More like a half-mile, but my lungs complained just the same.

Once I'd labored up the last dirt mound, throngs of people swam into view. The deep thump of a bass drum provided the backbeat. The collective, high-pitched chanting reverberated, sending chills down my spine, as it did every time I heard those mournful cries.

Were they members of the Medicine Wheel Society? Or another Sioux tribe?

I craned my neck to see how far the crowd stretched.

The protesters had made an arc, which from afar resembled a crooked smile. The drummers were front and center, as were the sign carriers. Not many. Apparently they'd condensed their messages down to three basic points. I couldn't read the words from where I stood so I wound my way through the assembly until I reached the front.

The first sign read: **COWBOYS AND INDIANS UNITE**, and was held by a young rancher.

The second one, gripped tightly in an elderly Native woman's gnarled hands said, **MORE INDIAN GAMING DOES NOT = MORE PROFIT FOR TRIBES**.

The third, and biggest said, **KEEP MATO PAHA HALLOWED GROUND FOR ALL PEOPLE**.

Again, the amount of people and diversity of those people who were boldly and clearly showing opposition to the casino construction shocked me. I'd gotten used to apathy.

However, the owner of Brush Creek Construction wasn't indifferent or taking any chances. Five enormous road graders blocked access to the structure. Even those hulking steel machines wouldn't provide much protection if the mob decided to rush the building. Smart move, keeping the workers off site.

So where were the members of the Sihasapa tribe who'd pushed this casino through? Why weren't they here, defending their decision? The responsibility for this controversy was on their shoulders, not the construction company that was merely trying to complete the job they'd been contracted for.

I wended my way through the masses, and searched for familiar faces. Probably no one from my neighborhood was here.

I'd about given up hope when I recognized the motley group of ranchers, including Maurice Ashcroft, Don Anderson, and Dale Pendergrast.

Don's eyes met mine but his gaze skittered away quickly.

Great.

Didn't see Linderman skulking about. Didn't mean he didn't see me.

I kept moving. Out of the corner of my eye I caught a black, shiny flash. I wheeled around, afraid I'd see Reggie glaring at me in his usual crappy suit, but he wasn't there. My overactive imagination showing again.

A cheer spread when the drums finished. Two people brandishing bullhorns stepped in front of the crowd.

The group chanting began and grew stronger with each shouted, "Sacred Land! Sacred Land!" Drums joined the voices, clapping hands joined the drums and 500 people were united as one.

It was as scary as it was exhilarating.

Then the grayish black storm clouds drifted in from the west and spread across the sky, blocking the sun like a portent of doom. Electricity crackled in the air. Humidity hung like a wet sponge.

And just like that, the mood of the multitudes shifted.

The chanting died. An angry buzz started. A dirt clump flew toward the building. Followed by a rock. Soon everyone was whizzing chunks of earth at the building as if the concrete and steel girders were a living entity they could stone to death.

I ducked right before a clod nailed me in the side of the head.

Oh man. Sheriff Richards should've sent more deputies.

Individuals pushed, trying to get closer to the action.

The momentum of the mob would knock people to the ground. Then panic would ensue.

But Deputy John had taken control, facing the crowd with a bullhorn he'd appropriated.

"People. Listen to me. Stop throwing things or I'll start issuing tickets to everyone for destruction of property. This protest is officially over. I repeat: the protest is over. Begin moving toward your vehicles in an orderly fashion."

Lightning spiked, thunder boomed, and everyone scattered.

I hung around until most of the crowd dispersed. Maybe if I bugged Deputy John, he'd let something slip out about the murders. He wasn't nearly as closed-mouthed as the sheriff.

While I waited another black flash zipped past. Not the same one I'd noticed earlier, but definitely one I'd seen before.

Harvey.

What the hell was he doing lurking around?

I tried to follow him but he darted through the masses like a ninja, solid one second, a vapor the next.

Where was his bodyguard?

I'd about given up hope of finding him when I spied Harvey again, standing at the back of the clearing where it sloped into a steep drop-off.

This time he wasn't alone: He had his arm looped around Bud Linderman's neck and a pistol pointed at Bud's temple.

I unclipped my cell phone and scrolled down the contacts list until TM popped up. I hit dial.

He answered on the second ring. "Yeah."

"Martinez, it's Julie. I'm at the Bear Butte Casino protest. Harvey's here and he's got a gun to Linderman's head."

"Fuck. Hold on."

Dead air burned my ear for so long I thought we'd gotten disconnected.

Then, "Julie? Hang tight, I'm outside of Piedmont."

"Wait! What is going on?"

The connection crackled. "Big Mike said Harvey got a call and he took off. We've been looking for him."

"Did Big Mike know what the call was about?"

"We're assuming information on Rondelle."

It appeared Harvey was following through with his threat to find out who'd killed his sister. "What should I do?"

"Stay as far away from him as you can."

He hung up.

"Easier said than done," I grumbled to the dial tone.

I held my palm over my stomach to quell the sick feeling bubbling up like lava. My whole body was leaden, my feet dragged, kicking up gravel as I targeted the small

345

knot of people surrounding Harvey and his hostage.

Linderman's cowboy companions were off to the right side, guns lying in the dirt, useless.

Deputy John was trying to persuade Harvey to put down his weapon.

Harvey's mouth stayed shut while the deputy rambled. He didn't so much as twitch. His gaze constantly flickered between the crowd, the cop, and his hostage.

Finally the deputy went silent.

His radio squawked; he ignored it.

Jesus, Martinez, hurry up

"There are people who can help you. People who *want* to help you," Deputy John tried again in his best negotiator's voice.

"Is that right?" Harvey said.

"Yes. No one has to get hurt."

Harvey laughed.

Someone needed to warn Deputy John before *he* got hurt. He didn't know the last rational part of Harvey had died with Rondelle.

"Let me help you."

"You know what would help me out a whole bunch?"

Finally, Harvey was responding. "Anything. Just name it."

Harvey's grip on Linderman's throat increased. "If this motherfucker would just admit that he murdered my sister."

"I told you. I didn't do it," Linderman croaked.

"See? You *can't* give me anything I want, Deputy, so that makes you just as much of a liar as this cocksucker."

"Okay, okay, calm down. Maybe I can't give you that." He paused. "How do you know this man killed your sister?"

"How do I know?" He blinked, frowned at the deputy like he was an idiot. "A little bird told me."

Harvey had gone totally bonkers.

But Deputy John didn't miss a beat. "What did the little bird say, Harvey?"

"That this asshole," he pressed the gun deeper into the skin above Bud's ear, "was responsible."

"And you believe that?" Deputy John asked.

"Yep."

"Why?"

"'Cause everyone knows he's a manipulative bastard."

While Deputy John had been talking, two other deputies—Al and Jerry—had arrived on the scene and positioned themselves within shooting range, guns drawn. But neither had a clear shot.

Harvey had planned this pretty well for a crazy man.

Sporadic raindrops bounced off the dirt, kicking up the scent of wet chalk. I didn't look up at the sky. No one else paid attention to the weather.

"Tell them," Harvey demanded.

Linderman repeated, "I didn't do it."

"She worked for you, didn't she? You sent her to Trader Pete's to spy on them, didn't you?" His voice had returned to a calm cadence. "What'd you threaten her with, Bud*hole*, to get her to do your shit work?"

Linderman's wide-eyed gaze darted to Deputy John and he began to sweat profusely.

Was the sweat from fear? Or guilt? Harvey's level of agitation had jumped about 100 percent.

"Tell them!"

We held our collective breath for a lifetime, afraid of what would happen next.

"You are chickenshit *and* a liar," Harvey said at last. "Tell them how you threatened to hurt her daughter, an innocent little girl, if Rondelle didn't do what you wanted."

No reply.

"Were you there when the top of Rondelle's head was shot off?" He shifted the gun to Linderman's forehead. "Like this? Is this where you placed the barrel?"

"Come on, Harvey," Deputy John said. "This isn't helping anyone. Put down the gun."

Harvey gave no indication he'd heard him.

"Did you look into her eyes as you fucking killed her? Tell me or I'll blow your fucking brains out right now."

Linderman blubbered: "I d-d-didn't d-d-do it."

A disturbance broke out behind me. I didn't have to turn around to know Martinez had arrived.

He blew right past the armed deputies and stopped next to Deputy John.

Big Mike wordlessly moved in on one side of me, No-neck the other, keeping Al and Jerry from having a clear shot at Martinez.

"Hey, man," Martinez said to Harvey, "what's going on?"

Harvey didn't seem particularly surprised to see him. "Just taking care of some personal business."

"This isn't the way to do it, hombre."

"It's the way this fucker took care of Rondelle."

Martinez shook his head. "You don't know that."

"Yes, I do. He killed her. *He's* the reason she's dead."

He carefully weighed Harvey's response. "Killing Linderman will only cause problems for you, Harvey, not him. He's not worth it."

"That's funny. Don't you always say, 'What goes around comes around'?"

"Yeah. But nothing is gonna bring Rondelle back around."

Harvey's sad, broken smile leached the hope right out of me.

"Wish it would. I shoulda told her . . ."

"Doesn't matter man, she knew."

Harvey's face was wet. From tears? Or rain?

"You know how this works, Martinez. Price needs to be paid."

"It will be."

Harvey and Martinez exchanged a long, silent look.

"Not today," Martinez said. "Let him go."

Just like that, Harvey unwrapped his arm from Linderman's neck. Keeping the gun aimed at Bud's head, he shoved him to the ground.

Linderman scuttled away like a cockroach.

The sky opened; rain poured down. The rich scent of wet dirt rose up as water sizzled on the hot earth.

Despite the flashes of lightning and answering cracks of thunder, no one ran for cover. We hung in suspended animation, part of this, yet not.

Harvey said something I couldn't make out.

"I can't hear you," Martinez shouted.

"I'm sick of this," Harvey shouted back.

"Sick of what?"

"Sick of nothing ending up the way it's supposed to be!"

Silence.

"Then I'll fix it."

Harvey shook his head.

"I thought you trusted me." Martinez said. "So let me help."

"You can't," he said. For a second Harvey wavered.

"What's different this time?"

"You don't know what it's like!"

Martinez threw up his hands. "Jesus! How can you say that? To *me*?"

Harvey frowned.

Everyone seemed equally baffled by the cryptic conversation. The usual hushed whispers to try and decipher it were conspicuously absent.

"Come on, Harvey. Give me the goddamn gun."

The loud exchange made the scene even more illusory; normally neither Martinez nor Harvey raised their voices.

"Man, I'm sorry."

"Don't be. We'll work it out."

"Not this time."

Martinez took a step forward. "Just give me the gun, okay?"

Harvey raised the gun at him.

No-neck and Big Mike were by Tony's side before Harvey had leveled the barrel.

"Back off, Martinez."

"Give. Me. The. Gun."

"You can have it when I'm done, *hombre*."

By the time his meaning had sunk in, it was too late. Harvey jammed the barrel in his mouth, closed his eyes and pulled the trigger.

CHAPTER 28

MARTINEZ WOULDN'T LET ANYONE COME NEAR HIM. He hadn't said boo since we'd left the sheriff's office except to quietly insist I drive him to Fat Bob's.

I almost didn't recognize the place. The neon motorcycle atop the bar wasn't spinning. The flashing beer signs and floodlights were off, leaving the parking lot barren. Maybe the rain amplified the bleakness.

Maybe the building grieved for Harvey.

I parked in back by the fenced-in beer garden. Without a word, Martinez slipped from the car.

Time dragged as I watched him through the rhythmic slap of the windshield wipers. He stood in front of the door, oblivious to the driving rain.

My heavy exhalations fogged the windshield, partially obscuring him from view.

What was he thinking? What was he feeling? What was he waiting for?

What was I supposed to do? Help him? Ignore him?

Drive away?

He hadn't asked me to stay.

Then again, he hadn't told me to go.

I wrestled with indecision.

He needs time alone, the rational part of my brain insisted.

I never listened to logic.

I switched off the ignition, and jumped from the safety of the car into the deluge.

With my shoes already soaked, I slogged through the puddles. Martinez didn't acknowledge me as I splashed up behind him. Rain pelted us, not a warm tropical shower, but cold, relentless, stinging drops that seemed to slice right through my skin.

With the wind howling outside, and lost in the grief screaming inside him, he'd isolated himself completely.

I had to get through to him.

Shivering, I bumped him hard with my hip. "You forget the alarm code or something?"

He faced me. Water clung to his long, dark lashes even after he blinked with confusion. "What?"

"Are we going inside?"

"Yeah." An automaton, he unclipped his keys and started flipping the locks. Six in all. He jerked the steel door; it squeaked open and he disappeared inside the dark building.

Fluorescent lights flashed, blinding me as I followed the wet leather jacket pulled taut across his back.

He punched in the code to deactivate the alarm.

The wind whipped the door shut with a deafening

bang; I nearly leapt to the rafters.

He didn't notice.

Methodically, he slid the deadbolts home and locked us in.

Guess I was staying.

His bootsteps echoed *squish squish* as he tracked slop across the concrete floor to his private office. Only one of the five locks was engaged and he'd entered the room before I could catch up to him.

A phone rang. Once. Twice.

Stopped abruptly mid-third ring.

A telephone base and receiver sailed out the open door and crashed; plastic exploded like shrapnel.

The plug-in end of the cord still had a piece of Sheetrock attached from where it'd been ripped from the wall.

His grief hit me; my knees buckled from the force of it.

Martinez reappeared and steadied the door with one hand, while he angrily wrote with the other.

My feet finally moved. I inched closer, to see the angry black letters he'd scrawled over the door:

STAY THE FUCK OUT

Our gazes crossed. In his I saw unmitigated rage.

I didn't know if I could handle this situation, let alone handle him.

Sensing my hesitation, he chucked the black Sharpie toward walk-in coolers, and cocked his hands on his hips.

"You comin' in or what?"

Heart thundering, I nodded and crept past him.

A series of locks tumbled behind me.

Water dripped from my clothes. I stayed put, making nervous puddles on the carpet.

Martinez bypassed me and headed straight for the bar cart. He wasn't choosy about his anesthetic. He pressed the bottle to his lips. Drank quietly, but steadily. When he drained the last of his self-prescribed painkiller, would he throw the empty at the wall?

I know I would have.

I primed myself for the explosion of glass and fury that didn't happen.

All at once he remembered himself. He slowly turned toward me. The bottle of Jack Daniels dangled from his fingertips. His gaze raked me from stringy hair to soggy feet.

"Sorry. You'd probably like to get out of those wet clothes."

I shifted, not yet able to articulate the words he needed to hear.

He pointed to the dark hallway. "There's extra towels in the closet. Feel free to use whatever you need." He lifted the bottle, drank. "I'm hitting the shower."

The Jack Daniels accompanied him to the bathroom and the door clicked shut.

Inside the bedroom, I peeled the sodden clothes from my body as quickly as my numb fingers allowed. After I toweled off, I slipped into a white cotton robe I'd found on the back of the door.

I didn't snoop, although technically Martinez had given me free rein. Any other time I would've seized the opportunity to glean secrets about El Presidente, but I wasn't in the mood. Wasn't anything in the windowless room besides a king-sized bed and a small dresser.

Gathering my sopping things, I returned to the main room and dropped them on the plastic carpet protector beneath the office chair. My restless gaze zeroed in on the bar cart.

The round, wooden cap exclusive to Don Julio tequila rose up like a beacon.

Tempting, but one of us needed to stay sober. I took a bottle of water from the mini-fridge and my eyes sought my purse, in dire need to feed my nicotine habit.

Crap. I'd left my smokes, my keys, my cell, hell, everything in the car. With the Fort Knox security system in this place, I couldn't sneak out to retrieve my cigarettes or "borrow" a pack from the bar. I was screwed.

Couldn't drink. Couldn't smoke. No TV. What the hell was I supposed to do?

Wait, which I don't do well under the best circumstances.

These were far, far from that.

I tucked my clammy feet under me and secured the robe over my knees. Nestled my neck in the cushions and closed my eyes. Time on my hands gave me time to think. I didn't want to think. The ghastly images of Harvey's last moments flickered behind my lids.

Big Mike, No-neck, and I had grabbed Martinez to try and stop him from going to where Harvey had fallen.

He'd shaken us off like lint.

No one had come near him as he stood over the body. He wouldn't leave Harvey. He watched until they zipped the bag and loaded him into the back of an ambulance.

Even then he hadn't uttered a sound.

At the sheriff's department he'd let his lawyer do the talking.

If I was having a hard time blocking it out, what was Martinez going through?

When the shower shut off, I knew I'd find out soon enough.

One door opened, another closed.

Humid, pine-scented air wafted in. Muffled noises drifted from the bedroom.

And I waited.

Surreal stillness amplified sounds. The bottom of the bedroom door scraped against the carpet as it swung open. The fabric of his clothing brushed the tweed couch when he walked past me. Then the suctioning pop of the mini-fridge door, followed by the snick and hiss of a carbonated can.

Finally I found the guts to look at him.

Martinez stood in the center of the room, staring sightlessly at the exit sign above the door, a Coke can clutched to his naked chest. Baggy silver boxing shorts exposed his muscled stomach and skimmed his knees. His feet were bare.

My stomach roiled. I'd never seen him like this, half-dressed, half-lost, totally vulnerable.

"Tony?"

He turned toward me, his face shuttered.

"Do you want to talk?"

He shook his head.

"You want to get drunk?"

"No."

"Then what can I do?"

He drained the Coke and crushed the aluminum between his hands as easily as a gum wrapper. "Can you make it go away?" He whipped the spent can at the garbage pail. "Jesus, Julie. Can you tell me why he did it? Make me forget he's fucking *dead*?"

I winced at the hard slap of his words.

God, I hated this. I didn't know why I'd come or why I'd stayed. Why I thought *I* could help him. Being here just reinforced the sad truth that I was the *last* person qualified to hand out advice on how to deal with gut-wrenching, soul-stealing loss.

No wonder Kevin hadn't confided in me.

I unfolded from the couch and tiptoed to the pile of wet clothes, my single thought to escape. I grabbed my cold jeans only to have Martinez snatch them from my hands and fling them back to the floor.

"What are you doing?" he demanded.

"I'm leaving."

"Like hell you are."

"For Christsake, Martinez, I suck at this. How am I supposed to help you when I can't even help myself?"

I whirled away to hide my humiliation; my mouth had no such shame and ran unchecked.

"Ben has been dead for three *years*, my mother for almost twenty, and I'm still seriously fucked up. I can't sit here and coo sympathy and lie that it'll be all right. It

358

won't be all right. Nothing will ever be the same."

My voice cracked, then broke completely. "Your life will have a big, black, gaping hole in it that nothing or no one on this earth will ever fill. But you already know that, don't you?"

Being strong and tough was an illusion. Far more appealing to crawl in that hole and howl like a wounded animal.

His hands curled over my shoulders. "Julie—"

"Don't." I tried to shrug him off. Jesus, I was a pathetic, self-centered excuse for a human being. I was supposed to be consoling him, not making it worse, not making it about *me*.

He spun me back around.

I didn't have a chance to see sorrow or pity or anything else because his mouth was on mine.

And I didn't do a single damn thing to resist.

As Martinez kissed me, so sweetly, so completely, so perfectly, my tears fell.

I fell.

I'd expected tongue-thrusting, teeth-grinding passion from him, not tenderness. Not bewilderment. Not this intimate glimpse into his frailty.

The deeper we took the kiss, the more he let me see his raw, battered state. I recognized it. Understood it. Gave into it.

My blood, sluggish from the cold rain, heated and raced through my system, vanquishing my tears but not my doubts.

His mouth broke away in slow increments; he slid

his warm, soft lips to my cheek. "Stay." Hands knotted in my wet hair. Ragged exhalations teased the skin below my ear, sending goose bumps cascading down my body. "Please. Just stay, okay?"

I knew it was wrong. I should've pushed him away. Taken the opportunity to put him back at arms' length where he belonged. Even as my conscience blasted warnings, I whispered, "Okay."

The sweet kisses disappeared.

His hands, always so gentle and tentative with me, were idle no more. Rough fingertips and palms slipped down my face, my throat, then inside the robe and caressed my bare flesh from the curve of my belly to the curve of my ass.

I wound my arms around his neck, threading my fingers through his damp hair. I couldn't get close enough to him. I wanted to share the same breath, the same mind, the same skin.

His forehead burrowed into the tender spot where my collarbone connected to my neck and he went still.

"Tony?" I murmured.

"Make it go away." His hoarse whisper cut across my skin, cut *through* it. "Can you make it go away? Make me stop thinking about it?"

His anguish ripped the air from my lungs.

I pressed my body against his, cradled his face in my hands, grazed my lips across his cheeks, the corners of his eyes, his temples, the lines on his forehead, the rigid set of his jaw.

When our lips met again, and his mouth freely

opened to mine, I poured myself into him. Offered him the understanding of his grief that I couldn't verbalize.

With this, I could make him forget, make us both forget.

What little control he had shattered.

He unknotted the belt and pushed the robe from my shoulders until it pooled at my feet. Grabbed the back of my bare thighs and lifted me against the wall.

My senses were awash in his heat, his scent, his urgency. My legs circled his hips. I arched closer, letting my head fall back as he trailed hot, wet kisses down my throat, buried his face between my breasts.

"Yes or no, blondie. Tell me now."

This was wrong, wrong, wrong. We both knew it.

And yet, I still answered, "Yes."

Our eyes met and there was no going back.

I hooked my fingers inside the elastic waistband of his boxing shorts and yanked until there were no barriers between us.

He drove inside me and nothing else mattered.

Later, in the complete darkness of the bedroom, we didn't communicate beyond the sounds of lovers.

We didn't have to. We didn't want to.

Martinez rested his head on my belly, one hand clasped in mine on the mattress; the other idly stroked my leg from knee to the inside of my thigh.

My fingers sifted through his hair, smoothing the

soft strands from his brow, the tensed line of his neck, the heavy set of his shoulders.

His silent tears dampened my stomach. As he pretended not to cry, I pretended not to notice.

CHAPTER 29

I WOKE ALONE, SPRAWLED FACE FIRST ON THE MATTRESS. Naked.

Without a hangover.

There went the excuse for my behavior last night.

Did I need an excuse?

No.

So I'd slept with him. Big deal. Pointless to shut the barn door after the cow had gotten out. Besides, Martinez and I had been headed this direction since our first meeting in Dusty's months ago. Circumstances had just accelerated the process.

When I remembered those circumstances, my insides grew tight, my head pounded, and nausea spread like I *had* been knocking back tequila.

Harvey was dead.

God. I could not believe he'd done it. How he'd done it. And now that my brain was a bit clearer, it pissed me off. What a selfish goddamn thing to do. In front of his best friend. Harvey knew it'd scar those left behind far more than the millisecond of pain he endured right after the gun discharged.

No matter how invincible Martinez acted, he wouldn't be able to shove it aside.

Had he disappeared because he regretted opening himself up to me? Or for another reason entirely? Was he the type of guy that now that the chase was over, he'd set his sights on bedding someone else? Was I just another notch on his handlebars?

The idea I'd been taken for a ride didn't sit well. I sighed and rolled, taking the twisted cotton sheet with me. I'd just scooted back to the headboard when the door opened.

Martinez walked in.

My heart kicked hard.

Even though he was fully dressed in his usual biker finery, I didn't bother to cover my nakedness like some Victorian maiden. We'd gone far beyond normal embarrassment last night.

We'd gone *way* past a professional relationship.

He shut the door, braced his wide shoulders against it and crossed one booted ankle in front of the other. He stared at me unabashedly, not with sexual intent, but as if he was trying to read my mind.

No trace remained of the despondent man from last night. Yet, the haunted sorrow was there, lurking beneath the surface.

I wanted to soothe that ache even when I knew he wouldn't welcome it now, or want to talk about it. I never had either. Scary, that we were more alike than I'd imagined.

Did he see that similarity when he looked at me?

Neither of us seemed particularly anxious to break the awkward silence.

"Your clothes are still wet," he said finally.

Soggy clothes were better than driving home bare-assed in my Sentra, in a lame impression of Lady Godiva.

"Are they in the other room?"

"No. I moved them to the tub." He angled his head toward the closet. "I've got some extra workout sweats. They'd be big, but you're welcome to wear them."

I said, "Thanks."

Martinez sighed. He didn't fidget, just kept his gaze steadily trained on me.

"Regrets, blondie?"

Why lie? "I don't know," I admitted. "You?"

"I don't regret a damn thing."

I swallowed. Didn't help my dry mouth but kept it shut.

My silence surprised him.

Then he surprised me by saying, "You want to talk about it?"

"Why?" My eyes narrowed. "You gonna profess your undying love for me now, Martinez?"

"Ah. There she is. I wondered which Julie I'd en-counter this morning."

"What do you mean 'which Julie'?"

"I expected you'd pick a fight, giving you a reason to storm out, which I gotta admit, I'd prefer to the polite control I'm seeing you use now."

I jerked the sheet closer. "Nice, that I'm so predict-able."

"Wrong." He pushed away from the door but was strangely cautious, stopping at the foot of the bed. "Just when I think I've got you pegged, you shock the shit out of me."

I didn't know what to say.

His dark eyes latched onto mine and wouldn't allow me to look away. "You've got to know you were more than a warm body to me last night."

I *really* didn't know what to say to that.

A door slammed in the outer room and I jumped. Apparently we were no longer alone. Good time to change the subject.

"Doesn't sound like your warning kept people out of your office."

"It did for a while." Martinez sauntered to the closet and slid the track doors. He reached on the top shelf and pulled down two pieces of neatly folded black fleece clothing. Dropped them on the pillows beside me.

I grabbed the sweatshirt. "What happens now? With the Hombres, I mean."

Again, he didn't pretend he wasn't watching me get dressed. "We'll hold a memorial service when everyone from the other chapters gets here. Then we'll have a meeting to figure out who's applying for Harvey's job."

"Don't you just pick a successor?" I said, yanking the sweatshirt over my head.

"No. We consider the candidate's loyalty, and let's

say their *qualifications*, then we vote."

"What do you have to do to be considered a candidate?"

He lifted a brow. "Why? You interested in a different position?"

I blushed. Crap. So much for acting casual. I snagged the sweatpants and threw back the sheet, angry at my bout of modesty.

"I don't do this, Martinez."

Guilty thoughts slapped me. Seemed like a year ago I'd been with Kell when it'd been less than a week. Martinez and I had borne more nasty shit together in the last few days than most people experienced in a lifetime.

"I don't care about anything you did before last night," he said.

That told me nothing. I slid to the edge of the bed. Shoved my feet in the leg holes and shimmied them over my hips to my waist.

"Will you come to Harvey's memorial service with me?" he asked, out of the blue.

My fingers fumbled with the drawstring. Martinez rarely asked me for anything. It figured he'd want the one thing I couldn't give him.

I met his gaze head on. "I don't do funerals either."

One tiny twitch of his left eye was the only sign I'd given the wrong answer.

"You went to Shelley's funeral." When I didn't respond, he prompted, "What about your partner's girlfriend? You plan on going to that one, don't you?"

"No." I smoothed my hand over my scalp. Fuck it.

My hair was as messed up as this situation, and just as pointless to try and straighten out right now. "What do you want from me, Martinez?"

"Don't insult me by pretending you don't know."

How was that an answer? And why wasn't he invading my space and messing with my hair like he usually did?

He tossed an unopened pack of Marlboro Lights and a book of matches on the bed. "Figured you might want these. I'll clear the guys out of here and give you some privacy."

Then he exited the room and left me staring after him in total confusion.

Martinez didn't attempt to dissect the night we'd spent together.

Despite the awful events that had led us there, every time my mind wandered that direction, my stomach got swoopy. We might not see eye to eye on everything, but we were definitely compatible in bed. Very compatible.

Not helping you focus on the real the situation, Julie.

If Martinez could let it idle for a while, then so could I.

He'd told me he'd tentatively planned a joint memorial service for Rondelle and Harvey, hinging on when I found Chloe, or if the mysterious people hiding her came forward once they found out Rondelle was dead.

Noble, that Martinez didn't want to bury the child's mother without giving her a chance to say goodbye. But didn't he understand standing over the coffin wouldn't give her closure anyway?

I couldn't fathom the abandonment issues that little girl was facing. Had her father sent her away without explanation? Chances were good Donovan could come out of the coma with severe brain damage. Chloe could essentially be an orphan.

With Harvey gone, what would happen to her? Would a member of Donovan's family step up and take on the responsibility of raising her? Or was she doomed to follow the same path as Rondelle; shuffled from foster home to foster home on the reservation without any family support?

That possibility turned my stomach and made me more determined than ever to find her. Even if I had to go against Martinez's instructions and go to the cops.

On the way home I attempted to piece together what I'd learned yesterday with what I already knew.

Bud Linderman had sent Rondelle to work for the Carluccis under the threat of harming her daughter. I knew this, Martinez knew this, so how come Harvey hadn't? Had Martinez decided it was best to keep that information from Harvey?

Obviously it'd backfired. Big time.

So, someone had called Harvey, and shared the information about Bud Linderman's threats.

Why now that Rondelle was dead?

Revenge?

Who?

A little bird told me, buzzed in my head like an

369

annoying bee.

What the hell could that mean? It had to mean something, right?

Not necessarily. It'd probably been gibberish from a man crazed with grief.

But the phrase kept pecking away at me. *A little bird, a little bird . . .*

I was desperate for something to make sense in this case. A sign. Anything. I looked up through the windshield at the cloudless sky. It stretched far and wide; in that dazzling robin's egg blue that often follows a violent summer storm.

And then it hit me so hard I slammed on the brakes.

A little bird wasn't some nonsensical phrase babbled by a madman.

A little bird was a person.

Robin.

Rondelle's friend from Trader Pete's.

I stepped on the gas and headed for Deadwood.

Since Rondelle had told me Robin was her boss, I hoped like hell Robin worked the day shift.

With summer tourist season in full swing I had a decent chance to sneak in under the Carluccis radar. Yet, if I did find Robin, I had no guarantee she'd talk to me.

When I found a free parking spot right behind The Golden Boot, I knew it was my lucky day.

Inside Trader Pete's I planted myself by the wall in

the quarter slots section behind an artificial ficus tree. Pained me to shove twenty bucks in, but it was the smallest bill I had.

Down to my last three bucks, the constant *ding ding ding* of the machines was driving me nuts. A stoop-shouldered cocktail waitress with steel gray hair finally spied me.

She didn't attempt a smile. "Can I get you something to drink?"

"Nah. I'm good."

Her lips pursed. With the school marm hairdo, I wondered if she carried a metal ruler to whap my knuckles. Nope. No pencil behind her ear, either.

As she turned away, I said, "Can you tell me if Robin is around today?"

"Didn't you see her? She's working the cage."

"No. I hadn't been over there yet."

"You a friend of hers?"

No. "Yeah."

"If you want, give me your name and I'll tell her you're here."

"That's okay, I wouldn't want you to go to any trouble. I'll wander up there in a bit."

"Suit yourself."

I cashed out and relocated to another machine that offered me a clear view of the money cage. Robin wasn't hard to distinguish; the other person working with her was a dead ringer for Buddha.

Robin was tall, pixie stick-thin, with dark blond hair, and a phony smile.

As I fed quarters into the slot, I wondered how to approach her. I didn't want the Carluccis to see us together. I'd purposely stayed as far out of camera range as possible.

I considered and discarded several scenarios. Money gone, I made my way to the bathroom. The outer lounge area, an explosion of tufted pink velvet and laden with the scent of rose air freshener, was empty. I pushed through the swinging door into the section with the stalls.

Caught sight of myself in the mirror and nearly screamed.

I looked worse than Kevin's dotty Aunt Mildred. Martinez's jumbo sweatshirt hung past my knees, my hair stuck out at all angles broadcasting the fact I'd recently tumbled out of bed.

My eyes were puffy black circles from crying last night and—Good God! Was that a *hickey* on my neck? I peered in the mirror. Oh yeah, that's just what I needed, proof of my stupidity.

The door swung open. Robin came in and glared at me.

"Who are you? I don't know where you get off claiming we're friends—"

"I'm not a friend of yours, I'm a friend of Rondelle's."

Her indignant mouth snapped shut.

"Yeah, I didn't think you wanted me to share that information with Flo, the cocktail waitress."

Robin slumped against the wall. "Who are you?"

"Julie Collins."

"What do you want?"

"Answers. I was hired to find Chloe, which I haven't been able to do. So now that Rondelle and her brother Harvey are both dead—"

"Harvey's dead?"

"You didn't know?"

She swallowed. "How?"

"Shot himself in the face."

"Omigod. When?"

"Yesterday."

"Why?"

I watched the panic build in her. "He took Bud Linderman hostage after the protest march by the Bear Butte casino. Obviously, it didn't go well."

"Did he hurt Linderman?"

"Linderman probably crapped his Wranglers while Harvey had the gun to his head. But in the end Harvey let him crawl away."

"No!" escaped on a gasp before she clapped a hand over her mouth.

"Didn't see that one coming when you called Harvey yesterday, did you?"

Her face went milk white and little by little she slid all the way to the tile floor. She shook her head back and forth. "Oh my God. I never expected . . . I didn't want . . . I thought he would . . ."

"Thought he would what, Robin?"

Eyes the color of quicksilver flicked to mine. "I thought he'd beat the shit out of that bastard Bud Linderman, like he deserved, not—"

"Not kill himself in a fit of grief?" I said harshly, as

the sound of that fatal gunshot echoed in my head.

Tears tracked her ashen cheeks. "No." Her strangled voice caught on a sob. "Oh God. I shouldn't have called him. I wouldn't have called him if I'd have known."

"Why did you call him?"

No answer. Just the *drip drip drip* of a leaky faucet over her tears.

My patience snapped. "Robin?"

So did hers. "Because I was pissed off when I found out Rondelle was dead, okay? I know that fucker Linderman had something to do with killing her. I just know it. And since Rondelle wouldn't tell her brother about Linderman's threats while she was alive, I thought now that she was dead he had a right to know."

"You don't think Rondelle had a legitimate reason for keeping Linderman's threats from her brother?"

"No!" She threw up her hands; her knuckles hit the metal electric hand dryer but she didn't notice. "Harvey could've helped her. He could've saved her. She wouldn't have had to keep lying to Linderman. But she was so damn stubborn, and now she's dead!"

I stared at her in disbelief. Wanted to wrap my hands around her skeletal neck and shake some goddamn sense into her.

"And you didn't think Harvey, an enforcer with the Hombres, would do more than just 'beat the shit' out of Linderman? For Christsake, the Hombres aren't known for their negotiating skills! How could you be so fucking naïve?"

When her head drooped to her chest, and the hiccupping sobs became wails, I knew.

Shit.

I took a deep breath, and settled across from her on the cold floor, wondering how long it'd take until she'd calm down.

When her sobs softened to weak sniffles, I tossed her a paper towel.

She blew her nose with gusto. Clenched the soggy brown paper in her fist. The Black Hills Gold rings adorning her fingers were vivid against the stark whiteness of her knuckles.

"You wanted Harvey to kill Linderman, didn't you?"

She nodded.

"Robin, that's why we have cops—"

"Don't give me that 'let the authorities handle it' line of bullshit. Don't you get it? Guys like him, guys like the Carluccis, they can do whatever the fuck they want, to whoever the fuck they want, whenever the fuck they want and they never have to answer to anybody. Never." Eyes closed, she pressed her head back into the wall. "The cops or the legal system can't touch them. They *always* get away with it."

An unsettling thought struck me: Was Martinez one of those guys that gets away with everything too?

I pushed it aside and let her words, her anger sink in. She was absolutely right. But that didn't mean she'd done the right thing.

"You should've seen her face when Linderman sent those pictures of Chloe with those men. It's a parent's worst nightmare that something so sick could happen to their kid." She shuddered and hugged her knees to her chest, practically becoming one with the wall. "I worked for Linderman at that old time photo place in Spearfish Canyon for a while. He's a manipulative bastard, he would've done every single thing he threatened. The fucker would've enjoyed it too."

"Didn't you think about what might happen to Harvey if he killed Linderman?"

"Yes. But I didn't think he'd go after him in such a public place. I thought . . ." She looked straight at me. "I thought Harvey could just make Linderman disappear."

"But if he'd gotten caught?"

"Don't be so fucking naïve, Julie," she retorted, throwing my words, my tone back in my face. "You know the Hombres' lawyers would've gotten him off."

I wasn't so cocksure. Then again, Martinez's lawyer, the invincible Mark Adderton, *had* been waiting for him in the parking lot when we'd gotten to the Sheriff's Department last evening. He'd seen to it no charges had been filed against anyone. He'd made sure Martinez only had to answer the most basic questions. He'd handled all the arrangements for Harvey's remains.

"What about the Little Joe? Didn't you consider him? She actually had proof of him raping her."

"You know about that?"

"Rondelle told me."

"What else did she tell you?" Her red-rimmed eyes widened as if she'd just thought of something. "Hey, how did you get my name?"

I didn't want to drag her into this any deeper, so I

didn't ask about the missing money. "When she told me about the disk, she said you were her only friend here."

A fresh wave of tears spilled out. "Some friend. My brilliant idea made a man kill himself."

The, "There, there, sweetie, it's not your fault," words she wanted to hear were firmly stuck in my throat. Maybe Harvey would've figured out a way to deal with Rondelle's death, but we'd never know now.

"But you helped her get the disk, didn't you?"

She nodded.

"Do you know where the disk is now, Robin?"

"No. And before you ask, I don't know where Chloe is either."

She scrambled to her feet. Splashed water on her face.

Our eyes met in the mirror. "I've got a girl the same age as Chloe. If it'd been me getting those pictures I'd have done the same damn thing. That's why I helped her. Makes me sick that nothing will ever change and no one cares."

At the door, I turned back and looked at her. "You are wrong. I care. Whoever did this will pay. Count on it."

CHAPTER 30

THE TREK TO DEADWOOD HADN'T PANNED OUT THE WAY I'd imagined. Robin had made the call—which may or may not have been the final straw for Harvey. Since he'd learned of Rondelle's murder, he'd been a ticking time bomb. Who's to say something else wouldn't have set him off? Maybe with even more disastrous results?

The inside of my car was like a furnace. I didn't mind, I welcomed the warmth since a strange chill had settled inside me.

My mind was going a million different directions as I merged into the surprisingly light traffic. Where had all the tourists gone? I squeaked through the last traffic signal and my four-cylinder Sentra struggled up the steep hill. Although I was anxious to get home, I hugged the guardrail in the slower right-hand lane.

At the top of the hill, the road gently curved before it began the deep descent into the canyon. I'd kept my speed at an easy 30 mph until I reached the last sharp corner where the road dropped.

I tapped the brakes.

Nothing happened.

I hit the brakes again, harder.

Nothing.

Crap.

What the hell was going on?

Don't panic. My foot kept pumping the brake, like it would miraculously catch and bring me to a sudden stop.

It didn't.

I glanced down at the speedometer. My speed was now at 35 mph.

And I'd just started the descent.

For a second I gave into my growing distress and jerked the steering wheel.

My tires connected with loose gravel and the back end shimmied as I corrected the skid and kept the car as far to the right as possible.

Okay. Stay calm. Consider the options. Quickly.

Another big curve loomed ahead. If I remembered correctly, it leveled off into a small meadow.

If I could just get there before I gained more momentum . . .

Trees whizzed past. Thoughts moved through my head like lightning.

I was going to crash. No doubt about it. But if I could control the crash, and keep my car from plowing into another car, at least innocent people wouldn't suffer for my bad maintenance habits.

The speedometer stayed steady at 40 mph.

I tested the brakes one last time.

The brake pedal went all the way to the floor.

Fuck.

One option left.

My right hand palmed the emergency brake between the bucket seats. I pressed my thumb into the button and eased the stick up, holding my breath.

Please, please, please.

The tires grabbed and the car slowed slightly.

A semi-truck full of logs passed me, nearly blowing me off the road.

I glanced at the speedometer. Thirty.

The highway flattened, straightened.

This was my only chance. Rock walls and deep drop-offs lined the remainder of the road as it wound down through the sleepy canyon.

A ditch ran along one side, a steep, empty creekbed along the other. The ditch was lined with barbed wire fence, the creekbed with boulders.

No brainer which side I'd choose.

Again, I pulled the emergency brake. Slowly.

No head-on traffic. No one behind me, either.

I crossed the median to the shoulder of the opposite lane.

My speed had dropped to 25.

At the last second, I tried to drop the gearshift into the lowest gear. It was stuck in "D." Frustrated, I bore down with all my might and the damn thing finally slipped gears.

The engine made a horrible grinding, crunching sound. Ignoring it, I jerked the hand brake and aimed for the ditch, hoping like hell I wouldn't roll this sucker before it stopped.

I clutched the steering wheel with only my left hand and held my breath.

Tires screeched. Then I hit the backside slope of the ditch. My body bounced inside the car. Dirt and grass flew over the windshield. Someone screamed.

The last thing I remembered was the airbag exploding in my face and far off, in the back of my mind, I thought it was strange, how that loud BANG sounded exactly like gunfire.

Cool hands touched my skin. Followed by sharp needles jabbing into my skull.

Ouch. God. Stop it.

I attempted to move, to get away from the pain. I couldn't. I was paralyzed. I struggled to talk, but nothing came out. Felt like my throat was coated with glass.

The sharp needles turned into burning spikes.

Goddamn. Quit it. That fucking hurts!

"Hey, hey, where's the fire?" Those same cool hands curled around my bare shoulders. "Relax."

"Hurts," I managed.

"I know, sweetie. But if you hold still it won't hurt as much."

"'Kay."

I drifted back into the blessed blackness where there was no pain.

381

"Julie Collins? Come on. Open your eyes for me."

A dull throbbing echoed inside my head. "I can't."

She tsk, tsked. "You didn't even try. Come on. I need to see those pretty blue eyes again."

I squeezed my eyes shut.

She laughed, a girlish high-pitched squeak. "I knew you'd be difficult the minute they wheeled you in here."

Story of my life. "Where am I?" I asked, without opening my eyes.

"Mmm. Not surprised you don't remember." She paused. Metal clanked on metal next to my ear. "You're in the Lead hospital. You were in a car accident."

Then I remembered. I peeled my eyes open. One at a time.

A white flash cut into my retinas like a laser. "Fuck. Can you cut the goddamn stadium lights? You're frying my fucking eyeballs."

She tittered again. "Oh it's not that bad. Hang on. Let me look at the other side and you're done."

"What're you doing?"

"Checking your concussion."

My eyes watered. "And what's the diagnosis, doc?"

"I'm not the doc. Just a lowly nurse."

Her icy hands disappeared. Rubber shoes chirked against the linoleum. Breathy voice connected with a face as she swam into focus.

Five foot nothing. Long hair the color of goldenrod.

Soft, purple eyes that reminded me of a spring pasque flower.

And about twelve years old.

Okay. More like eighteen. Manners forgotten, I demanded, "How old are you?"

"Old enough to be a real nurse with a real degree and everything." Her generous mouth curved. "And a really, really big needle if you get smart with me."

"How long have I been here?"

"A couple of hours."

Hours had passed? "What happened?"

She became briskly efficient. "Hang on. I'll get someone who can answer that." She pulled the curtain aside and vanished.

I looked down at my body. Ugly pale blue hospital gown covered me to the knees. An IV stuck in my left arm. I scooted up. Groaned. God. It felt like someone had whacked me in the chest with a barstool.

My face hurt. I lifted my right hand to my nose. Swollen, but not broken. Ran my tongue around my teeth. Whew. All intact. My neck was sore and my head didn't even feel like *my* head, but a very heavy cement block teetering atop a flimsy aspen limb.

The curtain parted. A Lawrence County Deputy stepped forward, Styrofoam cup in hand.

"Hi. Julie? I don't know if you remember me—"

"Dave Tschetter, right?"

He nodded, and I could tell he was a bit surprised. What? Did everyone suspect I had brain damage?

"I'd say it's nice to see you again, Dave, but that

would be a complete lie."

He smiled. "Gotta say, you looked a helluva lot better at the county law enforcement conference last year." A pause when the intercom paged Dr. Danielson. "You in the private sector full time now?"

"Yeah."

"Pity. I think Sheriff Richards had always hoped you'd take the test and become one of us." He didn't sip his coffee, he drained it. I'd never met a cop who didn't live on caffeine. "Do you remember what happened today?"

"I thought you were here to tell me."

"I can tell you one thing: Your car looks like a crumpled pie tin. Wrecker service hauled it to a garage in Sturgis. Probably pointless. It's totaled."

I reclined my head back in the pillows. "My purse?"

"Undamaged, surprisingly. Cell phone made it through too."

"Thanks."

"I gotta admire your driving skills. Few people could've come out of that crash still breathing."

"Glad I paid attention during Driver's Ed," I said dryly.

"You remember how fast were you going when you hit?"

"Somewhere between the speed of light and a deadstop. Everything was in slow-mo until the last second." I inhaled to calm the sudden spike in my breathing. "Probably twenty-five."

He nodded. "Why were you in Deadwood?"

"Following a lead for a case. I got in my car and

started down the big hill. When I hit the brakes nothing happened."

"Had any mechanical problems with your car recently?"

"I sure wouldn't have driven up here if I had."

"No problems on the way up?"

"Nope. My brakes worked just fine."

He sighed. "Unfortunately, going up isn't the problem. Coming down is the tricky part. You might not have noticed if they were acting strange."

"True."

"Well. That's it. I don't have anything else to add except you oughta buy a lottery ticket today, Ms. Collins."

I fidgeted. It hurt. I didn't move. It hurt. More than anything I wanted to hurt in my own damn bed. "Any chance I can get you to spring me from this joint, now that I've been officially cleared of any wrongdoing?"

Another broad smile. "I'll send in Nurse Ratchet. She handles the discharge papers."

I glared at him. "How can you compare that sweet little thing—"

"That 'sweet little thing' can bench press 200 pounds and bring a man to tears with her razor sharp tongue." He tossed the cup in the garbage. "I oughta know. She's my wife."

Wife? Candy-striper cutie? No way.

She materialized by his side. She only reached his armpit. "Bad mouthing me again, sweetheart?"

"Never."

The look he gave her made me want to cry. No man had ever looked at me like that. No man probably ever *would* look at me like that. Add in the fact she looked back at him the same way made me feel like my life was complete shit.

Jesus Christ. Had they given me painkillers or hormones? I never had this overwhelming urge to weep. I certainly never gave into it when I did.

Maybe I did have brain damage.

After he'd left and they quit making goo-goo eyes at each other, I said, "Can you bring me the discharge papers so I can go home now?"

"I don't know. You're pretty banged up."

"Is 'banged up' an official diagnosis, nurse?"

Her kind eyes hardened. "No. But my recommendation to the doctor is to keep you here overnight, and he listens to me even if you won't."

"But I can discharge myself, right?"

"Only if you've got someone who can sign you out and take you home." She checked the bandage on my head. "*Matrix* driving maneuvers aside, this isn't an injury to be taken lightly. No matter how tough you think are, your body *will* need time to recover."

"I know. I'll take it easy."

She studied me. Knew I was lying through my teeth. "Is there someone you can call?"

And again, there was that temptation to bawl my eyes out.

No. And thanks for pointing out the sucky emptiness of my life.

I couldn't call Kevin.

I refused to call my father.

Jimmer? Maybe.

Martinez? No. Wouldn't want him to think I was stalking him after last night.

I picked Kim.

But what if she said no?

Then I'd toss a chair through the window and make my own escape. I couldn't stand another fucking hour in this damn hospital.

I gave Nurse Tschetter a charming smile, though it stung like a son of a bitch. "Would you hand me the phone?"

Two hours later I held the discharge papers in my lap as I sat in Kim's Volvo. I went comatose and didn't stir until she woke me in my driveway.

"Come on, sugar. Even though your ass is skinny, I ain't hauling it up the stairs. You gotta walk. That's it. Slowly."

I hurt everywhere. I barely made it to the couch before I collapsed.

"I shouldn't have let you talk me into this. You should be in the hospital, Jules."

"I'm fine."

She harrumphed and her footsteps faded. A minute later she said, "Lift your head," and tucked a cool pillow beneath my neck.

I exhaled a bliss filled sigh.

"Can I get you anything else?"

"Painkillers. And tequila."

"You wish." She handed me two pills and a luke-warm glass of water to wash them down.

I closed my eyes and willed the damn drugs to kick in.

Kim pressed her soft hip on the couch beside mine. Didn't say anything for a time. Her fingers gently pushed my matted hair away from the bandage.

"How many stitches they have to put in this hard head of yours?"

"Ten. Give or take."

She sniffled and I opened my eyes.

"What?"

Tears dripped, leaving black smears down her cheeks. "I'm just happy you're not dead."

"Kim, I'm fine."

"Oh shut up. Let me fuss over you a little, will you?"

I smiled. It didn't hurt at all. "Okay."

Then once again everything went gray.

I woke with a hellacious headache.

From a wild night?

No. From my wild ride yesterday.

The voices arguing in the kitchen added another layer to the constant throbbing. I listened but couldn't decipher specifics. Hearing loss? Or that pesky brain damage issue again?

I struggled to sit up. Mouth dry, I grabbed the glass of water. After a tiny sip, I reached for the Excedrin, knocked the bottle over, and it crashed to the carpet.

The arguing stopped.

Kim scurried into the living room, Martinez hot on her purple heels.

Great.

Kim said something; Tony said something back.

No wonder I hadn't understood. They'd been speaking Spanish.

"Julie, sugar, how do you feel?" Kim cooed.

"Like shit."

Nasty, pregnant pause.

"You didn't call me." This from Martinez.

I took another drink.

"Don't give me that bullshit about you not running to your *clients* for protection."

Meaning: We'd gone beyond client relations. I glanced at Kim to see if she'd caught the gist.

But she was too busy snapping, "What part of 'she had a head injury' don't you understand?"

He rattled off a phrase in Spanish.

She snarled one in return.

"English, please. Makes me paranoid that you're talking about me."

"Well, we are."

I looked at Martinez.

Kim pleaded, "Tony. Wait. Please. Don't."

"Don't what?" I said.

He got right in my face.

I shuddered at the cold fury in his eyes.

"Don't ask you why in the hell someone tried to kill you yesterday."

CHAPTER 31

I SLURPED ANOTHER MOUTHFUL OF STALE WATER.

"Kill me? Jesus, Martinez. Paranoid much? My brakes failed. That's it. No one tried to kill me except the damn Nissan Corporation and their cheap ass braking system."

He leveled me with that, "I'd-like-to-strangle-you-with-your-own-intestines" look.

"Wrong. After I found out, from someone besides *you*, that your car had been totaled in Boulder Canyon, I sent a mechanic up to Sturgis this morning to check it out. Know what he found?"

He paused for effect.

"Someone had sawed through your back brake cable and snipped the hose to both of the front brakes. You didn't have a chance."

The liquid in my stomach churned.

I dropped my head between my knees to fight off the dizziness, but the only thing that action did was drive a spear of pain further into my skull.

"Jesus, that fucking hurts," I said, wincing.

"I can't believe you told her like that! You are so heartless."

Martinez knelt in front of me. Strong hands cradled my head and lifted my chin slightly so he could peer into my eyes. "You all right?"

"No."

"Good."

Kim stamped within my line of vision. "This is how you help? By making her feel like crap? I wouldn't have let you in here if I had any idea you had such a lousy bedside manner."

Martinez completely ignored her tirade. His thumbs glided back and forth across my cheekbones. His intent gaze searched my face, my swollen nose, flicked to the bandage on my head, then back to my eyes.

The distress in his rocked me to my core.

Kim had it wrong. He was ruthless, not heartless.

Big difference.

My thoughts flashed to my time in the hospital. How alone I'd felt. How I'd wanted someone to count on, someone to lean on, even for a little while.

He was here. He *wanted* to be here, apparently, no matter how hard I tried to push him away.

So, I caved.

He knew the nanosecond it happened.

"Leave us," Martinez demanded.

"But—"

"It's okay, Kim, I'll be fine."

"I'll be right in the kitchen if you need anything."

"Bring us some coffee in a bit," he suggested.

She spun on her heel and rattled off something in Spanish that made him smile.

With his left hand he tenderly brushed my hair back over my shoulder. Twined a few pale strands around his dark fingers. His right hand slid carefully down my face. His palm was warm against my jaw. Solid. The pad of his thumb swept across my bottom lip in an erotic arc.

My breath caught.

In one smooth move he replaced his thumb with his mouth.

He tasted like sweet coffee. And he filled me with those sweet, sweet drugging kisses until I felt like my lungs might burst. I pulled back. But not too far back.

"Martinez—"

"Ssh," he whispered against my lips. "Just let me."

"This has to stop."

"In a minute." He kept the kisses gentle and comforting, never veering toward the demanding, hungry ones I'd remembered from the other night.

Finally, he broke the kiss and pressed his damp lips to my ear. "Not one word. But we *will* deal with this very soon, understand?"

I swallowed and nodded.

Martinez angled back. Stood. "Right now, we're going to talk about the car accident. Start with when you left Fat Bob's yesterday morning."

Kim bobbled the tray of cups she carried when she heard that tidbit.

Annoyed, I rattled off everything, not caring that Kim soaked in every word.

"Where did you park yesterday when you were in Deadwood?"

"On the back side of Main Street by The Golden Boot."

"Why? The parking garage is safer."

"But it's not free."

"Didn't I agree to pay your expenses?"

"You want to argue about money, Martinez?"

He hunkered down and said very softly, "You really don't want to push me right now, blondie."

Shit.

"You remember anybody hanging around in the alley yesterday?"

I glared at him. "Get real. It'd be too risky for someone to sneak under my car and tamper with the brakes in broad daylight."

"Not necessarily. They'd just lie if someone caught them and claim they were fixing mechanical problems."

Seemed like he had firsthand info on the best way to handle that specific situation. I didn't want to know how. "Could someone have messed with it while it was parked overnight at Fat Bob's? Or even at the Bear Butte Casino site? What about Linderman? Doesn't he own a couple of car dealerships?"

"Yeah, he does. But the point is, why?" His eyes bored into me. "Is there something else going on with this case you haven't told me about?"

I shook my head. Winced because it hurt.

"Enough," Kim said. "She needs to rest."

"I agree." Martinez stood and headed toward the door. He turned back. "If anything else happens, I want to know. Immediately. From you. Is that clear?"

I stifled the urge to snap off a salute. "Crys-tal clear, sir."

To Kim, he said, "Shove painkillers and sleeping pills down her throat, whatever the hell it takes, to make sure she stays put today and isn't out gallivanting around."

Kim nodded, face somber.

After Martinez had shut the door behind him, she burst into giggles.

"Gallivanting around? Oh my God. Where'd he come up with that phrase? It's so . . . quaint for such a badass."

"Beats me."

I reached for my cigarettes. The first puff made me feel sick. The second did too. By the third, my body had quit protesting and gave in to the inevitable poisoning.

Kim had sprawled in the recliner, feet up, my *Days of '76* mug in hand. "Does Kevin know?"

"What? About the accident?"

"No. That you're sleeping with Tony Martinez."

I choked when I exhaled.

"Don't bother to deny it. The fact he came *gallivanting* in here, ready to rip off my limbs to get to you today was a dead giveaway." She thoughtfully blew on her coffee. "But the hickey really clinched it."

Automatically, my hand flew to my neck.

"Not that one. The one above your right breast."

I froze.

"Didn't know about that one, huh?"

"How did *you* know about it?"

"I helped you get undressed last night, remember?"

I shook my head. Dammit. I had to stop doing that. It hurt. "Last night was pretty much a blur."

"So. How long has this been going on?"

My first inclination was to hedge. Except, I needed to talk to someone about this thing going on between Martinez and me. Was he another bad choice in a long line of my bad choices?

If he was completely wrong for me, why didn't it feel wrong?

"Jules?"

"Umm. Only one time."

Kim rolled her eyes. "Yeah, right."

I admitted, "Okay, more than one time, but it was only one night."

"When?"

"The night before last. After Harvey . . ." I ground out my smoke. "I'd never seen Tony like that. We were both pretty screwed up by it. This whole thing is screwed up. I'm screwed up."

"Are you going to tell Kevin?"

"That I screwed up? He already knows. Will I tell him about Martinez? I don't know." I groaned. "Who am I kidding? I won't have to tell him; he'll find out and then we'll have another big goddamn fight."

"*Another* fight?"

I didn't respond. With all the crap that had transpired in the last thirty-six hours, I'd hardly thought

395

about Kevin at all.

Where was my guilt? Used up because we'd fought and I was mad at him even though I knew he'd been right?

Kim's cell phone chirped.

I popped a painkiller, chased it down with cold coffee. Her brief conversation ended.

"What's up?"

"The hair dryers blew a fuse again. Jenny is freaking out. She's such a ditz, she can't even change a light bulb let alone find the fuse box." Worry creased her perfectly plucked brows. "Sorry, but I should check it out before she burns the damn shop down."

"Go. I'll be fine."

"You sure?"

I swung my feet up and snuggled into the couch. "I'm tired. I'll be out in about two minutes and won't know if you're here or not anyway."

"Glad to be appreciated."

Say thank you, Julie Ann, a voice strangely like my mother's prompted.

"Uh, so thanks for coming up and rescuing me last night, and for, umm, staying with me. You're a real North Carolina peach."

She blinked, startled by my gratitude. "You're welcome."

Before the door closed I'd fallen asleep.

My head was pounding. I sat up too fast and grabbed the coffee table to keep myself from passing out.

The pounding continued. Not only in my head. Someone was beating on the front door.

I wrapped the quilt around my shoulders and shuffled to the foyer. Throwing out a welcome mat without knowing the identity of my guest? Maybe that wasn't the smartest option.

"Who's there?"

"Don Anderson."

What? Why was he here?

I'd barely cracked the door when he pushed it open and bolted inside.

"Whoa. Don. What's going on?"

"I, ah . . . need to talk to you."

He tossed an apprehensive glance over his shoulder. I suspected he wanted to peek out my curtains before he jerked them shut.

"Let me guess: You don't want anyone to know you're here talking to me, right?"

"Right." His milky gaze took in my less than stellar appearance. "You look terrible. You okay?"

"Car accident. I'm fine now."

"Does your daddy know?"

"No. And let's keep it that way, shall we?" I motioned for him to take the recliner in the living room while I sank into the couch. "So, Don, tell me what's on your mind."

Arthritic hands crushed the bill of the vintage Zip Feed cap; he aimed his eyes at the pointed tips of his cowboy boots. "Doug said he tried to hire you to find who killed Red Granger."

"I'm hoping he also told you I can't do that because of the legal restrictions."

"That's a pretty smart rule. But you can follow somebody, right?"

"Usually. Mostly it depends on the situation. Why?"

Don glanced up. "Does it cost a lot?"

I kept my impatience in check. "Again, it depends. Who do you want followed, Don?"

He didn't answer straight off.

A strange thought struck me. "Is it my dad? Did he do something wrong?"

"No! He'd never do anything like that."

"Like what?"

"Like, mebbe killin' someone."

My headache roared back with a vengeance. "Stop beating around the bush and tell my why you're here or leave."

He blurted, "I think Dale Pendergrast might've killed Red Granger."

"What?"

Don slumped back in the chair. "You heard me. I think Dale might've killed Red and I want to hire you to follow him and see what he's been up to. I'm worried 'bout him."

This was beyond bizarre. "Okay. Why don't we start with why you think Dale is responsible for killing Red?"

"Ever since they started building that casino, Dale

and Maurice have been actin' mighty strange. Both been complainin' that Red isn't doing his job, and if he was, accordin' to them, that 'abomination' wouldn't be there."

"Dale might've killed Red because he thought he was a crappy politician? Seems a pretty slim motive for murder."

"Not when you consider a coupla things. Dale is a real boot-licker when it comes to Maurice. And Maurice ain't made no bones 'bout the fact if *he* was on the county commission, he'd see to it that casino would be gone. With all the hullabaloo going on, I'm afraid Dale decided if he shot Red, it'd get blamed on one of them other groups."

He slid me a sly glance. "Didn't you tell us that Indian fella got shot? Think it's a coincidence Red got shot right after that? I'm bettin' that might've been what gave Dale the idea. Red wouldn't think nothin' of it if Dale pulled up while he was fixin' fence. And boom. Right in the ticker."

I opened my mouth, but now that Don was on a roll he'd forgotten I was in the room.

"With Red outta the picture, Maurice could get that seat on the commission he's been eyein' for the last few years."

With my head throbbing it took a second to organize my thoughts. "But county elections aren't held for another eighteen months."

Don beamed at me, the star pupil. "That's why the head of the commission would have to appoint someone to fill Red's seat. Know who's the head of the commission?"

"Hark Taylor."

"Maurice's huntin' buddy. So who do you think old Hark's gonna appoint to fill Red's seat?"

Maurice. "But what would Dale get out of it?"

He slanted forward, eager to gossip. "Oh, he wouldn't have done it just for Maurice. No. It'd give him a chance at buyin' Red's land. Ain't no secret Red and his wife Viv have been having problems. She told my wife last year she was tired of ranching, been buggin' Red to retire so's they could move to Arizona and be closer to the grandkids. Guess Red flat out refused."

"That gives Viv a pretty solid motive."

"I know. Them deputies have been out to talk to her twice. Confiscated all of Red's guns. The minute she ain't a suspect, she'll sell that land and Dale will be the first one in line."

"Dale's a little old to be turning into a land baron. Why's he want that ranch land so bad?"

By his look of horror, I figured I'd just tarnished my star pupil badge. "How could you live in this county for so long and not know nothin' about grazing rights?"

I held up my hand to stop the lecture. "Because I don't care." I fished out a cigarette but didn't light it. "I fail to see how following Dale is going to disprove anything. Sounds pretty cut and dried to me."

"But—"

"But what I want to know is why you haven't taken this information to Sheriff Richards."

Don folded his lips. They stayed that way.

"Not talking now, huh?"

"I've said too much already. Besides, everybody knows—"

"Don't give me the crap argument that everything you've told me is common knowledge around these parts. For the last three years *nobody's* kept this county's secrets better than me, and I couldn't have put this together with a map."

His hands twisted his hat.

"Don?"

"I didn't go to the sheriff because Dale is my friend, okay? He's been my friend and neighbor for more'n forty years! I'm jus' s'posed to forget about that and turn him in like he's some kind of common criminal?"

"Yes."

He vehemently wagged his head. "I cain't do that."

"Then you shouldn't have come here." My brain protested the shift forward. "You not turning him doesn't absolve Dale of *his* crimes, Don. It makes you an accessory after the fact for withholding information from the authorities."

"But—"

"I don't give a damn if he's right up there with the friend you have in Jesus, because he *is* a common criminal if he killed Red Granger."

I was breathing so hard and fast I didn't need to smoke.

Don stared at me, misery etched in the lines of his worn face. Lines that seemed even more cavernous than when he'd arrived. "You gonna tell the sheriff?"

"No."

His hangdog expression brightened until I said, "You are. I'll give you until tomorrow morning. If you haven't marched your butt into Sheriff Richards' office by then and shared this information with him, I will."

"I'll deny I ever said anything to you."

I shrugged. "Won't matter. With the basic outline, the sheriff is smart enough to connect the dots."

"I never shoulda come here," he mumbled.

"Then why did you?"

"Because I thought you could help."

"By covering up a murder? I don't think so."

But hadn't I done that once before? By taking the blame for Meredith Friel? Why couldn't I do that now?

Because this time it was wrong.

He stood; his hunched body shook with anger. "Maurice and your dad was both right. You ain't got no loyalty."

Startling, how much that comment didn't sting.

"Wrong. I just don't give my loyalty to people who don't deserve it."

When he reached the foyer, I said, "Tomorrow morning, Don."

He slammed the door.

Made my head scream.

I swallowed a painkiller. Chased it with a sleeping pill. As I drifted off I wondered if the day would ever come that my life wasn't one fucked up mess after another.

CHAPTER 32

As it turned out, Don Anderson didn't have to rat on his friend.

Sheriff Richards called the next morning to check on me, since Deputy Tschetter had blabbed to him about my car accident. After the inevitable discourse on my risky behavior, he told me there'd been no change in Donovan's condition. Then he filled me in on the really big news in Bear Butte County.

One of the guns confiscated from Red Granger's place, a Ruger mini-14, commonly referred to as a "varmint rifle," matched the ballistics of the bullets taken from his body.

They'd arrested Viv Granger and were holding her in the Bear Butte County Jail. No bail. She didn't have an alibi and swore up and down she was innocent.

That's what they all said.

But the strange thing was the sheriff, who assumes everyone is guilty, seemed uncertain about Viv Granger's guilt. He wouldn't give me additional details. In truth, I was amazed he'd told me as much as he had.

I wasn't feeling well enough to go into the office. I called and checked the messages. Seven from clients, one from Kevin.

Yay. We were now communicating through voice mail.

He'd informed me yesterday that Lilly's funeral was tomorrow. Which meant today.

I couldn't go. Not that I wanted to. Lilly's family didn't need me there. Besides, Kevin hadn't asked.

What did it mean that Martinez had asked me to accompany him to Harvey's service?

Further, what did it mean I seriously considered going?

I debated on leaving Kevin an equally dispassionate response about my car accident, but I didn't want to fight with him. I missed him. I missed us.

Why had it taken me so much time to realize Kevin's grief would be a personal matter he'd deal with on his own? Why had I thought trying to prepare him for Lilly's death *before* she died would somehow be easier? Damn. That was just morbid. In hindsight, it was a good thing he hadn't attempted to talk to me because I would've isolated him even further.

I couldn't speed up the process, even if my sole intention had been to save him from the pain.

He'd loved Lilly, even when I didn't understand it. Just because I didn't *want* him to love her didn't mean he hadn't.

Maybe that's what hurt the worst. Even when I knew Kevin loved me. He knew I loved him. But what did that mean?

Our friendship has always been hard to define. We'd relied on each other during the confusing transition from childhood to adulthood. We'd lost touch for some of the years we were married to other people. The underlying attraction we've never acted on, although the opportunities have always been there, constantly tugged at us. We both tended the tiny seed of hope in the back of our minds that someday, when the moon, the stars, the universe, my life and his were all in perfect synch, we'd take that chance.

Ironically, we had taken our relationship to another level, not an intimate one, but a business partnership. Lately I've wondered if that wasn't somehow harder.

As I half heard the mechanical prompt, part of me grieved we'd only be friends and partners for the foreseeable future. Part of me was relieved to move on.

I hung up quietly without leaving any message at all.

I showered, even though I wasn't supposed to. The stitches got wet even though they weren't supposed to. I rationalized I'd needed to change the bandage and held my breath as I peeled away the gauze to gauge the damage.

An angry red gash stared back at me, a crooked line from the corner of my left eyebrow up to my hairline. Great. The zipper-shaped scar made me look like the *Bride of Frankenstein*. Maybe Kim could cut my hair to hide it. If not, I had Halloween covered for the next few years.

My cupboards were bare. Worse, I was out of coffee and soda and almost out of cigarettes. A quick trip to the

405

store was a necessity.

The horror of yesterday hit me anew when I stumbled outside and didn't see my Sentra. I went back inside and grabbed my gun.

My old truck ran like a champ. I'd made it about two miles down the service road when I glimpsed a black car in my rearview mirror.

Didn't mean anything. Lots of people drove black cars.

To be on the safe side, I removed the Browning from the holster and shoved it down the crack between the bench seats.

After parking in the back lot of the convenience store, I entered through the front.

No angry men barreled in behind me. Actually, the store was devoid of customers, and anything resembling real, fresh food. Seemed Kell had influenced me after all.

Diet Pepsi, cigarettes, small can of Folgers, and a couple of packages of Twinkies in the bag, Melinda let me slip out the back door.

I'd just tossed the groceries on the floorboard when tires crunched in the gravel behind me.

Heart pounding, I pulled out the gun and the motion reminded me of the injuries I'd been ignoring. My ribcage protested, as did my neck, shoulders, knees, and everything in between.

I turned around, slid the gun in the small of my back and propped myself between the open truck door and the truck bed.

A vintage cherry red Corvette had parked sideways, blocking me in. Little Joe Carlucci unfolded from the driver's side and beat feet toward me.

Christ, I was sick and tired of this. I wanted one day, one lousy fucking *hour* without drama.

"You stupid bitch. Where the fuck do you get off accusing me of stealing from my father?"

I held up my left hand to keep him from coming closer. "Whoa, whoa, whoa, hold on a second, Junior."

Reggie's nickname appeared to make him more hostile. "I oughta—"

"You oughta calm down right now and stop right there."

Amazingly, he did. Then he demanded, "What did you say to him?"

"First things first. How long have you been following me?"

"I don't got to answer that."

"Did you think it'd be funny to cut the brake lines on my car?"

He blinked confusion. "What the fuck are you talking about?"

"Don't play stupid; answer the question."

"No." He hitched his shoulders back and pointed at me. "You owe *me* some answers."

"I owe you *nada*. If your father wanted you to know what he and I talked about then he would've told you."

"Yeah? Well, he's been a little busy since Tommy was found wearing a bullet shirt. Between the cops, and the family, and all the other shit." He scowled. "Big Joe asked me, he actually fuckin' asked me if I'd killed Tommy."

"And Rondelle and Luther," I pointed out.

Little Joe didn't catch the distinction. "He knows me an' Tommy was like brothers. We played ball together, graduated together. It's ripping me up that someone shot him like a goddamn mark and Big Joe thinks *I* coulda pulled the trigger."

I couldn't tell if he'd done it, if he was sorry he'd done it, or just sorry his father had figured out he'd done it.

"You and Tommy were pals? I thought Reggie and Tommy were tight."

"Reggie and Tommy?" he repeated, confused, which seemed to be a natural state with him. "Nah. They hadta work together at the casino, but that's it."

Not my overactive imagination that they'd been in synch when threatening me and torturing Kell. "But weren't they—"

"What don't you get? Big Joe ordered Reggie here from Jersey to keep an eye on me. Like I need a fuckin' babysitter, especially an uptight asshole that thinks he's better than me. All's he does is bitch about bein' stuck here, when he's not runnin' his big mouth off to Big Joe about how I fucked up again."

He crossed his arms and glared at me. "But we ain't talkin' about that. Tell me why you told Big Joe I'd ripped him off and lied about it to cover my ass."

"FYI: I didn't accuse *you* specifically of stealing the money. I just pointed out to your father what a lame ass story you'd told him about how the money ended up missing."

"How the hell do you know anything about what happened? You weren't there."

"Please. I didn't have to be there to know the 'She tied me up'," I mimicked in a falsetto, "was a piss-poor attempt at putting the blame on Rondelle for what you really did to her."

He didn't say a word.

"*You* left the safe open. *You* forgot about the security cameras. *You* were too cheap to put in a decent surveillance system upstairs in the first place. Don't blame her, me, or anybody else because *you're* so stupid. And don't think for a minute your father didn't have doubts about it before I talked to him."

"He sure didn't act like it until you showed up."

"Again, Junior, not my problem."

"See, that's where you're wrong. You made it your problem when you stuck your nose in it. So, I expect you to make it right." His lips twisted into a grotesque grin. "You can do it on your own, or I can make you."

"Make me what?"

"Tell him I didn't have nuttin' to do with takin' the money."

I laughed. "Why would I do that? Someone got away with a whole pile of your daddy's cash because of your deviant behavior. The shit is coming down on you, as it should."

"Oh I see. You're all bent out of shape about me givin' it hard and fast to Rondelle." He shrugged, a cocky roll of his shoulders. "Might've been a little rough, she fought at first, but in the end she liked it. She always liked it."

And I lost any control I had on my temper. For

Rondelle, for me, for every woman who's suffered through the attitude that we secretly liked being forced.

"A little rough? You fucking raped her, you piece of shit."

"So?"

"So, it's all on the disk. The Lawrence County States Attorney's Office would be very interested in it. You're gonna do time for this one, Junior, and no one's gonna enjoy watching you burn more than me."

"*No one's* gonna bother arresting me now that she's dead." He edged closer, as if he'd grown a spine. "And without the disk, no proof."

I acknowledged my stupidity and the danger of the ultimate bluff even as the words tumbled from my mouth. "How do you know I don't have the disk?"

He stopped. The smug grin fell away. "What?"

"You heard me."

"You tellin' me *you* have the disk?"

I didn't answer. Let him draw his own conclusions, wrong as they may be.

"Bullshit."

"Believe me or don't, I don't give a rat's ass." I placed my hand on my right hip. "But remember: If I've got the disk, then I also know who snuck into the office and ripped off the money."

His pupils shrank. "Who did you see?"

"That's between Big Joe and me."

Slight pause.

"Wrong answer, bitch."

He reached for me; I reached for the gun.

I had the safety off and the barrel pointed at his greasy face before he'd taken a single step.

"Back the fuck off, Junior. Now."

He took a step back.

I saw the second his male ego realized he'd backed down from a woman. Followed by the mean glint in his eye when he decided to rectify the situation.

The ugly, violent part of my brain took over. In the back of my mind I wondered if I'd somehow died in that car accident and was having an out of body experience.

I watched myself embrace what I'd shunned in my father. I'd spent years controlling, suppressing this vicious, nasty side of myself to no avail; in the blink of an eye it filled me and fit like a second skin.

His nasal whine brought my attention back to him.

"Who do you think you are? Calamity Jane?"

"More like Annie Oakley. She was a better shot."

He laughed; it oozed over my flesh like crude oil.

"You ain't gonna shoot."

Lightning fast, I sited the Corvette's back tire and fired. Whatever noise it made as it deflated was lost in the deafening sound of close range gunfire.

Little Joe jumped back. "Jesus Christ!"

Anger burning, I calmly put another bullet in the Corvette, above the wheel well. The third shot right beside it.

Gunpowder hung in the air.

I aimed the gun at his head again. Had to talk loudly over the ringing in my ears. "Don't think I'll shoot?"

God. He was stupid. His macho side still wasn't

with the program. Back straight, he glared at me.

So I blasted the ground next to his feet. Three times. Dirt and rocks kicked up and mixed with the gray haze of gunpowder.

When he'd quit high stepping like a Rockette on acid, he gaped at me. With the barrel sited to his empty head, and my complete lack of conscience, I saw fear.

Finally.

"Stop following me," I said. "You come near me or my house and I guarantee I'll fire every fucking clip I've got into you, and then some. They'll be picking chunks of you outta my lawn for weeks."

He muttered something.

"What? Didn't quite hear that."

"Fuckin' psycho. I'm callin' the cops."

"You do that, Junior. With what I've been through in the last few days, I'll take a nice, quiet jail cell over dealing with assholes like you any day."

"This ain't over."

"Wrong." I motioned to the blacktop behind his car. "On the pavement. Now. I wanna see those fish lips kissing the dirt."

He hesitated.

I fired so close to his loafers that the tassels smoked.

Little Joe hit the ground.

I backed up. Kept the gun trained on him as I climbed in and slammed the door. "Stay there, right like that until I'm gone. Then stay the hell away from me."

I started the truck, threw it in reverse and burned rubber.

Without conscious thought I drove to the ranch. By the time I reached the turnoff I realized what an utterly asinine thing I'd done by taunting Little Joe Carlucci with the false information I had the disk, and then taking potshots at him.

I definitely had brain damage.

My dad was sitting on the porch, almost as if he'd been waiting for me. We hadn't spoken since the day he'd been in the office. As usual, I had no idea how he'd react to me being there.

I climbed out of the truck and trudged up the steps.

"Heard you wrecked your car," he said.

I managed, "Yeah," before I sank into the fluffy cushions on the porch swing.

He didn't ask if I was all right, just stared pointedly at the bandage.

Birkenstocks kicked off, I tucked one foot beneath me and used the other foot to push against the porch and set the swing in motion.

"Where are Trish and the kids?"

"She left to take 'em to church camp. She'll be back later tonight. They'll be gone for the rest of the week."

The swing bumped into the railing behind me, rattling the chains. I slowed down the swinging motion to a gentle, easy glide.

A crow called an alarm; another answered.

I said, "Heard they arrested Viv Granger for shooting Red."

He snorted. "Didn't take 'em long to make a mess of it. Got the wrong person in jail. No way did Viv shoot Red."

My gaze lit on the vegetable garden. The *tick tick tick whirr* of the sprinkler provided a soothing background. Water clung to the dark maroon leaves of the sweet potato vines; the droplets glistened in the sun like gems. A slight breeze brought the loamy scent of wet soil, and the soapy sweetness of rose blooms. I drank it in, savoring the rare moment of tranquility.

Dad sighed. The wicker chair cracked and groaned as he altered his position.

Finally, I said, "Can I tell you something?"

He looked at me strangely and nodded.

"I don't think the sheriff believes Viv did it either."

"Then why did he have her arrested?"

"Had enough evidence to make an arrest. He'd have caught more heat if he'd ignored it." The painted slats were cool beneath my foot as I pushed back and forth.

"What was the evidence?"

"Red's gun."

"That's it?" he scoffed. "Don't mean nothin'. Everybody in the county knew he kept that gun in the barn. I've even gone over there and borrowed it a time or two when I'm out in the field."

"Don Anderson know about it too?"

"Yeah. Why?"

"Don came to see me yesterday. At my house."

"What'd he want?"

"Wanted to hire me to follow Dale Pendergrast."

A frown appeared. "Why? What's he think old

Dale's been doin'?"

"He's afraid Dale might've had something to do with Red's death. Thought if I followed Dale around, I could, shall we say, allay his fears that his buddy was a murderer."

"Don tole you he thinks Dale killed Red? What for?"

Succinctly as I could, I repeated my conversation with Don. Dad's anger escalated to epic proportions. When I reached the end of the tale I was afraid he might have a stroke.

He exploded. "For cryin' out loud, most days Dale can't find his butt with both hands. He ain't smart enough to come up with that kinda scheme, and he don't even take a crap without runnin' it by Maurice first."

The way he'd sneered *Maurice* caught my attention. "I thought you and Maurice were pals."

"You'd know I don't have much time for him anymore if ya came 'round more often."

I ignored the taunt. "But when I came to dinner last week you were ticked off about Maurice losing calves because of the dust from building the casino."

"Don't like to see nobody's livestock dead."

He pushed back his black cowboy hat and stretched out his long legs. He wore his usual workday clothing, long-sleeved, light weave cotton shirt, ripped and stained once dark blue Wranglers, not skintight like rodeo cowboys and western singers preferred, but baggy, with the cuffs frayed and dirty from dragging in the pasture.

His work boots caught my attention. Dust covered, the color had faded from brown to creamy tan, soles worn thin, heels worn down, the leather weary and cracked. A hole by the ball of his left foot allowed a piece of his white sock to stick out.

I had the oddest sensation, looking at that dirty, stained sock, like I was seeing a secret part of him that he didn't realize was exposed.

Before I could analyze that weird feeling, Dad slapped his thigh. "Damn ticks are everywhere this year."

"They been bugging the livestock too?"

"Not as much as the dust." He sighed. "No matter how much of a know-it-all pain in the rear Maurice has become, he don't have money to spare to replace them calves or to pay the vet to keep comin' out. Not since the shooting range project went belly up."

"How'd that affect him? Wasn't it going on county land?"

"Yeah, but he'd sunk a lot of money into building improvements, figurin' with his land being closest to the range, plenty of people who like to shoot but don't have no access to huntin' grounds would pay to hunt on his property. Didn't work out that way. Had to sell a chunk off in order to pay off his loan and the property taxes."

I rocked. Listened to the *clank clank* of the swing chain. From the oak trees behind the barn came the loud buzz of cicadas. The drone tapered to a hum when the wind rose and fell. Pungent, hot, aromatic outdoor scents swirled around me until I sucked the sweet musk of summer into my soul. I relaxed for the first time in days. With my father of all people. Go figure.

Strangely enough, I kept the conversation going

instead of taking my leave. "Is that why Maurice is so hot to get on the county commission? Wants to lower property taxes?"

"I think most of the reason he wants to get on the commission is so he can get his acreage borderin' the county rezoned commercial. He can put his *own* shootin' range on it and that holy group that caused all the problems can't do a thing 'bout it because it'll be on private land."

Something didn't fit. "If he's so broke, where's he going to get the money? Wasn't it supposed to cost the county around 200 grand to build it?"

He shrugged. "Evidently he's taken on a silent partner. Been kinda cocky 'bout it, which is one of the reasons why I can't stand to be 'round him no more."

The hair on the back of my neck stood up. I pretended to consider his response. Asked with forced casualness, "Remind me again of the name of the holy group?"

"I dunno." He scratched his forehead. "Medicine Wheel something. All them Injun names sound the same to me. Another thing that bugs me about Maurice is that he's suddenly 'put aside' his differences with them. Seems a man oughta stick to his principles, not shove them away when it suits him."

My blood ran cold.

Dad claimed anyone could've waltzed into Red's barn and lifted the gun.

Including Maurice. Who would've known exactly where the gun was kept. And where to find Red on his vast ranch.

What if part of what Don Anderson had told me was true? I agreed with Dad: Dale wasn't smart enough to pull off such an elaborate con. But I also didn't believe Don was bright enough to put it all together himself either.

I'd bet Maurice planted the seeds about Dale's guilt in Don's head, knowing full well Don wouldn't rat out his longtime friend. Maurice had a big ego. He'd have to tell someone.

It made more sense that Maurice killed Red to get on the county commission and then framed Red's wife for it. With Maurice's hunting buddy on the council, a recommendation for Maurice to fill Red's vacant seat was pretty much sown up.

Then he'd get his damn shooting range.

The implications brought back the queasiness. I stopped rocking the swing.

What if Maurice had shot Luther Ghost Bear because of his involvement with stopping the shooting range, and it was *Rondelle* who was in the wrong place at the wrong time, not Luther, like I'd originally suspected?

Would Maurice really wait two years to get revenge on the members of the Medicine Wheel Society?

Hell yes. Guys like him had a long memory and could carry a grudge for generations.

That still didn't explain how had Tommy gotten involved. Another victim of wrong place, wrong time? Maybe Tommy had been tasked with following Rondelle and had ended up in the crossfire.

Could he have been Maurice's silent partner? As a lower level thug, and a friend of Little Joe's, I doubted

Tommy had the cash to fund Maurice's enterprise.

Unless he'd recently come into some money.

Had Tommy been upstairs at Trader Pete's when the bookkeeper was in the office? Little Joe would've trusted him to make sure the safe got shut when he stormed off and raped Rondelle.

Instead, Tommy could've seen it as easy money and grabbed it. Shut and locked the safe knowing the cash wouldn't come up missing for a week. If he destroyed the security disk, both he and Little Joe would've been in the clear for their separate crimes.

Big Joe wouldn't have suspected either of them.

But Rondelle had gotten to the disk first.

When Rondelle reviewed the disk, she must've seen that Tommy had stolen the money. Had she blackmailed him? Is that why he'd decided to kill her?

Then how had Tommy ended up dead?

By trusting Maurice.

Once Maurice had gotten his money from Tommy, he probably decided he didn't need a partner. Bang. Partnership turned into a sole proprietorship.

"What's wrong with you all of a sudden?" my dad asked sharply. "You look sick."

I perched on the edge of the swing. "Still feeling the effects from the car accident. I should get home."

After Don Anderson's reaction yesterday, I knew I'd get a similar one from my father if I shared my suspicions about his former buddy Maurice. I didn't need the lecture. I also didn't need Dad running off at the mouth before I had a chance to talk to Sheriff Richards.

As I shuffled to my truck did my dad wish me well? Or say something snarky?

Hell. He didn't say anything at all. Not even good-bye.

CHAPTER 33

On the way home, I ate two Twinkies, slurped a can of warm soda, and smoked a cigarette. Didn't alleviate the churning emptiness in my stomach.

I couldn't get my brain to shut off either. Something didn't fit, but what?

Cue the cheesy game show music. I was about to play another round of "What If?"

Round one: I'd connected Rondelle to Luther via the Medicine Wheel Society. Luther to Maurice via the Society getting the shooting range banned. Rondelle to Tommy via Trader Pete's.

But Tommy to Maurice? That was a stretch.

According to my father, Maurice had been talking about his silent partner for months. If Tommy had just taken the money from the Carluccis, he could've only bought into Maurice's business proposal days before his murder. Maurice wasn't the type to wait around.

Who else had enough money to help fund the

shooting range?

The Carluccis, obviously. Although they'd been opposed to the Bear Butte casino—same as Maurice—I doubted Maurice would've trusted them. Not only weren't they local, they were from the east coast; an *ethnic* group from the east coast, which was worse.

But greed had no national boundaries.

So, if the Carluccis were lower on the totem pole of potential silent partners, who were the other possibilities?

Not Maurice's cronies, Dale Pendergrast and Don Anderson. They'd have been bragging to everyone in the county about their big plans. Their assets were tied up in their land.

Same went for my father.

Red Granger had money. Yet, he'd been one of the few honest politicians I'd known. He would've seen a conflict of interest in personally investing in a privately held shooting range—especially if he had to recommend rezoning to the Bear Butte County Commissioners to allow it to get built. He was out, too.

I coasted to the end of my driveway and stopped.

Local person, with money, wanting to make more. Hoping to make himself look good. Good old boy who believed in God, country, and the NRA.

Bud Linderman.

Ding ding ding. Jackpot! Julie Collins, you are the winner of round two!

Ah hell.

I rested my forehead against the steering wheel, as, once again, the implications made me dizzy.

Rondelle had double-crossed Linderman. Tommy worked for the hated Carluccis. In this scenario, Luther *had* been in the wrong place at the wrong time.

With a few blasts to the head, through Maurice, Linderman had eliminated a couple of problems.

Oh, I didn't doubt Maurice had been the triggerman in either scenario. He'd always struck me as a sociopath capable of extreme violence for no reason other than he had a bevy of firearms and a desire to use them. A result of post-traumatic stress disorder from Vietnam? Maybe, but even combat flashbacks weren't a valid excuse for the brutal deaths Luther, Tommy, and Rondelle had suffered at his hands.

What now? What proof did I have? None. I knew Sheriff Richards would (grudgingly) listen to me, but until tangible evidence surfaced, all my "what ifs" and theories didn't mean squat.

Plus, if I called him, he'd probably demand I come in and explain why in the hell I'd shot up Little Joe Carlucci's car.

Better to save that phone call for later.

The adrenaline from practicing my shooting skills on a live target, and spending time with my father had taken a toll on me.

I dragged my aching body in the house. Left a message for Martinez to call me. Same for Kim.

After locking the doors and placing my Browning within reach, I downed a pain pill and sacked out on the couch.

Cool air drifted over me as the quilt was peeled back from my body. Strong arms separated me from my cozy cocoon and picked me up.

Groggy, I stirred and inhaled: leather, a subtle pine cologne, a whiff of machine oil, all mixed in with the musky male scent of warm skin.

"Martinez?"

"Go back to sleep."

I yawned as he carried me down the hallway. "You taking me to bed?"

"Been waiting months to hear you say that, blondie."

My heart began to pick up speed. "You know what I meant."

He rubbed his cheek over my crown. Gave it a warm, soft kiss. "Same goes."

If this was a dream, I didn't want to wake up.

Smoothly, he set me down on the cool mattress.

I opened my eyes to the near darkness of my bedroom. "What time is it?"

"A little after nine."

"God. I've slept away the day."

"You needed it." At the window he twisted open the plastic blinds, then shut them again. Turned on the knock-off Tiffany lamp by my bed.

"Where are your bodyguards?"

"Interviewing enforcer candidates."

They'd decided to let El Presidente waltz around alone after all that had happened lately? Wrong. "You ditched them, didn't you?"

"Yeah."

I focused on his economy of movements, soothing, yet sexy as hell. "Hey, how did you get in here? I know I locked the doors."

"I noticed that." He shoved the rumpled mound of bedcovers to the other side of my bed. "I also noticed your gun is on the coffee table." After piling two pillows together, he said, "You really should clean it after it's been fired."

I sighed. "I suppose you want to know who I fired it at today?"

Martinez froze. "You shot *at* someone today?"

"Yeah, and before you get all pissed off, I'd planned on telling you, okay?"

"Start telling me now."

I did.

When I'd finished, he spun on his heel, paced to the door, stopped and came back. Dropped to his haunches in front of me. Pressed his forehead against my knees and began to laugh. Hard.

"What?"

He grinned at me and curled his hand around my head like he always did. I was beginning to get used to it.

"I don't know why I bother to worry about you."

"You worry about me?"

"Yes." His fingers brushed away the wisps of hair that had stuck to my cheek. Then those rough-skinned knuckles traced my jaw line, up one side and down the other.

425

His touch was electric shock therapy; my aches and pains miraculously disappeared.

"Tony, why are you here?"

He didn't answer right away. He kept stroking my face, watching my reaction with those dark, dark eyes. "Do you want me to go?"

I shook my head.

"Good."

Unnerved by his continued stare, I dropped my chin. "Stop staring at me. I look like crap."

"You think I care?"

I looked up at him skeptically.

"See? I knew you wouldn't believe me if I told you it didn't matter."

"You really don't care about the stitches and the bruises? I'll probably have scars."

He kissed the corner of my mouth, my swollen nose, the skin around my stitches. "Scarred or not, I'll take you any way I can get you."

My stomach did a little flip. "You *do* know what you're getting yourself into with me, don't you?"

"I could say the same to you."

I hadn't forgotten Martinez lived by his own rules. Not the ones set by the law. Not even the same rules I followed. Could I ever come to grips with what he did as president of the Hombres?

Probably not.

But as he kneeled in front of me, I didn't see the outlaw, just the man. I knew he saw me for who I really was. Maybe he was one of the few who ever had.

I lightly fingered his worn leather vest, covered in those intriguing patches. "So, you remember the other night?"

"Vividly."

"Well, I don't."

He waited.

"I mean, I don't remember vividly. It was so dark I didn't really get a chance to look very closely at—"

"At what?" Impatience flashed in his eyes.

I pressed my lips to his temple. Waited a beat. "At your tattoos."

He shivered as I blew a stream of air inside his ear.

"How about it, Martinez? Wanna show me your tattoos?"

I felt his grin on my cheek before he gently lowered me back on the bed.

Hours later, when we were both exhausted and he was wrapped around me like a vine, he'd become quiet. More so than usual.

"Are you okay?" I asked.

"Not really."

Strange, how he'd known I was thinking about Harvey, not the change in our relationship.

"Sucks, doesn't it?"

"Yeah."

"You *can* talk to me."

His hold on me increased. "I know."

427

"I wish this was over. After I find Chloe I want to . . ."

"What?" he murmured.

"Get away. Forget."

He didn't say anything.

I yawned. Shifted closer to him to absorb his body heat. He continued to play with my hair. I didn't understand his obsession, but I counted myself lucky he was a hair man, not a breast man. I had lots of hair.

"You didn't finish telling me what happened after you shot up Little Joe's manhood," he said.

"Huh-uh. You distracted me."

"Ah. The guided tour of my tattoos." He nipped my shoulder. "I think you missed a couple."

"I'll look again later."

"Mmm. I'm holding you to that."

He sounded tired. The sooner I told him how I'd spent my afternoon the sooner we could melt away.

"I went out to the ranch."

His caresses lulled me toward sleep. I had a hard time staying awake while I told him what my father had said and the conclusions I'd drawn.

The last thing I remembered was Martinez placing a soft kiss on the back of my neck and whispering, "Thank you."

I woke up alone around noon. If not for the hastily scrawled, "I'll call you," note he'd propped next to my cigarettes, I wouldn't have believed last night had happened. Hard to fathom Tony Martinez and I meshed, in and out of bed.

After I'd showered, I dressed in baggy shorts and a tie-dyed T-shirt. Threw my hair into a ponytail. I didn't plan on going anywhere. Actually, I was sort of scared to leave my house.

The day dragged on. I ordered a pizza. Watched TV. Waited for the phone to ring.

I'd called Sheriff Richards first thing only to find he'd taken a well-deserved day off. I didn't want to bug him at home since Mrs. Richards was nearly as big and intimidating as he was.

Missy had promised to have him call me if he checked in.

I waited some more.

My cell phone rang just after dusk. I didn't recognize the number. I answered anyway, hoping it was the sheriff.

"Hello?"

"Julie Collins?"

"Yes?"

"Listen carefully. We have the girl. You have the disk. We're willing to make a trade."

My knees failed and I sank to the floor.

Oh my God.

"Who is this?" I said. "Let me talk to her. Right now."

"You aren't in a position to make demands."

I dry heaved. When I regained control, I said, "Okay. Tell me what you want."

"Bring the disk to the Bear Butte Casino. Bottom

door. Basement. East entrance. Come inside. Wait there for further instructions. Come alone. Come unarmed. If you fail to follow a single instruction, she dies. You have twenty minutes."

Click.

CHAPTER 34

I STAYED SURPRISINGLY CALM.

Since I'd bluffed my way this far there was a slight chance I could keep it up long enough to get Chloe to safety.

I dug in my entertainment center and yanked out a blank CD still in the case. Tossed my home office until I found an unused manila envelope and slid the CD case inside. I threw my gun (cleaned, with a fresh clip) my knife, cell phone, and a package of Twinkies (for Chloe) in my purse.

Before I ran out of the house, I left a vague message on Martinez's voice mail.

Only when I was in my truck and on my way did I allow myself to think about Chloe. She'd better be okay. They'd better not have harmed a single hair on her little head or I'd kill them.

Even when I didn't know who "them" was.

Fuck. I floored it.

Scenery blurred past. I'd made it to the turnoff when I hit the brakes. The seatbelt caught, throwing me forward, and the back end skidded sideways in the gravel.

Damn that hurt.

No sense barreling up there. They were expecting me.

I whipped down the embankment and parked my truck in the ditch. Killed the lights. I dropped the stun gun in my purse, and slid from the cab.

The stars weren't yet at full brilliance. The moon hadn't risen. The bitter scent of skunkweed arose as I carefully picked my way across the field. At the last hill I stopped and caught my breath, about 500 yards from the building.

The heavy equipment that had served as a blockade was gone. Didn't look like the builders had made much progress in the last few days. Wait. They had put in the windows.

I wasn't dumb enough to try and sneak my Browning or my stun gun or my knife in with me. But I wanted them close, just in case. A saw-toothed shaped rock poked up, ten yards to my right. I hid my purse along the back side of it in a lone clump of tall grass.

At 100 yards, I removed the two small, flat nylon restraints from my front pocket. Wrapped one around my ponytail holder, and slipped the spare, with the rhinestone glued on the clear plastic block, over my hand to my wrist. I squinted. Looked like a friendship bracelet.

Envelope clutched in my hand, I forced my feet to move. One step at a time. I could do this. I *had* to do this. Chloe's life depended on me being able to do this.

No back up. No last minute rescues. Just me.

Hey, no pressure.

Shades were drawn in the office trailer. The recent rain had left mud puddles across the empty parking lot.

Bear Butte loomed in the background. Silent. Watching.

The front of the building was spread out, and appeared to be a single level, except off to the right side it sloped sharply to reveal a walk out basement.

I should've veered to the right. Instead, I went left. I don't know how I thought coming in on the wrong side would give me the element of surprise, but it would give me a vague idea of escape routes if Chloe and I needed to run.

Boulders lined the slope around a sea of pea-sized gravel. Had to be some kind of drainage ditch. Chloe and I could probably hide behind those big rocks if we had to, but it was too close to the building for my peace of mind.

Sturgis was too close for my peace of mind.

I started downhill. Every step jarred my ribs. I slid in the mud, righted myself by touching the cool cement blocks of the foundation.

I'd reached the end of the left side of the building. I peeked my head around the corner. Couldn't distinguish the lumpy shapes. Listened, couldn't hear anything over the rapid staccato of my heart.

I turned the corner.

Discarded construction materials littered the area. I had to slowly pick my way through a footstep at a time lest I step on a nail or broken sawzal blade. I'd made it halfway when a low hissing registered.

I froze. Just what I didn't need, a rattlesnake hunting out here in the dark. Damn things always hissed a warning before their rattles signaled a strike.

I willed the blood to quit rushing in my ears so I could listen again.

Nothing. Maybe I'd imagined it.

I gave the remaining junk a wide berth anyway and rounded the last corner.

Since my eyes had adjusted to the darkness, I noticed a five-pound bucket of Sheetrock mud held the steel door ajar.

What was I supposed to do now? Go in? Wait out here?

A latex glove clapped over my mouth. Cold steel pressed into my neck.

Fear seized me, hard.

The hand moved. The knife stayed.

"Spread out and hold still."

I closed my eyes, suffocating with helplessness.

A strong male hand thoroughly patted me down. Up my left side, then my right. Over and under my arms, neck, and head. Down my back, and the back of my legs. Between my legs, up the front of my thighs, across my hips, belly, my breasts, collarbones, and shoulders.

I had to focus on something besides the nauseating sensation of unfamiliar, unwanted hands on me. Why hadn't he taken the disk?

He moved the knife under my chin. "Swear you

ain't got no weapons or nothin' on you."

"I swear," I whispered.

"Come on then."

I still didn't recognize the voice, but I obeyed.

Once inside, my bare knees hit concrete when he shoved me to the floor. The disk flew from my hand and the envelope skidded. Tears stung my eyes as I scrambled away. I kept crawling until my back hit the solid cement wall.

"She's clean," he said.

Footsteps faded.

A floodlight burst through the doorway, momentarily blinding me.

A new voice said: "Glad to see you finally learned how to read a clock, Ms. Collins. You made it in eighteen minutes this time."

I blinked.

Not Linderman. Not Maurice Ashcroft.

Reggie.

I should've known. Any man with such bad taste in clothing had to be a slimy fucker.

My fear mixed with rage. "Where's Chloe?"

No answer.

"I want to know now."

Frankie Ducheneaux marched forward, around the light he'd set on the floor. Reggie jerked him back. "You will. In due time."

He wanted to play games. Draw out the drama a bit. Well, too fucking bad. I wanted to see Chloe to make sure he hadn't hurt her.

435

I focused on Frankie. Didn't see that he had a gun, just the knife. "How much is he paying you, Frankie? How much did he pay you to sabotage this building? How much did he pay you to betray Rondelle?"

"He ain't payin' me nothin'."

"You're doing this for *free*? You have any idea how much time you'll do for kidnapping?"

"Kidnapping? What the fuck are you talkin' about?"

"Ignore her." To me, Reggie said, "Maybe I should've gagged you first."

"Maybe you should tell me where the hell Chloe is. I did exactly what you told me to. What else do you want?"

"To make sure you didn't tell no one where you were going." He considered me. "That freak Jimmer rolling up in his Hummer?"

"No."

"How 'bout your buddy the sheriff?"

"No."

"Burrito boy don't know where you are?"

Not even the mention of Martinez's name stopped the dread from growing. If he showed up it'd be too late. I found it hard to breathe.

Reggie jeered, "Knew you were a soft touch, pretending to be such a tough bitch. Figured mentioning the girl would get you here in a hurry."

Then I knew. Chloe wasn't here. She never had been here. Reggie had been bluffing.

Relief flowed through me. Followed by a river of fear. I swallowed. "Well, Reg, gotta hand it to you; I fell for it." I purposely let my eyes stray to the dark corner where the envelope holding the disk had landed. "I don't imagine you're gonna let me live, now that you've got what you want. Gonna kill me like you did your buddy Tommy? Or you gonna blow my head off like you did with Rondelle?" My eyes met Frankie's and I took a chance. "And Luther Ghost Bear?"

Frankie's startled gaze flew to Reggie.

"Didn't know that, did you, Frankie? That your pal, Reg, blew away Luther's face? Shot him in the chest first. And knowing the kind of wise guy Reg is, I'll bet Reg laughed at him and tried to make Luther beg for his life."

"Shut up," Reggie said.

"Thing is, Luther probably willingly gave it—"

"You *shot* him?" Frankie yelled at Reggie, leaping between us. "You fuckin' shot a Lakota holy man?"

"No, I didn't shoot him. See what she's—"

"If you din't, who did, huh? Tell me! That wasn't part of the deal!"

"Easy." Aware Frankie wasn't going to let it go, Reggie said, "Rancher named Maurice Ashcroft shot him, okay?"

"But you paid him," I piped in while I had the chance. "They all knew you'd taken the Carlucci's money. Rondelle and Luther because they'd seen the disk. Tommy probably saw you coming out of the office. Did he ask you for a cut? Or did he threaten to tell Big Joe about your disloyalty?"

"You said this wasn't 'bout money!" Frankie railed, waving around the knife. "It's 'bout keepin' Bear Butte holy, and pure and safe from greed!"

I laughed. "And you believed him? Jesus, Frankie. It's *always* about money."

"Is it? Was everythin' you told me a big fuckin' *lie*?"

"That's how it is?" Reggie said patiently. "After all I've done for you, you're gonna believe her now?"

Frankie turned sullen.

"Let me explain something. Sacrifices gotta be made, you knew that. They'll make that dead holy man a symbol. Don't you think that's what he would've wanted? To further the cause of your people?

"Don't listen to her. We're still going through with it. You're gonna be a hero, my man. After tonight no one will have the balls to question your loyalty again."

That perked Frankie right up.

I wanted to vomit. Whatever Reggie had convinced Frankie to do didn't have the approval of the Medicine Wheel Society.

"Everything's set, right?" Reggie waited a beat, then said softly, "Hand me the knife, bro."

Frankie passed it over.

"Go on outside and double check everything. Carefully. The way we talked about. We don't need no surprises at this point."

He slipped out the door.

"Nice performance," I said.

"Shut up." Reggie glared at me. "I'd like nothin' better than to plug you in your big fuckin' mouth. Maybe when he gets back I'll drag you outside and do it."

Even with my mouth dry from sheer terror, I said,

"You sure he's coming back? Doesn't seem to me like he trusts you much."

"Don't matter. He'll stick around until he gets what he wants."

"Which is?"

"This place gone."

"What do you mean 'gone'?"

"Gone as in Kaboom!"

A bomb? There was a fucking bomb in here? Where?

He mocked my wild-eyed expression. "Don't smell it, do you?"

"Smell what?"

"Propane."

Oh Jesus.

"Don't take much to leach the scent out. Even in new construction. Little trick I learned back east."

Blood slammed into my head. The hissing sound I'd heard. An open valve from a propane tank. Had Frankie shut it off when he heard me sneaking around behind the building? Or had that been the last hiss as the tank emptied?

The air in here had seemed heavier, but I'd attributed it to my fear, not liquid gas.

Holy hell. How much propane had they flooded this place with?

Like if I knew the exact ratio it would matter.

The volatile properties of propane danced in my mind. All it took was one tiny leak and ignition in one form or another. Fire. Electricity. Then boom.

No wonder he wouldn't shoot me. A single spark

and this place would blow.

I didn't know the effects of breathing it; how long before I passed out? My muscles turned to jelly. God. I was going to die. Close to where Ben had.

I focused my hatred on Reggie. "Why? Why would you do this? You don't give a fuck about this being holy land."

He laughed. "You're right."

"What did you promise Frankie to sucker him into helping you?"

"I didn't sucker him into anything. Was *his* idea. He wanted to prove himself to the Medicine Wheel Society. Just gave him some suggestions and the opportunistic fucker ran with it."

"Suggestions like cutting my brake lines?"

"No. I did that. How'd you like the way *I* validate parking, smart ass bitch?"

"You tried to kill me for one little comment I made?"

An alligator smile. "I've killed for much less."

"Then why'd you hire Maurice?"

"Ashcroft volunteered." Reggie cracked his neck side to side. "Tommy helped him round up Rondelle and Luther. Tommy shouldn't have pushed me 'bout getting a cut of the money."

"What do you get out of it? Just the money you stole?"

"The money don't mean shit; it was just an opportunity I couldn't pass up. Never was about the money."

"Then what was it about?"

"Was about me getting to go home."

"This is a *suicide* mission?"

440

"Jesus Christ, no. Last place I wanna die is in the middle of butt-fuck South Dakota. I'm talking about home to Jersey."

He scowled at the door, then at me. "How can you people stand livin' here? There's no buildings, there's no people. There's no nothing. Don't even have a decent sports team or restaurant within 400 miles. This place is nothing."

"Gonna miss Jersey a lot goddamn more from a jail cell."

His voice dropped to a deadly whisper. "That right? How do you figure? You and Frankie won't be nothing but pieces. Ashcroft, that trigger-happy fucker, gets his precious council seat, and his revenge for the money he lost over the shooting range deal. I guarantee he'll keep his big trap shut."

"No one will believe it."

"Yeah? Other casino owners in Deadwood are already suspicious of the Carluccis. And Junior has stupidly dicked with the Hombres territory too."

"Martinez won't let this slide if it messes with his business plans." Or with me.

"Asshole didn't get caught with his hand in the cookie jar because the damn cops were jerking off, or he wouldn't be a problem either."

"You called him with the anonymous tip? Why?"

"Faster them bodies turned up the faster I can get outta here. Junior's pissing his pants cause Big Joe thinks he done the murders, even though he ain't got the balls. That, along with Junior letting 150K disappear, and Big

441

Joe is finally ready to haul Junior's ass back home. Once he does, my babysitting duties for that worthless motherfucker will be over for good."

Took about ten seconds for the reality to sink in. "That's what this was about? You had four people fucking murdered because you hated your *job*?" My voice remained steady even as my temper spiked. "Dozens of lives are decimated, businesses destroyed, property ruined, and holy land desecrated because you couldn't get a goddamned canoli?"

He crossed the room and hauled me to my feet by my shirt. Shook me like a dog's chew toy.

"Shut your goddamned mouth."

I didn't. "You're forgetting one thing, Reg. When Big Joe finds out it was his trusted nanny who ripped him off, your life won't be worth a wooden nickel. Here or in your beloved *Jersey*."

"How will he find out, huh? You told Junior you had the disk. Now I have it." His gaze flicked to where the envelope should have been. "Don't tell me it's a copy. Those security disks are encoded and can't be copied."

When I didn't respond, he relaxed his hold on me.

"You're not the only one who can bluff, fucker. Rondelle never gave me the disk. I don't know where the hell it is."

Disbelief lit his eyes. He roared and dropped me.

The knife flashed, pain followed.

I'd braced myself, but the spot where he slashed my left arm was quickly overshadowed by his right uppercut.

The Milky Way exploded behind my lids, burned in

my mouth and down my throat. I dropped to my knees.

Oh God, it hurt, hurt, hurt. Jesus.

Reggie was muttering something behind me as he headed for the disk.

I didn't have time to loll around in pain.

I crawled toward the portable light on the floor. Averted my eyes when I picked it up. Wobbled as I lifted it above my head. I backed up until the door was between Reggie and me.

Firming my grip, I aimed the light in his eyes.

"Stay right there, Reggie. You know there's enough electricity in this battery to spark the propane."

"Not much. You think I'm stupid enough to take a chance on blowing myself up?"

"Nothing is foolproof."

He advanced, holding his hand in front of his face to shield the light. "You're bluffing."

"Not this time. I swear, I'll fucking hurl it at the ground if you so much as breathe my direction again."

"You won't."

"I will. If I'm going out in a blaze of glory, I'm taking you with me. I'd do it just to doom your black soul to spend eternity in butt-fuck South Dakota."

That gave him pause.

Blood poured down my arm and dripped off my elbow to the concrete.

Our voices had brought Frankie back into the fold. When he saw me, he froze.

"Over there. Next to Reggie." When he didn't budge, I yelled, "Now!"

My arms were getting tired. If they saw me shaking, I'd be screwed.

With the deadly potential of one spark of static electricity ending the standoff, I eased backward slowly, one rubber-soled foot behind the other until I reached the doorframe. My heel caught on the weather stripping on the bottom, and for the briefest second, I bobbled the light.

They both dove for the ground.

I slipped out the door. Gently set down the light.

And ran like hell.

CHAPTER 35

I'D MADE IT TO WHERE I STASHED MY PURSE WHEN I heard:

Click click click.

Whump.

BOOM!

And the building blew.

The ground shook. A pillar of fire shot into the air.

I curled into a ball and tried to protect myself from the heat and flying debris.

When I heard the crackle of flames, smelled smoke, I lifted my head and peered around the rock.

The building had blown. The whole damn thing POOF like it'd never been.

Jesus.

My lungs hurt. I didn't know the potential hazards of sucking in propane instead of oxygen, but I wasn't about to light a cigarette any time soon to find out.

Dazed, I stumbled to my feet.

It looked like a war zone, not a holy place.

Most of the wreckage began fifty yards from where I stood. Pieces of the roof littered the ground. The chunks of pink insulation fluttering in the air were reminiscent of scorched cotton candy. Slivers of wood poked out of the ground like pongee sticks. Shards of glass glistened in the red glow of fire.

The steel girders had peeled back, turning the building into a lopsided sardine can.

Why had the building blown?

Had Frankie decided to finish the job anyway?

With Reggie inside?

One could only hope.

I shivered. When I attempted to wrap my arms around myself a sharp sting reminded me Reggie had sliced my arm with the knife.

Glancing down, I saw blood oozing out. Hadn't even scabbed over yet. Seemed like hours ago I'd been in the building.

The sticky red goo made my stomach pitch. My vision doubled.

I yanked off my T-shirt, teetered until my butt hit the rock. I tied it around the wound, figuring it'd hold until someone could stitch it up.

Any second I'd hear sirens. I debated on whether I had the energy to return to my truck when I heard a *whomp swish whomp swish.* Another explosion?

My startled gaze zeroed in on a man galloping toward me.

Reggie brandished a smoking two-by-four, and

446

screamed, "I'm gonna kill you!"

Oh shit. I blindly reached inside my purse. But before my hand had closed around any type of weapon, Reggie was on me.

I'd barely had time to roll away when he jammed the stick into the ground, trying to shish kebab my leg.

"You are dead! You hear me? Dead!"

He'd gone absolutely stark raving mad.

Injured, I wasn't in much of a position to fend him off.

The odds maker in my head started a tally.

We were both operating on pure adrenaline.

I could outrun him.

He outweighed me by 100 pounds.

I had limited hand-to-hand martial arts skills.

He was a former boxer.

He had a big stick.

I had a big gun.

The odds were slightly in my favor, but only if I could get to that gun.

I rolled to my knees.

He swung.

I ducked and hit the dirt again as Reggie charged me.

Ow. Fuck. I smacked my forehead into the rock and felt the stitches pull. Saw stars.

Get up get up get up.

I got up.

Eerie silence was punctuated by the crackling and groaning of the burning building.

He'd stopped yelling.

I didn't have a drop of adrenaline left in reserve.

Maybe he didn't either.

Keep moving. Keep him talking.

"Reggie. Its over."

He lunged at me with the stick.

As he forced me to retreat, we were getting farther away from my gun.

I expected him to feint right; he feinted left and whacked me in the arm where he'd cut me. I shrieked with pain and scrambled backward, managing to stay on my feet through the white haze of agony. I was tired of hurting. I just wanted to give up, curl up in a dark room, and lick my wounds.

You ain't so tough.

Quit being such a baby.

Come on, you're stronger than this.

You're a survivor.

You gonna cowboy up, or are you gonna lay there and bleed?

My mind cleared away all the voices in my head. I'd do what I had to do.

Reggie reared back and charged.

I was ready for him. When he reached me, I dove at his feet and knocked him down. He bounced on his belly like a bowling pin after a strike.

The stick went flying from his hands.

Stunned, he didn't move.

I did.

I jumped on him, and ground my knee into the middle of his back to immobilize him. Figured I had about a ten second window to make this work.

I slipped the nylon cord from around my ponytail holder, grabbed his right arm and jerked it behind him. Slid the restraint over his right wrist.

He bucked beneath me like a wild bronc.

I held on.

I spun sideways, grabbed his left arm, pulled it and slid the other loop over his left hand to his wrist. I wrenched his arms together as hard as I could. Yanked the small clear plastic block down and cinched the nylon cuffs tight.

Under eight seconds; better than a champion calf roper.

"What'd you do to me?" he yelled into the dirt as he flopped around. "I'm gonna kill you when I get loose!"

"You won't get loose from a Tuff-Tie, asshole."

I stood, and nearly crashed to the earth again. I had to stay alert until the cops arrived.

Wakey, wakey, Julie. Come on.

I took a step and my knees gave out.

Fuck.

Reggie glared at me. When he realized I was down for the count, his lips morphed into an evil grin that cut me to the quick.

I'd learn the meaning of torture if I didn't get away.

He attempted to come to his knees by sawing up and down like a kid's rocking horse.

Made my head reel.

With one last burst of energy, I crab crawled to the rock, glowing yellow in the reflection of the fire. Patted the ground until my fingers brushed the gun.

Through my increasingly wavering vision I crept

forward, slow as a snail, every centimeter I moved sending a lance of pain to my knees, arms, head. But I didn't stop. Couldn't stop.

Reggie was lying on his ugly face. Wiggling. Sweating. Panting. Helpless.

I fought for purchase in his oily hair. I twisted his head back.

The loathing in his eyes meant nothing to me except a challenge to remain focused.

Breathing hard, I leaned close so he wouldn't miss a single word. "I fucking hate you. I hate what you've done. I hate what you are, an ignorant, condescending piece of shit. I should let the Carluccis have you, let them carve you up like a cheap fucking ham. That's what you deserve. But not this time. This time you will pay."

I let his head flop to the ground. Placed the gun between his shoulder blades. Pressed the button on the stun gun and zapped him.

Twice.

When he stopped twitching, I crawled as far out of his reach as I could before I collapsed.

Flat on my back, I stared at Bear Butte silhouetted in the background, mocking me, before I went unconscious.

CHAPTER 36

THE MAN WAS STATIONED BENEATH THE HALOGEN LAMP, whistling softly to himself. Twisting a section of chicken wire into a small cage. Planning. Dreaming. Scheming.

The barn door screeched open.

When would that danged woman quit pesterin' him?

"I ain't hungry. Told you that once. Just go on to your meeting."

"She's already gone."

He looked up. Two men he didn't recognize. One flanking him on each side. "This is private property. You can't just—"

"Yes. We can." The third man, the speaker, was hidden in the shadows of the horse corrals.

"What do you want?"

"You know."

The man swallowed. Refused to give anxiety a foothold. "Now, hold on."

"No. Hold still."

He shook his head and backed up. Tripped over his own boots before he stumbled over a milking stool.

Two hulking shapes hauled him upright. Held him while the third man, the shadow man, inched forward, but not enough to reveal himself.

A whip cracked by his ear.

He flinched. Angry at his spineless response, he said. "I don't have to—"

Rusty wire appeared at his throat.

"You will do what you're told."

He shook his head again.

That piece of wire was jabbed into the back of his neck.

"Try again. You will do what you're told."

When he didn't reply fast enough, hands grabbed his balding head, pushed him forward. The wire was jammed deeper into that same wound, and twisted into the muscle like a corkscrew.

Intense, flaming hot pain got his attention. "Okay," he screamed.

"Good choice."

He slumped, breathless. Fearful. He could bide his time by pretending to go along with whatever they'd planned. But these cocksuckers had no idea who they were dealing with. "What do you want?"

A scrap of paper materialized.

"Write this down."

"Why should I?"

Repeat of the wire entering his flesh. He was sweating, panting. Reluctant.

"Cooperate and it won't hurt."

He hesitated. Burned with fury. Who did they think they were, barging in and threatening him? Poking him like he was a piece of meat? Telling him what to do?

"Again," shadow man instructed.

Same wire, same hole. Deeper this time. Twice as painful.

Despite his hand turning into a paint shaker, and the blood trickling down his back, the man wrote. In his rage, the words he scrawled didn't register.

After he finished, the bigger of the two guys wrapped a clothesline cord around his belly, holding his arms at his sides.

"Gag him."

One of the men yanked his oily bandana from where it stuck out of pocket of his jeans.

"Wait."

A different bandana sailed through the dust motes and landed at his feet, kicking up hay particles and the odor of manure.

"Recognize it?" shadow man asked.

It was the one he'd lost that day at the settlers cabin.

Before he could wrap his mind around the meaning, they wiped the liquid snaking down his neck and stuffed the blood-covered rag in his mouth. Lightly tied the other bandana around his face to hold it in place.

"On the stool."

With the taste of death in his mouth and his desperation clouding the air, he began to struggle.

His head was jerked back. A piece of wire dug into

the corner of his eye. He screamed as hot blood obscured his vision.

No one heard the muffled sound.

They hoisted him on the stool, then tied his legs together.

Shadow man yanked a rope from above the workbench.

He twirled it. Threw it over the rafters like an experienced roper.

Blinking away the blood, he saw the guy on his left tug the rope taut and fashion a loop. The noose was dropped over his head. Secured around his neck.

He wouldn't give these lowlife thugs the satisfaction of seeing him crack. He was a soldier. He'd been through worse. He'd *done* worse.

Defiant, he opened the eye that wasn't caked with blood.

They untied the rope around his arms. Made him unbutton his shirt until it draped around his waist. He complied with precisely measured movements so as not to topple off the stool. The rope wasn't tight enough to offer a quick, painless snap of his neck. He'd choke to death. Slowly. Puzzling why they'd demanded his flesh was exposed.

Then he remembered the whip.

Saw the rusty nails. A twisted chunk of barbed wire already discolored with his blood.

The men retied his arms using his shirt as a buffer so the rope wouldn't leave burn marks.

Leave evidence this wasn't a suicide.

The reality, the words he'd written finally hit him, and his wild eyes sought those of the shadow man.

He stepped into the light.

The man's bladder released and he knew terror.

"Price must be paid," shadow man said softly.

He could do nothing but stand helplessly, covered in his own piss and wait for a gruesome death.

"Pick up the cords and remove the gags before you hang him."

His atonement day had come.

No one would mourn him. No one would seek vengeance for his death.

Everyone would believe he'd died a gutless coward.

Shadow man moved closer. "One more thing."

Maurice forced himself to lock eyes with his judge, jury, and executioner.

"I lied."

He gestured to his men to pick up the instruments of torture.

"Make it hurt," he said, before he disappeared back into the shadows to watch.

CHAPTER 37

I FLOATED IN THE ATMOSPHERE WATCHING THE SCENE unfold below me.

Martinez had handcuffed Reggie to the arm of a slot machine and chased him in circles.

With a black bandana tied around his head, gauzy black pants billowing into big black boots, Martinez was the grim reaper. On his bare chest the maze of tattoos morphed from a treasure map into a skull.

A long, curved silver sword sliced the air.

"I warned you what would happen if you touched her again."

Martinez raised the gleaming blade. Brought it down hard and separated Reggie's hand from his arm.

Reggie screamed.

My arm throbbed in response. I gasped and my eyes flew open.

"Easy, babe," a soothing voice said. "You're safe." Warm, dry fingers stroked the top of my hand. "Just a

456

bad dream."

The room swam into focus. One white wall, a bland curtain hanging from the ceiling, a small steel sink. A scent of antiseptic lingered behind the plastic smell of adhesive and the cool rush of purified air.

I glanced down and saw my toes poking from beneath a tan wool blanket. A metal rail stuck up at the end of the hospital bed.

The hand holding mine squeezed.

I turned my head.

Kevin sat in the chair beside me.

"Hi," he said.

"Hi," I said back.

He seemed at a loss to say anything else. He wrapped both hands around mine and kissed my knuckles. Pressed his stubbled cheek there, and stayed like that for several minutes.

"How long have I been here?"

"Thirty six hours or so."

Hours? Again?

"They've kept you sedated."

I warbled, "Thirty, thirty, thirty six hours a day . . ."

"At least your quirky sense of humor didn't get blown to hell."

Beep beep beep echoed behind the curtain. A nurse answered the call of the person in the other half of the room. Voices murmured.

"You *do* know you're lucky to be alive."

Tears swam up but I battled them back.

"Jesus. Can you tell me what happened?"

"Got a couple of days?" I took a deep breath. "I don't want to talk about the explosion right now."

"Okay." His concerned gaze traveled to the bandage on my forehead. "You were in a car accident too?"

I nodded. Fidgeted a little. Didn't want to talk about that either.

"I won't ask you why you didn't tell me, because I know why." His sad, somber eyes sought mine. "I'm sorry. It's a piss poor excuse when you're lying in the hospital cut up, bruised, and hurting, but I am sorry that I wasn't there."

"You would have been there if you could have, Kev, I *know* that."

"But—"

"You've been by my side for damn near every one of my life crises. Major and minor. So you missed one, big deal. If I get knocked down again, you'll pick me up. You always have."

He kissed my hand. "I always will."

"I know."

"I hate that I let you down."

Silence stretched.

"I hate that you shut me out." I slumped deeper into the pillows. "It hurt, okay? And I'm not used to you being the one that hurts me."

"I'd rather cut off my own arm than hurt you, babe."

I tensed, flashing back to the dream about Martinez.

He blew out a long, slow breath. "I never understood the finality of death before. Sounds stupid. I've watched you grieve, for your mother, for Ben, and I thought I

458

knew what to expect when it happened to me. I didn't. Not even fucking close.

"It'd be easier if I knew what to do. But you could give me a detailed manual and it wouldn't apply to me. Of all people I thought *you'd* understand." He rested his cheekbone on our joined hands. "I have to muddle through losing Lilly in my own way, Julie. In my own time frame."

Not yours.

He didn't say it; he didn't have to.

I pointed to the water pitcher. "Pour me a shot, will ya?"

Kevin released my hand, gave it one final kiss and recognized the conversation was over.

It'd gone better than I'd hoped.

Bright bouquets of flowers were scattered around. "Well, aren't I just Miss Popularity? Who are all these from?"

"This one," he held up a *Winchester Ammunition!* coffee cup jammed with grassy strands resembling ditch-weed, "is from Jimmer. The yellow roses are from Trish and Doug."

Had Dad stopped in? I didn't ask.

"Kim dropped this off." He frowned at a small stuffed tiger. "That's bizarre. Almost looks like she purposely scorched the fur in some places."

She probably *had* torched it to make it look more like me. Kim did possess a strange sense of humor. It was also her clever reminder that although I was frayed around the edges, I'd survived.

In an oblong opaque vase, filled with indigo marbles,

seven delicate stems of orchids branched out, each stalk laden with a different colored set of blooms.

"Those are from me," he said.

"They are absolutely stunning, Kev. Thank you."

Nothing from Martinez.

I swallowed my disappointment.

"You're welcome." He sauntered over to the window. Sunshine shimmered around him. He kept his back to the room, to me. "He's been here, you know. Prowling the hallways."

My heart beat faster.

"He's the one who called and told me about you being in the hospital after the explosion. I wouldn't have known otherwise."

"Martinez did?"

"Yes."

Thick silence.

"I won't pretend I understand why you're with him, Jules."

I tensed. This was another conversational avenue that was a dead end. Kevin had no right to expect an explanation from me, and I had no intention of giving him one.

"You are with him, aren't you?"

"Yes."

Kevin's sigh of exasperation with me was actually sort of nice. Normal for us.

"As your friend I think you're making a huge mistake, but that's nothing new for you. As your partner, from now on, you *will* keep your relationship with him strictly on a personal level."

I'd be happy to sit at my desk and research employment histories at Wells/Collins Investigations for the next ten years if I never had to live through anything like the last ten days again.

"Take some time off. You deserve it." He shoved his hands through his hair. "Can I ask you something?"

"Umm. Sure."

"Does he go anywhere without a bodyguard?"

I smiled. "I can think of a few places."

He angled back toward me, but with his face in shadow I couldn't read his eyes. "Just be very careful. I couldn't take it if anything happened to you."

The nurse came in and started poking me.

Kevin disappeared and not long after I drifted away.

"Hey. Come on, Collins, wake up."

I recognized the sheriff's gruff voice. "I'm not waking up unless you brought me a present."

He snorted.

My eyes opened. As usual, he was right in my face. The man had no clue about personal boundaries.

"Glad to see you'll continue to make my life hell." His eyes softened. "Girl, you give me ulcers."

"Your job gives you the ulcers, not me." I stretched and sat up. "Speaking of, what happened after I blacked out?"

"Why don't you get right to the point?"

461

"Hey, I've been out of it for a day and a half. I deserve to know. And please don't tell me you can't tell me."

Surprisingly, he launched right into it. "Saw your truck and me and John went running up there. We found Reggie first. Then I saw you. Bleeding, passed out in your bra. Decided there must've been a reason you'd tied him up—nice cuffs by the way—so we left him trussed until you were loaded in the ambulance."

"Frankie?"

"In Federal custody, same as Reggie. It was a zoo. The FBI showed up, along with the ATF. Kicked us off scene, which was all right with us."

"Did Reggie tell you he hired Maurice Ashcroft?"

"He's talking to the Feds about lots of stuff."

Bet the Carluccis weren't happy. "But Maurice is in your jail, for killing Rondelle, Luther, and Tommy? And Red Granger, right?"

He sighed and pushed back away from the bed.

"What?"

"Maurice Ashcroft is dead. Suicide. Left a note and everything."

"Holy shit."

"Yeah."

The holy shit wasn't for the suicide. Holy shit was because I knew in my gut Martinez had been involved.

And he'd gotten the information from me the last night we'd spent together. Smart move, blabbing my theory on Maurice.

Talk about deadly pillow talk.

How was I supposed to feel? Sorry? Used? Angry?

Disgusted?

My emotions ran the gamut. Mostly I felt . . . relieved.

Maurice *had* killed four people. Probably for sport as well as greed. Many would argue his murder was warranted. An eye for an eye. What goes around comes around. The end justifies the means.

Even if in the end it meant vigilante justice had served it?

I honestly didn't know.

I'd used those same rationalizations myself. Lying, breaking into places I shouldn't, hacking into secure sites, withholding information from the cops, from clients, from my partner. Verbally and physically threatening people if they didn't cooperate with me. Firing a gun at someone just because I could. So far I hadn't stolen anything but hey, it was early in my PI career.

Who was I to pass judgment on anyone else when I was clearly guilty of breaking the law? On more occasions than I cared to admit? Was lying for my own gain worse than lying to help someone else? It's all lying, isn't it? Is there a degree of separation? Who decides what it is?

Where *does* one draw the line?

Killing for the greater good? Or murder for hire?

I hadn't killed anyone for revenge.

Yet, I'd let Meredith Friel walk free after killing Bobby Adair for revenge. And I'd taken the blame for it.

That made me guilty on a whole different scale.

The sheriff interrupted my internal war.

"Maurice hung himself. Wife found him in his

463

barn. Coroner was puzzled by the puncture wounds all on his upper arms and torso. Decided they were probably just from him fixing barbed wire fence and from a rusty wire chicken cage he'd been working on."

Or from the Hombres torturing him. Was that part of the enforcer qualification process? Retribution?

Was Martinez vindicated now that he'd gotten revenge?

Yes. This time.

I suspected there'd be other times. But I sure as hell couldn't judge him on what might happen in the future. I closed my eyes. Our worlds were so different.

Then again, we were both willing to do what it took to make things right, whether or not that action fell outside the law.

Was I making excuses for him? Maybe. We'd clicked on several intimate levels, on some I never had with any man. Would he try to change me? Probably not. I didn't want to change him.

So where did that leave us now that the case was over?

" . . . in my mail."

"Sorry. What did you say?"

"Said I finally got a chance to open my mail yesterday. With all the things happening it was on the bottom of my list of priorities. Was nearly a week behind." Hooded eyes watched me carefully. "Had an interesting item in one package."

My fingers pleated the bedcovers. "Yeah? What?"

"A security disk from Trader Pete's. No name on the return address, though. Curious, doncha think?"

Rondelle. Oh my God. When she'd asked me to name the one person I'd trusted above all others . . . I'd thought it was a casual question. My heart ached that she'd had no one in her life she could trust.

"What did you do with this disk, Curious Tom?"

"Gave it to Dave Tschetter. Lawrence County isn't my jurisdiction, you know that. Dave will do right by her."

Doubtful Little Joe Carlucci would do time. I so wished he'd have gotten a taste of his own medicine in prison.

"There's another thing you should know."

My eyes were afraid to meet his. What else? Had Little Joe Carlucci whined about me shooting up his precious car? It'd be the ultimate miscarriage of justice if he escaped doing time for rape and I was arrested for discharging a firearm in public and destruction of private property.

"What?" I managed.

"Maurice also shot Donovan Black Dog. Another ballistics match with the Ruger Mini-14 he used to kill Red Granger. Can't believe Red was shot with his own gun."

We chewed on that sad fact for a second.

"Speaking of . . . Donovan came out of his coma yesterday. You want me to take you down there so you can talk to him?"

I nodded.

The nurse helped me into a wheelchair; I wasn't happy about that but she swore it was hospital policy.

We rode the elevator down.

The sheriff only made one snide comment about my

lovely prison-striped hospital gown. When he saw the concrete burns on my knees, the scratches and gouges on my shins, and the scrapes on my forearms from trying to escape from Reggie, he became awfully quiet.

Donovan had more tubes and machines and medical junk surrounding his bed than I'd ever seen.

He was awake when the sheriff wheeled me in.

"Hey," he said. "If it ain't my guardian angel. They wouldn't let me come up'n see you."

"I'll be outside," the sheriff said, and vanished.

"You look good," I lied.

"And here I thought you could bluff. You don't look any better than me." His gaze searched my face. "Is the building really gone?"

"I guess so."

"So's my job, then. Brush Creek will hafta declare bankruptcy."

"Don't they have insurance?"

"Some. But it won't cover the cost overruns. They sure won't be able to rebuild the casino."

All those people, out of work. Didn't seem fair. No one had won in this situation.

He closed his eyes. "I get tired real quick so I'm jus' gonna say this. Thanks for savin' my life."

"You're welcome. Where's Chloe?"

"*Shee*. Still lookin' for her? Like a wolverine on the trail, ain't you?"

"Can't close my case until I know where she was . . . is."

He didn't draw out the drama.

"Won't matter if you know now. She's at one of them

466

private summer camps for Native kids up'n Minnesota. Two months of campin' in a tipi, fishin', learnin' Lakota and the old ways." A slightly crooked smile. "Run by my great uncle. She was so excited. Didn't have no idea why I was sendin' her there. She jus' thought she'd gotten lucky, been real good or somethin', getting to spend the summer runnin' free with her cousins. Without me and Rondelle fightin' over her."

"So the whole time I've been busting my ass looking for her she's been roasting marshmallows, telling ghost stories and having a good time at camp?"

"Yep."

I laughed. "Man, am I glad to hear that. We were all freaked something bad had happened to her."

"Told you she was safe. I told you ya wouldn't find her."

He frowned, and I could tell it took effort.

"She don't know 'bout Rondelle. Sad thing. Rondelle lost her mama, now Chloe has too." His breathing deepened. "My family is gonna wait 'til I get there next month to tell her. I told them jus' to let Chloe be a kid for a while more. She'll grow up soon enough."

I thought on that for a moment.

I reached for his hand and said, "Be well," and waited to leave until he fell asleep.

After the sheriff had returned me to my room, he left.

I admired my flowers. Stared out the window at the shimmering lights of Rapid City and Ellsworth Air Force Base and beyond to the plains and Badlands. Brooded that I had one more night in this place before I could go home. Alone.

The prospect didn't fill me with joy.

On impulse I picked up the phone and dialed.

He answered on the second ring.

"I found out where Chloe is. I'm ready to wrap up this case."

I hung up, closed my eyes, and waited.

CHAPTER 38

UNCOMFORTABLE IN THE CRAMPED HOSPITAL BED AND my own skin, I rolled to my side and whacked my arm into the metal railing.

Pain raced up and down, hundreds of fire ants biting me from my fingers to my shoulder.

"Fuck! Stupid fucking thing!"

Might as well be in a damn coffin. I pushed my hair out of my eyes and sank into the concrete pillows.

Then I saw him leaning against the doorjamb.

My heart did that swoop-roll-flip thing.

"Problems, blondie?"

I growled.

He sauntered in and melted into a silhouette.

"I called you hours ago." Didn't I sound like a fishwife?

"Sorry. We installed the new enforcer tonight. Couldn't get away until now."

"Who was the lucky winner?"

"Guy named Jackal from Colorado."

"*Jackal*? First or last name?"

In the dark, Martinez's white teeth flashed. "Only name." His smile dimmed. "You wanted to talk about wrapping up the case?"

Say no, Julie. Tell him why you called.

Naturally I talked about Chloe's case. Tied all the loose threads and wrapped it up in a tidy little package.

He didn't seem particularly happy with my present.

"Glad she's all right. Won't be surprised if Harvey left everything to her," he said.

"Harvey had a will?" I said.

Martinez sighed.

He did that a lot around me.

I couldn't think of a single thing to say, which burned my ass because I *so* wasn't a beat-around-the-bush girl.

More uncomfortable silence.

"So you'll send me a bill for the rest of the charges?" he asked. "Or should I pay you now?"

And . . . I lost it.

"A *bill*? Fuck you, Martinez! There isn't enough money in the world to pay me for what I've been through. Threats and dead bodies and nasty images I'll never be able to erase. Look at me! I'm beat to shit! I even totaled my goddamn car. Although, it was crap, it was still my—"

He loomed over me, gently placed his fingers over my mouth before I'd worked up a really inventive set of swear words.

"It is you. I'd begun to wonder if I'd gotten the wrong room."

"Ow, let go of me," I tried to say, but it came out, "Owwllggmm."

His hand fell away. "What?"

"Umm. It hurts where Reggie, ah, punched me."

His gaze iced over and dropped to my jaw.

I lowered my chin.

"Let me see."

"It'll just make you mad."

"Too fucking late. I'm already mad." He tilted my head back, and sucked in a harsh breath when he saw the bruising.

I closed my eyes. Willed the tears away.

The warm gentleness of his lips shocked me, as it always did. He placed a string of tender kisses up my throat and over my jaw.

I started to cry. I hated to cry. "Shit," I said through my sniffles.

"Let 'em rip, blondie. I'll still think you're tough."

I laughed and cried some more.

Martinez kissed me until my eyes were dry. Took a long, long time.

With his forehead nestled against my neck, he said, "Stay out of exploding buildings."

"I'll try."

"Christ. That's reassuring."

His breathing was a steady, soothing stream of warmth across my chest. His fingers were entwined in my hair, twisting the sections into long spirals.

"The memorial service?" I asked.

"Had it this morning."

I listened to the nurses chatting at the kiosk. "I'm sorry. I would've gone with you."

He raised his head and stared at me. Smiled in that sexy way that sent my pulse tripping.

I touched his face, let my hand linger. "What are we doing here, Martinez?"

"Hell if I know."

"You any good at this relationship stuff?"

"Not so much."

I sighed. "Me either."

"Wanna give it a shot and see what happens?"

"Yeah. I do."

"Good." He turned his head and kissed my palm.

In that moment did I think about any of the scary things that defined badass businessman Tony Martinez?

No.

Did he worry about getting involved with a woman who had more issues than the Sierra Club?

He didn't appear to.

Neither of us was naive; we knew we'd have to address our differences sometime.

Just not now.

"Come away with me," he said softly. "For a couple days, a week."

"Where?"

"A secluded beach." He paused as my hand drifted down his arm and I felt his muscles tense beneath my fingers. "You interested?"

I stroked the dragon tattooed on his bicep and pretended to consider it. My mean streak showing? Hell

472

yes. I wouldn't want El Presidente to think I was easy.

"Maybe. When you thinking?"

"Tomorrow."

I laughed.

"Seriously. A guy I know has a place in Florida. We could be there by sunset. Surf. Sunshine. It'll give us time to . . . "

He let me fill in the blanks.

I did. Not with, "Time to figure this out." Or even, "Time to roll around naked and sweaty." Though both of those scenarios were likely.

No. I knew what we both needed more than anything.

Time to forget. Time to heal a little. Time to just be.

"I'd like that," I said. "But not tomorrow, okay? Give me two days? Something I've got to do first."

Martinez didn't ask what. He tucked me in, lingered with a good night kiss that left me dreaming of sand, sun, and nothing else for a change.

Once again Kim signed me out of the hospital. Sensing my melancholy, she hadn't fussed much.

I slept the whole day and through the night. I think Martinez checked on me at one point but he hadn't stuck around.

The next morning I made prayer pouches with pieces of fabric from my favorite Van Halen T-shirt and tobacco from a crushed pack of cigarettes. When I finished, I realized I hadn't smoked in three days. A sign it was time to quit?

Nah.

Later as I stared at the trailhead I didn't think it would matter. This climb was a bitch even for crusading nonsmokers.

In all the years I'd lived in South Dakota, I'd never hiked Bear Butte. Never had the chance to before Ben's death, didn't want to afterward.

First, face your fear head on.

My mind traveled as I started the ascent.

I thought about my mother as I tied the first bundle to a small chokecherry bush. It'd been easy to forget her life against my father's anger over her death.

Kevin. Donovan. Chloe. Martinez. One each for their grief.

Kim. For filling a void in my life I hadn't realized existed.

Frankie Ducheneaux. Although he was a deadly mix of ego and ideology, he shared a pouch with The Medicine Wheel Holy Society. I hoped their quest to keep this chunk of earth a sacred place wouldn't get lost in politics and the personal motives some people masqueraded as principles.

None for Reggie, the Carluccis, Bud Linderman, or Maurice Ashcroft. They didn't deserve prayers, mine or anyone else's.

I tied individual bundles to a large pine. One for Rondelle, Luther, Harvey, and Red.

Still, I didn't feel relief as if my load had lightened. Instead, my temper rose. Why was Bear Butte at the root of so many needless deaths?

Mato Paha was slow in answering.

I began to scale the beast, slowly, one step at a time.

The higher I climbed on the twisting path the more urgent my questions seemed. The more intense the pain seemed, both the physical pain from my face-off with Reggie, and the emotional pain I'd been hanging onto for years.

The chunks of rock and shale lining the path rattled beneath my feet, suggestive of walking on ancient bones. In other places the path gleamed, polished by the footfalls of many. I stopped on a small plateau and watched as two red-tailed hawks dove, then caught an updraft and hovered above me. Weightless and free.

I wondered what that felt like.

Heat radiated from the sage plants, releasing a tangy scent. Yucca, cactus, Black Sampson dotted the steep landscape on the front side. On the backside, pine trees charred black from fire stood in a perfect line like a broken-toothed comb. The path leveled in the shade, then began a series of steep switchbacks which led to the top.

The summit is invisible until you're there.

I climbed the last set of wooden steps. After my lungs quit aching and my calves quit burning, I walked the perimeter of the pine deck, able to see all four directions.

I was unprepared for the impact of the rugged beauty. The wide sky was an endless palette of blues, lavender, and grays, extending above the magnificent sweeping vista where black hills met golden plains.

Little wonder this majestic place was considered holy.

How could anyone believe this was nothing?

Bear Butte had survived fire and floods. Had seen the rise and fall of nations. Would still stand tall and proud through the human cycle of birth and death. Love and hate.

I clutched the remaining prayer bundle in my fist. The one I'd made for Ben.

Standing on hallowed ground, I didn't feel the measure of peace I'd expected. Or experience a sudden realization that my hatred for this sacred place had been misguided.

There was no catharsis for me. I knew in my heart there wouldn't be any until I found out who had murdered my brother.

I studied the bundle. It'd keep until that time when I could truly let go.

I tucked the pouch in my pocket, turned away from the grandeur spread out before me and began to make my way back down the rocky slope to the bottom.

THE END

*A Special Presentation of Lori G. Armstrong's first novel
from Medallion Press,* BLOOD TIES:

PROLOGUE

DEATH HAS NIPPED AT MY HEELS like a disobedient dog since I was fourteen.

A drunk driver killed my mother the autumn of that year. She was hit head on. The extent of her injuries, including massive head trauma, excluded the option of an open casket.

I felt cheated. I believed then, if I'd touched her hand or stroked her cheek one last time, acceptance of her death might have offered me comfort or closure. It didn't ease my pain that she didn't suffer. It didn't ease my sense of injustice that the drunk also died upon impact. And it didn't ease my father's rage that the man responsible was Lakota.

After my mother's death, my father's hatred of Indians deepened, spreading wide as the Missouri River which divides our state. He'd never hidden his prejudice, but in the aftermath, the racial slurs flew from his mean mouth with regularity. *Prairie niggers* and *gut eaters* were flung out heedlessly. In those public moments I cringed against his harsh words. In private I fumed against him. I found it puzzling that a man with such a deep-seated loathing for an entire race had sired a son with the same blood.

Apparently my father believed he was absolved of his part in the creation of that life when he signed away paternal rights. The child's mother believed the boy would never know the truth about his white father.

They were both wrong.

My half-brother, Ben Standing Elk, arrived on our doorstep shortly after he'd turned nineteen.

When my father leveled a look of pure disgust upon the Indian darkening his door, I was horrified, and demanded an explanation for things I didn't have the ability to understand. His stony silence mocked me. I expected him to yell back. I expected to be grounded for showing disrespect. But the last thing I expected was the hard, stinging slap he delivered across my face.

We never spoke of that day. By some miracle, probably of my mother's making, I forged a relationship with my brother.

Good old Dad was conspicuously absent whenever Ben came around. I'd gone beyond caring. I loved Ben without question. Without boundaries. And without clue to the consequences. With him I found the bond I'd been lacking. A bond I counted on years later when the tenuous one with my father finally snapped.

Blood ties are strong. But the strands can easily be broken, whether tended with love or ripped apart by hatred. My father chose his means, fate chose mine.

Fate and death seem to be intertwined in my life. After recent events, I realize nothing about death ever offers closure, regardless if it is accidental or premeditated. I still feel cheated. But I'm older now. Wiser. More determined that justice will be served, even if that justice is a brand of my own making. I won't blindly give in to acceptance until I know the truth. Even then, I doubt it will bring me peace.

Ben helped me deal with my mother's death. I grieve that there is no one to help me deal with his.

The dog is quiet once again, sated somehow. But I know it won't last. It never does.

Three years later . . .

CHAPTER ONE

"ALMOST, JUST A LITTLE LOWER. Right there. Oh, God, yes, that's it."

I'd shamelessly splayed myself over the filing cabinet, but the warm masculine hands caressing my vertebrae froze.

"Knock it off, Julie. Sheriff hears you moaning like that, he'll think we're doing it on your desk."

"Al." I sighed lazily. "If I thought you could find my G-spot as quickly as you zeroed in on that knotted muscle, we *would* be doing it on my desk."

"Smart ass. Don't know why we put up with you."

I twisted, heard the satisfying crack and pop of my spinal column realigning itself. No more sex on the kitchen table for me.

"You put up with me because I file, but I'm not dedicated enough to devise my own system."

My blond, waist-length hair curtained my face as I slipped my heels back on.

"Besides my pseudo-efficiency, I look a damn sight better manning the phones than Deputy John. Admit it, tiger," I added with a snapping, sexy growl.

Al colored a mottled burgundy, a peculiar habit for a forty-five-year-old deputy. He adjusted his gun in a self-conscious gesture, which made me wonder if he'd finger his manhood in front of me as easily. In law enforcement the size of your gun was closely related to the size of, well, your gun. Hmm. Was Al's private stock an Uzi? Or a peashooter?

"Regardless," he continued, unaware of my question-

ing gaze on his crotch. "If my wife heard me trash-talking with you I'd be sleeping in the den for a month."
I set my hands on his face and slapped his reddened cheeks while I maneuvered around him.

"I've seen your den. And your wife . . . Wouldn't be much of a hardship."

Light spilled across the mud-crusted carpet when the steel front door blew open. All five-foot-one inch of Missy Brewster, my 4:00 relief, sauntered in.

My tolerance level for Missy was lower than a stock dam during a drought. She embodied the skate-by-with-a-minimum-amount-of-effort civil servant attitude, versus the work ethic my father had literally pounded into me and which I couldn't escape, no matter how menial the job. Lazy, whiny, and petty were Missy's least annoying characteristics.

I guessed she'd compiled her own list of my irritating quirks: punctuality, humanity, a stubbornness born of desperation.

Her crocheted handbag thumped on the filing cabinet. She peeled off her NASCAR jacket, and slung the silver satin over the chair with a loving touch before adjusting her cleavage with a slow overhead stretch. A haughty look followed.

"Hey, Julie. Stud boy is waiting. Said something about you getting your ass out there pronto."

I watched Al's gaze linger on Missy's mammoth breasts, crammed tightly into a pink t-shirt. My eyes followed his, but I refused to glance down at my own 36C chest in comparison; there was none.

"Stud boy? You call him that and flash those boobs in his face?"

Her lips, the color and consistency of candied apples,

turned mulish.

"I didn't flash him."

"But I'll bet he looked."

"Honey, they all look." With a fake sigh of resignation, she squeezed her big butt in my chair and swiveled toward the computer to clock in.

She reached for a pencil, deigning to answer the phone on the fifth ring.

"Bear Butte County Sheriff's office." Her tone oozed sweetness. "Hey, Gene."

Yuck. I added disinfecting the receiver with Windex to my list of duties for tomorrow.

"Yeah, I just came on."

Missy flicked an irritated glance my direction.

"No, she's still here." Pause. "He's probably messing with his computer. Want me to ring him?" A minute of silence followed; her false eyelashes batted with apparent panic.

Al, sensing Missy's damsel-in-distress signal, stepped forward.

I stayed put.

"Well, glad it didn't happen here." She muttered a bunch of "uh-huhs" before adding, "No problem. I'll tell him straight away. Bye, now."

"What's up?" This from Al, the brave, blushing warrior.

Missy's shifty gaze wavered between Al and me. "Nothing in our neck of the woods."

Skirting the desk, she hustled down the hallway, Al hot on her Ferragamo heels as she rapped daintily on the sheriff's door.

I got the distinct impression Missy wanted me to leave. So, naturally, I followed the merry little band into the inner sanctum of Sheriff Tom Richards' office.

He didn't respond immediately to our interruption. His back, roughly the size of a Cadillac hood, greeted us, a constant *click clack click clack* echoed from the keyboard. The plastic slide-out tray bounced, and although I didn't see his hands, I knew they fairly danced over the keys. My typing skills are half-assed on a good day. It amazed me thick fingers could be so nimble when it came to office drudgery.

"Sheriff?"

His acknowledgement was a harsh grunt.

"Gene Black called."

"Yeah? What did he want?" *Tap, tap, tap.*

"They found a floater."

His movement stopped; his spine snapped straight as an axel rod. He turned. "When?"

"This morning. Some fly-fishermen hooked it in Rapid Creek."

He scowled at the clock. "He's just calling me *now*?"

Missy's fleshy shoulder lifted; the gesture a nervous twitch, not a casual shrug. "Wanted to give you a heads up before the media did."

"Whereabouts was this?"

She plucked a loose paperclip teetering on the desk edge. "Up in the Hills, off Rimrock." Her pudgy fingers twisted the metal into a caricature of modern art.

"Pennington County claimed jurisdiction, but Rapid City PD was on scene as a courtesy. Then a whole mess of people showed up."

The sheriff chugged his coffee, gorilla hands dwarfing the cup.

Being around him every day makes me forget how immense, how out of proportion he is with the rest of the world. At six-foot nine, he has the distinction of being the biggest sheriff in the state. His arms, legs, and torso are perfectly balanced, but his huge head isn't: It resembles an overgrown honeydew melon with ears.

His button nose is centered in a grayish face; his coffee-colored eyes withhold any trace of softness. Spikes of black hair protrude from his head and chin, reinforcing the ogre-like image from a fairy tale. The knife scar connecting the right side of his mouth to his jaw line creates a constant scowl and discourages most comments, either about the state of the weather up high, or whether or not he plays basketball.

"Gene said they weren't allowed to move the body right away," Missy continued. "They called in the DCI from Pierre. Which also caught the interest of the Feds."

"The Feds and DCI? Why not the NPS, too? Who the hell did they find up there?"

Don't go there, my brain warned, but my mouth ignored the plea. "With that much manpower?" I said. "I'll guarantee it wasn't another Indian."

Ugly silence followed, thick as buffalo stew.

In the past two years, five transient Lakota males — varying in age from thirty to seventy — had become life-sized bobbers in Rapid Creek, which twists from Pactola Lake and zigzags through Rapid City before dumping into the Cheyenne River. Despite the toxicology reports of the drowning victims, which revealed blood alcohol levels approaching blood poisoning range, cries of outrage among the Sioux Nation and resident supporters fell on deaf ears.

It seemed neither local law enforcement nor federal agencies were spurred into action, especially the FBI, still smarting from Yellow Thunder Camp in the 1980's and the controversy surrounding the 1972 siege at Wounded Knee. Not even the appearance of Native American activist/Hollywood actress Renee Brings Plenty, who'd lodged a protest march down Main Street to the Pennington County Courthouse, had changed the status quo.

The "so-what" local attitude remained: Another dead, drunken, dirty Indian out of the gutter and off the welfare rolls.

Who cared?

I did.

Three years had crawled past since the discovery of my brother Ben's body in Bear Butte Creek. Unlike the other Native Americans, Ben hadn't drowned, no alcohol or drugs showed up in his tox reports. With his throat slashed, his body discarded like garbage, he'd washed to the bottom of Bear Butte Creek, an area the Lakota consider sacred.

And like my mother's death, I hadn't gotten over it, I hadn't moved on. In fact, I'd moved *back* to South Dakota from Minneapolis for one specific purpose: to find out who had killed my brother and why.

Probably masochistic to abandon a promising career in the restaurant industry to apply for a secretarial job in the miniscule county where Ben had been murdered.

In my pie-eyed state following his funeral, it'd made sense. With unfettered access to legal documents, I suspected I'd uncover a secret file on Ben — like on those TV detective programs — detailing why, how, and whodunit, and I could get on with my life.

There wasn't any such file. So, here I am, years later, stuck in a rut that's developed into a black hole: a dead-end job, sexual flings that masquerade as relationships, and the tendency to avoid my father and his new family like Mad Cow disease.

No one understands my anger, frustration, and the sadness wrapped around me like a hair shirt. Some days, I didn't understand it. Time hadn't healed the wound of grief; rather it remained an ugly sore, open for everyone to gawk at and for me to pick at.

In the immediate silence, Missy's globes of cleavage turned into blushing grapefruits. She avoided my eyes, but her clipped tone was the voice of authority. "They prefer to be called 'Native Americans'."

I snagged the mangled paperclip and pointed it at her, hating the saccharine tone she bleated in the presence of testosterone. "No, they don't. Most of them prefer their tribal affiliation. Native American is a politically correct term."

"Whatever," Missy said with a drollness she'd yet to master.

"So, fill us in," I said. "What color *was* the body they found?"

Al shifted toward the fax machine, away from me. Missy furnished me with a view of the bra straps crisscrossing the folds of her back. "White. Young, female, about sixteen, fully clothed. The body wasn't decomposed, according to Gene."

"Suicide?" Tom asked.

"Didn't say. They're keeping the details quiet."

A disgruntled sound cleared my throat before I stopped it.

Missy whirled back to me, coquettish manner forgotten. "Don't start. This doesn't have a thing to do with your brother's case." She whined directly to Al. "See?"

Hands shoved in my blazer pockets, my fingers curled longingly around the pack of cigarettes stashed there. Damn those crusading non-smokers.

The sheriff shot me a withering look, but asked Missy: "She been identified yet?"

"They notified next of kin."

"What else did Gene tell you?" His gaze swept the bulletin board overwhelmed with official notices and the never-ending explosion of papers on the desk. "I don't remember seeing any reports of a missing local girl."

In a community our size, a missing dog is big news. A missing child is tantamount to calling out the National Guard.

"That's why they're keeping it low key. The girl was a minor living in Rapid City, but for some reason her parents didn't report her missing."

Again, my mouth engaged before brain. "Well, lucky thing we've got local law enforcement, the Feds, DCI and everybody and their fucking dog concerned about this one dead white girl."

The sheriff gaped, hooking his thumbs in his gun belt loop. His sigh was a sound of utter exasperation. Touchy, feely crap was not his forte' but I didn't give a damn. Let him flounder. God knows I'd done more than my fair share.

"Aren't you off shift now? Go home. Forget you heard any of this."

"I think that's why Gene waited to call," Missy offered slyly. "He knew *she'd* react this way."

Again, my reputation for resentment had eclipsed the real issue.

"This case doesn't affect us," Sheriff Richards said. "Ben's death is irrelevant."

"Irrelevant to whom? Not to me." My thumb ran along the grooves of my lighter. In my mind I heard the click, watched the orange flame fire the tip of my cigarette. Mentally I inhaled.

"Surface similarities, but we don't know the details. Besides, your brother's case is cold, so I'm missing the connection."

"Come on," I intoned, rookie teaching a veteran a lesson. "A death in *any* local creek is a connection. Maybe now that one with the right skin color has surfaced, Ben's case will get the full investigation it deserved."

The ogre in him bellowed, "Julie, will you stop? Jesus! We did a full investigation. Everybody and their fucking dog — as you so eloquently put it — busted ass on his case."

Paws slapped his desk, sending a family picture snapped at an old time photo studio in Keystone crashing to the carpet.

"You know the BIA and AIM still sniff around, so don't give me that 'we don't care because they were Indian' line of bullshit."

So much for the short-lived touchy, feely crap. I struggled not to flinch under the discord distorting the airless room.

He sighed again. "Take the weekend to clear your head; get drunk, get laid, whatever it takes to get you out of here until Monday."

His finger shook in the same manner as my father's. I braced myself for the slap that wouldn't land, waited for the invariable *but*.

"But I hear one word you were up there playing PI at the crime scene, or asking questions of any agency involved and I'll suspend you without hesitation and without pay, got it?"

In my mind's eye, I zoomed inside the safety of my

TV screen, a cool cat like Starsky, blasé about getting my ass chewed. There, in the perfect fictional world, the stages of grief were wrapped up within the allotted hour. I wished it were simple. I wished I didn't live every damn day with sorrow circling my throat, choking the life out until my insides felt raw, and hollow, and left me bitter.

So, for a change, I didn't argue with him, press my viewpoint or try to change his; it was useless. Recently, even *I'd* grown weary of my combative stance and reputation. Unfortunately, my uncharacteristic silence didn't help the sheriff's disposition. He'd brought meth-crazed bikers to tears with his practiced glower, which quite frankly, right now aimed at me, tied my guts into knots that would make a sailor proud.

"Get some help," he said. "Grief counseling, anger management, whatever. Deal with your loss and stop making it some goddamn," he gestured vaguely, plucking the appropriate word from mid-air, "*soapbox* for racial injustice."

Neither Al nor Missy spared me a glance. Wasn't the first time he'd broached the subject, nor would it be the last. At this point it wasn't worth my crappy job. Playing PI indeed. I *was* a PI — albeit part-time. Although Sheriff Richards disapproved, legally, he couldn't do a damn thing about it.

I smiled pure plastic. "Fine. I'll drop it. As far as grief therapy? I'll be doing mine at home, in my own way, but gee, once again, thanks for your overwhelming concern." Self-indulgence aside, the door made a satisfying crack as I slammed it on my way out.

BLOOD TiES

LORi G. ARMSTRONG

Blood Ties. What do they mean?

How far would someone go to sever . . . or protect them?

Julie Collins is stuck in a dead-end secretarial job with the Bear Butte County Sheriff's office, and still grieving over the unsolved murder of her Lakota half-brother. Lack of public interest in finding his murderer, or the killer of several other transient Native American men, has left Julie with a bone-deep cynicism she counters with tequila, cigarettes, and dangerous men. The one bright spot in her mundane life is the time she spends working part-time as a PI with her childhood friend, Kevin Wells.

When the body of a sixteen-year old white girl is discovered in nearby Rapid Creek, Julie believes this victim will receive the attention others were denied. Then she learns Kevin has been hired, mysteriously, to find out where the murdered girl spent her last few days. Julie finds herself drawn into the case against her better judgment, and discovers not only the ugly reality of the young girl's tragic life and brutal death, but ties to her and Kevin's past that she is increasingly reluctant to revisit.

On the surface the situation is eerily familiar. But the parallels end when Julie realizes some family secrets are best kept buried deep. Especially those serious enough to kill for.

ISBN#1932815325
ISBN#9781932815320
Gold Imprint
US $6.99 / CDN $8.99
Available Now
www.loriarmstrong.com

For more information

about other great titles from

Medallion Press, visit

www.medallionpress.com